Peter Watt has spent time as a soldier, articled clerk, prawn trawler deckhand, builder's labourer, pipe layer, real estate salesman, private investigator, police sergeant and adviser to the Royal Papua New Guinea Constabulary. He speaks, reads and writes Vietnamese and Pidgin. He now lives at Maclean, on the Clarence River in northern New South Wales. Fishing and the vast open spaces of outback Queensland are his main interests in life.

Peter Watt can be contacted at www.peterwatt.com

T0348207

Also by Peter Watt

The Duffy/Macintosh Series
Cry of the Curlew
Shadow of the Osprey
Flight of the Eagle
To Chase the Storm
To Touch the Clouds
To Ride the Wind
Beyond the Horizon
War Clouds Gather

The Papua Series
Papua
Eden
The Pacific

The Silent Frontier
The Stone Dragon
The Frozen Circle

Excerpts from emails sent to Peter Watt since his first novel was published:

'I've never contacted an author before but after reading *The Frozen Circle* I felt I needed to congratulate you on an outstanding novel, your best yet and I've read them all. The way you combine your fictional characters with history is amazing.'

'I've just finished reading your *Cry of the Curlew* series and it was absolutely fabulous! I had trouble putting the books down.'

'I have really enjoyed all your books.'

'I have a lot of trouble putting [your books] down. The only problem is nothing gets done around here when you write one. Can't wait for the next.'

'You make history come alive . . . I especially enjoy the human side of war you portray in your stories.'

'Another brilliant read.'

'I love the way you have intertwined the characters through all the books so far and tied them all into the early settlers in this country. The history has been great and the stories superb!'

'I have just finished reading *The Frozen Circle*, [and] in my opinion this is your best work yet. I loved the way you used time and distance to bring your story to a suspenseful and unexpected end . . .'

'I wish to convey my congratulations on the quality of your stories. I find them difficult to put down and look forward to reading the next one. Well done and may there be many more.'

'I have now devoured every one of your books and am eagerly awaiting your next publication . . . Thank you for the hours of pleasure you have given me.'

'[*Eden* is] one of the greatest books I have ever read.'

'I have recently discovered some of your wonder-ful stories and have been captivated by the characters, their lives, loves and exploits. Your love for the histori-cal adds such power to your books, you almost feel you are there. . . . [*Papua*] brought me to tears on more than one occasion.'

'Keep the pen writing, my man!'

'Thank you for your wonderful tales. I have just fin-ished *The Stone Dragon* . . . You bring the characters alive and make me feel part of the story. Thank you for many, many hours of pleasure.'

'Your books make me look forward to getting on the train in the morning. Keep up the good work!'

'Love your work.'

'*Cry of the Curlew* kept me reading into the small wee hours by candlelight . . . I was so engrossed in your story telling . . . Good on you for telling your tale . . . it has given me a greater sense of being and more so a strong ambition to impart on my children self worth and strength in their beliefs!'

TO
TOUCH
THE
CLOUDS

PETER
WATT

PAN
Pan Macmillan Australia

For Naomi and Monique,
with all my love

First published 2009 in Macmillan by Pan Macmillan Australia Pty Ltd
This Pan edition published in 2010 by Pan Macmillan Pty Limited
1 Market Street, Sydney

Reprinted 2011

National Library of Australia
Cataloguing-in-Publication data:

Watt, Peter, 1949–.
To touch the clouds / Peter Watt.

ISBN 9780330425827.

A823.3

Set in 13/16 pt Bembo by Post Pre-press Group
Printed by IVE

For his eyes have been full with a smouldering thought;
But he dreams of the hunts of yore,
And of foes that he sought, and of fights that he fought
With those who will battle no more –
Who will go to the battle no more.

'The Last of His Tribe', Henry Kendall

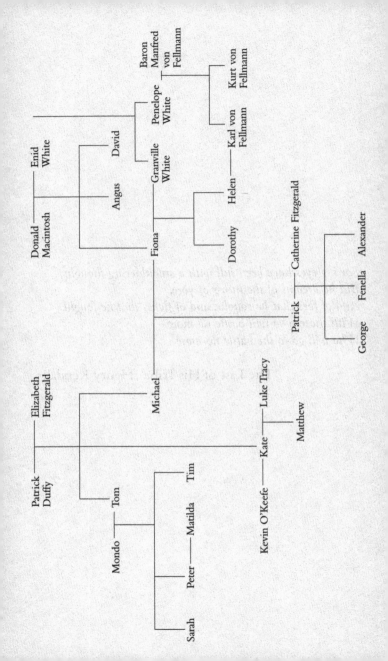

Prologue

**Glen View Lutheran Mission Station
Central Queensland
1934**

His black and scarred skin hung from his skinny bones and his eyes were opaque with blindness. The old warrior's beard was white and his teeth stained yellow from years of the white man's tobacco. Wallarie sat cross-legged under his favourite tree as the sun rose on his face. He could smell the dry, red earth around him and strained to hear the fading cry of the curlew deep in the brigalow scrub surrounding the mission station. He sensed his life was almost spent and he waited to join so many of those he once knew – now long gone. Locked in his memories spanning almost a century he toyed idly with the battered old wood pipe in his hand. It was empty and he hoped that someone would come and give him tobacco to light and suck the smoke into his lungs.

There was a sound and Wallarie cocked his head. The noise came from something the old Aboriginal had never seen but had smelled and heard many times in the past couple of years. An automobile, the Pastor called this new thing, that came to Glen View station carrying people on its back. It ground to a halt not far away, raising a fine film of dust to swirl around him as he sat beneath the bumbil tree.

'Wallarie, are you well?' the man's voice asked politely. It was a young voice, a lad in his late teens. 'I thought you might like some tobacco.'

Wallarie's face broke into a broad grin as he turned his blind eyes to his visitor. 'You got baccy,' he replied and reached out to receive the precious gift.

Although he couldn't see the young man squatting in front of him, Wallarie knew he was waiting patiently until the pipe bowl was plugged, tamped down and lit from a box of matches Wallarie carried with him. He could feel the warmth of the sun flow over his body. As the young man waited for him to speak he sucked contentedly on the pipe until he could feel the euphoria the nicotine brought to his old body.

'You want to hear the rest of the story?' Wallarie chuckled, knowing that the young man scoffed at the curse of the ancient cave on the hill at Glen View. 'Well, it was about twenty of your years ago,' he said, knowing that his words would mesmerise his listener, for not only was Wallarie of the Darambal people a great warrior in his youth, but in his old age he had become a wondrous storyteller. 'It was the time before you had the Great War,' he continued, carrying the listener back across the years with his hypnotic words. 'They had all forgotten the curse ... except one . . . until it touched them. I will tell you of those times when the whitefella touched the clouds and lightning came down on the earth for many years. The whitefella who flew with the eagles knew that he must learn to do this ahead of what you whitefellas called the Great War.'

I

Office of the Secret Service Bureau
London
December 1913

A light flurry of snow was falling outside the
plainly decorated office of the young, studious-
looking man. He was in his early twenties, with
thinning sandy hair. Before him on his desk lay
sheafs of paper both in German and his own translation handwritten in English. Although the man
was dressed in a well-cut civilian suit he was in fact
a British naval officer and held the lowly commissioned rank of ensign. Ensign Rutherford placed his
pen by the bottle of ink and rubbed his eyes. Outside
his office he could hear the clop-clop of horse-drawn
carriages and wagons making their way through the
fall of soft snow. He had worked diligently on his
translation of the German naval papers for most of
the day, to ensure that he had not made any mistakes.
It had been a valuable intelligence coup. The translated document had to go upstairs to the commander

of the Bureau before he could sign out and join his family for the Yuletide break away from his naval service to His Majesty.

Ensign Rutherford stood to stretch his long legs. He walked stiffly to the window of his office to gaze down on the light traffic of the London street. He was deep in thought about what he had just translated and wondered how important the Imperial German naval operational order was to the welfare of the British Empire he served. After all, the documents did not relate directly to a threat to England's naval security. He was not aware that the original volume of German papers had arrived on his desk via a tortuous path from a French brothel to the British naval attaché in Berlin, and then on to London through diplomatic couriers. They referred to a plan by the Imperial German Navy to attack specified targets in far-off Australia and New Zealand in the event of war between Great Britain and Germany. As a mere ensign who happened to be fluent in the German language, he guessed the translated documents would most probably be filed and forgotten. How important could the former colonial towns of Brisbane, Sydney, Melbourne and Hobart be? And as for some place called Gladstone in Queensland and Westport in New Zealand, who in Hades had ever heard of them?

Ensign Rutherford returned to his desk and shuffled the papers into their respective piles. Since they were classified as *Top Secret* he knew that he would still have to handle the task he had been seconded to very carefully. When the papers were collated he placed them in a Bureau-issue leather satchel and left his office, locking the door carefully behind him.

'I need to deliver these documents to the Chief,' he said to a tough-looking former Royal Marine, now wearing civilian dress and sitting behind his desk screening people coming and going to the secretive offices of Britain's counterintelligence.

'Very good, sir,' the former marine replied. 'Just wait here.'

Obediently, Ensign Rutherford stood stiffly by the desk while the guard disappeared down a dimly lit corridor to return moments later.

'He will see you now, sir,' the guard said, resuming his post.

Rutherford marched smartly down the corridor. At a door he knew was the office of Commander Mansfield Smith Cumming, he knocked. A voice bade him to enter.

Rutherford stepped inside. The office was more elaborately decorated than his own and had a coal fire in the corner, warming the room sufficiently to make it comfortable. As he was in civilian dress he was not obliged to use the traditional salute, but braced as required by military etiquette.

'What have you for me, Mr Rutherford?' the middle-aged naval officer asked gruffly, placing a pen down beside papers he had been signing.

'Well, sir, I have completed the translation of the German papers and gleaned that it is an operational order by the Imperial Navy concerning their intentions towards some of our former colonies in the

Pacific in the event of war between Kaiser Willie and the King.'

The senior officer looked sharply at the tall young man standing before him and the young ensign regretted that what he had said could be perceived as flippant. 'Our good regent and the German Kaiser are related, and the Kaiser deserves the respect due to him, Ensign Rutherford,' Mansfield Cumming Smith rebuked. 'Kaiser Wilhelm was, after all, our late Queen's favourite grandson.'

'Yes, sir. Sorry, sir,' Rutherford said, blushing. 'I meant no disrespect.'

'Anyway, man, what did you conclude from your translation?' the head of the Secret Service Bureau asked, changing his tone.

'Well, sir, from what I read the Germans have a plan to destroy the towns of Brisbane, Sydney, Melbourne and Hobart using cruisers from their fleet on the China Station. They also intend to capture the coastal ports of Gladstone in Queensland and Westport in New Zealand to supply coal to their warships.'

'Westport has a particularly high grade of coal,' Smith Cumming muttered, looking down at the translated documents Rutherford had placed before him. 'That will not do.'

Rutherford did not really care. His mind was already on making his way to his parents' home in Portsmith for the Christmas festivities. 'Yes, sir,' he replied dutifully.

'Anyway, Mr Rutherford, you have done a good job and please accept my good wishes for the season,' the secret service chief said. 'That is all.'

Rutherford braced once again, thanked the senior officer for his good wishes, turned on his heel and marched out of the office leaving the British head of intelligence to ponder the significance of what lay on his desk. An attack on the former British colonies in the Pacific region in the event of war could seriously jeopardise a British victory against the growing might of one of their main rivals in Europe. Australia and New Zealand provided much of England's imports of primary produce, along with other essential war material. The Royal Navy might have to divert precious resources to defend the shipping channels across the Indian Ocean, leaving the North Atlantic denuded of essential warships. Something had to be done to counter any German implementation of such an operational order.

Smith Cumming quickly scribbled a memo, signing the document in green ink with the letter C. Colonel John Hughes, currently attached to the relatively new Australian Army, was a man he had satisfactorily dealt with before. All he had to do was locate his current whereabouts and bundle off the information to him. For an army man, Hughes was relatively intelligent, Smith Cumming mused. He would leave it in his hands. Now he could also leave the office, go home for a Christmas of good cheer and look forward to 1914 as a year of goodwill towards all men.

2

It floated rather than flew, Colonel Patrick Duffy
mused as he watched the fragile Bleriot monoplane rise over the desiccated paddock. The nose
of the canvas-covered, timber-framed, single-seat
aircraft dropped and the tiny machine dived at a shallow angle towards the ground.

'What the Dickens is he doing?' Colonel Duffy
asked the tall young man in his early thirties standing
beside him.

'Just watch and see, Colonel,' the man replied in
the distinctive Yankee drawl that had earned him the
nickname Texas Slim from his Australian friends. He
had in fact been Randolph Gates when he had been
born on the vast plains of Texas to a struggling cattle
rancher and his school teacher wife.

As Patrick Duffy watched he saw a small object
disengage from beneath the belly of the Bleriot

9

and hurtle on an angle towards the dusty paddock. It smashed into the earth and exploded in a puff of white powder. The aircraft was already raising its nose and drifting into a circle overhead so the pilot could observe the point of impact.

'Not bad,' Randolph Gates observed. 'Looks to me he was only about five yards off his target.'

'What caused the white dust?' Patrick asked.

'Matt used a bag of flour,' Randolph answered, waving his arms above his head.

The signal to land brought the little aircraft into a sweeping circle overhead as it approached a cleared area of the paddock. The Bleriot touched down, bounced a few times and came to a halt only twenty yards from where the two men stood. Dust trailed its landing as the bamboo tail skid-ploughed a small furrow in the earth. The engine spluttered into silence and Matthew Tracy – now better known as Matthew Duffy – eased himself from the cockpit to clamber to the ground. He wore goggles and a leather skullcap and his face was splattered with black oil. Beneath the grime of the flight was a face many women found appealing and the young man also had the muscled body most men envied. Matthew walked towards the two observers, taking off his goggles to reveal his eyes still untouched by the oil from the engine.

'We have a visitor,' Randolph said, walking towards his friend. 'Colonel Duffy.'

As he approached the tall, broad shouldered man in his early fifties Matthew held out his hand. There was no mistaking the bearing of the military man he had been – and still was – when he returned Matthew's firm handshake.

'Sir, it has been a few years since we last met,' Matthew said with a broad smile. 'It is good to see you.'

'It is good to see you, young Matthew,' Patrick said, releasing his grip. 'What, ten, twelve years?'

'Thirteen, I think,' Matthew answered just a little sheepishly. 'I should have kept more in touch with the family.'

'At least your mother has kept us up to date with news of your adventures,' Patrick said, reaching into the pocket of his jacket that he'd slung over his shoulder. He wore expensive suit trousers, a clean-starched shirt, braces and a straw boater hat. 'Can I offer you a cigar?' he asked, producing three fine Cubans.

'No thank you, sir,' Matthew replied. 'I am just a little dry in the throat after the flight.'

'Kate, your mother, wrote from Queensland to say that you were doing something with your Bleriot down our way,' Patrick said, offering the third cigar to Randolph who accepted it gratefully. 'Although you took great pains to conceal the importation of your aircraft into Australia I was informed of its existence. As you had not broken any regulations with our Customs the matter was not of any concern to the civilian authorities. But it did pique my interest – especially as it was by a cousin in the family of a well-known adventurous character. You know, you worry my Aunt Kate to death with your escapades overseas.'

'I don't mean to,' Matthew said. 'My mother is a good old stick.'

Patrick smiled at the young man's reference to his mother. Even in her late fifties Kate Tracy was a very good-looking woman with considerable wealth and power in the state of Queensland. Many eligible men attempted to court her but Kate Tracy, once also known as Kate O'Keefe and originally Duffy, thwarted all advances. Her life was lived for her only son and the financial empire she ruled over.

'So, what was that all about?' Patrick asked, gesturing with his cigar towards the paddock where the bag of flour had been dropped.

'I was experimenting with the idea of using aircraft to drop bombs,' Matthew answered. 'Texas rigged up a latch system that I could operate from the cockpit to release the bag, which under other circumstances might have been a modified artillery shell with fins to assist a more accurate flight.'

'You realise that Harry Hawker has just last week flown his Sopwith off the Caulfield race course in demonstration flights and has made some good money for his efforts. You could have done the same.'

'That Yank Harry Houdini beat us all to the first demonstration flights in Australia.' Matthew shrugged. 'What I have in mind here will be more important than financial gain when we go to war with the Germans.'

'So you believe war is imminent in Europe?' Patrick asked, drawing on his cigar.

'I have toured Europe – even Germany – and I can feel it coming,' Matthew answered, glancing at his tiny monoplane parked only a few yards away.

'I know aeroplanes will be vital in winning the war when it does come.'

Patrick smiled. 'Maybe, as a means of observing the enemy and directing cavalry formations against them.'

'More than that,' Matthew said with passion creeping into his voice. 'They will be used to bomb and machine-gun the enemy in places where we cannot reach them with our current arms. Only the lack of development of better aircraft prevents us from equipping planes to carry out those tasks already. We both saw what those rapid firing weapons could do to us in South Africa,' Matthew continued, referring to the time when he had enlisted under-age and fought as a mounted infantryman at Elands River while his cousin Patrick Duffy served as an officer with the mounted infantry in many battles of the Boer War. Matthew's youth had been eventually revealed and he was sent home to Australia. 'I think the days of the mass cavalry charges are over. Aeroplanes will become the new cavalry to swoop on targets and support our infantry.'

'You know, you are talking military heresy,' Patrick cautioned, grinning. 'The gentleman of the cavalry will never admit to being upstaged by mere machines.'

'Mounted infantry will still have a role,' Matthew consoled. 'I just see that the invention of the aeroplane is going to change warfare beyond our wildest dreams.'

'Matthew,' Patrick said, 'it is getting late and I have to return to Sydney for an important company meeting but I need to talk to you at more length about your ideas. There are people I want you to meet and I am offering for you and Mr Gates to come to my place on the harbour. You know where my house is. If it is possible I would like to have you both attend – say, next Sunday at 3pm. We have important business to talk about.'

Matthew sighed. He always felt that the time might come when he would eventually be forced into a meeting with his estranged Sydney family. It had been many years since he had met with Fenella Macintosh on a beach at Manly to say farewell. He vividly remembered the pain in her eyes as he walked away and out of her life.

As if reading Matthew's thoughts Patrick added with a smile, 'Fenella will be at dinner that day with her young man.'

'I am glad to hear that, sir,' Matthew answered.

'I am your cousin,' Patrick continued. 'You may as well call me by my name. After all, you no longer have any connections to the army that I know of.'

'I think that I would be more comfortable calling you by your first name, Colonel.'

Patrick slapped Matthew on the shoulder, understanding the military joke between them. Despite their blood link the younger man was paying his cousin the respect due to a highly decorated and experienced soldier. It would not be Patrick but Colonel that Matthew would continue to call his cousin.

'As you wish,' Patrick replied, turning to walk back to his car which he'd parked at the end of the paddock by a newly constructed sturdy tin shed. 'I will see you both next Sunday for dinner.'

As Randolph and Matthew watched him stride away Randolph turned to Matthew. 'What was that all about?'

'I am not sure,' Matthew answered, shaking his head. 'It has been years since I last had contact with the family in Sydney and now the colonel suddenly turns up out of nowhere. Whatever it is, I am sure we will learn over a good meal and port wine at the Macintosh mansion on Sunday. In the meantime, we have to put the old girl to bed.'

Matthew and Randolph strode towards the little Bleriot. Hooking up ropes, they pulled it towards the shed they'd especially constructed to house the aircraft. As they towed the Bleriot Matthew could not take his thoughts off Fenella. It had been so many years and they had both changed so much. Matthew had one advantage in their meeting, however. He had seen her while sitting in the darkened auditorium of a picture palace in Sydney. She was not at the time in the theatre, but actually on the screen. Fenella Macintosh was making a name for herself as a famous film actress.

The young woman slumped at a wooden table with her head in her arm did not appear to be aware of the man standing behind her, armed with a long-bladed knife which he held raised ready to stab her.

'Okay, cut. We will try that again from a different angle.' The young woman raised her head from the table to glance at the man who had called the direction. 'We need to see the grief in those big, beautiful eyes of yours, Nellie.'

Fenella Macintosh turned to her would-be killer and took his hand. 'Darling, you have an invitation to dinner next Sunday night at my father's house,' she said. 'A long-lost cousin will be the guest of honour.'

Guy Wilkes smiled down at Fenella. He was a handsome, dashing figure with dark, oiled hair parted in the middle and piercing eyes highlighted by the excess of stage make-up. Fenella was similarly made up, highlighting her most expressive features so as to convey her feelings to the audience, without recourse to sound. 'I don't think this script will work, Arthur, old dear,' Guy complained to the older man who joined them at the table.

Arthur Thorncroft frowned. He was a solidly built man but carried his sixty years well. He still retained the bearing of a man who had fought as an officer with the New South Wales contingent that had been sent to the Sudan. Thirty years earlier he had faced the fierce Dervish warriors. There too he had met a young colonial serving with the British army by the name of Patrick Duffy and an unlikely friendship had blossomed between the two men. In Arthur's world he would have liked their friendship to have developed into a more physical and intimate relationship, but Patrick Duffy was not that way inclined. Despite their differences, the two men remained close friends and Patrick's daughter, Fenella, was the nearest thing Arthur had to his own daughter. 'My dear boy,' he sighed, 'to stay in business

16

we have to make something a little more sophisticated than bushranger films. The unwashed masses want melodrama from our studios – otherwise the Americans will crush us out of existence.'

Now it was Guy Wilkes' turn to frown. He had hoped to be portrayed as a sadly heroic figure fighting the evil establishment of colonial Australia instead of a maniacal, jealous husband bent on killing his unfaithful wife. After all, had not the portrayal of bushrangers packed the tents and community halls in rural Australia and the newly built picture palaces in the cities? Had not those same films made him the heart-throb of women who swooned whenever he appeared in public? On the other hand, he might be able to identify with the character he was portraying when he looked into the wide eyes of the young woman at the table. Fenella Macintosh received the same adoration from half the male population of Australia; the other half was yet to see her on the silver screen.

'The crew feel that we should pack it in for today,' a young man said to Arthur. 'We can have an early start tomorrow.'

Arthur turned to the young man whom he had appointed as his assistant film director, script supervisor, location selector, and manager of film props and lighting. 'Yes, well, if that is the feeling we will call it a day,' he agreed to the relief of the small group of people on the film set. The cameraman carefully dismantled his hand-cranked camera in its wooden box on a tripod and took the cumbersome apparatus away. Soon he'd develop the footage of film they had shot that day.

'Did I hear you tell Guy that you were having a long-lost cousin over for Sunday roast?' Arthur asked. 'And, if I had to guess, would I be right in saying it was young Matthew Duffy?'

'It is, Uncle Arthur,' Fenella replied.

'Ah, how is Matthew?' Arthur asked with genuine concern. His memory of Matthew was of his camera assistant bent on joining the contingents steaming across the Indian Ocean to fight the Dutch farmers in South Africa. Matthew had succeeded and found his war at the Elands River battle.

'You must tell him to contact me when you see him,' Arthur sighed. 'It has been a long time.'

'I will,' Fenella replied. 'I am sure that he will come and visit us on the set.'

'Well, I will let you lovebirds enjoy the rest of the day and bid you a fond farewell.' Arthur turned to walk away and his assistant fell into step, chatting with his boss and lover about the requirements for the next day's filming of *Love Lost and Found*.

Arthur's exchange with Fenella had aroused Guy's curiosity. 'Who is this cousin of yours?' he asked with a churlish note to his question, sensing something intimate from the past.

'He is the son of my father's aunt,' she said, using a cloth to wipe away the excess eye shadow from her face. 'He left his home in Queensland when he was about fifteen to travel to Sydney and for a short while worked with Uncle Arthur as his assistant.'

'So, he is one of them,' Guy said smugly, dismissing

the mysterious cousin as any threat to his hold on Fenella.

'I strongly doubt that,' Fenella retorted. 'He was able to lie his way into the army and fought in South Africa very gallantly, so my father has told me, before being revealed as under-age. He was sent home and, from what I have heard, worked his mother's cattle properties in Queensland as well as travelling the world to some very exotic places. Father has told me that Matthew is now an aviator.'

'None of that does not say your cousin is not one of Arthur's mob,' Guy snorted dismissively.

'Well, Matthew used to send me love letters from Africa – when he was a soldier,' Fenella replied, knowing full well that her reply would upset Guy. It did not hurt to remind the man in her life that he always had competition for her affections. Her statement had its effect and Guy Wilkes, debonair actor of the silver screen, fell into a surly silence as he wiped the make-up from his face.

Arthur Thorncroft was last to leave the film set. He had paid carpenters to construct the shell of a living room, open on one side to allow natural light to filter in assisting the cameraman do his work. The window on the back wall was in fact a painting to save on construction costs, and when the scene had been completed in his melodrama about a wife in love with another man, it would be replaced with another picture.

Arthur was very good at hiding his emotions

and none of his staff were aware of what a financial dilemma Arthur's film company faced. From 1907 to the previous year profits for his films had meant for an optimism that had proved to be falsely based. Developments in the thriving Australian film industry were being sabotaged by the emergence of more cheaply produced foreign films swamping the local market. Also a system had developed in the Australian industry where the separate entity of the distributor – a middleman who could more efficiently supply the exhibitor with a steady supply of imported movies – was cutting producers like Arthur out of the distribution of their own films to cinemas. To keep ahead of the strangulation of his films by the powerful distributors Arthur had been forced to borrow heavily for production costs so that his own films could impress even those middlemen distributors. Arthur had always relied on the Macintosh family – headed by Patrick Duffy – and financial support had always been forthcoming. Patrick had allowed his children to assume the Macintosh family name on his maternal grandmother's dying wishes and Patrick had even accepted a conversion from his Irish Catholicism to that of his grandmother's stern, Protestant beliefs although he did not demonstrate any real adherence to religion in his life. Lady Enid Macintosh had been a formidable woman in her time and this trait continued in her great-grandson George Macintosh, whom Arthur was scheduled to meet at the set this evening.

George Macintosh was punctual. He arrived in his expensive, chauffeured car, stepped from the vehicle, adjusted his tie and glanced around the empty lot. With purposeful strides he walked to Arthur's cluttered office.

'Hello, Arthur,' George said coldly, not bothering to offer his hand. 'You and I have some business matters to discuss.'

Arthur gestured to a chair. George Macintosh was around thirty years of age, with an aristocratic demeanour and handsome appearance. He stood at average height and carried no excess weight considering the playboy life he led among Sydney's most respectable society. He had the suave good looks that attracted even married matrons and many had used their feminine charms in an attempt to win his favour. But George Macintosh had an eye for young, single women and was very successful in his endeavours to bed them.

Appraising the man sitting opposite him, Arthur experienced the usual chill of apprehension he always had in George's company. Arthur remembered an old Macintosh rumour that somehow the family had brought down on their heads a terrible curse for an atrocity committed on their property of Glen View in central west Queensland over half a century earlier. Looking at George, Arthur wondered if the curse was the younger man himself. He wished Alexander, George's younger brother, had been more motivated to take on the management of the Macintosh financial empire of shipping, rural properties, stocks, shares and real estate development. Now that empire could be said to include shares in the blossoming film industry. But Alexander was very much like his father, Patrick, a man driven more by adventure than business.

'By business, I presume you mean the profits of my last film,' Arthur offered.

'Should we say, the lack of profits,' George replied, steepling his fingers under his chin.

Arthur knew from past experience that this gesture usually spelled something he would rather not know about. 'This film will recuperate that loss,' he said defensively, not really believing what he had just stated. 'But I will need more funds to complete shooting.'

George rolled his eyes dramatically. Maybe he should have been the actor and not his sister, Arthur thought, watching George's pained expression. 'I am not sure that lending any more to you would help,' George said. 'As I see it, the options are either closing down your company and selling off all assets to a rival or replacing you as the producer.'

Arthur had half expected that he would be put on the mat over the losses but did not expect to be sacked. He was stricken by the thought. 'What if I spoke to your father,' he suggested, sweat oozing on his hands. 'He and Lady Enid initially backed me in setting up the company.'

George's smile lacked any semblance of warmth. 'My father has delegated all financial management to me – as you well know – and at the moment he is too preoccupied playing soldiers to be interested in any decisions that I might see fit to make. You have no other choices than those I suggest. So what is it to be? Bankruptcy or bail out while you can?'

Arthur rose to his feet, his face reddening. 'If you just give this film a chance we will be back in the black,' he said, controlling his rage at the smug, young man smiling at him from his chair. 'After all, your own sister's career is at stake. Would you deny her a chance to rival Lottie Lyell?'

'But you are no Raymond Longford,' George said, referring to the well-known and respected Australian film producer. He rose to end the meeting. 'You have twenty-four hours to reflect on my offer. Good evening, Arthur.'

In a fog of despair, Arthur watched George leave his office. How could such a good family as the Macintoshes produce such a callous bastard like George? Twenty-four hours to find a solution to the problems facing his production company was not enough time. He would keep the news from his crew until the last moment.

3

The tropical sun was almost at its zenith over the territory of the Morobe District in German New Guinea as Alexander Macintosh observed the young New Guinean labourer endure his flogging in courageous silence. The long cane rod rose and fell with ferocious rapidity ten times before the punishment was over, and the blood ran in rivulets where it had broken the shiny black skin of the boy's back. The young man was bent over a wooden structure and a huge, bearded white man towered over him, sweat staining every part of his dust-grimed white clothing as he wielded the long cane.

Sweat also trickled down Alex's clean-shaven face beneath his wide-brimmed floppy hat. He stood at just under six feet tall, had the broad shoulders and chest of his Scottish forebears and a pleasant, open face. The white tropical suit that he wore was also stained with sweat, the result of standing in the hot, midday sun of the tropics. Single and twenty-five years of age, Alex had steamed to the German port in New Guinea to trade and the Macintosh trader, the *Osprey II*, now lay at anchor in the placid waters just off the coast.

'Ja, that will teach him,' an older man with a neatly trimmed beard muttered beside Alex. Switching to the German language, he continued, 'His punishment is necessary to ensure that the kanakas understand the meaning of an honest day's work.'

Alex did not comment. He was a guest of Herr Schumann's hospitality on his copra plantation although personally he found the severe punishment brutal.

'Release him,' Schumann hollered to his foreman, a burly German who had administered the prescribed punishment to the labourer who had committed the crime of missing work for two days among the coconut trees of the German planter's property. 'Put a salve on his wounds and send him back to work.' Turning to Alex, the planter said, 'As you can see, Herr Macintosh, we are not barbaric in our treatment of the natives. The man was being punished for breaking the rules and now I will have him receive medical treatment.'

Alex bit his lip. He wanted to ask whose rules, but said nothing. His mission into German territory was on behalf of the family's financial interests in extending trade to the European colonisers north of the Australian-administered territory of Papua. He had to admit that many Australians in Port Moresby agreed with the corporal punishment administered by their German counterparts in New Guinea to control indentured workers, many of whom worked as virtual slaves to the Europeans. 'It is not my place to comment on Governor Hahl's policies in your territories,' Alex tactfully replied in German. It was a language that all members of his family had studied because of their links with Prussian relatives, one of whom was a Lutheran missionary with his station at the family property of Glen View.

'Hahl is too soft on the damned kanakas,' Schumann said, wiping his face with a clean handkerchief. 'Ah, we will have coffee on the verandah away from this damned sun.'

The German plantation owner was in his late fifties and very fit for his age as the scourge of malaria had acted to keep his habit of eating to excess under control. Both men turned to walk towards the sprawling timbered house with its encompassing wide verandahs and shuttered windows left open to catch the tropical breezes drifting in from the coast nearby. The house was silhouetted against the great, lushly covered green mountains to the west bordering the river valley that stretched into the hinterland. White clouds billowed above the mountains, promising a cooling afternoon downpour.

A young housemaid wearing a colourful wrap-around skirt delivered the coffee to the two men now seated in comfortable cane chairs on the verandah overlooking the rows of coconut trees. Both men had removed their hats. Albert Schumann produced a collection of fine cigars from a silver container and offered one to Alex.

'This is a tough country to break,' Schumann said, sucking on his cigar to produce a plume of blue-grey smoke. 'The kanakas are forever murdering our people – even missionaries, who have only the best intentions for them. Yet Berlin hardly grants any support to bring civilisation to the natives and protect our interests in these islands. We are a backwater in the Kaiser's empire. He has more interest in our African and Asian colonies than those in the Pacific. We are expected to support ourselves.'

'But your copra production is second to none,' Alex said to flatter his host.

'This is true,' Schumann answered, nodding his head. 'It is the reason you are here, yes?'

Alex took a long draw on his cigar and gazed out over the men toiling under the hot sun among the coconut trees. 'I represent business interests that can pay you a good price for your product,' he said.

'I know that your companies have the shipping to transport our product to Brisbane and Sydney,' Schumann said. 'What price are you tendering?'

Alex made an offer. For a moment Schumann did not answer. 'My wife and daughter will be arriving today, Herr Macintosh,' he finally said, as if ignoring the offer. 'Maybe we will talk business when you have had time to think about the figure you have put forward. But, in the meantime I would like to extend our hospitality to you and request that you stay over for a couple of days. You can observe how we manufacture the copra for export. I am sure that my wife and daughter would be impressed with our guest from Sydney who has relatives in Prussia. My wife is from Prussian aristocracy and may know your relatives.'

Alex knew that Schumann had considered the amount too low and was politely giving him time to come up with another offer. He was also surprised that his host knew so much about his family and, as if to answer the startled expression on Alex's face, Albert Schumann continued, 'There are many German businessmen in Sydney. We have a competent intelligence system when it comes to trade. It is always good to know who you are dealing with. I requested information on your companies when you wrote to me requesting this meeting. It is because you have links to my country that I am even considering your contract price.'

Alex smiled. Albert Schumann was a shrewd man and the negotiations would be hard fought.

Under a cooler, late autumn sun over Sydney, George Macintosh came off the tennis court, wiped his brow and reached for a tumbler of iced water. He swallowed the cold liquid and gazed across the spread of neatly manicured lawns to a spectacular view northwards over Sydney's harbour. Sailing boats, ferries spewing smoke and little clinker-built fishing boats dotted the serene, sparkling waters.

'You did not offer me a drink,' a female voice said petulantly beside George.

'You didn't play well,' George growled, turning to his tennis companion, Miss Coral Gregory-Smith. She wore a long, lightweight cotton dress to her ankles and the cumbersome dress required by young ladies even when playing a vigorous game such as lawn tennis had hindered her. The hurt expression on her face at the rebuke mattered little to George who hated losing at anything. Before she could reply, he added, 'We should get changed. Father is having a formal dinner for some guests including my long-lost cousin tonight. I am sure you will enjoy the company.'

Coral turned on her heel and, in an unladylike gesture, tossed her tennis racquet towards a neatly trimmed hedge, muttering tearfully words that a well-bred young lady from a good Sydney family should not know. George watched her stride away and shook his head. She was only the latest in a string of socially acceptable ladies he had courted and he wondered how long she would last when she came to learn more about his ideas of carnal pleasure.

When she had reached the doors of the sprawling Macintosh mansion, George pursed his lips in contemplative thought. This house would be his solely one day. Neither his sister, Fenella, nor his younger brother, Alexander, had any rightful claim on the Macintosh estates – at least in his opinion. After all, Fenella swanked around Sydney involved in nothing more than displaying herself to the public, while Alexander was just as weak as his father with his taste for adventure. His siblings had no real interest in furthering the family fortunes and, as far as he was concerned, they would only squander what his ancestors had fought hard to build into a financial empire in the colonies of Australia.

As he stood sipping a second glass of iced water

he saw his father in the company of a man George knew from previous visits as Colonel John Hughes, currently detached from the British army. Both men wore expensive suits and walked deep in conversation through the gardens at the edge of the estate as the waters gently lapped against the sandstone outcrops of the tiny, picturesque harbour inlet.

George frowned. His father hardly took any interest in the day-to-day running of the companies anymore, so preoccupied was he with his military duties as commanding officer of a militia regiment in Sydney. He seemed to spend more time in his uniform than in his business suit. George shrugged. Maybe that was a good thing. Now he was virtually the master of all decisions affecting the future of the family companies. So why was it that his siblings should have equal shares in all his hard work? Oh, what he could achieve without having to drag them along.

George placed the empty glass on the silver tray and hefted the racquet over his shoulder. He would go to his room, change for pre-dinner drinks and make idle conversation with his father's guests. The matter of Arthur Thorncroft's financial troubles would not be of any interest to his father. In fact, the situation could be used to destroy his sister in a devious way that only George could engineer. Fenella was the apple of his father's eye; he adored his only daughter. George brooded. Fenella could wrap her father around her little finger. All George had to do was open his father's eyes to who she really was – or, more accurately, what George would make her.

A smile slowly came to George's face as he walked towards the two-storey sandstone house with its many lavishly decorated rooms. All he had to do was first take his sister out of the family and then concentrate on how he could remove his brother. Alex was somewhere up in the wilds of New Guinea. Hopefully he would encounter some wild, savage headhunters, even cannibals, thereby solving George's problems. The idea flashed through George's mind, comforting him. He knew that his brother and sister were no match for his cunning. Nor was his weak father whose only claim to any fame was his military record, fighting first the Queen's enemies and later those of the King.

When George approached the front door he was greeted by his father's personal valet, a former Scottish soldier his father had fought alongside in the Sudan almost thirty years earlier. His name was Angus MacDonald, a tough-looking, broad-shouldered man in his mid fifties. His face was scarred from bar room brawls and his red hair now thinning. Patrick had located the former soldier down and out in a Glasgow slum on a visit to the British Isles ten years earlier and immediately given the former soldier he had shared so much with on the battlefields of Africa a job, raising him from the destitution of a retired sergeant major on a meagre pension.

'Hello, Angus,' George said, passing the valet by the door.

'Sir,' Angus replied, acknowledging the greeting coldly. 'I hope you had a good game.'

Angus watched the eldest son of the man he

would have given his life for many times over and shook his head. How could the finest soldier he had ever served have spawned such a loathsome creature? But the Scot was privy to many family secrets and well knew that Patrick Duffy had a habit of not wanting to know too much about his eldest son's private life.

Fenella arrived with Guy Wilkes on her arm and dazzled with her beauty, highlighted by an array of tastefully worn diamonds. She was greeted by her father who made a great show of paternal love. Next in line was George whose coolness towards his sister was cleverly masked by a man in control of his emotions.

'Hello, Nellie,' George greeted, without any attempt to kiss her on the cheek. 'This is Miss Coral Gregory-Smith.' His partner for the evening was also expensively dressed for the occasion. 'I believe Coral is an ardent admirer of your films.'

Coral, a very pretty young woman of twenty years, flashed a smile. 'I have seen all of your pictures,' she said in a gushing way. 'I think that you are very beautiful.'

Fenella accepted the compliment and returned the smile warmly. She noticed Coral's eyes fall on Guy and the young woman continued, 'I have also seen all your pictures, Mr Wilkes, and think that you are our best actor.'

Guy warmed to the words and pushed forward to take Coral's hand in his. He did not let her fingers go until a little longer than the necessary time expected by the formalities of introduction.

Fenella glanced across the dining room to see Matthew and Randolph standing side by side looking a little awkward. Both men wore the required dinner suits and she could not think how Matthew had grown even more handsome in the many years since she had last seen him. But then he was hardly more than a fifteen-year-old boy who had escaped the hell of war. Immediately, she moved gracefully across the room to greet him.

'Hello, Matthew,' she said, extending her hand. 'It has been a long time.' She thought she saw a blush under his deep tan.

'Nellie,' Matthew said, accepting her gesture. 'It is wonderful seeing you all grown up although, I have to admit, I have had the chance to see you on the film screen.'

'Why did you not keep in contact with us in Sydney?' Fenella asked, gently chiding him. 'We are, after all, family.'

'I, ah . . .' Matthew fumbled. 'This is Mr Randolph Gates, a good cobber of mine,' he said, turning attention away from his cousin's question. 'He is also an ardent admirer of your performances on the screen.'

Fenella turned to the man standing beside Matthew. He was tall with a ruggedly handsome face and when he introduced himself she detected his slow American drawl.

'I think that Guy would have competition from you, Mr Gates, if you ever chose to be in films.'

Matthew was surprised to see how his hard-bitten,

hard-drinking, two-fisted womanising friend looked suddenly vulnerable at the attention he received from the famous Australian film star.

'Ma'am, most of my friends call me Texas Slim,' he replied.

Matthew smirked, sensing that his American friend was smitten by Fenella's beauty and charm. Both men had travelled the world together and had formed a bond as close as that between blood brothers. In a sense, Randolph had been both father and brother to a young man growing to adulthood without knowing his long-dead American father, the legendary gold prospector Luke Tracy. But Matthew always remained the boss, his mother having first employed the American cowboy before the turn of the century to assist in managing her many cattle properties in Queensland. Like Matthew, Texas Slim was also a veteran of a military adventure, having fought in the American army in Cuba against the Spanish in the brief 1898 Spanish–American war.

Before they could enter into further conversation, Patrick entered the room with Colonel John Hughes, a distinguished-looking man with thick grey hair and a curling moustache waxed at the ends. Both Patrick and John Hughes held the rank of colonel – Patrick being a lieutenant colonel and John Hughes a full colonel, thus outranking Patrick by one level.

Patrick announced dinner would be served and Matthew escorted Fenella to the place at the table marked for her beside Guy Wilkes. In turn, all members and guests of the Macintosh family took their places at the long, polished timber table which glistened under the flicker of the rows of candles placed along the centre. Expensive silverware lined the table beside crystal goblets.

When all had taken their place, Patrick stood to give a welcoming speech and reached for his goblet of wine. 'To the King,' he said, raising his glass. All stood to raise their glasses in the traditional toast to the monarch. 'And to those who have in the past given their lives for the Empire.'

A mumbled repetition of Patrick's words echoed in the large, candle-lit room. Chairs scraped as people resumed their seats. Two maids entered the room to ladel soup into the bowls in front of the guests. Matthew and Randolph had found themselves seated near Patrick and Colonel Hughes. All were soon introduced to each other and the various courses of the evening came and went in an atmosphere of light conversation, jokes and laughter.

As the plates for the final course were cleared away, Patrick once again rose to his feet and cleared his throat. 'Ladies and gentlemen,' he said. 'I think it is time that the men withdrew to partake in cigars and port. Guy and George, I think that you should keep the ladies company so that we do not appear to be just old chauvinists. Thank you.'

Patrick turned to Matthew and Randolph. 'Gentlemen,' he quietly said, 'I think this is the time to have a discreet conversation in my library with Colonel Hughes.'

★

Patrick closed the door behind him and took down a decanter of port from a shelf. He distributed port glasses and opened a silver box of fine cigars. All four men helped themselves.

'Take a seat, gentlemen,' Patrick gestured, his lit cigar in one hand and port glass in the other.

All found large, comfortable, high-backed leather chairs and sank into them. 'I would like to say how good it is to have you both as my guests,' he continued, addressing Matthew and Randolph. 'It is no accident that I should catch up with you after so many years, Matthew.'

'We were wondering, Colonel . . .' Matthew said, taking a swig of the good port served.

'Possibly I should intervene here,' John Hughes said. 'It was I who prompted Patrick to contact you after a conversation a couple of years ago in Greece with an old politician friend of mine, Winston Churchill. Winnie also likes a good port and we were discussing some matters when he happened to mention a young Australian colonial with an interest in flying aeroplanes and his Yankee companion who had delivered him an excellent report on that war between the Italians and Ottomans in Libya. He was especially interested in the young colonial's views on the Italian use of dirigibles and aircraft to drop bombs on the Turks. Anyone come to mind?' Hughes asked with the trace of a smile on his face.

Both Matthew and Randolph noticeably squirmed in their chairs at the question.

'I knew Mr Churchill had been a correspondent in South Africa when I was there,' Matthew replied.

'He had also been a soldier before that and I had read of his interest in military matters, particularly the navy. We were not far from Greece so I thought the British might have an interest in what we saw in Libya and Tobruk.'

'I must say that your observations about the successful defence of Tobruk against the Italians by some young Turkish captain by the name of Mustafa Kemal was very interesting, considering it was written by someone who had never held a commission in the army.' Hughes continued, 'You should consider taking one in Colonel Duffy's Sydney regiment in the future.'

'I was once a soldier, sir,' Matthew replied. 'Some things on the battlefield are universal – like recognising military skill in a leader.'

'Well said,' Patrick interrupted. 'Do not think that we are in disagreement regarding your invaluable work assisting the Empire. On the contrary, we feel that you are far more valuable to our cause than you realise. I presume what you two observed has also been passed on to our American friends.'

'Colonel, if Texas is going to share the dangers then he shares the information. Yes, he has passed on our observations to his government. I feel that in the future we may have to turn to the other side of the Pacific for help against future enemies.'

'Highly unlikely the Yanks will rush to assist us in the event of a war in Europe,' Hughes said, puffing on his cigar.

'I was thinking about enemies in this part of the world,' Matthew replied. 'I feel that the Japanese may one day pose us a serious threat, considering their extraordinary navy and the rise of military influence in their society as a result of giving the Russkies a good thrashing. I dare say that one day they will be forced to seek territories in the Pacific region if they are to sustain their growing industries and population.'

'What you say might have merit,' Patrick mused, aware that Matthew and Randolph had spent some time living in Japan. 'In a sense that is why we are having this conversation. I already know that you are certain war will break out in Europe and that Britain will be drawn into any conflict there. That means us as well.'

'You Australians do not have to rush to defend British interests,' Randolph said quietly. 'After all, if the Limeys get into a shoot-out with the Austro-Hungarian Empire and its German allies, that does not really concern you guys over here. You would be better off staying out of it and making a fortune supplying both sides.'

'I am afraid we would not have any choice in the event of a war between England and Germany,' Hughes said. 'I cannot reveal sources but we do know of a German plan authorised by the Kaiser to attack eastern seaboard settlements in Australia in the event of war between Germany and England. The Imperial German Navy stationed in China has been tasked to make raids on the coast from Gladstone to Hobart and also on New Zealand centres of population. They see Gladstone – and Westport in New Zealand – as sources of coal for their shipping. Any bombardments of our settled areas could mean a severe cost to life and property that would force England to send a substantial part of its navy here to counter the threat. That would then weaken any chance of placing a blockade on German war supplies in the Atlantic. In the event of war we will be well and truly committed. Our first task will be to cripple all German bases in the Pacific to prevent the Imperial German Navy putting its operational plan into action. That is where you two come into the scheme of things.' Hughes paused to observe the reaction of Matthew and Randolph and allow Patrick to take over the conversation.

Patrick sipped his port and leaned forward towards Matthew. 'You are a civilian and not under any military jurisdiction. But of all the men I know I feel that you and Randolph are the most capable to carry out a mission for your country and the British Empire that could just prevent the Germans from carrying out their bloody plans to kill innocent men and women here. You see, Colonel Hughes and I go back a long way in our army careers and we are both thought of as unconventional outsiders. I suppose that is why we have included you two in an operational plan that is not exactly sanctioned by either the British or Australian governments. It involves a very touchy subject – espionage, and probably sabotage to boot.'

Matthew took a deep breath and glanced at Randolph who made a slight shrug of his shoulders. 'You already know that my ideas on the use of aircraft in war are somewhat unaccepted at this time,' Matthew replied. 'Then, I guess that I am in good company.'

Both Patrick and John Hughes broke into smiles,

raising their glasses to Randolph and Matthew. 'Gentlemen, welcome to the dirty world of spying,' Patrick toasted.

'Believe me,' Hughes said, 'you will receive no glory or even recognition for what you are about to do. You may even end up dead and buried in some place none will know of. Be assured, what you will be briefed on could change the course of history in our favour and save countless lives for the King and his Empire.'

'As a citizen of the good ol' USA, I am kind of not doing it for your king and his empire,' Randolph cut across the stirring words. 'But I will do it for my cobber, Matthew Duffy.'

Matthew took Randolph's hand and gripped it. 'Thanks, old chap.'

'And now to what we need you to do for us,' Patrick said, rising from his chair and walking over to a desk. He removed a map from a drawer. Spreading the map on the table he held down the edges with the decanter of port and his own glass. The other three men clustered around. On the map of the South West Pacific the German-occupied territories were highlighted.

'Here,' said Patrick, stabbing with his cigar at a place Matthew could see marked as the town of Rabaul in the German territory of Neu Pommern, 'is the target.'

Fenella and Coral were engrossed in a conversation about current fashions. George was bored and found

Guy's prattle about fashions for men equally as dull and inane. He sipped very little of his port wine as imbibing alcohol was something that held little interest for him – partly because he had strict rules for his workers to remain sober and felt he at least should set an example and partly because he knew the over-use of alcohol inhibited his ability to make clear decisions. He wondered at the meeting being conducted behind closed doors in his father's library. Why were the two guests in attendance? George knew that his father was somewhat careless when it came to concealing documents in his library, however, and was sure that in time he would, in a roundabout way, learn of the matters being secretly discussed. As business manager of the family companies George considered that he must know of everything his father was involved in, especially if he were to be on top of matters, even the military matters his father dabbled in. George turned to Guy and noticed that the man appeared to be fidgeting more than usual.

'If you will excuse me, ladies,' Guy said. 'I must leave your company for a moment.'

George watched the actor depart the room and noticed that he was not going in the direction of the mansion's bathroom. He waited a moment before also excusing himself to follow the path taken by Guy and found himself outside on the dimly lit verandah overlooking the harbour. At the far end Guy was sitting in one of the comfortable cane chairs. As George approached him he noticed that the man was sitting, staring with vacant eyes at the lights of the boats still plying the harbour waters.

'Is everything all right, old chap?' George asked, but Guy was slow to react to his presence. George closed the distance until he was an arm's length away. In the seated man's lap was a small brown paper sheet. On it George could see a powdery white substance and from his experience dealing with slum tenants he had a good idea what it was.

'How do you administer heroin?' George asked in a matter-of-fact tone.

Guy glanced up at him, focusing his eyes. 'I snort it,' he replied, wiping at his brow with the back of his hand. 'It helps with the pain. But that is something private, old boy.'

George sat down in an adjoining cane chair. 'Does my sister use the stuff?'

Guy turned to him with an expression of euphoria. 'Your sister does not know that I have recourse to Mr Bayer's fine product. She is a very moral lady.'

Not if she is with you, George thought, but refrained from verbalising his view. Instead he said, 'That is good to hear.' A secret smile crossed George's face, unseen by Guy. 'I would like to talk to you about something I expect you to keep to yourself.'

'What would that be?' Guy asked, carefully rewrapping the white powder in the brown paper sheet.

'I expect that you will be told in the next twenty-four hours that you no longer have a job. You may find yourself out on the streets.'

Despite his feelings of wellbeing, Guy reacted to the statement with a visible look of alarm.

'Because of my use of heroin?' he asked.

'No, no,' George said, raising his hand reassuringly. 'I do not judge a man's private life,' he lied. 'Your employer, Arthur Thorncroft, is up to his neck in debt and will probably be bankrupt very soon. He does not have the funds to finish his film.'

'What can be done?' Guy asked, turning to George.

'I was hoping that you would ask that,' George replied with a smile. 'But I will need you to do me a personal favour. I can assure you it will be worth a lot more money to you than what Arthur is currently paying you. I have only one question: how much money would it take for you to fall out of love with my sister?'

George's question startled Guy. He blinked, his mind muddled by the effects of the opiate. 'That is a strange question,' he said slowly. 'I doubt that you would have enough money to make me give up Nellie.'

'So you admit that money might change your mind,' George said, sensing that the man on the verandah was essentially a weak, vain man who could be bought. 'How about the figure of two thousand pounds.'

Guy's eyes widened. It was a small fortune, a lot more than he made working as an actor. 'I would have to think about it,' he mumbled, breaking into a sweat.

'You have until you leave tonight,' George said, rising from his chair. 'After that, you will not only be out of a job, but will not hear my offer again. It is your only real option.'

'Is that what giving up your sister will cost?' Guy asked.

'I did not say that,' George replied. 'I asked how much it would cost to fall out of love with my sister – not leave her.'

Confused, Guy stared at the dim figure before him. 'What would you expect of me – if I accepted your offer?'

'If you take my money then I expect that you will honour what I ask of you,' George replied, walking away. 'Just give me your answer before you leave tonight.'

Randolph was pleased to be back in the company of Fenella when the meeting was over. He was even more pleased to see that she was alone.

'Mr Gates,' Fenella said, smiling at the American, 'I see that my father has released you to our company.'

'Your father is a very interesting and charming man,' Randolph replied. 'But I must confess that so are you.'

Fenella blushed at the compliment and chided herself for doing so. She could not remember the last time a man had been able to make her feel more like a young, naive girl rather than a worldly woman of the world. 'I have been informed by Uncle Arthur that you Americans are renowned for your flattery.'

'There is a difference between a statement of fact and idle chatter,' Randolph replied.

Fenella found herself appraising the tall American with an uneasy interest. He had an aura about him of strength, courage and gentleness which was very appealing. 'I hope that we get the opportunity to meet again,' she found herself saying, noticing Guy returning to the room and immediately making a line towards Randolph and Fenella.

'I hope so, too,' Randolph said, seeing Guy approach. 'I think that I should excuse myself. Your beau has returned.'

As Randolph walked away to join the men standing in the room Fenella could not help comparing the man at her elbow with the one now with his back to her. Maybe it was a good thing that she had met Guy before Randolph, she thought with a touch of guilt, and quickly dismissed the thought.

As the evening came to an end and each of the guests departed Guy Wilkes shook George's hand. 'You have a deal,' he said quietly.

4

Patrick's family and guests had departed leaving only the servants and his friend John Hughes, who was with him in the library to share a bottle of good port wine. Cigar smoke filled the room with its pungent but not unpleasant odour.

'Do you think that your choice of men for this important operation has been wise?' Hughes asked, rolling the ruby red liquid in his goblet. 'I can understand why you have assigned Alexander to the mission as he is a commissioned officer in your regiment, but Matthew Duffy is a civilian.'

'Matthew may be a relative of mine and a civilian,' Patrick replied, 'but his background and grasp of military technology has equipped him to carry out the task probably better than my own son Alex.'

'I am not sure if it is proper to have the American tag along,' Hughes said.

Patrick shrugged. 'I doubt that we could have asked Matthew without asking Mr Gates,' he replied. 'I suspect that the Yanks are already keeping a close eye on developments in this part of the world. They don't trust the Japanese. After all, the visit of their Pacific fleet here a couple of years ago was to impress the Japanese as much as to show us who is master of the Pacific. The Japanese victory over the Russians back in '05 has made everyone a little nervous and from reports we have received it appears the military is assuming a greater role in Japan. They are shaping up to be the Prussians of the East.'

Hughes nodded his head in agreement. As the principal intelligence officer in the Pacific region for the British government he was very much aware of the rapid Japanese armaments progress, but so far the Japanese government had remained cordial to His Majesty's government. The Japanese had based their navy on the British model but they had also used the German model to build a formidable army. Hughes also knew that the Japanese reaction to any war in Europe would be critical to the future of Australia and, in turn, critical to Britain's strategic interests. The Japanese naval ports were in close proximity to those of the German cruiser squadron in the Chinese harbour of Tsing-tan. 'My people in London do not feel that we should get ourselves entangled in any war that might break out on the European mainland,' Hughes said. 'The PM has intimated that we will only be drawn into a war there if the Germans violate Belgian territory. Otherwise, the Froggies and the Prussians are welcome to maul each other like they did back in '73.'

'We can't take the chance that England will stay out of any war in Europe,' Patrick said, gazing at a curling wisp of cigar smoke that rose around his head. 'We have very little in the way of land or naval forces to resist an attack on our coastal cities. That operational order for the Australian station gives clear intentions of what the Germans will do to us in the event of war with England. It will not just be a matter of rallying to the Mother Country but a matter of survival. Matthew's mission is vital to sabotaging any first strike by the Imperial German Navy. We will have to move first and very fast if we are to prevent the German cruisers currently stationed in China steaming south from their base to bombard our main centres of population.'

Patrick's views were guided by his knowledge of a summarised and translated paper that Colonel Hughes referred to as *document twenty-two*. Its contents had been cabled in code to Sydney early in the new year. Hughes was not authorised to reveal how the sensitive German document was intercepted, such was the importance of protecting the source of the intelligence. It was like a giant game of chess but with both Hughes and Patrick Duffy playing as a team against their unseen if not unknown German adversaries. As the German Pacific empire stretched across Australia's northern borders the threat was very real to Australia's very own survival should war break out between Germany and England. Both professional soldiers had witnessed the terrible effects of bombardments on the minds and bodies of men in past conflicts. They had seen the horrifying effects that great shards of red-hot steel could inflict on a man's body, tearing it to shreds, disembowelling and ripping away limbs. Neither man wanted to see such sights on Australian soil; they did not want Australian men, women and children suffering under a German naval bombardment of their homes and places of work. Now, the two men would embark on a mission that just might tip the balance against the orders contained in the German document. But it would be a dangerous course of action. It could cost two close relatives and a neutral American their lives.

'Well, old chap,' Patrick said, raising his glass, 'here's to the success of the operation – and that God might be on our side in this venture.'

Hughes smiled, raising his glass in response. 'Here is to three brave young men with a sense of duty. May God protect them in the difficult days ahead and furnish us with a victory.'

Both men swigged from their ports, engrossed in their private reflections of what together they had plotted to change the course of history, a plan unauthorised by their respective governments. Colonel John Hughes knew that the chief of intelligence in London would not want to know about it – especially if things went wrong. Both men in the room were acutely aware that their reputations and careers were on the line as much as the security of their beloved countries.

In the back seat of Patrick Duffy's chauffeured car, Matthew Duffy and Randolph Gates remained silent.

Patrick had arranged to pick up the two men from the Emu Hotel in Chippendale where they were staying while in Sydney and then take them back after the dinner. The men's thoughts were in turmoil; the proposition put forward for their assistance in a scheme to spy on the German military to the north of Australia occupied Matthew's mind, while the meeting with Fenella Macintosh at the dinner hours earlier filled the American's thoughts.

The car stopped in the dark city street dimly lit by a gas light in front of the hotel, a two-storey building well known to country visitors. Thanking the driver, Matthew and Randolph alighted to knock on the door and be ushered inside by an elderly night porter who recognised two of the younger guests of the establishment.

'I know it's late but is there any chance of getting a bottle?' Matthew asked. 'It will be worth a bob for you.'

The porter was a man experienced in the needs of hotel guests and had a thriving little business on the side, supplying their requests ranging from after-hours liquor to discreet visits from certain shady ladies. He also had contacts with starting price book-ies and a good knowledge of social gossip. 'Would you prefer rum or whisky?' he asked.

'Whisky would be fine, Harry,' Matthew answered. 'Could you deliver it to my room as soon as possible? I think Mr Gates and I could do with a stiff drink before retiring.'

The porter shuffled away to fill the order, leaving Matthew and Randolph to make their way up the stairs to Matthew's room. Unlocking the door, they entered the room already lit by a gas light. Now it was time to talk.

'Are we going to actually go along with the colonel?' Randolph asked, slumping down in a comfortable chair by the window overlooking the empty city street below. He'd had time to let the ramifications of what they were embarking on truly hit him during the car journey back to their hotel.

Matthew pulled out a chair behind an elegant desk and sat down. 'I said we would,' he answered. 'But I do not expect that you have to stick with me on this one, old friend.'

'God damn you, Matt – you think I would let you go alone on this one?' the American growled. 'Your mother would hunt me down and skin me alive if anything happened to you.'

Matthew grimaced at the mention of his mother. For years he knew she had accepted her only son's wanderlust and thirst for the dangerous as something he had inherited from his father, Luke Tracy. Matthew knew that as a young woman his mother had faced danger every day of her life forging her fortune on the wild Queensland frontier. And he guessed she had accepted that exposure to war had changed her son, and had expressed gratitude for the fact that, for a couple of years upon returning from South Africa, he had at least worked one of the family cattle properties in Queensland under the watchful eye of her chief manager, Randolph Gates. Eventually, Matthew had gone to her and begged for a substantial allowance to pursue a life travelling the world. He knew that his mother had agonised over his plea to be set free to wander. At first she had resisted but after a year she relented, setting one proviso: Matthew could only travel in the company of Randolph Gates. Matthew gladly accepted the condition. Over the years he and Randolph had formed a mutual respect for each other. That had been the first step on Matthew's path to roaming the world and learning how to fly in Egypt, and Randolph had honoured his promise to his employer that he would keep in touch by letter informing her of Matthew's welfare.

'I promise that I will see Mother before we go on this little job for the colonel,' Matthew replied.

A knock at the door alerted the two men to the fact that the porter had delivered their bottle. Matthew thanked Harry and slid a note into the grateful man's hand. When they were alone again, he poured the whisky neat into tumblers, handing one to Randolph. Matthew raised his glass in the manner of a toast. 'Here's to beautiful women, a long life and the success of our mission,' he said.

Randolph responded in silence by raising his glass. He had been thinking about Fenella Macintosh and could not get her out of his mind. He also felt uncomfortable as he was aware of Matthew's romance with her some years earlier. Taking a long swig from his glass, Randolph said casually, 'You must have been pleased to be able to meet again tonight with one whom you must be very fond of.'

Matthew stared blankly at his friend in the flickering light of the room. 'Who ... oh, you mean

Nellie,' he replied with a knowing grin. 'That was a long time ago and I was surprised at my feelings towards her tonight when we were together. I have to confess that all I felt was a very strong affection for my cousin, but nothing more than that. Nellie was merely a school boy crush.'

Inwardly, Randolph felt his spirits soar. So only that effeminate actor, Guy Wilkes, stood in the way of him convincing Miss Macintosh that he would like to see more of her. Randolph's opinion of the actor was low. As a man of action, he considered all men who could not rope a steer and brand a cow to be pansies. He doubted Guy Wilkes could do those things. 'I am sorry,' Randolph said.

Matthew blinked. 'You old devil,' he chuckled. 'I was right when I thought you had a bit of a thing for Nellie tonight. I could see the way you were hanging on to everything she said and the way you were looking at her with cow eyes.'

'I think that Miss Macintosh is one of the finest ladies I have had the honour to meet, that's all,' Randolph answered, dismayed that his interest in Matthew's cousin was so obvious.

'Well, you have a bit of competition for Nellie's affections,' Matthew continued. 'Guy Wilkes is very popular with the ladies.'

Randolph did not reply immediately but took a swig of his whisky. 'What do we do next?' he asked, changing the subject.

'We have six weeks to get matters organised before we are due to steam from Sydney in company with my cousin Captain Alex Macintosh,' Matthew replied. 'In that time, we can stow away the Bleriot and make a trip to visit my mother.'

'A good idea,' Randolph agreed. 'It has been at least a year since Miss Tracy last saw you. It will kind of prove that you are still alive.'

Matthew winced. It had always been his friend who had sent the letters from different parts of the world to keep Kate Tracy up to date on where they were and some of what they were doing. Randolph knew that he could not tell his boss that her only son was popular with many of the ladies they encountered from Shanghai to Moscow and had indulged himself in the charms they offered. Nor could he tell Kate Tracy of the times that he had been called on to tend to the wounds her only son received as a result of the occasional bar room brawls and small wars they stumbled into in the course of their wanderings. From what Randolph knew of the extended family history, trouble was a constant shadow in their lives. Kate's brother Michael Duffy had lived as a mercenary soldier from the battlefields of New Zealand through the end of the Civil War in Randolph's country and Mexico to the veldt of South Africa. Patrick Duffy, Kate's nephew, had served fighting from Egypt through the Sudan to South Africa as well. And Matthew too had served as a soldier in the war against the Boer farmers. Even now, Randolph could see that the young man's experiences in South Africa had left an indelible mark on his soul. His fanatical interest in the use of aviation in warfare was only an extension of his past. But one thing stood out about Matthew – he was a patriot to his country and born to soar with the eagles.

'Then we carry out our mission in Neu Pommern and come home.'

It sounded simple, Randolph thought. But what Colonel Duffy outlined earlier that evening was fraught with danger. The American brooded that he was participating in a mission that was of little concern to his own country. After all, a war among the Europeans that dragged their colonies into the conflict would not involve America, which had stated its neutrality in European politics. Only his friendship with Matthew dragged him into the plot.

Guy Wilkes angrily paced the carpeted floor of Fenella's small house located not far from Arthur Thorncroft's film studio. Patrick had purchased the house for her years earlier and because of its proximity to Arthur's studio it had witnessed many parties to celebrate the completion of a project. On a narrow, tree-lined avenue, the house was situated in a pleasant, middle-class suburb within walking distance of the trams that rattled through the city streets. Fenella sat at a mirror in her room set apart from the small living room where the actor fumed in his jealousy.

'You seemed rather enamoured of that bloody Yank tonight,' Guy said in a fury when he ceased pacing the floor. 'Don't try to deny it.'

Fenella stopped brushing her long, lustrous hair. 'I was not showing, as you are implying, any more interest in Mr Gates than I do in any of my admirers,' she sighed. 'From what I have been told by my father of Mr Gates he has led an interesting life.'

'There are thousands of women out there,' Guy said, entering the bedroom and waving his hand in the air, 'who would give their right arm to bed me. You are a fortunate woman to have me court you.'

Fenella felt her anger rise. 'Do you think that I have not many admirers?' she snapped, turning away from her reflection in the mirror. 'What were you before Arthur employed you – a good-looking draper's son from some godforsaken country town with big dreams of fame and fortune in the city. Well, you might have that, but you do not own me.'

Guy realised that he had over-stepped his mark. 'I did not mean it that way, Nellie,' he said, attempting to reconcile. 'What I meant to say is that we are both lucky to have each other. As Arthur has often said, we are the darlings of the film-going public.'

Fenella placed the brush on the dresser in front of her. 'I don't give a damn for what the public think of us as a couple,' she said slowly, choosing her words precisely. 'I am with you because I love you – not because you are Guy Wilkes, the dashing thespian. No more or no less than that. I do not care if Uncle Arthur feels our relationship is good for business.' She stood and walked towards Guy, whose eyes were still glazed from the withdrawal of the heroin he had inhaled. She touched his face with the tips of her fingers. 'You have to trust me or we have nothing together.'

Guy was surprised that her caress felt condescending rather than affectionate. Carefully keeping his emotions under control he raised his own hand to grasp her fingers and draw them down to her side. 'I do trust you,' he said quietly, turning away from her. 'It is time that I left to return to my place.'

As Guy made his way to the front door he congratulated himself on agreeing to George Macintosh's request. Fenella Macintosh was as traitorous as all other women that he knew – just like his own mother who had deserted his father and him when he was only five years old. When he was able to really confront himself, Guy had to admit that he despised women for their nature. It was ironic, he mused, that women loved him for his handsome looks and charm. Destroying Fenella Macintosh would teach her a lesson she would remember all her life, he thought as he closed the door behind him. It did not hurt that he would be richly rewarded for his services. Fenella needed to learn that she was a mere woman who should not upset him with her flirting ways. Yes, she would pay dearly.

George Macintosh slipped the gears of his Buick two-seater into neutral and left the car at the front of the old horse stables, now converted to a shed to garage his cars. He would let his manservant park the car inside as he did not want to bother himself with the effort. Miss Coral Gregory-Smith was safely at her home and it was time to retire to his grand house – once the property of his relatives, Granville and Fiona White. The house was smaller than the Macintosh mansion but still built of sandstone and two storeys high, with ivy creeping up the front and framing the array of windows looking out to the harbour. Alighting from the car George walked across the fine, gravel driveway to open his front door where he was met by a sleepy, older man dressed in a much-worn dressing gown.

'Sorry, Mr Macintosh,' the elderly manservant apologised. 'I thought that you might arrive home earlier. I seem to have dozed off.'

George eyed his manservant. Maybe he was getting too old for the job, he thought, and might best be replaced. He did not reply to the older man but pushed past him with a grunt of acknowledgment. When he had reached the bottom of the ornate stairway he turned to the servant. 'I am expecting a visitor around eleven o'clock tonight, Curtiss,' he said. 'Please ensure you are awake to allow her entry. Oh, you can put the Buick in the stables,' he added, tossing the key to the old man who fumbled with them, dropping the key to the floor.

'Very good, Mr Macintosh,' the servant replied, rising from his knees after retrieving the key and shuffling out the door.

George climbed the stairs to his library and found a bottle of fine Scotch whisky in a cocktail bar adjoining the wall-to-ceiling shelves of musty books collected by the Whites over the years they had resided in their Sydney house. Given what George anticipated would fill the rest of his evening, he broke his strict rule on the consumption of alcohol and sat down in a chair behind his desk to gaze about the library, reflecting for a moment on the previous owner. George had heard the family stories about Granville White. A man of peculiar tastes, was the way his father had described Granville, leaving the rest to the imagination. George somehow felt that he might have liked the man if he had still been alive.

He poured a generous shot of whisky and his attention returned to a ream of papers stacked neatly before him. They were the financial statements of Arthur's film company and did not reflect a good showing for the Macintosh companies to which it was indebted. George took a swallow of the fiery liquid and flipped a page of the report while removing his tie and loosening the top button of his crisply starched shirt. In the morning he would visit the bank that held the lien on the film company and either transfer funds or agree to fold the enterprise. Guy Wilkes' agreement to help him in his special project to discredit Fenella in her father's eyes had changed matters considerably and George knew that he would keep Arthur's project alive for the moment.

He turned over the page that he had been viewing and stared into the dark recesses of his library. His eyes rested on an array of old Aboriginal weapons – spears, shields and nulla nullas attached to the wall. For a brief moment the thought of a curse on his family flitted through his mind. Something that his grandmother Lady Enid Macintosh believed in, he mused, sipping at the Scotch. So much so that she had the collection moved to the house he now occupied. George did not believe in the power of superstition.

A gentle knock at the door alerted him to the fact that his guest had arrived.

'Come in,' he called from his chair and the door

opened to reveal a young woman he guessed to be in her late teens. 'You must be Florence,' he said, not bothering to rise from his chair. 'A mutual friend recommended your services.'

'I am,' she replied, attempting to appear confident.

George rose from the chair and strolled across the dimly lit library to stand before her. He could see that she wore the heavy make-up that stamped her trade on her face. 'Pull up your dress and lay across the table,' he commanded, walking to a corner of the room where a hollowed elephant's foot contained a collection of canes.

The girl moved uncertainly to the desk, bent over, revealing her naked backside. She watched George across her shoulder, her confidence mixed with fear. 'You will not hurt me,' she pleaded.

George flexed a thin cane as he returned to stand alongside the girl. 'That is why you are being paid so well,' he sneered. 'I may hurt you, but I will not harm you.'

The cane swished through the air, striking the girl painfully on her bare buttocks. She yelped and buried her head in the blotting paper on George's desk. Tears of pain flooded her eyes and, biting her lip, she reminded herself that this form of perverse entertainment was worth a month's pay to a working man.

George's face contorted with his pleasure at inflicting the pain on the helpless girl. His eyes bulged and the flush of excitement rose in him like a raging bushfire. Five more times the cane rose and fell until the girl could no longer restrain the tears that flooded her eyes. When the caning ceased she was aware that he was behind her with his pants to his ankles. Grunting like an animal, George spent himself in the girl who offered no resistance.

'That, my love,' George gasped, 'is what money can buy. Your body and soul.'

The young prostitute did not answer but bit back the pain. George was only warming up and felt a rush of ecstasy for the further pleasures that lay ahead before the sun rose.

5

Alex Macintosh had met many beautiful women in his quarter century on earth but Giselle Schumann was probably the most exquisite woman he had ever seen. At twenty years of age, her sun-gold hair, striking blue eyes, slender neck and pert nose sprinkled with freckles from her time living in the Southern Hemisphere were not her only attributes. She had a fashionable hourglass figure and moved with the grace of an aristocrat. Although she was not tall in an elegant way, being a head shorter than Alex, he knew from the moment his eyes met hers he was smitten by the young woman.

She stood with her mother at the bottom of the stairs leading to the plantation house, surrounded by suitcases as a couple of native servants manhandled the luggage from Schumann's car. Albert Schumann was obviously delighted to see his wife and daughter and after an exchange of warm greetings Schumann turned to Alex standing at the top of the stairs and introduced him.

'This is my beautiful wife, Karolina, and my equally beautiful daughter, Giselle,' he said proudly. 'I would like you to meet a guest of ours from Sydney, Mr Alexander Macintosh.'

Both women smiled and Alex attempted to read Giselle's expression. It was warm and he thought he saw a glimpse of a challenge in her eyes.

When the luggage was stored away Schumann arranged for coffee and cakes on the verandah. Alex was struck with the warmth of the family to each other and they were inclusive of his presence as well. When Albert Schumann was forced to excuse himself to attend to an urgent matter on the property Alex was left with his wife and daughter.

'My husband has informed me that you are related to the von Fellmanns from Prussia,' Karolina Schumann said in German. 'I know the Count and his wife well.'

'I must confess that I have not kept contact with that side of the family,' Alex replied, sipping delicately from a fine china cup. 'A relative on my grandmother's side married into the von Fellmanns and one of their sons currently has a Lutheran mission station in Queensland. I met him many years ago when I was with my grandfather.'

'They are a very wealthy and respected family in east Prussia,' Karolina continued, keeping Alex's attention. He could see where Giselle inherited her beauty. 'But so much for idle chatter concerning

63

family,' Schumann's wife said, placing her coffee cup on the cane table. 'My husband has also informed me that the ship we noticed in the harbour belongs to your family and that you are here to negotiate a cargo of copra before you leave us.'

'That is correct,' Alex replied, glancing at Giselle who had so far remained out of the conversation. 'We only have to agree on a price.'

'I hope that you and my husband are able to arrive at one that is mutually agreeable,' Karolina said. 'In the meantime, I trust our hospitality meets with your satisfaction.'

'Your husband has proved to be more than a kind host, Mrs Schumann,' Alex said. 'And it has been a privilege to meet you both.'

'You must excuse me, Mr Macintosh,' Karolina said, rising and straightening her long, flowing cotton dress. 'I must organise with our servants for the dinner tonight. I am sure that you and my daughter are able to carry on a conversation.'

Alex rose from his chair as Karolina departed to go inside the house. He sat down and turned to Giselle who was smiling enigmatically at him. 'What is funny,' he blurted, sensing that he had done something to amuse the young woman.

'Your German,' she said with the noticeable trace of an educated English accent. 'It is not very good.'

Alex blushed. He should have known that Giselle spoke English. Her father had informed him that not only was she born in Australia but had spent all her schooling there in an exclusive ladies' college in Sydney. 'Well, I was tutored in your language with the aid of a cane,' Alex said, reverting to his native language. 'It did not endear me to German language lessons.'

'But you do have German relatives if not our blood,' Giselle said, raising her cup to her lips. 'I must confess to you that I feel more English than German although I would never tell my parents that. I have spent most of my life living among English speakers in your country and have come to admire your way of life so far from our home in Prussia.'

'Have you visited your home in Germany?' Alex asked, pleased to be able to slip into a conversation with the young woman in his own language.

'Yes,' Giselle replied. 'We have spent the occasional Christmas at home. My father has done so to remind me of my roots and our culture, but I am afraid the snow was not as pleasant as walking on the beach in summer in Sydney.'

Alex was surprised at how Australian Giselle was, considering that she was classed as a German by the fact of her parents' heritage. He was aware that she was watching him with a decided interest and then and there decided that Giselle would remain in his life forever. Fate had sent him to this remote German outpost in the Pacific to meet the woman whom he would share the rest of his life with. Her presence caused his real mission to fade away as easily as dust before a storm.

The review of the island's defence force was over, and upon entering the Garrison Officers' Mess at the Rabaul Club, Major Kurt von Fellmann removed his cap and placed it on a hat stand. He glanced around the room with its timber plank walls adorned with the occasional stuffed deer's head and high ceilings providing circulation of the humid tropical air. The club was obviously an attempt to remind the German planters and civil servants of their Fatherland, which had flung itself onto a wild and sometimes savage frontier. His eyes settled on a similarly dressed officer wearing the tropical uniform of a reservist captain.

Kurt strode forward. At thirty-five years he had the martial bearing of his profession. He had inherited his Australian mother's blonde hair and blue eyes – as had his twin brother, a Lutheran pastor working among the Aboriginal people of central Queensland. The captain rose from his chair at a table, stood to attention and clicked his heels together in the traditional German salute.

'You may resume your seat, Hauptmann Hirsch,' Kurt said, taking a chair opposite the German captain, a man in his late twenties with an open, pleasant face and a shock of red hair. He wore his field uniform stained with sweat and was of medium build and average height. He did not stand out in a crowd except when he was in command of men and then his true character as a leader prevailed.

'What did you think?' Dieter Hirsch asked with a frown.

'Fifty reservists and a contingent of around six hundred native police are no match against the English in Australia,' Kurt replied in disgust. 'The damned government in Berlin has absolutely no idea how important the radio station here is to our naval strategy in the event of war with the English. We should have at least a couple of regiments of regular army, supported by artillery, garrisoning these islands – not what could barely be considered a company of troops.'

'You can see that we are forgotten out here,' Dieter Hirsch replied, pouring schnapps into two glasses. They were virtually alone in the club in the mid afternoon as the population of the modern, well-set out town of timber and iron-roofed houses sweltered under the fierce tropical sun. In the shadow of the ever-present volcano that dominated the pretty township on the harbour of Blanche Bay, avenues of mango trees provided some shelter to pedestrians walking the streets. The German trading town was prosperous, the hub of colonial administration in the German Pacific empire. 'The Kaiser prefers his African empire to that so far from Germany in the Pacific.'

Kurt accepted the tumbler of fiery liquid from the German reservist officer who, when not parading with his fellow colonists wearing their slouch hats and shouldering Mauser rifles, was a civil servant working for Governor Hahl. 'I can see that, and upon my return home will be lobbying to reinforce these islands.' He raised his glass in a silent toast and Dieter Hirsch responded by doing likewise.

'Do you think that there will be war with France?' Dieter asked gloomily. He had grown to love his single life in the tropics away from the cold, closed areas of his native Munich. War would mean an end to his idyllic life. He would be mobilised for the conflict and possibly sent home to serve.

'Eventually,' Kurt replied, with less than reassuring words for the German civil servant. 'All of Europe is a vast depot of arms and armies. The British challenge our right to rival them at sea and the French hate us in Europe. All it will take will be a spark to set us all off in a war.'

'It does not seem that our civilian population is as aware of the situation as we in the military are,' Dieter said. 'And if there was a war with France I have read that the English will possibly stay neutral.'

'That it may be,' Kurt replied, swigging at the schnapps. 'They traditionally have no love for the French. If that is so, my friend,' he continued, 'you will not have to worry about your position out here in the wilds of our Pacific frontier.'

'I will drink to that,' Dieter said, raising his glass. 'To peace in the Pacific and a glorious victory to us – if we eventually fight the French.' Kurt did not want to disappoint this very likeable reservist officer and so joined him in his toast. 'Oh, I almost forgot,' Dieter said, reaching into the pocket of his trousers and retrieving a telegram. 'This arrived a few hours ago.' He passed the slip of paper to Kurt. 'It appears that we are to expect an Australian trading steamer in port next week with a passenger who is related to you, a Mr Alexander Macintosh from Sydney. He is currently visiting with Herr Schumann in New Guinea. Schumann is one of our more influential plantation owners.'

Kurt scanned the inked words on the paper and

folded it neatly. It appeared that his country's intelligence services were well and truly active in this backwater of the Kaiser's empire and he guessed that his distantly related Australian family were aware of his whereabouts in the Pacific from his itinerary posted at the German consulate in Sydney. It was not a military secret that he had been tasked by Berlin to make a tour of German defence outposts on behalf of the Imperial German Army. He had been chosen as he had a good grasp of the English language and the culture of the European settlers of the Australian continent. He was also tasked to end his tour with a goodwill visit of German settlements in Australia. He had a vague idea about his relations in Australia from the letters his brother Karl had written to him. There had been an interesting story about a trek his brother had undertaken in the company of the legendary Michael Duffy when Alexander was only a boy. It seemed that Alexander had not known that Michael Duffy was in fact his grandfather. Now he was about to meet the young man who he also knew held the King's commission with an Australian militia unit.

'I hope that the visit from Mr Macintosh will prove to be a happy one for you, Herr Major,' Dieter said.

'Oh, yes,' Kurt replied. 'I have not had the pleasure of meeting him before. It will be interesting to catch up on the English side of my family.'

When the glass was empty Kurt rose to excuse himself. He had much to do to record his findings for the overall analysis required by his superiors in Berlin. In the light of what he had read it would be a scathing report as required by document twenty-two. How in hell did Germany expect to win the war in the Pacific if the English used their Australian allies to strike first at the vitally important radio stations that were scattered throughout the German islands and which supported the Imperial German Navy ships operating out of their China base? Kurt shook his head, placed his cap on his head and stepped into the blaze of the tropical sun.

Alex woke slowly to the sounds of the copra plantation stirring for the day's work. He rubbed his eyes, pushed aside the mosquito net covering his bed and reached for his trousers hanging on the brass knob of the bed end. The chatter of Melanesian workers trudging to the rows of coconut trees was mixed with the raised voice of the housemaid chiding her young assistant over the matter of the cooking fire going out.

The previous evening spent with Albert Schumann celebrating their final agreement for a cargo hold of copra had taken its toll on Alex. He had a hangover and wished that he had not been so lax in watching his alcohol intake. But Herr Schumann had invited neighbouring planters to share in the celebration of the contract with the Macintosh companies. Alex had a vague memory of spending as much time as he could in the company of Giselle until he was steered away to speak with Schumann's guests.

Alex stumbled to a bureau on which a porcelain dish containing warm water stood and fumbled for his razor and shaving brush. Lathering the stick of soap, he shaved, using his reflection in the mirror fixed to the wall behind the bureau to guide his hand. With water from another dish he wiped the soap from his face and combed his hair. Finished with his morning preparations he made his way through the rambling house to the dining room where he was met by Albert Schumann and Giselle at their breakfast. He was greeted warmly.

'It will be a pity to see you leave us, Herr Macintosh,' Schumann said, looking up from a plate of sausages and eggs. 'You have now been with us for almost three weeks and will always be welcome to visit us in the future. I will ensure that we see you off before you depart today but I must excuse myself for the moment to attend to plantation matters.'

Alex nodded and sat down at the large, polished table decorated with sprays of colourful tropical flowers. Giselle sat opposite him, nibbling on a slice of bread and jam. Alex smiled weakly at her, agonising over whether he had acted foolishly the night before.

'If you are wondering, Mr Macintosh,' Giselle said when her father had left them alone in the dining room, 'you were the perfect gentleman last night – despite the amount of alcohol you had consumed.'

Alex blinked at her in surprise. It was as if she were reading his mind. 'I, ah, was not sure,' he said, poking at a plate of eggs placed before him by the housemaid who immediately left the room. 'I think your father has bested me in the deal. I was attempting to drink away the thought that I will have to face my brother George in Sydney and explain why we have paid so much for the cargo.'

'It would not have anything to do with currying favour with my father, would it?' Giselle asked with the trace of a smile on her face.

Alex knew exactly what she was alluding to. His interest in her over the weeks must have been very obvious, he cursed himself. He had already surmised that a young woman of such beauty and poise must have many suitors in her life.

'No,' he sighed, pushing aside the uneaten eggs and reaching for a ripe mango in a silver dish on the table. 'I do not have much aptitude in business dealings. That is the domain of my brother. No doubt he will have me on the carpet for the deal but I don't particularly care. At least the voyage brought me to a place where I could meet you.'

'I am surprised that we did not meet in Sydney,' Giselle said with a twinkle in her eye. 'But I suppose you have little to do with the German community there.'

Alex sliced at the mango, peeling away the skin to expose the succulent yellow flesh. Juice ran down his fingers. 'Strangely, we do have a lot of contact with the German community in Sydney,' Alex replied. 'My family has many business dealings with German agencies and this deal was organised from Sydney with a German broker.'

'Well, it is indeed a pity that we did not meet in Sydney,' Giselle said. 'Then you could have taken me on picnics and to the theatre and also to the pictures to see your sister on the screen. I like her performances.'

Despite the throbbing in his head, her words penetrated sufficiently to make him forget his hangover. There was a mutual attraction but time had run out for him. He was due to steam to Rabaul that afternoon. 'Miss Schumann,' he said, forgetting the slice of mango in his hand, 'there is nothing more in this whole world I would like better than to spend time in your company. Is it possible that you are able to travel to Sydney in the future?'

'My mother and I are planning to travel to Sydney this September for the spring season,' Giselle replied. 'We have many friends there and hope to attend the horse racing carnivals. My mother is a great lover of good horse flesh as my grandparents breed fine horses in Bavaria on their estate.'

Alex felt his spirits soar. But September was at least half a year away, he despaired. A dark thought entered his mind. Giselle might develop a romantic attachment to one of the plantation owners' sons that he had met the evening before. He remembered one young man, a fine and handsome planter, a widower, being very attentive towards Giselle. Alex had experienced pangs of jealousy even then. Dirk Keller – that was the man's name. 'What will you do between now and then?' Alex asked, attempting to sound nonchalant despite his turbulent feelings.

'Oh, amuse myself around my father's property,' Giselle answered. 'I also attend to the medical needs of my father's workers. I hope one day to study to be a doctor of medicine and hopefully qualify as a surgeon.'

Alex was surprised at her revelation. He did not

see Giselle as a nurse but when he examined her face he could see more than just physical beauty. There was also a gentleness in her eyes he had overlooked.

'That sounds like a very honourable thing to do,' he answered lamely. 'Where would you study?'

'Sydney University,' she replied. 'I am currently awaiting word on whether my application for admittance has been approved.'

'Oh,' Alex exclaimed, realising that if she were successful she would be living in Sydney for a long period completing her studies. 'That would be grand.'

'You have mango juice dripping into your lap, Mr Macintosh,' Giselle said with a broad smile, causing Alex to blush and glance down. 'I am afraid that I am not yet a doctor,' Giselle said with a smirk, 'so it would be inappropriate for me to wipe away the juice from that part of your anatomy.'

Alex glanced up and broke into a laugh. Giselle was certainly a young lady with more sides to her than he had already seen in the days that they had shared company and conversation. It had been a wonderful time of horseback rides to the edges of the jungle, reserved chatter and evenings spent on the verandah joining in the late afternoon drinks as the sun set. At no time had Giselle intimated any interest in him until this moment when they were alone in the dining room and he was about to steam away. But at least he had hope and was already scheming to see her before September. He knew his plans would mean a confrontation with his older brother but he did not care. After all, what could George do to him?

★

The day went too quickly for Alex. It was spent away from Giselle supervising the transfer of the copra bags down to the beach and onto the ferry boats of the Macintosh coastal trader. The little coal-burning ship lay at anchor a few hundred yards from the beach and was already building up steam for the voyage to Rabaul. Black smoke curled from her funnel and the derricks swung over the side to lift the heavy nets containing the white flesh of the coconuts that would eventually find itself compressed into oil for the market in Australia.

When the loading was over, Giselle rode side-saddle down to the beach on a tough little pony. She wore a straw hat and long white skirt pinched in at the waist.

'My father has sent his apologies for not being able to bid you a bon voyage personally,' Giselle said, dismounting with easy grace to stand before Alex, sweating under the late afternoon sun. 'We are having some trouble on the western border of the plantation with some natives from further up the valley. He has been forced to fetch our local constabulary. But I have come to say goodbye – for the moment.'

Alex removed his hat and wiped his brow with a bandana from around his neck. 'I may be back this way sooner than you think,' he said. 'I must say that you are the most beautiful and remarkable lady that I have ever met.' Surprising both of them he suddenly reached out and drew Giselle to him. She did not resist and his lips met hers in a kiss that sealed his spoken words. Her arms went around his neck and she bent her body into his.

'Good on yer, boss,' a rough male voice yelled from the boats where a gang of men loaded the cargo, making Alex acutely aware that they were being observed by both the plantation workers and his own European crew. Although it was the time this was not the place to reveal his feelings.

They drew apart and Alex could see a slight frown on Giselle's face. 'You should have done that days ago, Alexander,' she said. 'Could you not see my feelings for you?'

'I didn't know,' he blurted.

'Well, if you are able to return before I travel with my mother to Sydney that would be very welcome,' Giselle said, standing back from Alex on the beach. 'For now, you must leave me, but I know in my heart, we will soon be together.'

'I don't want to leave,' Alex said. 'I love you and want to spend the rest of my time in this paradise on earth with you.'

Giselle looked at Alex with sad eyes, knowing that reality was his temporary absence from her life. 'Your ship must sail,' she said gently. 'Time will pass and we will meet again.'

Reluctantly, Alex turned to walk to the last row-boat leaving for the steamer in the harbour, acutely aware that the ship had only a small window of time to steam away on the tide. He was met by his Scottish engineer, a short but solidly built man in his early forties with a freckled bald head and a myriad of freckles on his pale grinning face. 'Don't say anything, Jock,' Alex cautioned, stepping into the boat.

'I was just going to say that you have good taste

in lassies, Mr Macintosh,' the engineer replied, shoving the stern of the boat off the beach and leaping aboard. 'You should think about snatching her and taking her with you.'

Alex turned to his friend and employee with a dark look but the suggestion had merit. Maybe Giselle might welcome being kidnapped by him. His expression silenced the jovial sailor and Alex turned to gaze at the beach now under the soft shadows of the setting sun. Giselle stood holding the reins of her pony, staring back at him. She waved and Alex returned the gesture. But soon enough she disappeared on her mount into the rows of palms on the beach and his boat was bumping the side of the cargo ship.

Aboard, Alex was met by the captain, a tall, gaunt Englishman in his fifties, Ernest Delamore. 'We have a radio telegram for you,' he said in a less than welcoming tone. 'Sydney is wondering what has held you up here.'

Alex glanced back at the darkening shoreline. He knew the answer full well but did not offer any explanation, other than to say it had been business. Delamore shook his head and walked away, leaving Alex to continue gazing at the shoreline, willing Giselle to make one more appearance. The ship rocked gently on the tropical seas and, with a clanking of anchor cables shuddering through the iron deck, the Macintosh ship prepared to steam northeast to Rabaul, leaving Alex's heart on the beach.

As the ship chopped through a rising sea off the shore Alex chose to go below to his cabin. What the heck, he thought, climbing down the metal stairs to the deck below. It did not matter how much he paid for the cargo and George could go to hell. After all, he was on a mission for his father. It was just a pity that his older brother could not be brought into the operation. George was under the impression that he had sent his younger brother on a voyage to make even more money for the Macintosh empire. But this was not the case. Alex opened the door to his cabin and felt a twinge of guilt as he slumped onto his narrow bed attached to the bulkhead. He had not really thought about it before but he was, in fact, betraying the trust of the Schumann family and their friends. And sadly that also included Giselle.

6

Although the studio was running smoothly that balmy, late autumn day in Sydney, Arthur Thorncroft was distracted. As the scene was being filmed he sat in his canvas folding chair, his thoughts drifting to the reprieve the injection of money had made to the survival of the film and his company. George Macintosh provided no explanation as to why he was continuing support for the project and Arthur had not asked, although the film maker suspected that the young man he intensely disliked must have an ulterior motive. All that mattered was that the film would be finished and sold to the distributors.

'You think that will do, Mr Thorncroft?' the young cameraman asked from behind his camera.

'What? Sorry,' Arthur answered vaguely, his thoughts interrupted. He glanced over at his two stars. Fenella and Guy were staring back at him. 'What do you think, Miss Birney?' Arthur asked the stern-looking, middle-aged woman with greying hair tied back in a bun.

She stood to one side of the set holding a clip board and adjusted her spectacles in an irritated manner. 'If you ask me, Mr Thorncroft,' she replied indignantly, 'I think that they are ruining my work.'

'I need a clearer explanation,' Arthur said.

The scriptwriter rolled her eyes. 'Obviously you were not concentrating on the scene,' she said impatiently. 'Otherwise you would have noticed how wooden Miss Macintosh's performance was during her supposed loving embrace of Mr Wilkes. I could not feel the passion between them at all and think that you should re-shoot the scene.'

'Sorry,' Arthur sighed. 'I was somewhat distracted but I will speak to Guy and Nellie.'

'Good,' the woman replied, satisfied that her hard work was being respected.

Arthur waved Guy and Fenella to him. They stepped out of the set that would soon be dismantled and the pieces converted for another shoot at a later date. Arthur rose from his chair and placed his arms around Guy and Fenella's shoulders, huddling them to him. 'What is going on between you two lovebirds?' he asked in a paternal manner. 'Where is the love between the two of you that the Australian public has come to expect?'

'I don't know what you mean,' Guy scowled while Fenella remained silent.

'I have noticed a certain amount of coolness

between you over the past week or so,' Arthur said. 'Has something happened I should know about?'

'We have just had a small spat,' Fenella answered. 'I am sure that it will pass.'

'I hope so,' Arthur commented. 'Because in our business, imparting feelings to an audience – who believe what they see up on the screen – is real. That is what we call acting. I cannot afford to have you bring any personal differences to the set.'

Guy and Fenella nodded and Arthur broke the embrace to glance over their shoulders at George Macintosh who had appeared on the set. Beyond him, his chauffeur stood idly by the Buick. George signalled for Arthur to join him.

'Good afternoon, George,' Arthur greeted. 'I have not had the opportunity to thank you for extending funds for the completion of the picture.'

'You know my only interest is that you turn a profit for all the money the Macintosh companies have put into the project,' George replied. 'I am only here today under instructions from my father that you use your contacts to buy the best movie camera you can with the additional funds I will allocate for its purchase.'

Arthur raised a brow. 'What Patrick asks will cost quite a lot,' Arthur answered. 'But I can fulfil his request and, all going well, have the camera at the studio next week.'

'No sooner?' George frowned.

'What you are asking is not sold in a grocery shop,' Arthur replied quietly. 'It just so happens that I know of a cancelled order for such a camera. It's being shipped to Sydney and should arrive early next week. I will be on the wharf with the money to ensure it does not fall into any other film-maker's hands. May I ask why your father has requested an extra camera for the company?'

'He did not enter me into his confidence,' George sneered. 'Just contact me as soon as you have your hands on the merchandise and I will inform Father. Now, if you will excuse me, I need to speak with Mr Wilkes.'

George walked over to Guy who sat sprawled in a deck chair sipping from a silver hip flask. Arthur watched the two men huddled in a conversation they clearly did not want him to be privy to. Arthur was curious but shook his head and walked back to the office at the end of the studio as the crew went about preparing to shoot the scene again. In Arthur's opinion, whatever the two men were discussing boded no good.

West of Sydney, in an isolated rural area, Matthew Duffy was in a state of near ecstasy, standing in a grassy paddock and gazing at the object that had his full attention.

'Can you fly it?' Patrick Duffy asked.

'Matthew can fly anything that has wings stuck to it,' Randolph answered in lieu of his friend.

'A BE.2,' Matthew said, walking towards the newly assembled canvas and wood biplane with its huge, four-bladed, wooden propeller. Designed as a two-seater, it had two cockpits. He stroked the metal engine. The men who had assembled the aircraft had done a good job; all the cross-wiring was taut between the struts.

'I am afraid that the aircraft is only on loan from the chaps at Point Cook for the duration of the mission,' Patrick said, noticing the avaricious look in Matthew's eyes. 'Colonel Hughes was able to convince the Prime Minister that it should be seconded to us for a matter of national security and the aircraft no longer exists in any records. I suppose that makes it a ghost aeroplane. No doubt you are eager to try it out,' he said, reaching into his pocket for a cigar despite the strong acrid smell of fuel. 'I have been informed by the mechanics that the winds are right and you have enough daylight to take it for a flight. But you will have to fly low and keep out of sight of any habitation. She is, after all, a ghost.'

Matthew was well aware that the newly assembled aircraft bore no registration markings. It had been painted a dull green above and a light blue below along the fuselage and wings to blend with the earth below or the sky above depending on the perspective of observers. He took the goggles and leather skullcap from Randolph. Hauling himself into the rear cockpit, Matthew quickly assessed the controls and jiggled the moving parts that controlled his flight. Satisfied, he nodded to Randolph who moved into a position to swing the big propeller, activating the engine. It only took three hefty swings on the prop to cause the engine to splutter into life, spewing out a strong smell of oil and fuel from the exhausts along the engine.

Randolph jumped to the side and Matthew let the aircraft bump and jolt over the levelled earth of the paddock that had been prepared as an airstrip. Randolph held up a rag to indicate wind strength and direction. Matthew nodded, snapped off a mock salute and pulled out the choke, causing the engine to roar to life. The biplane roared down the strip until its tail rose and finally the aircraft itself lifted gently into the afternoon air, rising slowly to drone towards the west.

'I told you he can fly anything with wings,' Randolph said smugly.

Patrick was obviously impressed with how quickly Matthew appeared to master the unfamiliar aircraft as he rose higher in the sky. 'For your sake I hope you are right,' he replied with a slow smile, finally lighting the cigar cupped in his hands, 'because tomorrow morning you are going up as his passenger to practise for the mission.'

Randolph already knew where they would be going but had not been informed of what they were meant to do when they reached their target. Nor was he fully aware of their specific role in this possibly very dangerous mission. 'What would be my part in this mission, Colonel?' he asked as they both watched the tiny aircraft dip and disappear beyond a low tree-covered ridge.

'What skills do you have operating a film-making camera?' Patrick asked, puffing on the cigar while watching the ridge line to the west.

'I have snapped a few photographs in my time,' Randolph replied.

'No, I mean a film camera – like they use to make moving pictures.'

'None at all,' Randolph answered.

'Well, that is going to change,' Patrick said, turning to the American. 'Next week, I will arrange to have my friend Arthur Thorncroft organise for one of his cameramen to teach you all about using a camera. In the meantime, while we are out here, you and Matthew will get familiar with the BE.2. You will be using it in the job ahead of you.'

'May I ask what that will be, Colonel?' Randolph questioned.

Patrick gazed for a moment at the ridge he had seen the tiny aircraft disappear behind. The plane suddenly reappeared, droning up into the sky and rolling to one side in a turn. 'All in good time, old chap,' he answered.

Randolph knew that he would be wasting his time asking any more questions. Was it that the Australian colonel did not trust him because he was a Yank? Maybe he had a right to, Randolph realised. From what he had experienced of his own country's history, the United States of America would not let itself become embroiled in any European conflict. After all, the Europeans had a history of two thousand years of fighting among themselves.

A pleasant thought popped into the American's mind. If he was to be trained to use a camera it just might place him in the company of Fenella. He was smiling at the thought when Matthew brought his aircraft soaring back to the makeshift airstrip. The two men instinctively ducked as the aircraft sailed overhead and turned to return for a perfect landing.

'I think it is time that we retired to open that

bottle of Scotch I have brought to celebrate the first stage of our operation,' Patrick said. 'But keep in mind, tomorrow you are going to commence lessons on how to strip and assemble a BE.2, so you will need to keep a clear head.'

Randolph watched Patrick turn on his heel and stride towards the farmhouse that had been converted into a secret base for training operations. Good food and other supplies had been transported from Sydney and it was obvious that the Australian army officer was a thorough man. That gave the American some faith in the success of whatever had been planned for him and Matthew.

'It will help you relax,' Guy said soothingly to Fenella, who eyed the white powder piled on the brown paper with suspicion. 'It has strong medicinal properties and it cannot harm you.'

They were alone in the bedroom of Fenella's cottage. The tension between them was causing a rift that widened with each waking moment.

'Is it heroin?' Fenella asked.

'Yes, but it is no more than a strong pain reliever,' Guy said, leaning forward to snort a puff of the powder up his nose. He sighed and leaned back in his chair, allowing the chemical to enter his system.

'I know that your father frowns on the stuff but it has done me no harm and I can name many respected people who avail themselves of the powder. People your father holds in high esteem.'

Fenella stared at Guy. His face reflected a dreamy

86

serenity. In the past she had wondered at his mood shifts and felt for some time that the drug may have had something to do with his unpredictable behaviour. She had fallen head over heels in love with this handsome, charming son of a country draper, despite her father's disapproval. He had instinctively disliked the young man with the oily manners and little demonstration of the manly attributes of hard work, ambition and a sense of being true to others. Patrick did not consider that a man should live off his good looks or make a living pretending to be something he was not – although he did not think acting was beneath his daughter's ambitions. After all, what other choices did a woman have in life before she assumed her role as a wife and mother? Acting was a way for a woman to fill in time before assuming her intended vocation.

'You swear on our love that heroin is not like opium?' Fenella asked. Guy nodded his head. Fenella leaned forward and snorted the powder up her nose, forcing herself not to sneeze. As she sat on the bed the chemicals began to control her feelings. Now she understood why her lover had advocated the drug's use. The eventual euphoria made her feel so good; worries simply melted away.

Guy watched the tense expression on Fenella's face slowly wilt to be replaced with a look of wonder and peace. Why her brother had asked him to introduce the young woman to the world of heroin was a mystery to Guy. Once it hooked a person there was no going back. But the money he was being paid to carry out the service to George Macintosh was huge.

Guy Wilkes had decided that he no longer had need for the beautiful young woman in his life and the deal he had made with George not only released any lingering feelings he might have toward Fenella but also paid handsomely. So why was it that he experienced feelings of jealousy whenever he thought of Fenella showing interest in other men?

Guy rose from the chair. Fenella was now lying back on the bed. With practised smoothness he began removing her clothes. In her euphoric state, Fenella did not resist his advances. She was in a world of sheer pleasure and nothing else mattered.

In the week that Randolph and Matthew spent on the farm they had learned the mechanics of the BE.2 biplane under the watchful eye of two aircraft mechanics detached from the army at Point Cook. They were instructed not only on its maintenance but also spent a couple of days learning how to strip the aircraft down into transportable parts and then re-assemble it. When the biplane was ready to fly Matthew and Randolph conducted exercises in low level flight and at times Randolph had taken the controls. Even Patrick had gone aloft with Matthew for a flight around the countryside and remarked when they had landed that he could see the young aviator's vision of the aeroplane being deployed as a future weapon of war.

Satisfied that this stage of the operation had achieved its aim of familiarisation with the aircraft, Patrick declared that the biplane would be stripped down and packed in wooden crates for transport back to Sydney where it would be placed in secret storage until next required.

The five men then cleaned up around the farmhouse and departed in a couple of trucks to the nearest village for lunch and beers at a pub. They did not speak of their time at the farm but shook hands with the two men from Point Cook who would now take a train from Sydney to Melbourne and rejoin the aviation school at Point Cook. Both these men had also been sworn to secrecy – knowing only that they were to assist in the exercise at the farm.

When Matthew and Randolph returned to their hotel in Sydney Matthew picked up the mail from the front desk. Among the letters was a gilt-edged invitation.

'It appears that the colonel is rewarding us for our contribution to his mission,' Matthew said, scanning the stiff card. 'You and I have been invited to attend his regiment's annual ball for officers at one of Sydney's finest hotels.'

Randolph dropped his swag on the floor of the hotel foyer and took a seat in one of the comfortable leather chairs. 'Do you think that Miss Macintosh will be attending?' he asked, attempting to sound casual.

'I am fairly sure she will,' Matthew said, glancing at his friend. 'But she will probably be escorted by her beau.'

'Probably,' Randolph answered, attempting to keep the disappointment from his voice.

'But as we are to report to Arthur's studio tomorrow I am sure that you might have the opportunity to speak with Nellie and ask if she has been invited to the ball. You never know . . .' Matthew could read his American friend like a book and saw the hope glimmer in his demeanour at the suggestion. Matthew had never seen Texas Slim as taken by any woman like this before. He was more like a little school boy than the tough adventurer Matthew had come to know. Matthew hoped that Randolph would be successful in his bid to woo Nellie. He had disliked Guy from the moment he had felt his limp handshake upon their meeting.

'Well, old chap,' Matthew said, 'I think that it is time to retire to the bar and catch up on the drinking we were denied at the farm by the colonel.'

The following day, the men shuffled into the studio to be met by Arthur Thorncroft whose lips pursed in annoyance at their dishevelled appearance.

'You two must have had a good night,' he said, turning on his heel and indicating that they should follow him.

The celebration in the hotel bar upon their return to Sydney had ended in a brawl with a couple of station hands down from Queensland who happened to hail from a rival property near Kate Tracy's. Honour and the reputation of her ringers had been insulted and the ensuing fist fight drew in innocent bystanders to the point of men spilling into the city's streets and gutters and leaving teeth and blood behind in the bar.

By the time six police had been dispatched to deal with the brawl Matthew had settled all damages with the publican and the two rival parties stood side by side discussing the merits and superiority of Queensland horsemen over those in any other state. The police left shaking their heads. Still the short, fierce fight with fists and feet had left Matthew with a split lip and Randolph with a black eye and bruising to the side of his face.

Arthur led them into a room scattered about with bits and pieces of camera parts. They were greeted by a pleasant young man in his late twenties. He had an open, warm smile on his clean-shaven face and wore a woollen vest with the arms cut away.

'Bob Houston,' the cameraman introduced himself, shaking Matthew and Randolph's hands firmly. 'I am Mr Thorncroft's leading cameraman and pleased to meet you both. Mr Thorncroft has informed me that you were once an apprentice to the trade of the camera, Mr Duffy.'

'I will leave you in Mr Houston's capable hands,' Arthur said, preparing to depart. 'I am sure you will quickly update your knowledge, Matthew, and Mr Gates appears to be an intelligent man despite being born an American. If you need to see me, I will be in my office.'

On a table in the centre of the room was a wooden box with an extendable lens and at the side of the box a brass cranking handle. 'Mr Thorncroft has briefed me that you gentlemen need to learn how to use this camera we have just purchased,' the cameraman said, guiding them to the table. 'Of course there is a lot more to filming than just simply cranking the handle and pointing the camera at the subject. You need to be fairly proficient before the camera is handed over to you. But what exactly do you need to know about the camera's specific use?'

'How it can be used from an aircraft flying approximately five thousand feet from the ground – or lower,' Matthew said quietly between the hammer blows in his head.

'Interesting,' Bob Houston uttered. 'May I ask why you want to film from an aeroplane?'

On instructions from Patrick, Matthew had already prepared his cover story. 'We have been asked by a wealthy landowner for aerial film of his property. It appears he wants to use the bird's eye view of the terrain to assist him in planning water storage from natural watercourses on his land.'

'Not a bad idea,' Bob commented, already opening the wooden case to expose the mechanical workings of the camera. 'I have never heard of that being done before. I heard that you are an aviator. It might have been handy when I was in South Africa chasing those Dutch farmers during the war when I was with the New Zealand Mounted Rifles.'

Despite his hangover, Matthew was amused at his own ingenuity. Maybe there was a future in aerial photography for mapping terrain and assisting the future of Australia's vital agricultural industry although his passion for the potential use of aircraft in combat was still his priority. But he was also interested to learn that the cameraman was a New Zealander and had served in the same war as he.

'I served with our army in South Africa,' Matthew replied. 'What rank did you hold?'

'Sergeant,' Bob replied. 'Unlike you Australians we had to prove that we could supply our own horse, rifle and equipment before they would recruit us. Every young bloke in New Zealand wanted to join up but originally they only took those who could prove they could afford to fight and die for the good old British Empire. You look like you might have been pretty young to have served.'

'I was,' Matthew replied with a grin. 'When we get the chance you and I should swap a few stories. One of them is how I got sent home.'

For the next couple of hours the cameraman took both Matthew and Randolph through the mechanics of the camera and how it operated. He cautioned them about the flammability of the cellulose film and said that developing the film was a lesson for a later date even though Matthew was already experienced in such matters from his time with Arthur many years earlier.

When both his students demonstrated to his satisfaction that they could load and unload the film from the camera, Bob called a break for lunch. He suggested a counter meal at a hotel nearby and Matthew and Randolph readily accepted his invitation to join him.

To Randolph's delight, Fenella appeared on the set outside the camera room just as they were departing. She was in discussion with Miss Myrtle Birney, the scriptwriter, over changes to the script. She glanced up at the three men and an expression of concern shadowed her face when she noticed the two in company with the New Zealand cameraman. Randolph suddenly felt embarrassed. His battered appearance was not presenting a good image for the woman he hoped to impress.

'Cousin Matthew and Mr Gates,' Fenella said mischievously. 'Have you both been involved in the same accident?'

Matthew grinned. 'You might say that,' he replied. 'But, as they say, you should see the other blokes.'

Fenella smiled sadly at her cousin. 'I can see that you have changed little since I knew you as a young soldier. Fisticuffs prowess seems to be a trait of Macintosh and Duffy men. And I can see that you have drawn poor Mr Gates into your wayward life. I had the impression that Mr Gates might be a gentleman,' she sighed.

'Oh, Texas can mix it with the best of them,' Matthew said with some pride. 'Don't let his Yankee charm and ugly looks fool you. I could tell you some stories about our adventures but think I will not, lest you blush.'

'Mr Gates,' Fenella said, turning her attention to the American standing quietly to one side, 'I am sure that we have something in make-up that will conceal the bruises to your face.'

Randolph stepped forward, sweeping his Stetson hat into his hands. 'I truly appreciate your offer, Miss Macintosh,' he said. 'But I have come to learn how to live with cuts and bruises in the company of your cousin.'

'Come, Mr Gates,' Fenella persisted, reaching out

to lead him by the hand. 'We have a dressing room near Uncle Arthur's office and I am sure that he would not begrudge me repairing the damage that your friendship with my wayward cousin has caused your fine looks.'

Randolph glanced at Matthew, who shrugged. 'Sounds like Nellie might be able to finally do something to make you look handsome,' he said. 'I will go to the pub with Bob while Nellie patches you up.'

As Fenella led Randolph away. Matthew grinned. The unexpected silver lining to the brawl was that it created an opportunity for the American to make conversation with Nellie. Who knows where that could lead, Matthew thought as he followed the cameraman off the set.

Fenella sat Randolph down in a chair. A large mirror covered the wall and the room had a strong smell of grease paint.

Fenella found a jar of pale-coloured grease, applying it delicately with her fingers to the bruised areas of his face. Randolph could smell the scent of her perfume as she leaned over him.

Fenella stood back to admire her work. 'There, Mr Gates, you can hardly see the bruising anymore.'

'Thank you, Miss Macintosh,' he said. 'It has been a long time since I can remember such a soft and gentle touch from a woman.'

'That is sad to hear,' Fenella said, impulsively touching his face with her fingers. 'I would have thought that such a charming man as yourself would have known the touch of many beautiful ladies.'

'Not much time for that,' Randolph replied. 'My life has been mostly spent in the company of rough men or roaming those places in the world hardly on the map.'

'You are a very interesting man, Mr Gates,' Fenella said. 'I am sure that you have the opportunity to share your time with female company.'

Randolph was aware of how close Fenella was. His attention was drawn to the moist outline of her lips. He reached out and drew her to him, kissing her with tenderness.

'Mr Gates!' Fenella gasped, breaking the embrace to draw away from him. 'I do not think that was appropriate.'

Randolph silently cursed himself for his impetuous action. 'I am sorry, Miss Macintosh,' he mumbled in shame. 'It is just that you are the most beautiful woman I have ever met.'

Brushing down her dress, Fenella stepped back, indicating that the American should leave the room. Randolph understood her gesture and, hat in hand, departed the room without another word being spoken between them.

'God damn you, Gates,' he muttered as he placed his hat on his head. 'You deserve to be horse-whipped, tarred and feathered, and run out of town on a rail.'

When he found the hotel where Bob Houston and Matthew were washing down their cheese sandwiches with a cold beer he strode across to their table.

'Did you ask Nellie to escort you to the

regimental ball?' Matthew asked, glancing up. But his friend's sorrowful expression answered his question. 'I take it she must have said no.'

'Worse than that,' Randolph said, taking a seat at the table. 'I doubt that Miss Macintosh will ever speak to me again.'

Randolph stared at the working men crowding into the bar for a meal and ale. What he would have given to have had a steady job and the chance to prove his worth to Miss Fenella Macintosh.

7

Patrick Duffy sat alone at the dining room table by the large French window that overlooked the well-manicured gardens below. In front of him was an article reporting that the Australian Prime Minister, Mr Joseph Cook, had called a double dissolution of both houses of Parliament. He had complained to the Governor-General, Sir Ronald Munro Ferguson, that his Liberal Conservative majority of one in the House of Representatives and minority in the Senate were unable to govern properly. The PM's adversary on the Labor Party opposition, Billy Hughes, had stood and predicted that the Liberals would be cast out of power. Patrick pondered on what a change of government might mean to their mission and so absorbed in the article was he that he was hardly aware his son had entered the room carrying a cup of tea.

'Good morning, Father,' George said, standing by the window to gaze out on what was shaping up to be a beautiful, clear and warm winter's day in Sydney.

'George,' Patrick said, glancing up from the paper he now folded neatly on the table. 'What brings you here this morning?'

'Oh, I have brought some papers for you to sign . . . nothing of great importance . . . and thought that I might ask what is going on with cousin Matthew and his Yankee friend. In my opinion, there seems to be a lot of cloak and dagger stuff underway. I just hope that it does not jeopardise any of our German trading interests.'

'You know better than to ask me about my work,' Patrick replied. 'I can reassure you that none of it puts our financial affairs with the Germans in jeopardy.'

'You really think that a war is coming?' George asked, taking a sip of his tea.

'I know that to most people there appears no real sign of war but in my business I am paid to be ready. Yes, I think that we could very easily be at war with Germany sooner rather than later.' Patrick spoke in a measured tone, silently reflecting on the arms race between Britain and Germany for naval supremacy.

'Does my brother think the same way?' George persisted. 'He is, after all, one of your officers in the regiment.'

'I have not had much opportunity to discuss the matter with Alex,' Patrick answered. 'You seem to have tied him up with company matters.'

'If I remember rightly,' George continued, 'it was you who insisted that Alexander undertake the trip to

New Guinea and Rabaul when you heard that I was looking at expanding our operations with the Hamburg merchants. You have never done that before.'

Patrick was growing uncomfortable with his eldest son's questions. They were infringing on his military role rather than that of chairman of the family companies. It was a father's duty not to differentiate his love for his children but in the case of George, Patrick knew this was not so. From childhood the man before him had exhibited disturbing traits of coldness and cruelty. He had demonstrated many times that his only interest was his own pleasure and the acquisition of power. Nor had George any sense of duty. He had refused to take a commission in Patrick's militia regiment and had insisted on taking possession of Granville White's house for his sole use. Patrick had agreed because he had to admit that his eldest son was very good at managing the many companies Patrick had inherited from his grandmother Lady Enid Macintosh. Patrick had little interest in the world of banks and trading, preferring to spend most of his time in the company of fellow soldiers. He had been promoted to command a militia battalion of infantry in Sydney with Scottish traditions and his duties as commanding officer to his soldiers called on most of his time. He had been delighted when his youngest son had shown a keen interest in soldiering and taken a commission to rise to his current rank of captain acting as a company commander. Patrick suspected that the influence of his own father, the legendary soldier of fortune Michael Duffy, had a lot to do with Alexander's choice. Alexander knew all the stories of how his mysterious grandfather had fought – from the New Zealand wars through the American Civil War to the arid lands of Mexico's revolt against the French and finally in South Africa against the Dutch farmers. Along the way Abraham Lincoln had personally awarded his grandfather the Congressional Medal of Honour. Patrick himself had fought in colonial wars in Africa, commanding the fierce Scotsmen who had enlisted in the English army after the Highland clearances. Soldiering was very much in the Irish-Scottish Celtic blood of his ancestors.

'I thought that the sea voyage would be good for Alex, that is all,' Patrick finally replied, dismissing any further attempts at interrogation from his son. 'I have to change and attend duties at the regiment,' Patrick continued, rising from the table.

'Do you know that we have a German relative visiting our shores?' George said. 'Major Kurt von Fellmann is currently on a Pacific tour to inspect military installations and part of his inspection brings him to Sydney to meet with members of the German Australian Station.'

Patrick paused at the doorway to the dining room. 'You mean Penelope's son, brother of Karl?'

'Twin brother, I believe,' George answered, smug in the fact that he was privy to news that not even the formidable military intelligence apparatus he suspected his father of being part of was yet aware of. 'I could offer him an invitation to the regimental ball when he arrives.'

Patrick could see the smirk on his son's face. 'How did you find out about his visit?' he asked, suspicious.

'I have friends in the German consulate here in Sydney,' George replied. 'They are, after all, not enemies of Australia.'

'Leave an invitation for him,' Patrick said. 'He is related, albeit distantly.'

George placed his empty cup on the table. 'I already have,' he said, wiping his mouth delicately with a linen napkin from a silver holder. 'I anticipated that you would like to meet him. After all, you are both officers with much in common.'

Patrick wanted to say something about his son's presumption in extending the invitation before consulting with him but let it slip, accepting that his eldest son was a very clever man despite all his darker traits. In a sense, George was attempting to please him, which was not something he often did. After signing the papers on the table before him Patrick departed, leaving George alone in the dining room.

A damned war with Germany was the last thing his family's financial interests needed, George thought. He had just invested heavily in German chemical production and that money could easily be lost in the event of war. The loss might not be enough to send the family to the poor house but could cause some tightening of belts. George had good reason to show his distant cousin hospitality. The man belonged to a powerful Prussian family and if war broke out he just might be in a position to help save any investments in Germany. But George also suspected that any deal he might be able to arrange with the von Fellmanns would come at a cost. But what it might entail was of little relevance to him so long as it meant money.

He dismissed the tiny voice in his head that warned him he might be treading the delicate line between patriotism and treachery.

For the moment he was more interested in his plot to discredit his sister. The first stage appeared to have been enacted and, according to the weak Guy Wilkes, it had not taken very long to reach the second stage. The thought of his sister being disowned by his father brought a smile to George's face.

The winter sun was at its zenith and Arthur Thorncroft was angry. He paced the sandstone cliff, stopping occasionally to gaze down at the Pacific breakers swirling over the rock platforms below. Hours had passed and Fenella had not arrived for the final scenes to be filmed. His crew lounged about in deck chairs smoking or just simply dozing in the warming sun. Arthur's leading man chatted to a small cluster of people who had wandered onto the outdoor set and, recognising their Australian film idol, engaged him in conversation.

'Guy,' Arthur called from the edge of Sydney's South Head. 'I would like to speak to you.'

Reluctantly, Wilkes disengaged himself from his adoring fans and wandered across.

'When you last saw Nellie she was well?' he asked, brushing back hair that had blown onto his face.

'I do not see her all that often now,' Guy shrugged. 'But the last time I saw her . . . the day before yesterday . . . if I remember rightly, she appeared well.'

'That is all,' Arthur said, dismissing him.

Guy promptly returned to his adoring gathering of young ladies all eager to report to their friends that they had spoken to the famous Guy Wilkes. He had hardly joined his followers when a black sedan pulled into the end of the road. It was Fenella's chauffeur-driven car. The driver held open the passenger door and Fenella alighted.

Arthur waited until Fenella had exchanged a few words with her admirers and made her way to him.

'You are a half a day late,' he growled. 'This project is costing me by the hour.'

'I am sorry, Uncle Arthur,' Fenella said, touching his arm with her gloved hand. 'I was not feeling well.'

'You do not look well, dear girl,' he answered, softening in his anger. 'I am prepared to cancel the work today and possibly resume tomorrow.'

'Oh, do not do that,' Fenella countered. 'I will make my preparations and we can shoot the scene before the light is gone.'

Arthur stared into Fenella's face. Something there disturbed him. He had a terrible thought, desperately wanting to be wrong. 'Are you using opiates?' he asked softly.

Fenella's startled expression answered his question and her initial surprise turned to a look of haunted sadness. 'I only use a little when I have had a stressful day,' she replied, attempting to deflect the disappointment she could see in Arthur's face.

'Is it opium that you are using?' he asked, gently grasping her arms.

Fenella shook her head and looked away. 'No, just a little heroin from time to time.'

Immediately Arthur thought of Guy. He had suspected for some time that his leading actor was using the substance and the thought that he had introduced Fenella to the white powder infuriated him. He had the urge to walk over to the man, pick him up by the waist of his pants and toss him over the side of the headland. But he was on the verge of completing his film and recuperating the money lost in the last project. He needed both his stars to finish the film. After that, he could look around for someone to replace Guy Wilkes.

A dark thought crossed Arthur's mind: what if Patrick learned that his cherished daughter was becoming addicted to the drug? What would be his reaction? Would he hold his friend responsible for allowing his beloved daughter to mix with the wrong crowd in the film industry? Arthur shuddered. He could remember a young officer of the Queen many years before who had survived in the wild deserts of the Sudan, killing the Bedouin with a knife and covering himself with their blood. Patrick Duffy was not a man one would want as an enemy seeking vengeance. It would be up to him to steer Fenella away from the drug before her father could discover her growing addiction to the narcotic.

'We will call it a day but I would like to speak to you about what you are doing to yourself,' he said gently.

Fenella hesitated. 'You will not tell my father,' she pleaded tearfully, reaching out for Arthur's hand.

'I will not tell your father,' Arthur replied. 'We have been friends for too long and shared a battlefield when we were young. No, but you must start to resist using the drug to satisfy your needs, my dear child, or your life will change for the worse. I have seen it happen to others.'

'I promise that I will try, Uncle Arthur,' Fenella said, sniffing back her tears just as Guy Wilkes ambled over to join them.

'Ah, Nellie, I see that you have finally decided to join us,' he said with a self-satisfied smirk.

'Shut up, Mr Wilkes,' Arthur snapped. 'I think we can all take the day off and go for a stroll along the beach. After all, we have lost the sun,' he growled, glancing at the clouds gathering over the sea and threatening heavy rain.

Guy threw up his hands to imitate hurt from the rebuke. 'I will tell the crew,' he said.

Glowering, Arthur watched him walk away.

Matthew could see a stranger staring back at him. At least the reflection in the window of the carriage appeared to be someone he had not thought much about as the train travelled through the night to Brisbane where he would change trains to travel on to Townsville. There his mother awaited his arrival. His trip north was the result of a telegram delivered to his hotel in Sydney. It had been from the family doctor to tell him that his mother, Kate Tracy, had suffered a minor stroke.

Matthew had stood staring at the words on the slip of paper, suddenly realising that his beloved mother was not actually immortal as he had always thought. Here was the woman who had survived the wild frontier of the Palmer River gold rushes of the 1870s and built a fortune, a woman who had known the death of two husbands – the latter being his father, the American prospector Luke Tracy. She had always appeared to him to be so independent from the company of the many suitors who had attempted to court her after the disappearance of her husband Luke in the harsh and mostly unexplored interior of Queensland.

Matthew could see the flicker of tree tops silhouetted by the full moon casting its shadow over the hills and forests of Australia's eastern seaboard. He had immediately organised this train journey and briefed Randolph that he was to remain in Sydney and keep contact with Colonel Patrick Duffy. It would take many days for him to reach Townsville in Queensland's far north and Matthew prayed that his mother would not die in the time it took to reach her. The doctor had instructed in his telegram that she was in relatively good health, but guilt flooded him as he reflected on how he had spent so much time roaming the world instead of being by his mother's side and assisting her in managing the family estates. But now his indestructible mother was ill and it had been over four years since he had last seen her face.

Matthew's guilt went deeper when he considered that he had used his mother's money to finance his wanderings of the globe in search of the elusive thing called self-meaning. His mother had once told him a story. The wandering Aboriginal people of the Julia Creek district where he was born in the shadow of a bullock wagon had said that he, the infant, was fated to soar with the eagles. That part appeared to have been fulfilled with his love of flying. He had always yearned to fly above the earth and touch the clouds. But that had not been enough. He was part warrior and part eagle. Both had come together to guide him in his life as he sought a means to make the new flying machines instruments of war. His restlessness in his years of seeking to realise the dream of combining flight with war had cost him any chance of a stable life. He knew how much his mother wished for him to settle down, find a good woman and provide her with grandchildren. To that extent he had proved a failure.

Oh, there had been many women but they had come and gone as passing ships in the night, and none had been considered as a future wife. The way things were shaping up with the mission Matthew wondered if he would truly disappoint his mother by getting himself killed.

Pulled by the powerful steam engine pluming a trail of smoke the train bumped and rattled its way forward in the night. Passengers leaned their heads on seats and attempted sleep. Matthew did not like slumber. Sometimes those terrible days at the Elands River siege came back to him with memories of screaming artillery shells exploding around him, shredding and mangling men, of the crack of bullets, snatching the very life from the man beside him with little more than a grunt, of a final scream of pain and anguish. In the dark shadows of his life war was never far from the young man's mind.

'Casino ... change at Casino,' the tired-looking uniformed porter said, working his way along the rocking aisle of the carriage. 'All out for the Brisbane line.'

Matthew rubbed his eyes and prepared for the change on the long railway station in the Northern Rivers region of New South Wales.

When the German steamer docked at Darling Harbour and the gangplank lowered Kurt von Fellmann was met by a balding man in his mid forties sporting a sweeping moustache and dressed in a smart suit.

'Major von Fellmann, I have been sent by the consul to welcome you to Sydney,' the balding man said without offering his hand. 'I am Maynard Bosch, assistant to the consul here.'

Major Kurt von Fellmann was also dressed in civilian clothes and he too wore a smart suit. 'Thank you,' he responded at the bottom of the gangway.

'Is this your first time in Sydney?' Bosch asked, falling into stride beside the German army officer.

'Yes, although I do have a brother who has lived for many years in this country.'

'I know,' Herr Bosch answered. 'Your brother is a Lutheran missionary in Queensland. We had the good fortune to meet last year when he attended a conference we held in Sydney.'

'How did my brother look?' Kurt asked with genuine concern in his voice.

'He looked well,' Bosch answered. 'Considering he was still mourning the death of his wife.'

Kurt hesitated in his stride. This was news to him. 'I was not aware that my sister-in-law had passed away.'

'Yes, sadly it seems that I am the bearer of the news to you. It seems that she developed leprosy.'

Kurt shook his head. The disease was a horrible way to die. 'I presume that you are also here to brief me.'

Bosch glanced at the milling crowd of passengers disembarking from the ship – men in their suits and wearing straw boaters, the women in their long dresses flowing around their ankles and wearing an assortment of fashionable hats in many shapes and designs. Luggage was being piled for the passengers to retrieve on the wharf. 'I will brief you at your hotel,' Bosch said. 'Do you have much luggage to clear with Customs?'

Kurt travelled lightly. He had only one small suitcase to retrieve. When he stepped onto the street outside the Customs Office he was once again met by the assistant consul standing beside an expensive German-built automobile. Bosch helped Kurt load his suitcase into the car's luggage compartment and placed himself behind the wheel to drive to the hotel. They navigated busy streets where trams powered by overhead electric lines vied for space with horse-drawn wagons and the puttering, shiny new cars. Pedestrians weaved in and out of the traffic, dodging the variety of vehicles now competing for the narrow streets bordered by sandstone buildings, some rising to a height of five storeys. Kurt could see why Sydney was considered the nerve centre of the

Pacific trade. Office signs told their story of international enterprise and the clatter of vehicles was a noisy contrast to the serenity of the Pacific islands he had visited on his tour.

When they reached the hotel in the heart of the city Kurt admired its elegance. Bosch parked in a space on the street and assisted the German officer to check into the hotel. By the time Kurt had been given a room lunch was being served in the hotel's dining room. They were ushered to a table with a white linen cloth and a fresh flower in a crystal vase set in the centre. The waiter was well dressed, impressing Kurt with the civilised standards of the former British colony.

'The food here is excellent and I think you should find your time in Sydney enjoyable,' Bosch said, accepting the menu the waiter passed to him. 'I would recommend the roast lamb.'

Kurt accepted the assistant consul's advice and ordered the lamb. His English was excellent with little trace of an accent as it had been a language his English mother had taught him from the cradle along with his twin brother, Karl.

'Aside from your military duties I have this for you,' Bosch said, reaching into the pocket of his suit coat. Kurt accepted the envelope, opening it to see a gilt-edged invitation.

'A regimental ball for the local militia regiment,' he said, raising his eyebrows. 'How did their commanding officer know I was visiting these shores?'

'Not so much the Australian government,' Bosch chuckled. 'We have friends here among the English population. It appears that you have English relatives, the Macintosh family, and one George Macintosh had the invitation passed to us some days ago. You will be required to wear your uniform as our government has approved your acceptance.'

'Well, it will be interesting to meet my mother's family here,' Kurt responded, turning over the stiff cardboard invitation in his hand and placing it on the table.

'I have another pleasant surprise for you,' Bosch continued, leaning slightly forward. 'Your brother has also been invited, in appreciation of his fine work among the native people of this land. He has accepted and will be travelling down from Queensland.'

Kurt was surprised to hear this further news. It had been many long years since his brother had left Germany for the far-flung continent of Australia with his wife. 'I am looking forward to seeing my brother,' he said, hiding his pleasure at the news. Kurt had long learned not to display emotion in front of strangers. 'And now, what does the consul have for me?'

Bosch carefully unrolled his linen napkin as the waiter delivered two plates with the roast lamb in a gravy and served with baked vegetables. It smelled delicious and they remained silent until the waiter had left them. No wine had been ordered to accompany the meal as both men knew they were on official business that required a clear head.

'We feel that the acquisition of the Australian government of its battle cruiser, two cruisers and three destroyers does not constitute any real naval strength – except that balanced against our own fleet on the China Station, the Australians have now a more modern navy than our own cruisers. We may outnumber them but the Australians have better ships. This was not something factored into document twenty-two when it was distributed to us out here.'

The mention of document twenty-two signalled to Kurt that the man briefing him had been cleared by the Imperial German Navy. It was thus safe to enter into a briefing with him. 'I have considered the development of the Australian navy as a real threat to our plans in the event of war with the British,' he replied quietly.

Although they spoke in German Kurt was acutely aware of the possibility of spies being around them. He hoped that if this was so in the dining room of the hotel they were not fluent in his native language. 'My report has already identified that we are not capable of putting the operational order into action in the possible event of war with the British Empire. Our Pacific imperial interests are under-gunned and under-manned. I suspect that the Australians will already be considering their own operational order to cover the contingency of us and Britain going to war. I suspect that they will launch a force to seize our radio stations in the Pacific with the help of their New Zealand neighbours.'

'There may be something in what you say about the Australian government already anticipating the elements of document twenty-two,' Herr Bosch said, frowning. 'We have reliable information from one of our most valued informants that a Macintosh company ship, the *Osprey II*, is visiting Rabaul at this very moment. That would not be unusual except our source inside the company has informed us that aboard is another relative of yours – a militia army captain by the name of Alexander Macintosh whose father is the regimental commander of the militia infantry battalion here extending the invitation to you for the ball. Our source is not privy to exactly why the ship is posing as a trader for copra but does know something is highly suspicious about his travelling with the company ship. We have already alerted our people in Rabaul about his visit.'

'What do you suspect that my cousin may be up to?' Kurt asked, slicing away a piece of lamb.

Bosch shrugged. 'I suppose he will attempt to reconnoitre our military dispositions there,' he replied.

'Well, what do you propose to do?' Kurt asked, chewing on the succulent meat.

'If we confirm that Captain Macintosh is indeed a spy we will arrange for him to have a serious accident,' Bosch replied, wiping at his mouth with the white linen napkin. 'We cannot afford to arrest him and accuse him of spying. That would cause ill feelings towards our people living in this country. No, we would have to arrange for him to disappear and make it look like an accident. Do you have any problem with that?'

Kurt felt a slight chill. The assistant to the consul was talking about the murder of a man he was distantly related to. Despite his own unquestionable loyalty to his Kaiser, Kurt was also aware that the man he had never met was still a blood relative, and a soldier like himself. 'No,' he replied, also wiping at his mouth with his napkin. 'If you are able to prove he is a spy then I am sure Captain Macintosh has to accept the consequences of his actions.'

'Good,' Bosch said, resuming his meal. 'It is a delicate thing, complicated as it is by your affiliations with this family, but I am sure our source will be pleased to know that you have concurred with our decision.'

The two men finished their meal and separated. Kurt retired to his room to change. Now he would officially attend his consul to be met by his countrymen living in this vibrant part of the Pacific. As he walked the few streets to the German Consulate building he could not prevent himself imagining how a naval bombardment of the central heart of this city would bring down the buildings around him and kill all the civilians passing him by.

8

The *Osprey II* docked at Rabaul under a sky of soft white clouds. Alex stood at the rail, looking down onto the wharf. Islanders with glistening black skin toiled, loading bales onto pallets to be hoisted by the derricks of the ship adjacent to them into holds. Sweat dripped down Alex's chest under his shirt as he observed the busy German port going about its work for the day.

'Customs have cleared us, Mr Macintosh,' Jock McLeod, the chief engineer, said. 'We can go ashore.'

'Good show, Jock,' Alex said. 'I would like you to get a bit of your kit together for an extended time ashore.'

Jock turned to walk back to put together a few items while Alex pondered the mission ahead of him. His eyes scanned the dock below for any signs that the German authorities were suspicious of the

Australian-registered trading ship but could see none. Satisfied all was well he returned to his cabin to retrieve a few items of his own.

Ashore, the two men walked towards the centre of the town with swags over their shoulders. They found a hotel, a simple building with wide verandahs and a corrugated iron roof, where Alex arranged two nights' accommodation with the owner, a small, bearded, middle-aged man wearing an immaculate white tropical suit. Alex had noticed that all the Europeans he had observed on his walk to the hotel also wore similar, practical suits whereas the Islanders mostly wore lap-laps – except for the colonial Melanesian police, who wore a European-style uniform.

'You are English,' the hotel owner said, observing the Sydney address Alex provided on the register.

'Australian,' Alex corrected in German.

'It is the same thing,' the owner replied. 'Australians are English.'

Alex was tempted to tell the officious man that he did not think that his Scottish-Irish ancestors would agree, but refrained. 'I am looking for a missionary priest, Father Umberto,' Alex said. 'Would you be able to tell me where I might find him?'

'Why would you want to contact the priest?' the innkeeper asked.

Alex knew that he had to be careful in his reply. The owner was acting strangely, considering that they had not met before. 'My company intends to provide financial support for his missionary work among the natives. I would like to meet Father Umberto and speak with him,' he replied with a forced smile.

'Father Umberto has a place up in the mountains,' the owner answered, eyeing Alex from behind his thin-wired spectacles. 'He works among the dangerous savages there – the Tolai.'

Alex knew that the Tolai people of this part of the German empire were fierce warriors, forever rebelling against the German occupation of their lands. An intelligent people, they did not take well to German law. Twenty years earlier the German military had clashed with the Tolai tribesmen in bloody skirmishes. Only the use of mercenary groups from other parts of the island had eventually subdued them, but the resentment was always simmering among the proud men of the Tolai.

'Then it is a good thing that my company may be able to bring Father Umberto civilised products, to help show the Tolai that it is best to accept our way of life, rather than resist the good intentions of the Kaiser,' Alex said facetiously.

The owner did not reply, accepting the pen back from Alex and passing him two sets of keys. 'Rooms six and seven,' he said. 'The times for meals are inside your rooms. I do not tolerate visits to the rooms after 7pm.'

Alex nodded and handed Jock his key. As they walked inside the hotel Jock finally spoke. 'I get the impression that he was a wee hostile towards us.'

'It seems that he does not like the English much,' Alex replied.

'Nor do I,' Jock answered. 'You should have told the wee man that.'

Alex smiled. Jock had not understood the German that passed between him and the hotel proprietor. He wondered how he would keep the Scotsman in the dark about the mission and yet rely on his help. That was another problem he would consider as he went on his way. First, he had to find someone who would guide them into the mountains to meet the Italian priest. It did not appear that he would receive any assistance from the hotel keeper.

Alex opened the door to his room to discover it was clean and airy. It was not much different from the country hotels he knew from his days in Queensland, with its mosquito net hanging over the bed from the ceiling. The only difference was that all the signs were in German. Gecko excreta even stained the ceiling. He threw his swag on the single, sagging bed and walked over to a window with open shutters. The room had a view across the verandah to the corrugated iron roofs of the adjacent buildings. He had hardly turned from the view when there was a loud knock at his door. He guessed that it was not Jock as he could hear him moving about next door.

'Who is it?' Alex asked in German.

'Hauptmann Hirsch,' the voice replied. Alex recognised the military rank of his visitor. He opened the door to see a solidly built man of average height and red hair, wearing tropical civilian dress of a white suit.

'May I come in?' Hirsch asked politely but firmly.

'Your country,' Alex replied, stepping back to

allow the German captain to enter. 'From your rank I assume that you are army.'

'I am the same as you, Captain Macintosh,' Hirsch said, extending his hand. 'I am with the militia here, as you are in your own country.'

The German had a strong grip. 'You seem to know a lot about me considering that my ship has just docked.'

'Ah, I had the pleasure of meeting a distant relative of yours last month – Major von Fellmann,' Hirsch said with a warm smile. 'A great soldier and good man. I have come to extend the hospitality of the Imperial German Army to a comrade from another country. We have our own club here, what you would call an officers' mess. I would like you to join us at five o'clock this afternoon for drinks.'

'I must thank you for your courtesy, but I am here to seek out a missionary priest my company wishes to support in his crusade to bring civilisation to some of your more troublesome citizens.'

'Father Umberto,' Hirsch replied. 'If you join us this afternoon I may be able to assist you. Dress is tropical suit. You can be fitted out by our Chinese merchants a block from here. They can measure and produce your suit within a couple of hours. Now, I must return to my civil duties. I expect to see you in a few hours. You may bring your engineer also, but he will be required to be similarly dressed.'

'I doubt that Jock has ever worn a suit in his life so I will exclude him from joining us,' Alex said. 'Besides, my friend does not speak German.'

'Ah, a good decision,' Hirsch said, once again

extending his hand. 'Those of the other ranks do not appreciate the talk between gentlemen. Five o'clock then.'

Alex pondered the visit from a member of the German military. He had hardly arrived and yet he was known to the authorities, he thought uneasily. The visit was more than a courtesy, he was sure of that. He was obviously under observation and would be forced to accept the German militia captain's invitation to join him. Rustling in his pockets, Alex located the wad of notes. No doubt the Chinese drapers would accept Australian currency, so long as he tipped a generous amount. It was time to invest in a white suit.

Alex briefed Jock that he would be required to attend a club that night. 'You have permission to paint the town red,' Alex grinned. 'But be on parade no later than six in the morning.'

'Aye, aye, Mr Macintosh,' Jock replied with a mock salute. The Scotsman had served time in a Highlands regiment in his youth and risen to the rank of corporal. His background was one reason Alex had requested Jock to accompany him on this mission.

When Alex arrived at the club he was met by Hauptmann Hirsch who introduced him to the members, many wearing their military uniforms. The welcome was warm and Alex quickly learned that the German militia officers had much in common with their Australian colleague. He also discovered that he could not buy a drink as the conversation, alcohol and good feeling flowed into the evening. Alex kept to the excellent beer as he did not want to drink himself into a stupor as most of the members of the officers' club seemed to be doing. Throughout the evening Dieter Hirsch remained with Alex.

'It is time that we dined,' Hirsch announced, leading Alex to an adjoining room where a table was loaded with German delicacies. Alex helped himself to a plate of sausage, sauerkraut and boiled potatoes. The two men retired to another table where they took a seat facing each other.

'This is good,' Alex said, cutting a slice of sausage. 'It just so happens that I like pickled cabbage.'

Hirsch had piled a veal knuckle and sauerkraut on his plate. The meat was rich with gravy which he sopped up with a slice of fresh bread. 'Since you are seeking to meet with Father Umberto in the hills,' the German said, 'I may be able to supply an armed party of native police.'

'That is appreciated,' Alex replied, reaching for his tankard of beer to wash down the meal. 'I was hoping to hire a guide to take me and my engineer up there, but if you are able to supply an escort that will be even better.'

'It is dangerous to travel inland without an armed party. Some of the natives of that region are still hostile to our rule,' Hirsch said, pausing in his meal.

'I am sure that if I am able to indicate that I am not German they will not trouble me,' Alex answered.

'They will not differentiate. They will kill you on sight, believing that you are a German like us.'

Alex was uneasy. He was already guessing what would come next and was soon proven right.

'I will be sending a party of our police boys with you. I must insist, Captain Macintosh,' Hirsch continued. 'It would not give a good impression to your government if anything were to befall you of a bad kind. As a matter of fact, it is time that I made an inspection of Father Umberto's missionary station. It is part of my duties with the civil service here to carry out inspections of all the missionaries to ensure that their welfare is taken care of. We will collect you at 9am tomorrow. I will insist that the innkeeper reimburses you for the night you will not be spending in his establishment.'

Alex was trapped. He had the uneasy feeling that his every move was being monitored and did not know why. There could only be one reason that the German authorities knew so much about him and that was if there had been some kind of security leak from Australia. But that did not make sense. From what he had been briefed before departing on his Pacific tour only his father and Colonel Hughes were aware of his real mission to the German-held islands. It was highly unlikely that either of them would let his real purpose for being in Rabaul leak. Alex accepted that his mission had just become very complicated but there was nothing he could do. He was trapped and, if he was not careful, could seriously jeopardise not only his life but that also of his engineer. 'We will be ready,' he answered but without conviction.

★

Hauptmann Dieter Hirsch stood before the four Tolai police selected for the escort duty. They stood to attention, their rifles at the shoulder. Hirsch wore his field uniform and was armed with a pistol in a shiny, close-down leather holster. He accepted the salute from the senior member of the police patrol, stood them down to seek the shade of nearby trees, turned on his heel and marched over to the verandah of the civil service office where he usually worked. He was met by a portly man in his late fifties wearing a civilian suit. Hirsch instinctively saluted. The senior civil servant was once a regular navy officer who outranked him.

'Herr Marx, we are ready to move out,' Hirsch said stiffly.

Marx removed his hat and wiped his brow with a clean handkerchief. 'You are clear on your orders, Hauptmann Hirsch,' the portly man said.

'I am clear on my orders, Herr Marx,' Hirsch replied with a note of reluctance that brought a dark look from the man towering over him from the verandah.

'I appreciate you may feel that in carrying out the allocated task you may be viewed as a cold-blooded murderer. But you are a soldier and I need not remind you that our reliable information has revealed Captain Macintosh as a spy. We have no doubts whatsoever that he is contacting the Italian priest on a mission that may one day put our defence in great peril should we go to war with the English. I am trusting your usual clear judgement to ensure that if you are required to kill the two Englishmen

124

it appears to be a regrettable accident. You have the means to arrange such an unfortunate event.'

'Yes, sir,' Hirsch replied. 'I understand the danger the captain may pose to our defence. I will not hesitate to carry out my mission should Captain Macintosh show any signs of espionage.'

'Very good, Hauptmann Hirsch,' Marx said, satisfied his officer would remember his loyalty to the Kaiser. 'Carry on.'

Hirsch saluted one more time, turned on his heel and bawled to his men to get on their feet and assemble for the short march to the hotel. The Tolai police scurried from the shade to form a single file, rifles on shoulders. Hirsch then gave the command to march and fell into step alongside his small detachment. As he made his way to the hotel the German officer frowned. Even in the short time he had spent with him he had grown to like the Australian officer and knew that if the time came to carry out his orders to kill the man and his companion it would be done with regret. They had much in common in their attitudes to life and the man had a natural charm that could woo the devil's daughter. But if Alexander Macintosh openly flouted the laws of his country he knew he would have no other choice but to obey his orders to dispose of the Australian. Dieter prayed that this situation would not eventuate but was also aware that the security of his country in this forgotten part of the Kaiser's Empire was at stake.

As his detachment marched towards the hotel few people on the avenue of mango trees took much notice. Armed police were a common sight in the settlement. Dieter Hirsch saw the two men standing in the dusty street and even from a distance could see that they were the worse for wear from the previous night's carousing, Alex in his company at the officers' club and the tough-looking man beside him at some European-frequented bar in town.

Hirsch called an order for his police to halt and walked towards Alex. 'Good morning, Captain Macintosh,' he greeted with a smile. 'I notice that your friend has met some of our local lads.'

Alex grinned, knowing that Hirsch was referring to Jock's two black eyes. 'He informs me that his was a worthy cause. One of the men he clashed with called him an Englishman.'

'I am afraid that many of my people here do not realise that the Scots are as different from the English as a Bavarian is from a Prussian,' Hirsch said. 'I see that you are ready to proceed.'

Alex hefted his kit over his shoulder. 'Lead on, Hauptmann Hirsch,' he said.

The trek took them from the tiny coastal strip of Rabaul town into rugged rainforest surrounding the horseshoe-shaped bay. Hirsch had informed Alex that the journey could possibly take a full day and night to reach the mission station.

The small party wound its way along an almost indiscernible track used for generations by the Tolai people travelling down to the coast. The humidity in the dank forest was oppressive as was the silence in the shadows. Stops were made to rest and drink water and it was on one of the stops that Alex became aware that a fever was coming on him. He alternated between feeling very hot to shivering from a chill that almost brought him to his knees. When a severe headache quickly followed, Alex began stumbling. Dieter Hirsch noticed the physical change in the Australian. When Alex sank to his knees, dropping his swag, Hirsch called a stop to the arduous journey upwards. Jock was beside Alex with a canteen of water, attempting to force some between his lips. 'Here laddie,' he said with soothing words. 'Take a wee sip.'

'Malaria,' Hirsch said, kneeling beside Jock and placing his hand to Alex's brow. The terrible disease had claimed so many German settlers over the years that the symptoms were as common to him as those of a cold. He spoke to Jock in German but the engineer simply shook his head and said, 'I don't speak German.'

Hirsch frowned. He had very little knowledge of English. 'We carry,' he was able to muster in his limited grasp of English.

With orders snapped to his police, construction of a makeshift litter was quickly underway. Using their machetes the men cut saplings for poles and a blanket was quickly strung between them. Alex was lifted into the litter and the four police took an end each to hoist the improvised stretcher onto their shoulders. Hirsch made a decision. They were closer to the mission station than to Rabaul behind them and he knew that Father Umberto's clinic would most likely have a supply of quinine. The patrol slowly struggled through the thick jungle. Just after sunset they emerged on a plateau and saw lanterns burning in the huts at the mission.

The Italian priest was summoned by one of the Tolai residents and greeted by Hauptmann Hirsch. Father Umberto spoke German fluently and gave orders for Alex to be taken to a small, white-washed stone building.

Jock could see from the glass cabinets affixed to the walls displaying vials of drugs that the building was some kind of medical dispensary. Alex was placed in the single cot to one side of the one-roomed clinic. When the priest spoke his voice was a rich baritone. A man in his fifties with a mop of snow white thick hair, black bushy eyebrows and a tanned bearded face he was wearing a flowing white cassock but no clerical collar. He was indeed a man to be respected, Jock thought, and was disappointed to learn that the priest only spoke Italian, German and French. None of the languages he knew.

'What do you think?' Hirsch asked the priest, now bending over Alex who had fallen into a delirium and was mumbling unintelligible words in English.

'I do not like what I can see,' the priest replied, forcing a thermometer into Alex's mouth. 'I think that this man has little chance of surviving. I am sorry, Herr Hauptmann,' Father Umberto said, standing stiffly to examine the mercury tube. 'He will be lucky if he sees another sunrise.'

The German militia captain shook his head. He had a decision to make. If Captain Macintosh died of natural causes then his mission was over. He'd be relieved of a duty he did not relish. But if the Australian recovered then he would be forced to remain and confirm that Macintosh was indeed a spy. But Hirsch had an ace up his sleeve; the Italian priest was not aware of the fact but one of his staff close to him was an informant to the German administration. That person had the priest's confidence and would be able to report just about everything back to Hirsch.

Dieter Hirsch made a decision to remain until Alex either died or gained his health. He turned to the priest and requested quarters for himself and his men. When Father Umberto agreed that Hirsch and Jock could share his quarters and the police a men's dormitory in the station, Hirsch ordered his men to bunk down and they were guided away by one of Father Umberto's Tolai assistants.

'I will have one of the good sisters sit with Mr Macintosh,' Father Umberto said. 'My nuns will take turns keeping an eye on the man.'

Arrangements were made and two very black-skinned nuns wearing white dresses and veils were summoned and although they were young they appeared competent in their nursing duties.

Holding a lantern, Father Umberto accompanied Jock and Hirsch across a flat, open ground to a spacious Tolai-built hut with European verandahs. Inside his quarters Jock could see that the priest had surrounded himself with shelves of leather-bound books – mostly on medical procedures – and some items of European furniture. Geckos scurried into corners of the thatched ceiling upon their entry into the building. 'I presume that you might like a wine before retiring,' the priest said to Hirsch, lighting another couple of kerosene lanterns. 'It is not often that a most distinguished member of the administration pays our humble mission station a visit.'

Hirsch accepted the offer and Father Umberto produced a bottle of red wine from a cupboard along with three glasses. Hirsch gestured to the glass and wine. Jock understood the invitation and nodded his head. The three men sat at a sturdy wooden table and raised their glasses. Although Jock did not understand the words in German he did recognise Alex's name and presumed that it was a toast to his boss and friend recovering. 'To Mr Macintosh,' he responded, with feeling.

Meanwhile Alex was fighting for his life in the clinic across the open ground between the two buildings. Swigging back his wine, Dieter Hirsch wondered if he might yet have to kill the Australian and this soured the taste of the fine Italian red. Maybe the man was better dying from the tropical illness than recovering only to be killed at a later date.

9

The location for the meeting had been well thought-out. Busy Circular Quay with its milling crowds embarking or disembarking from the ferries of Sydney Harbour was a place to disappear in. Herr Bosch, the assistant to the German consul in Sydney, knew whom he was to meet. He stood by the exit to the Mosman ferry watching the ladies in their long dresses hurrying for shelter and holding down their hats against a wind flurry while gentlemen in suits and straw boater hats joined them.

As rain clouds gathered in the skies overhead Bosch waited patiently under the shelter over the pier until he saw the man he had come to meet.

'Mr Macintosh,' he said in English when the man wearing an expensive, tailored suit approached. 'We should walk and talk.'

George Macintosh fell into step with the

assistant consul. They made their way with their heads down against the southerly wind now blowing sleeting rain towards the streets of Sydney. Trams clattered into life, conveying ferry passengers to their places of occupation. 'You have news of my brother?' George asked.

'Ja,' Bosch answered. 'Our last report was that he has been intercepted in Rabaul and remains under the observation of our government there.'

'Have your people in Rabaul uncovered any signs that he is on a spying mission?' George asked, crossing a busy street filled with trams, horse-drawn wagons and automobiles spewing fumes.

'Not so far,' Bosch answered. 'But if we do I cannot be responsible for what may befall your brother. You must understand that his life is in dire peril if he is a spy.'

'I appreciate what you are trying to tell me and be assured that I would not hold your government responsible if my brother were to have an unfortunate accident in the jungle.'

Maynard Bosch glanced at him with an unconcealed expression of disgust. 'I cannot understand how a man could speak so lightly of the possible death of a brother,' he said.

'You must understand, Herr Bosch, before you judge me, that my feelings towards my brother come second to the future of the family fortunes. If my brother is on some foolish mission to commit a crime against your government then he must understand that he runs a terrible risk of jeopardising his own life and, worse still, our investments with your country. What is the sacrifice of one man worth in the interests of many?' George said.

Bosch nodded although he still did not understand why any man would betray his brother. 'My government is very appreciative of your assistance in the matter and hopes that your suspicions are unfounded. From what I have been able to glean about your brother, Captain Macintosh, he proved very popular with the officers in Rabaul. It would be a shame for the world to lose such a man.'

George listened but felt no emotion concerning his brother's fate. He had passed on the information to curry favour with the German government as well as solve his problem of Alex sharing in any future inheritance. His plan to discredit Fenella appeared to be progressing well and before the end of the year he aimed to have both out of the family – one way or the other – leaving him the sole beneficiary of the vast Macintosh fortune. The heavy investment in the German chemical industry was fast becoming a small fortune in its own right as the Germans were leading in this field. George could see their discoveries as the basis of a huge pharmaceutical industry in the future. If Lady Enid Macintosh had still been alive she might have approved of his concern for the family name and fortune, he thought. She had no time for the weak and approved of his ruthless strength. He could bide his time either until his father died or eventually handed him the total control of the companies.

'Do you have anything else for me?' George asked, stopping outside one of Sydney's more exclusive hotels.

'It would help us if you could uncover more of what your father and Colonel Hughes are plotting,' Bosch said. 'I am sure that you could make yourself present when they meet at your father's house.'

'I do not see them together there very often,' George replied. 'My father normally discusses military matters with Colonel Hughes at Victoria Barracks.'

'It is a shame that you do not have a commission with Colonel Duffy's regiment like your brother does,' Bosch said. 'You could prove to be invaluable to us.'

'I am not a spy like my brother,' George retorted. 'I have passed on the information that I had because I felt I had justification to do so. But I am not a traitor to my country.'

'I did not say that you were,' Bosch countered. 'What you have passed to us is really in the interests of peace between our two nations. It is better that the activities of men like your brother be neutralised to maintain stability in the region.'

George knew that the assistant consul was throwing up a feeble defence of counterespionage but did not care. So long as they helped dispose of Alex and remembered his favour in the financial dealings he had with their industrialists he was untroubled by what they said about his role in the affair.

'Well, if there is nothing else I will bid you a good afternoon,' George said. 'I have a luncheon meeting with my company directors. But I would be very grateful if you would inform me immediately if anything should befall my brother. In the meantime I can assure you my cooperation will continue.'

Bosch watched as George Macintosh entered the main entrance to the hotel. It was a place that would have cost him a month's salary just to eat one meal. Bosch was a straightforward man who loved his country and his family. The idea that a man could so easily condemn his brother to death was beyond him, no matter what was at stake. Bosch's own brother was a farmer in South Australia. Sadly, he was a professed patriot of his new country and unaware of Bosch's activities in espionage. If it came to war between Germany and England Bosch worried that the ensuing hostilities would divide him and his brother in their loyalties.

He shook his head in disgust and turned to walk back to the consul office. At least he had the powerful and influential George Macintosh over a barrel. To not assist him could have dire consequences for Mr George Macintosh.

With Matthew Duffy in Queensland, Randolph Gates found that he had a lot of time on his hands in Sydney. He had an excuse to stay around the film set and assist with the project because he needed to be expert in the use of the camera. But he also found the work interesting as they changed locations and he helped set up the props as backgrounds for the scenes in Arthur's epic love story of passion and betrayal. Fenella was not hostile to his presence but simply seemed to ignore him. But his persistence seemed to be paying off. After a week, Fenella fell into small talk with him between scenes being shot.

This day Arthur had selected a location on one of Sydney's more remote northern beaches where he owned a beach cottage. The entire cast and crew camped out there and an impromptu party began when the sun went down over a glorious autumn day. At least that is what the cast and crew thought. In fact, Arthur had a good stockpile of food and alcohol for the shooting of the last scene in his film. He saw the occasion as a way to celebrate the conclusion of what had almost been a terminated project.

Randolph impressed them with his ability to find driftwood in the tussock-covered sand dunes and build a bonfire on the beach, while Arthur truly endeared himself to his employees by producing big, succulent steaks to grill over the fire. Potatoes were thrown into the hot ashes to bake in their skins and slabs of fresh bread acted as plates. Crates of beer completed the abundant feast.

Bob Houston stepped forward to hand out the bottles, and Arthur made a small speech congratulating his people on the fine job they had done of turning a script into a visual story. A breeze gently stirred the sand around their feet as the stars mixed with sparks swirling skywards from the fire into the clear skies.

Randolph had noticed how Guy Wilkes hovered around Fenella and was astute enough to see that she was not encouraging his presence. The American sat on a large driftwood log sipping his beer and chatting to the cameraman whom he had befriended on the set. Bob Houston, his teacher and now a good friend, commented that he should consider a career behind the small wooden box cranking the handle. 'You have a gift, Texas Slim, that you should take seriously.' He raised his bottle to the stars. 'I am sure Arthur would find you a spot in the team.'

Randolph was only half listening; his attention was on Fenella and Guy Wilkes who were apparently arguing. He could see them silhouetted against the star-studded moonless sky and did not answer Bob.

'Are you going senile, or something?'

'Sorry, what?' Randolph replied.

'You're not listening, are you, cobber,' Bob said, prodding Randolph in the ribs.

'Just thinking about things,' Randolph said, swigging his beer from the bottle. Suddenly, he handed Bob his beer and rose to his feet. 'Just got something to see to.'

Bob watched as Randolph walked into the dark towards the beach. The American had noticed that Wilkes appeared to be getting very pushy with Fenella. He had his hands on her shoulders and appeared to be shaking her.

'Anything wrong?' Randolph asked, looming out of the night beside the couple. They were standing at the edge of the sea, water breaking around their bare feet.

Wilkes swung on Randolph, his hands dropping from Fenella's shoulders. 'None of your business,' he snarled. 'Get lost, Yank.'

As Randolph took a step closer, ready to fight, the actor noticed his threatening stance.

'Are you okay?' Randolph asked Fenella who

had her head down as if she had been crying. She responded by shaking her head. 'Maybe you should come with me back to the party,' he urged gently, ignoring Wilkes who he sensed was not about to take any action against him.

Randolph took Fenella's hand in his and led her away. She did not resist and as they were nearing the blazing fire he stopped to gaze into her face. He had been right in his guess; Fenella had been crying.

'I don't know what was said between you two,' Randolph said, producing a clean handkerchief and passing it to her. 'But I do not like to see you so upset.'

'It was nothing of any consequence,' Fenella answered, passing back the handkerchief after wiping away her tears. 'I will be all right, but thank you for your concern, Randolph.'

The American felt a surge of warmth hearing Fenella use his first name. 'Would you like to join me on my log?' he ventured lightly.

'I think that would be nice,' Fenella said, with a weak smile.

Randolph led her to where Bob remained with the two bottles of beer in his hands. When he saw Randolph with Fenella he handed the half-empty bottle back to the American and discreetly excused himself from their company.

'Do you have another bottle of beer?' Fenella sniffed.

'I did not think that ladies drank beer,' Randolph answered. 'But I will fetch one for you.'

'There is a lot that you do not know about me,

Randolph,' Fenella said quietly. 'A lot that you may not approve of.'

Randolph felt awkward. 'I doubt that anything you have done could shock an old cowboy like me,' he replied. 'I think that you are the finest lady I have ever met.'

'Oh, Randolph,' Fenella said, squeezing his arm impulsively, 'I wish that were true, but I think that you would change your mind if you knew what I would like to confide to you.'

'Does it have something to do with the argument you just had with Wilkes?' he asked, gazing towards the eastern horizon. When Fenella did not reply Randolph rose to his feet. 'I will go and get that beer for you,' he said.

When he found the crate of beer he also found Arthur.

'Is Nellie okay?' Arthur asked.

'Why would you ask that?' Randolph replied, scooping a bottle from the crate and removing the lid.

'I saw you go down to the edge of the beach. Guy just stormed past me headed for the cottage. I doubt that your intervention in whatever happened between them improved his humour.'

'Miss Macintosh is fine,' Randolph answered defensively. 'We are just in conversation.'

In the flickering shadows by the bonfire Arthur's expression of concern was visible. 'Take care, Mr Gates,' he said. 'Believe me, Nellie has a problem that is beyond your assistance.'

Randolph was intrigued by the producer's

warning, but knew it would not be wise to ask him any more on the subject. Surely Fenella would explain when the time was right.

When Randolph returned Fenella was sitting with her arms wrapped around her legs and her head on her knees.

'Your beer,' he said, passing the bottle to her. She accepted it and took a long swig from the slender neck. Randolph sat beside her with his back against the trunk of a tree that had washed ashore.

'If you want to talk about what is troubling you just consider me a shoulder to cry on,' he said quietly. 'I'm kind of used to being out on the range listening to the noises in the night.'

'Thank you,' Fenella replied. 'But I would rather you and I talk of things near and dear to our hearts – rather than about my problems.'

Randolph shrugged. If that is what Fenella desired, then so be it. Strangely, he found that she changed from someone beset by despair to the bright, young woman he had first met at the Macintosh house by the harbour. Without heeding time they talked and laughed together until the bonfire on the beach was only a smouldering glow of hot coals and the crew had crept away to sleep. The constellation of the Southern Cross was on the horizon before they realised the time and bade each other a good night.

Fenella leaned over and kissed Randolph on the cheek with more than friendly affection. 'Thank you,' she said, gripping his arm. 'You are truly a remarkable man with a beautiful spirit.'

Before he could reply, she rose and walked towards

the cottage, leaving him with two empty beer bottles and swirling thoughts. He remained in the dark, his mind going over the events of the evening. If Fenella was hiding something, it meant little to him. He was in love with her.

The following morning dawned a perfect day for filming with clear blue skies and a gentle breeze. The cast and crew moved sluggishly but cheerfully. A small gauge rail track was laid out along the beach and a hand-propelled trolley set up for the cameraman to move with the action. A saddled, spirited shiny black stallion was led down to the beach by its handler for the scene.

Arthur stomped around the beach issuing directions and checking angles. Randolph stood idly by, watching the commotion but mostly keeping an eye out for Fenella. He knew that this was the scene where Guy rode along the beach at full gallop, swung himself from the saddle and swept Fenella into his arms while she stood up to her knees in the surf.

'Nellie, you are late again,' Randolph heard Arthur chide.

Randolph turned to see Fenella walking barefooted down from Arthur's cottage. She was wearing a long, flowing white dress and no hat. He frowned when he saw Wilkes follow her, wearing jodhpurs and a silk shirt unbuttoned to the chest. He strode across to the horse and the big animal attempted to prance away when Guy reached out for it.

Randolph grinned. It was obvious that the actor

was going to have a hard time with his scene. From where he stood the American could see Guy berating the horse handler. Then he stomped angrily over to Arthur who was supervising the set-up of the camera with Bob Houston. More harsh words were exchanged and Arthur threw up his hands in obvious despair. Fenella sat down on the log that she and Randolph had shared the night before, watching the tantrums with a bemused expression.

'Texas,' Arthur called to Randolph. 'Could I have a word with you?'

Randolph walked across to the huddle of cameraman, director and actor.

'Do you think that you might be able to handle this horse?' Arthur asked with a pained expression, gesturing to the snorting stallion. 'I believe that you were once a cowboy in your own country.'

'And a stockman here,' Randolph added. 'I will see what I can do.'

He walked over to the horse handler who was holding the reins. 'What's the big fella's name?' he asked.

'Darkie,' the handler replied. 'He don't usually play up like this. Looks like he don't like the other bloke.'

'That means Darkie and I have something in common,' Randolph said, reaching out to touch the snorting horse on the nose. With gentle strokes, Randolph spoke softly to the horse as one would croon to a child. Soon the horse stopped its snorting and appeared to quieten. 'He and I will be good pals,' Randolph said, turning to the handler and taking the reins from him.

Arthur joined Randolph by the stallion. 'I know that I am asking a favour but do you think you could do this scene and ride at full gallop along the beach, leaping from the horse when you reach Nellie? I can substitute Guy in the editing and have him swooping Nellie into his arms and kissing her. All you have to do is ride like the devil and leap from the horse.'

'Sure,' Randolph said with an easy smile. 'What do I need?'

'Well, you will have to change into clothing to match Guy's outfit,' Arthur said with a tone of relief. 'We have a spare outfit up at the cottage that I think will fit you.'

'Won't it be obvious that it is me and not Guy on the horse?' Randolph asked.

Arthur broke into a broad smile. 'Dear chap,' he said, 'this is the magical world of movie making. We have ways to make it look like Guy. All you have to do is ride the horse, leap off into the surf and leave the rest to me.'

'Okay,' Randolph said, looking across to Fenella who was shading her eyes and obviously watching him. Randolph gave her a wave which she returned.

When he had changed and returned to the beach Fenella was already standing in the gentle surf, waiting for him to do his part in the scene.

Randolph swung himself into the saddle and the horse barely flinched at the stranger on its back.

'Take him down about a couple of hundred yards and when you ride towards us keep parallel with the track,' Arthur directed. 'Bob will be attempting to move towards you on the trolley.'

Randolph glanced down at Bob Houston kneeling behind his camera while two burly men crouched in a position to push him as fast as they could when the time was right. With a mock salute, Randolph swung the horse's head around and cantered down the beach. He swung the horse around and waited for Arthur's command.

'Go!' Arthur shouted through a megaphone.

Randolph kicked the big mount into action. He was pleasantly surprised to feel the horse react so well to his handling and charged forward. He could hear the crew cheering him on and before he knew it Fenella loomed up before him in the surf. With practised ease, Randolph swung himself from the saddle and swooped Fenella into his arms, kissing her passionately on the lips even as he could hear from the beach something about 'cut'. Fenella's surprise was such that she did not resist and melted against him, returning the passion. The kiss seemed to go on forever and Randolph could hear the cheering from the crew as they watched the unscheduled scene.

Breathlessly, Fenella finally broke the spell and drew back, a dreamy expression on her face. 'That was not supposed to happen,' she said with a warm smile.

'Sorry,' Randolph replied without really meaning it. 'I got a bit carried away with this acting thing.'

'I hope that you were not acting,' Fenella chided gently.

'I wasn't,' Randolph said, grinning down at her.

They both burst into laughter and Randolph lifted Fenella off her feet in a bear hug, carrying her back to the beach where the crew were clapping their appreciation.

However, Arthur was frowning. 'That was not part of your instructions,' he said and suddenly burst into a broad smile. 'But your acting was so good that I think we will have trouble editing it out. Well done, Texas.'

Randolph made a short bow and looked up at Guy Wilkes whose face was a mask of fury. Randolph grinned a challenge to do something about his bold advance on Fenella, but the actor simply turned on his heel. As he stomped away. Randolph realised that Fenella was still holding his hand.

10

Sister Bridget considered herself a dedicated nun, one whose life would most probably end in the jungles of the Pacific Islands, serving the needs of her church. She was the fifth in a family of eight girls and two boys, born into an impoverished life in Dublin. The Church had offered the young woman an opportunity for a life outside the soul-destroying slums of the Irish city. For the past twenty years Sister Bridget's only contact with her family in far-away Dublin had been by letters – mostly from her younger brother who followed her in the order of birth. As children they had been close, living and playing in the filthy back streets of the Irish capital. In those days Bridget had been her brother's protector but now he was dead. Liam had not died of natural causes, but from the bullet of a Lee Enfield rifle in the hands of a British soldier. For Liam had been a revolutionary, sworn to freeing his country from the occupation by the Protestant English.

Sister Bridget was now in the fifty-fifth year of her life and had witnessed first hand the suffering of the Tolai people under the yoke of German rule. She was fluent in German and also the Tolai language, and although she despised the German government she did not hate the German people. Liam had often stressed to her that if any country in Europe rallied to assist in the struggle for Irish independence from England, it would be Germany, a natural enemy of the British people.

'He rambles about clearing the jungle,' Sister Bridget said to Hauptmann Hirsch, standing in the shade of a grove of rainforest giants just a short distance from the clinic where Alex lay in a fever. 'I do not know what he means.'

'Thank you, Sister,' Hirsch said, himself also of the Catholic faith. 'I must confess that I also do not know what his ramblings mean. No doubt your closeness to Father Umberto might reveal if the man is a spy working for the English government. I fear that Captain Macintosh is not simply here for humanitarian reasons.'

'I must return to the clinic,' Sister Bridget said. 'Father Umberto will be taking patients very soon.'

Dieter Hirsch nodded and watched the nun walk unsteadily away with the aid of a walking stick. God did not spare nuns from arthritis and the good sister suffered badly in the hip from the debilitating disease. He pondered on what Sister Bridget had overheard during her nursing shift with the gravely ill Australian. *Clearing the jungle* . . . Why would the Australian army officer be fixated with clearing the jungle? It did not make sense. Hirsch shrugged. It was time to speak with Father Umberto and ascertain the patient's health.

As the German militia captain walked out of the shade of the trees he noticed one of his Tolai police running towards him with an expression of fear across his dark face.

'What is it, Buka?' Hirsch asked.

'The Tolai,' Buka answered. 'They stole a rifle and ammunition.'

'God in heaven!' Hirsch exploded. 'When, and whose rifle?'

'It was my rifle and it happened just now,' Buka answered, standing at attention. 'A bush kanaka took it when we were eating at the kitchen.'

Hirsch had some sympathy for the man confessing that he had lost his rifle. The Tolai policeman knew the harsh penalty he might incur for such a breach of regulations. Past cases of missing rifles usually suggested the policeman simply deserted rather than face a charge. But Buka had owned up immediately. 'Get the others to parade now,' he commanded. 'We will commence a search for the offender and when we find him he will answer for his crime against the government.'

Buka ran back to where his companions nervously awaited the outcome of his admission to their commander. Within seconds they tumbled onto the large cleared space between the buildings of the mission station. When Hirsch questioned his men as to what they had witnessed one of them said he thought he knew in which direction the offender had gone. He even recognised the man from a nearby village that they had once visited. Hirsch suspected that the thief would be making his way back there.

Father Umberto had already heard of the theft of the rifle and hurried across to the German officer. 'My people have told me that it was not one of them who took your weapon,' he said. 'They are a peaceful community and informed me that the thief is a man from the village east of here.'

'I know,' Hirsch said to ease the worry he could see in Father Umberto's face about possible reprisals from the government for the serious breach of internal security in his mission station. 'I will take my men and go immediately to the other village.'

Without any further thought of his duty to Alex Macintosh, Hauptmann Hirsch ordered his patrol to set off in pursuit of the thief.

By the time night fell over the mission station Hirsch had not returned. Alex was now out of the worst of the fever. He sat up and sipped from a bowl of vegetable soup prepared by the nuns and brought to him by Father Umberto who was sitting at the side of his bed. Jock stood in the background, relieved to see the young man recovering.

'Is it safe to speak in front of your man?' Father Umberto asked in German.

'He does not understand German,' Alex replied,

wiping with a cloth at some drops of soup that had missed his mouth. 'You know why I have come to meet you.'

'I only know that your father has promised a generous grant of money and medical supplies to my mission for something that could prove to be dangerous to all concerned.'

'I hope not,' Alex replied. 'But I would ask you to commit yourself to helping me with certain tasks that might be construed by the government here to be subversive. I do not know how the German authorities might react if they learned of what we have planned.'

'If it involves any threat to life here you know that I will not assist you in whatever you are going to propose,' the priest said, spooning the last of the vegetable soup into Alex's mouth. 'That would be against my principles and detrimental to the standing of the Catholic Church in this part of the world.'

'I can promise you that what we have planned involves no threat to human life,' Alex reassured. 'We want you to recruit some of your trusted parishioners to clear a strip of jungle on the east coast for us. I have the dimensions but it needs to be done secretly within the next two months. Perhaps you could convince them that they are preparing the land for a large vegetable garden.'

'Is that all?' Father Umberto asked. 'Just send some of my native boys to hack out a field down on the coast.'

'I have a map of where we need the clearing done,' Alex said. 'We would also need a crew of at least six of your most reliable men to remain behind to assist us with porter duties – they will be well paid for their services.'

'What is this "garden" to be used for?' the priest asked with a touch of sarcasm.

'The less you know the better,' Alex answered. 'Then you don't have to lie if you are ever questioned by the Germans about our activities on the other side of the island.'

'So long as your task will not unnecessarily endanger my community or any citizen of Neu Pommern I will assist you,' the priest replied, standing stiffly away from the bed. 'You need to rest for the night before you attempt to get on your feet. I will speak further to you in the morning. In the meantime, may God look over you.'

Alex thanked the Italian priest and turned to the Scot hovering close by. 'Well, Jock, it seems that I am not yet destined for the bone yard.'

'It was touch and go, laddie,' Jock said, moving out of the shadows. 'I was not keen to return to Rabaul carrying your rotting carcass. What was all that about with the dago priest?' The Scot had little time for Papists – and even less time for anyone who did not have Scottish blood.

'Nothing of any real consequence,' Alex lied. 'He was just saying that I was recovering well.'

Jock frowned. He could sense from the way the two men had been conversing that there was more to the conversation than mere trivial talk about health matters. 'Captain Hirsch has been called away on a job,' Jock said. 'I heard from one of the nuns that a bush native stole one of their firearms and the wee German laddie has shot through after the thief.'

'It could not have come at a better time,' Alex said without elaborating any further. 'Do we have any idea when Hauptmann Hirsch will be returning?'

'None that I know of,' Jock replied. 'How long are we going to remain here?'

'We leave tomorrow,' Alex said, attempting to place his feet on the floor and test his strength after the bout of fever. He found that he could stand but felt giddy. He took the priest's parting advice and sat down on the bed again. 'I would think around mid morning when I have completed my arrangements with Father Umberto. I guess we will have to be prepared to camp out in the bush overnight.'

'The sooner we leave the better,' Jock growled. 'I dinna like what's going on around here. Something tells me that it could be dangerous if we stay on and I dinna know why. Just an old sense I got from my grandmother when I was a wee laddie myself.'

Alex accepted his engineer's fears. His uncanny sense of impending trouble had proved accurate in the past when they had worked together. He only had to give Father Umberto a detailed briefing on the arrangements for the clearing and the assistance they would require and then they could leave – with or without the German officer currently away chasing a firearms thief.

After briefing the Italian priest the following morning, Alex and Jock prepared to make their way down the jungle-covered slopes of the mountain range to the coast and Rabaul. Hirsch had still not returned but Alex had decided to make his way back nonetheless. The priest provided them with some stores for the journey from his meagre supply and Alex thanked him for the anti-malarial drugs.

Alex and Jock had departed by a good six hours when Hirsch returned with his patrol of Tolai police.

'Where is Captain Macintosh?' he asked Father Umberto.

'On his way to Rabaul by now,' Father Umberto replied, noticing the expression of annoyance in the German officer's face. 'He left this morning.'

'Why did you not stop him from leaving?' Hirsch asked.

'I could see no reason to do that,' Umberto replied. 'Besides, my people have informed me that the path back to Rabaul is safe to use because of your visit to us.'

Hirsch removed his hat and wiped the sweat from his brow with the back of his sleeve. He knew that what may have transpired between the Australian and the missionary priest would be reported to him by Sister Bridget. He hoped for Captain Macintosh's sake that his mission to see the priest was no more than a goodwill visit but a discreet meeting with the Irish nun soon revealed information that caught the German officer's attention.

'He has asked Father Umberto to provide labour to clear a stretch of jungle on the east coast,' she said under the shade of a huge rainforest giant at the edge of the mission station. 'Father Umberto has asked me to assist him with the plan but says little more about it.'

'Do you know where and when this will take place?' Hirsch asked.

'That I do know,' the nun replied and gave the details.

Hirsch let the information sink in. Suddenly he realised what the Australian was up to. 'An airstrip!' he exclaimed.

'A what?' Sister Bridget asked, fingering the long length of beads around her waist.

'Nothing of importance,' Hirsch dismissed. He would need time to consider all the possibilities of why Captain Macintosh was planning to have an airstrip constructed in the jungle. What could it possibly achieve?

'Thank you, Sister,' Hirsch said, terminating their meeting. 'Your assistance in helping my government is duly noted and I am sure that it will go a long way in the future of a free Ireland for your people. I am also sure that if the English ever decide to make war on us we will assist your resistance movement against the occupiers of your country.'

Sister Bridget nodded. Liam might be dead from a British soldier's bullet but there were many of his friends who would appreciate her tiny contribution to cementing a relationship with a free Irish movement far away in the Atlantic Ocean.

Dieter Hirsch walked away to muster his men for the return to Rabaul. He no longer had a reason to kill Captain Macintosh and his engineer. It would be better that the Australian proceed with his plan. Later Hirsch could swoop with an armed force on whoever was assisting him – including the Italian priest. He knew where and when the plan was to be implemented but for the time being it was a matter of organising the resources to intervene in the English plot. A cruiser from the Imperial German Navy should be tasked to support an operation against the would-be invaders of his land, Hirsch thought, walking towards the cluster of buildings where his men awaited him.

As they steamed for Sydney Alex stood at the stern of the *Osprey II*, gazing at the headlands of Rabaul harbour. The mission had proved to be very successful so far, especially obtaining the assistance of the Italian missionary and his parishioners. He would be returning within a month but still his mind drifted to Giselle and he was tempted to have the captain alter course to once again see her on his way south, but he knew he must stick with the plan outlined by his father. He was joined by the Scottish engineer, now covered in grease from the engine room, who was wiping his hands on a rag.

'Glad to be out of there,' he said, taking a place beside Alex.

'You still have that bad feeling, Jock?' Alex asked, turning away from his view of the horizon gently bobbing under blue skies and a few high level clouds.

Jock stared across Alex's shoulder at the tiny stretch of huts and houses at the harbour's mouth. A thin plume of smoke rose from the volcano overlooking the settlement. 'I dinna know why,' he replied with a frown, 'but I have a bad feeling, something I cannot put my finger on. It's a bit like that wee volcano out there. I feel something is going to explode around me and I canna put it out of my mind.'

As Alex listened he wondered if things were going smoothly after all. He could not see the Italian priest revealing his plans to the German authorities. After all, only his father and a handful of carefully selected people knew of what was being planned. How could they be compromised? He attempted to reassure himself but the Scot's words of warning echoed in his mind. Who could possibly betray the scheme?

Matthew Duffy held the reins of his horse with one hand and a small, paper-wrapped parcel with the other, and stared up at the heat shimmer surrounding the craggy, scrub-covered hill. It was as if an invisible shield had fallen between him and the summit and he could not proceed any further. 'Bloody stupid,' Matthew growled, shaking his head at the superstitious fear he was experiencing. But no matter how much he wanted to climb the hill to that place where it was said was a sacred cave, he could not motivate himself to move his feet.

Matthew had visited his mother in Townsville and the reunion had been poignant. Kate Tracy held her son to her with all the maternal love a woman could muster and chided him for his long silences, while praising Randolph Gates for continuing to keep her up to date on his welfare. She had recovered her health although was under strict orders from her doctor to get plenty of rest.

Matthew remained only three days and nights in his mother's sprawling house in Townsville and after listening to her less than subtle hints that he should return, marry and produce children to carry on the name, he left with promises of returning within the year.

Kate had farewelled Matthew from the verandah of her house, watching her beloved only child walk off on his way to their property adjoining Glen View in central west Queensland. Matthew would first travel by train south and then by a Cobb & Co stage coach to his destination. When he was out of sight, she returned to her living room where she could sob in private. It was not that Matthew was selfish, she attempted to console herself, but that he had inherited his father's character. Luke had been a drifter, always searching for his mountain of gold, and his son was the living spirit of the father, searching for the intangible thing that meant putting his life on the line. The mix of the wild Irish and pioneering American blood was a terrible thing, Kate sniffed, drying her eyes and considering the lonely years ahead.

Matthew was met by the property manager and his wife and given quarters. They proved to be warm hosts and, sleeping in the guest room, Matthew was swamped with memories of his youth work-ing the Kate Tracy properties – from the horseback mustering of cattle to riding the fences. But his visit was not intended to remind him of the earlier life he led before he ran away to war. For the many years he had roamed the world he would often find himself dreaming of this hill that haunted him. It was as if the sacred hill of the Nerambura people was drawing him to it, no matter how much he attempted to resist its magnetism.

He knew about the hill and its eerie history from his mother – and the significance to both his bloodline and that of the Macintosh family. It was said that a curse had been placed on both families for a terrible incident that had occurred in the district over half a century before – a massacre of innocent Aboriginal men, women and children by the Native Mounted Police led by a Lieutenant Morrison Mort.

The mid-afternoon sun was softening the heat from the baked, spindly scrub. Matthew stood, staring up at the hill, seeking out the shadows that might divulge the whereabouts of the cave entrance. He had tethered his horse and took a few steps forward only to halt and scan the stunted trees again. Something from his days soldiering warned him that he was not alone in this vast sea of sand and scrub. From the corner of his eye he thought that he saw a bush move. Slowly turning his head to where he caught the movement, he could only see a patch of brigalow trees.

Matthew gasped, his heart suddenly pounding in his chest. There he was! He stood tall and almost naked where seconds before was only a small clearing; a young warrior holding a long, lethal spear – with its shaft in the sand and its deadly tip to the sky. The warrior was watching him silently as if contemplating whether he was friend or foe. Matthew slowly raised the parcel in his hand towards the Aboriginal warrior silhouetted against a strange shimmer of heat mist.

'Tobacco,' Matthew said loudly.

The shape shifted and when the warrior approached across the earth between them Matthew could see that what he first took for a young man was in fact an old man whose body bore many scars, most from his initiation as a young man when he belonged to a clan that roamed the plains now known as Glen View station.

Wallarie reached out and took the parcel from Matthew, sniffing it before lowering his spear. 'You Matthew,' he stated rather than asked. 'You boy who fly with my totem, great eagles.'

Matthew did not reply immediately but he stood awestruck before the old man. He could have sworn that he had seen a very young man but perhaps it was a hallucination in the shimmering heat. 'I am Matthew, son of Kate Tracy,' he finally replied. 'My mother said that the tobacco is a gift to you – her old friend.'

'Hill not let you go up it,' Wallarie chuckled, tucking the parcel into a small bag hanging from the only piece of clothing he wore – a hair-string belt with a woven bark bag around his waist into which was tucked two small wooden clubs. 'The ancestor spirits not let you go to the cave.'

Matthew felt sheepish. How could the old man

know of his superstitious fear? 'I came to give you the gift,' he replied as Wallarie turned to stride towards a well-worn path among the rocks at the base of the hill.

'You follow me,' he said over his shoulder. 'Ancestor spirits say it all right you walk with me.'

Matthew scurried to catch up with the Aboriginal he knew was the last of his people in the district. For an old man he walked with strong strides.

'How did you know who I am?' Matthew asked when he caught up.

'Station hand tell me you come to big house,' Wallarie answered with just a hint of humour for the young man's awe. 'Sometimes, by and by, they leave food at hill for me – but not much baccy. Your mother told me by and by that blackfellas from north of here say you fly with eagles. I hear that the whitefella have a machine that fly in the sky with the eagle. I hear that you fly in one of those whitefella machines.'

Matthew smiled. Wallarie was a wily old man who had both Aboriginal and European people fooled with his supposed mystical powers, he thought, but checked himself when he remembered how he could have sworn that Wallarie had suddenly appeared out of thin air in the form of a young man, only to change to the old man now beside him. It made the hairs on the back of Matthew's neck bristle. 'Do you know why I have come?' he asked.

Wallarie halted and turned to him, his opaque old eyes starting to show the initial signs of blindness. 'I know you believe in the curse,' he said quietly, looking quickly around at the slope of the scrub-covered hill as if expecting to see something frightening. 'You want to know if the curse is still on you and the others.'

Matthew was dumbfounded by the old man's perceptiveness. 'Yes,' he said equally as quietly, lest he also disturb something unseen around them.

'The ancestor spirits come to you in the night,' Wallarie said. 'They show you the hill in your dreams. You have the gift – like Kate. You know the answer already.'

'I don't,' Matthew protested. 'All I see is these strange dreams – and you are in some of them – but you are sitting under a tree as a very old man, talking to someone I cannot see.'

Wallarie turned and continued the climb up the winding track to the summit. Matthew followed. 'Where are we going?' he asked, frustrated by the Aboriginal's silent reaction to his question.

'We sit tonight and I smoke some baccy,' he replied. 'The ancestor spirits say you able to enter the cave. Only woman not allowed in the sacred place of the men. Maybe ancestor spirits visit us – maybe not. Maybe need more baccy for them to come.'

When at length they reached the summit Matthew could look out from the vantage point over a sea of flat, grey scrub. The sun hovered on a dusty horizon, undisturbed by any sign of a breeze. It was as if the bush had suddenly fallen into a silence, listening to the two men standing atop the only high point in the immediate area.

Wallarie ducked his head under an outcrop of rock partly concealed by the roots of a big dying gum tree that had long ago taken root in the crevices of the hill. Matthew reluctantly followed him inside, and immediately could smell the ancient mustiness of the place dimly lit by the last of the sun's rays. A tiny glow of coals shone at the centre of the cave marking a fireplace.

Wallarie tossed a few small dry sticks on the embers, causing tiny flames to flicker into life and cast dancing shadows on the walls of the cave. Matthew stood in awe of the tiny ochre-painted figures depicting long-ago hunts for kangaroos as well as other animals which were now extinct, like giant wombats and lizards. A stick-like figure of a hunter with spear raised had an old scratch through it as if someone had attempted to erase the figure from the panorama of life depicted in the paintings.

'We sit and smoke,' Wallarie said, squatting by his fire and reaching inside his bag to remove the package.

Matthew sat opposite the old Aboriginal, the fire between them. As if by magic, Wallarie produced a battered smoking pipe and plugged it with a precious wad of tobacco which he lit with a burning twig from the fire. Puffing contentedly on the pipe, he seemed to be unaware of any other presence in the sacred cave.

Matthew sat watching him and wondered at the sanity of his visit. Had it all been a waste of time? He could be halfway back to Sydney by now and looking forward to a cold beer with Texas Slim in the bar of their favourite hotel.

Then Wallarie began to sing in a language

Matthew guessed was that of Wallarie's people. Matthew listened patiently, thinking of an excuse to bid the old man farewell and make his way back to the Glen View homestead. Matthew did not remember anything else after that. For a time he imagined that he was on a brigalow plain and could hear the happy chatter of women digging for tubers and children playing at being hunters and warriors with their spindly stick spears. It was as if he had been transported to this place a long time before the uniformed men came on their horses to kill the people with rifles and swords. He found himself being lifted beyond the cave and drifting over a harsh land not dissimilar to that of the semi-arid plains of Queensland. He was flying like the great wedge-tailed eagle and knew that what lay below him was his destiny. Then came a blackness, so complete that it would take weeks for his memory to return to the events of that night, and by then he was a long way from the hill at Glen View and in a place of extreme danger.

The sun had risen when Matthew finally came awake in a sitting position opposite the now dead fire. He roused himself and realised that he was alone in the cave.

'Wallarie,' he called but received no answer. The old man had simply disappeared. When Matthew stepped outside the cave into the early morning light his attention was drawn to one of the majestic wedge-tailed eagles circling above the hill. Matthew smiled. 'Wallarie,' he whispered in a reverential tone.

Matthew made his way down the ancient track to find his horse at the bottom of the hill grazing on the shoots of the arid lands. Although most of what he had experienced in the night seemed on the outer edges of his consciousness he sensed that the old Aboriginal was looking over him in a warm and protective way.

Matthew swung himself into the saddle and kicked his horse into a canter. He knew at least one thing: Wallarie had opened a window into the future and somehow he had seen his destiny.

II

Rain swept the empty parade ground of Sydney's Victoria Barracks. The old sandstone buildings stood as a reminder of the state's colonial era when the military ruled with an iron hand. Standing at a window, Colonel John Hughes surveyed the empty parade ground. He stood with his hands clasped behind his back. In his British officer's uniform he looked every part a professional soldier, with boots so highly polished that they reflected the light like a mirror.

'Sir,' came a voice from the doorway of his office. 'Colonel Duffy, Captain Macintosh and Mr Duffy are here.'

'Thank you, Major Oaks,' Hughes replied to his aide, also a British officer and veteran of colonial wars for the Crown. 'Send them in.'

A uniformed Patrick Duffy entered first, saluting

his senior officer. Alex wore his uniform and Matthew a smart conservative suit.

'Good to see that you survived your mission into German territory, Captain Macintosh,' Hughes said, shaking the young officer's hand warmly. 'Your father informed me that you had a bout of fever while you were away.'

'Malaria, it seems, sir,' Alex replied. 'I have had a couple of relapses since returning – but nothing serious.'

The British colonel's eyes rested on Matthew. 'I have heard also from Colonel Duffy that you have mastered our flying machine with flying colours – forgive the pun – and that your friend Mr Randolph has proved to be rather a dab hand with the camera. I am sorry that we had to exclude him from today's meeting but protocols dictate that we cannot officially engage a foreign national in our mission, albeit a covert one. But I am sure that you will be able to personally brief him at a later date. Needless to say we cannot officially recognise his part in our operation.'

'I understand, sir,' Matthew replied. 'Mr Gates is just along for the ride.'

'Good man,' Hughes replied. 'I know that he will prove to be a valuable asset to our mission when the time comes. I only wish that Patrick and I could be with you on this one.'

Hughes walked across his office to where a blanket was draped against the wall. He pulled it aside to reveal a map of German territory in the Pacific. 'Our aim is to have Mr Duffy fly his aircraft along the length of the coast, with Mr Gates acting as the cameraman to provide a bird's-eye view of the possible landing places for a combined army and naval force,' Hughes said, pointing with his swagger stick to Neu Pommern. 'Needless to say if anything goes wrong we can claim that Mr Duffy and Mr Gates have nothing to do with the military of the British Empire and are simply adventurers acting on their own.'

When Hughes glanced at him Matthew nodded his understanding.

'Good,' Hughes continued. 'Captain Macintosh has made contact with the Italian priest east of Rabaul and has briefed Colonel Duffy that we will receive help from Father Umberto. Colonel Duffy has allocated one of his company's steamers to transport the aircraft in crates and unload the aeroplane for assembly in the area chosen. I believe we will have help from the natives of Father Umberto's parish.'

'That is correct,' Alex said. 'His services will be generously compensated.'

'So all we need to do now is get the aeroplane aboard and await confirmation that Father Umberto has carried out his part of the bargain,' the English officer said, once again covering the map with the blanket. 'And pray that none of this operation is revealed to anyone outside this room.'

'I am sure that our security is tight,' Patrick said. 'I cannot imagine how anything we are planning could possibly fall into German hands.'

'For the sake of the young men's lives I hope you are right,' Hughes said. 'Otherwise we will have hell to pay. Now, I think it is a good time to retire to the mess.'

Hauptmann Dieter Hirsch snapped to attention. The major dressed in full uniform did not at first appear very impressive. He was short and in his late forties, with an obvious liking for good food – his stomach strained against his waist-line – and he wore spectacles. He looked more like the mayor of a Bavarian town than an intelligence officer with a formidable reputation for gathering vital information in Germany's far-flung imperial outposts from Africa to the Pacific.

'It is a secure area to speak?' Major Paul Pfieffer asked, gazing around at the cluster of filing cabinets and pictures of the Kaiser hanging from the wall.

'Yes, sir,' Hirsch replied stiffly, still standing to attention although he wore his civilian clothing.

'You may stand at ease,' Pfieffer said in a friendly tone. 'Please brief me on the situation to date.'

Hirsch took a shallow breath and recited everything that had occurred with Alexander Macintosh when he was escorted to the Italian priest's mission station. He also informed his visitor of what he thought the Australian was planning and when he would be covertly returning.

'You think that the English are going to use an aircraft,' the German intelligence officer asked, 'to reconnoitre Rabaul? It is obvious that we would see the aircraft and its presence would attract immediate diplomatic action from our government.'

'I think that Captain Macintosh may be planning to use it to fly over our east coast, sir,' Hirsch countered. 'That way we would have little warning of it being in our territory. I strongly suspect that they will take photographs from the air – if that is possible.'

'It is,' Pfieffer replied. 'Our navy is examining ways to use aircraft with the fleet to provide early warning of enemy naval locations. It would assist an enemy to have detailed photographs of possible landing areas should they decide to invade.'

'Would it be possible to have one of our cruisers offshore when the English send their ship?' Hirsch asked.

'I doubt that would be approved,' Pfieffer replied. 'It would be better to use your local gunboat to assist in our counter-operation rather than a cruiser. If we task a cruiser it might alert the English and they could cancel their operation. No, better we catch them in the act and embarrass the English before the rest of the world, show them up as a warmongering nation bent on destroying the peace that currently exists. The situation plays into our hands.' Hirsch dutifully nodded. 'I believe that you have a very good officers' mess at the Rabaul Club, Herr Hauptmann,' the senior officer said with a smile. 'Shall we retire for the afternoon to avail ourselves of its comforts?'

Dieter Hirsch was surprised at the senior officer's invitation. The man was a likeable type, not the autocratic Prussian type of soldier he was used to. 'It would be an honour and pleasure, sir,' Hirsch replied.

★

The most expensive hotel in Sydney provided the venue for the regimental ball. The huge room flickered with candlelight that highlighted the jewels worn by the ladies with their sweeping long dresses. Their military partners had donned brightly coloured mess dress, and those who had seen service wore miniature medals on their chests.

A bagpipe and drum band provided the music while smartly dressed waiters circulated with trays of champagne and sherry in crystal goblets. It was a grand affair where civilian guests and their partners mixed with the soldier and sailor officers of Australia and those foreign powers who were able to accept the invitations.

Alex wore his mess dress of jacket and Scottish kilt. He was alone; although he had the opportunity to invite a partner, his memory of Giselle stopped him from doing so. His father was annoyed that he had not invited one of the many eligible young ladies from their social circle but Alex simply replied that he had been so occupied by his work after returning from German territory that he did not have time to do as his father suggested. In fact, Alex could only think of one person who should have been by his side.

Father and son were standing side by side, flutes of champagne in their hands, discussing mundane matters when they heard the announcement of Mr Randolph Gates and Miss Fenella Macintosh by a regimentally dressed sergeant at the entrance to the hotel ballroom.

Both Patrick and his son looked utterly surprised.

'Damn!' Patrick swore. 'When did that happen?'

Alex shrugged. 'I thought that Nellie would be with that actor, Wilkes,' he replied.

Both men thought that Fenella's choice of man to accompany her to the ball was a pleasant surprise; they both loathed the actor they considered a cad. As far as they knew, the American was a man of honour, quite acceptable as a beau for the woman they felt most protective of.

The next to be announced was Mr Matthew Duffy. Matthew also appeared alone. He wore a beautifully tailored dinner suit with the miniatures of his South African campaign on the left lapel. He muttered something to the sergeant standing rigidly by the door accepting invitations and the sergeant smiled briefly.

Matthew glanced around the ballroom. From the top of the stairs he could see Patrick and Alex. He immediately made his way to them through the swirling crowd of colour.

'Good evening, Colonel, Alex,' Matthew said, accepting a flute of champagne from a passing waiter. 'I see that it must be bachelors' night at the ball.'

Alex grinned, pleased to have an ally in his choice to attend alone. 'I am surprised that you have not been able to convince some young lady to accompany you,' he said to his cousin whom he had immediately taken to after so many years of not seeing him. They had met when Alex was a mere boy and his cousin only a little older, on his way to enlist for the South African campaign, albeit underage. Upon meeting up again when Alex returned they seemed to have forged an immediate friendship. Alex eyed Matthew's two miniature medals with some envy for the fact that he had seen action fighting for the Queen against the Boers. Here Alex was, a captain in an infantry regiment with no combat experience, although his father had often cautioned him not to be in any haste to go to war.

'Just been a bit too busy to look for any young lady foolish enough to accept any invitation I might offer,' he shrugged off. 'One never knows – the evening lies ahead.'

The next announcement caught their attention.

'Mr George Macintosh and Miss Louise Gyles.'

'So, George has a new lady in his life,' Patrick muttered. 'I wonder what happened to the last one?'

Matthew glanced at the young lady beside George. She wore a long silk dress that flowed around her ankles and a string of sparkling jewels around her neck. Her raven hair was piled on her head and interwoven with pearls. The effect seemed to accentuate her slender neck. Matthew's breath was taken away and the impact she had on him was noticed by his cousin.

'Rather a stunning woman,' Alex said beside him. 'I don't know how my wretched brother finds them.'

'Ah, yes,' Matthew answered absentmindedly, already considering how he might get his name on her dance card. 'Truly a beautiful young lady. Do you know who she is?'

'She is the daughter of a very good friend of mine,' Patrick cut in. 'Sir Keith Gyles. I am not surprised that she is here.'

Matthew made no further comment. He had the feeling that Louise Gyles was not a woman easily swayed by the flattering words of mere mortals such as himself. She moved across the highly polished floor with the grace of a royal princess.

'I suppose that I should pay my compliments to Sir Keith's daughter,' Patrick said. 'The last time I saw Louise was during her school days. She was just a freckled young lady then. All legs and gangly like a young filly.'

Matthew watched Colonel Duffy stride away and wished that he had volunteered to go with him. But he remained with Alex, looking around for Randolph and Fenella to greet them. The old dog, Matthew chuckled to himself. Texas Slim had not confided that he had been able to convince Fenella to accompany him to the ball. Come to think of it, Matthew thought further, Randolph had spent very little time at their hotel. He would be either working at Arthur's studio or find an excuse to disappear on the weekend. Matthew suspected that he had met a lady but never guessed it was Fenella.

When Colonel Hughes and his wife were announced Patrick met them at the bottom of the stairs. 'You are looking particularly regal tonight, Gladys,' Patrick said, taking Gladys Hughes' gloved hand. She returned his compliment with a warm smile. Gladys was the epitome of an English rose and although in her late fifties she had the complexion of a much younger woman.

'You are looking very dashing, Patrick. Do you have a lady on your arm tonight?' she asked.

'I did not invite any other lady. I knew that you would be coming with this old war horse and felt that I would be able to sweep you off your feet before the night was gone from the sky,' he replied.

'You are welcome, old chap,' Hughes said, entering into the banter. 'All she does is nag me about spending all my time at the barracks.'

'If you two gentlemen will excuse me,' Gladys said, 'I see an old friend that I have not seen for a long time. I shall go and speak with her.' With this she departed, leaving the two soldiers standing together.

'Have you heard the news?' Hughes asked, reverting to a serious tone. 'Your PM is calling a double dissolution in parliament. Apparently it is the first time that this has been done in your new government.'

'I have read about it in the papers,' Patrick replied. 'What do you think it will mean to our plans?'

Hughes nodded at a junior officer passing by. 'If there is a change of government it could mean that our plan will be cancelled. Or it may mean that we have to convince the new PM – whoever he may be, although I suspect that it will be the little Welshman, Billy Hughes – that it is essential to carry on with what we know about German intentions in this part of the world.'

The next guest to be announced caused both men to put aside their political speculation.

'Major von Fellmann of the Imperial German Army,' the sergeant announced.

'I think that we should personally welcome my

distant relative,' Patrick said. 'I am sure that you would like to meet him.'

Both men moved forward as the German officer stepped into the crowded room. He was dressed in full ceremonial uniform and his smart, foreign appearance caused one or two curious heads to turn.

'Major von Fellmann,' Patrick said, offering his hand, 'I am Colonel Patrick Duffy, and the gentleman with me is Colonel Hughes, on secondment to us from the British army.'

Kurt snapped his heels together, accepting Patrick's courteous gesture.

'Gentlemen, it is a pleasure to meet you both,' he said. 'My mother has told me much about you, Colonel Duffy.'

'Ah, Penelope,' Patrick said. 'How is your mother?'

'She is well and, from time to time, missing the warmer climate of Sydney,' he replied. 'But I know she would expect me to pass on her compliments to her Australian relatives.'

'I am glad that you were able to be here,' Patrick said, guiding Kurt towards a waiter carrying a silver tray. 'Can I interest you in a drink?

'I would like that,' Kurt answered, taking a flute. 'A toast to friendship between Australia and Germany,' he said, raising his drink. Both Patrick and Colonel Hughes echoed his words.

'Well, Colonel Duffy,' Hughes said after sipping his wine, 'I think that I should leave you two to catch up on family business and find my wife before some young cavalry officer sweeps her off her feet.'

The two men watched him depart and Patrick

turned his attention back to his guest. 'I must say that you are very much like your brother, Karl. But he is your twin brother.'

'People say that,' Kurt replied. 'I have yet to catch up with Karl but I have been informed he will be here tonight.'

'I have heard that you have been on an inspection tour of the Pacific,' Patrick said. 'I hope that all has gone well.'

Kurt looked at Patrick. 'I believe that your son, Captain Macintosh, has just returned from one of our territories.'

Patrick could see that Kurt was diplomatically deflecting the conversation away from his official duties. 'Yes, I must introduce you to him,' he said, glancing around to find his son and was lucky to see him only a short distance away. Patrick gestured to Alex to join them and introduced the two men.

'So, this is your first visit to Australia,' Alex said. 'What do you think?'

'I like what I have experienced so far,' Kurt replied. 'I think that your ladies are very pretty.'

The two men were on ground they could agree upon – women. Patrick left them chatting together and wandered off to see if he could get another drink before making his official speech as commanding officer of the regiment to welcome guests and fellow officers. Around him couples swirled as the band played martial tunes. It was a truly wonderful evening inside the ballroom and for some reason Patrick had a fleeting thought that on the eve of the Battle of Waterloo British officers had attended a gala ball.

There would be no battles in the morning, he reassured himself – except with hangovers. But he was acutely aware that they were teetering on the edge of global conflict, although the general public was oblivious to the tenuous peace. In the murky world of intelligence he was waging a war to gather information that would be critical to Australia's survival if Germany confronted the British Empire in the Pacific.

Matthew did not wait to be introduced to George Macintosh's beautiful partner for the ball. He made his way across the dance floor to where she sat at a table with George.

'George,' Matthew said, acknowledging his presence.

'Matthew,' George responded, without any enthusiasm. Neither man liked each other.

'Miss Gyles, I am hoping that you have a space on your dance card for me,' Matthew said, ignoring George's cold stare. 'If I may be as bold as to introduce myself, I am Matthew Duffy.'

When Louise looked up Matthew had to admit to himself that he could feel sweat on the palms of his hand. His nervousness was not apparent, however, as he had long learned to control signs of fear. 'Are you related to Colonel Duffy?' she asked in a well-modulated voice.

'Colonel Duffy is my mother's nephew, so I suppose that makes Patrick my first cousin.'

'I thought that I could see a family resemblance when I first saw you some minutes ago,' she said with just the hint of a smile. Matthew was aware that he was staring into her eyes and felt that he could easily be lost in them. They were deep and mauve and he could see just a sprinkle of freckles across her cheeks which only made her more appealing. That she had noticed him earlier caused his spirit to soar. 'That makes George a cousin, too,' he added.

'Don't you have a young lady to attend to,' George growled, sensing that his cousin was paying more than passing interest in his partner.

'I had to come alone,' Matthew retorted. 'Your father has had me a bit tied up with work for him.'

'What is your occupation, Mr Duffy?' Louise asked, realising that the two men were vying for her attention.

'I am an aviator,' Matthew responded.

'An aviator!' Louise exclaimed. 'I saw Mr Houdini demonstrate flying only recently. It looked very exciting – and dangerous.'

'It can be both,' Matthew said, feeling that he may just have an edge on his cousin who was now glowering at him from the table. 'But we could discuss it if you can make a place for me on your dance card.'

Louise glanced at her card and, with a small pencil, wrote in Matthew's name. 'I think that the next dance would be available, Mr Duffy,' she said sweetly. 'George can use the time to talk to his business colleagues.'

The band had struck up a Scottish reel and Matthew extended his hand. Louise rose and he led her onto the dance floor. With whoops and yells the dancers swung around the floor. Louise was light on her feet. All the time, Matthew did not take his eyes off his dance partner.

When the dance was over, Matthew reluctantly escorted her back to the table. George was not there and Louise invited Matthew to sit and talk to her.

'I can see that you have served in the army,' she said, glancing at the medals on his dinner suit. 'Are you still connected with the military?'

'No,' Matthew lied, putting aside his links with the colonel's covert operation. 'I am involved in exploring the possibilities of flight for our country's rural needs.'

'Oh, I see,' Louise replied. 'Why have you chosen to be an aviator?'

Matthew thought about her question for just a moment. No one had asked him so directly before why he loved to fly. 'Do you ever sometimes sit and look up at the clouds?' he asked.

'Often,' she replied. 'I imagine the clouds are creatures with their different shapes.'

'Well, so did I and now I am able to go close enough to touch those creatures.'

Louise laughed lightly at his explanation. 'How exquisite!' she said. 'I would love to do that.'

'With all going well, I may be able to make your wish come true,' Matthew said. 'I actually own an aircraft but alas, it is a single seater, but I intend to soon purchase a twin seater.'

'I would love to fly with you,' Louise said, leaning forward so closely that Matthew could smell her perfume. He was about to reply when George suddenly loomed above them.

'I believe the next dance is mine,' he said to

Louise as the band struck up once again. 'If you will excuse us, Matthew.'

Matthew watched as Louise accompanied George onto the dance floor. Deep in his heart he knew that he had established a rapport with the beautiful young woman. He would see her again. What the bloody hell could she see in that fool George? But his question was gloomily answered as he watched them dance together. George was good-looking, rich and a very eligible catch for any woman, whereas he was not independently rich and led a life that left little time for a permanent relationship.

'Are you about to join the bachelor regiment?' a voice asked from behind him. Matthew turned to see Alex in company with a German officer.

'Major von Fellmann, I presume,' Matthew said, rising from the table and extending his hand. 'Matthew Duffy, at your service.'

Kurt accepted the extended hand. 'I have heard of you,' he responded warmly. 'You fought our Dutch cousins in Africa.'

'You are well informed,' Matthew answered. 'Welcome to Australia.'

'The way things are going between my sister and Texas Slim,' Alex said, the effects of just one or two many champagnes becoming apparent as he spied the couple dance past, 'I doubt that we can include him in the bachelor regiment anymore. Who would have guessed?'

'Not me,' Matthew said, shaking his head. 'Your sister might be responsible for breaking up a grand team of men if Randolph keeps going the way he is.'

'Uncle Arthur has offered Texas a full-time job with his studio, doing the dangerous stunts for Guy Wilkes,' Alex continued. 'But that won't be possible until you two complete your mission for Father.'

'What mission is that?' Kurt asked.

Alex suddenly realised that the alcohol had loosened his tongue and that he was saying things in front of an officer from the very country that they were planning to spy on. He also noticed the warning in Matthew's eyes.

'Oh, nothing much,' Alex corrected himself. 'It's just a job filming some farmland west of here.'

'An interesting idea,' Kurt persisted. 'Why would you do that?'

'The farmer wants to know how best to set up irrigation on his property,' Matthew said, cutting across any further explanation from his cousin. 'How about we retire to the bar where we will be closer to the supply of these good wines?'

As the three men weaved their way to the bar, Matthew realised that he would have to keep an eye on his cousin who was quickly succumbing to the bonhomie of the evening.

Matthew was able to secure another two dances with Louise Gyles before the ball came to an end. More importantly, he had been able to convince her to leave her visiting card with him.

Hardly anyone noticed the announcement of Pastor von Fellmann's arrival at the ball later in the evening. Already the champagne and music had fired the revellers into a noisy, dancing, chattering throng. However, Kurt saw his brother, dressed in a simple black suit, step into the room and look around for a familiar face. Kurt excused himself from the table he shared with some young officers from Patrick's regiment and hurried across to his brother. Both men's eyes met and an immediate warmth could be seen in their expressions. Kurt stepped forward and thrust out his hand. 'It is good to see you, my brother,' he said, holding Karl's hand firmly in his own. Their strict Prussian upbringing forbade more overt expressions of fraternal love in public.

'Time has been good to you, Kurt,' Karl said, reluctant to let go his brother's grip. 'You must tell me how things are with our family in Prussia.'

Kurt allowed himself the gesture of placing his arm around his brother's shoulders and guided him to a quiet alcove where he briefed his brother on the situation he had left behind at their family home in Germany.

'You must realise that we could be at war with the English before the year is out,' Kurt said when the conversation concerning family had ceased. 'It is time that you considered returning to our Fatherland. Or you may become a prisoner here.'

Karl gazed at the happy revellers and smiled sadly. 'I am at home, brother,' he replied.

'But you are German,' Kurt reminded him. 'You were born a German and will die so.'

'My beloved wife Helen is buried up north in Queensland,' Karl responded. 'I wish one day to lie beside her for eternity.'

Annoyed, Kurt attempted to reason with his brother whom he loved dearly. 'The Australian authorities will not be so sentimental if we are at war with the British Empire. You may die in some concentration camp like our Dutch brothers did in the last war the British fought. You may as well be safely at home until it is all over. You owe them nothing for your selfless missionary work among the heathens of this desolate land.'

Karl responded to his brother's words with a gentle smile. 'Do you know, my dear brother, a few years ago I might have agreed with you but for the last years I have seen the face of God in the desolate lands that I have served for the Church. I think that I have taken on some of the native spirituality although I dare say my divinity teachers back home would find this heretical. I have been exposed to the solitude of a land in a way that is not unlike the experiences of the old time recluses who found their own peace in the deserts of the Holy Lands. Do you know, my spiritual guide is a heathen Aboriginal by the name of Wallarie. An old man, he is the last of his tribe after we Europeans slaughtered all his people many years ago. He comes to my mission station from time to time to sit under a tree and simply reflect on the world around him. At first I tried to bring the word of Jesus to him but he gently rebuked me. And now I find a peace in his words concerning our place in this world. Oh, don't get me wrong, I am still a good Lutheran pastor but I have also found a tolerance to all that I do not always understand. No, dear brother, I will die out there with my brother Wallarie. It has been foretold by him.'

'God in heaven!' Kurt exploded. 'Does our mother know of your plans never to return?'

Karl looked away. 'I pray that you will be able to explain to her why I must remain in this land.'

Kurt shook his head. 'You are my brother and I will do my best to explain,' he said sadly. 'Still, you must realise that if war comes we may never see each other again.'

'I know that you will carry on the family name,' Karl said. 'That is what is important to the family.'

Kurt was pleased when Patrick made his way to them. The German officer was having trouble restraining his emotion and knew well that it was not manly to display his true feelings. Before long, Karl was introduced to the rest of their distant Australian relatives and the night continued into the early hours of the morning.

Very few of the departing revellers took much notice of the two men saying goodbye to each other – one in the uniform of a German officer and the other in the dress of a Lutheran pastor. Had they taken more notice they might have commented on the remarkable likeness between the two men. But how different they really were; one followed the way of the sword, the other the way of the Lord.

12

The meeting between George Macintosh and the German consul official, Maynard Bosch, was less than friendly. They stood in the shadow of the 125-foot high obelisk with its Egyptian design near the Bathurst Street entrance to Hyde Park. The air blowing around the two men was as chilly as their feelings.

'You failed to carry out your side of the bargain,' George scowled, his hands in his pockets and his coat collar pulled up around his neck in the late afternoon. 'My brother is alive and well.'

Bosch shivered against the cold and gazed across the central park of Sydney. 'We are not murderers, Mr Macintosh,' Bosch replied. 'Your brother was not under our control when he departed our territory. We could not simply pursue him across the sea and then execute him.'

'But you had all the evidence that my brother is planning to carry out subversive activities in Neu Pommern,' George protested. 'Even I can guess that he is engaged in plotting to map out possible landing sites for an invasion of the island.'

'That may be so,' Bosch replied, 'but we are not at war and your brother is a highly placed person because of your father. We would need to have absolute proof before we took any action. We would appreciate it if you could reveal the precise dates that this plan would be put into place.'

'I can tell you when my brother will be shipping out next and with what cargo,' George replied. 'That is something I feel is worth a lot to your government.'

'To know would be very helpful,' Bosch replied. 'At this stage our source has only been able to provide an approximate time for the operation in our territory. More accurate knowledge would put less strain on our limited resources to catch your brother and his comrades in the act of subversion.'

'I will be able to do that for you,' George answered. 'But this time you must be able to eliminate my brother – and I mean I expect to hear that he is dead.'

Bosch looked at the Australian with barely concealed contempt. 'If that is all, I will bid you a good afternoon, Mr Macintosh,' Bosch said, moving away from the man he loathed.

George watched him walk away. His thoughts were consumed only with keeping his brother and sister from any chance of future inheritance. With some smugness he felt that he had at least been able to use

Guy Wilkes to ensnare his sister in the world of elicit drugs. According to Wilkes, Fenella was now verging on total addiction to heroin and it was beginning to show in her work. She was missing appointments on the set or, at best, arriving late. Fenella was becoming more and more fixated on how she would obtain the next dose of the drug to get her through the day and to that end Wilkes was her saviour.

Besides the small fortune George paid Wilkes to encourage Fenella into a world of drug taking, Wilkes himself was more than happy to assist. Fenella had dumped him in favour of the American and the actor did not take kindly to being rejected.

In their last conversation Wilkes had suggested that perhaps George could make his move. Fenella's condition was ripe to exploit, George mused. Maybe it was time to visit his father and pour out his heart about dear Nellie's unfortunate situation. He could already anticipate his father's reaction to the news about his one and only daughter's slide into drug taking. George smiled. His weak siblings would never see it coming, he thought. They were too stupid to understand why he alone must rule the family.

George Macintosh strolled across Hyde Park through a swirl of crisp brown leaves under naked trees. He had an appointment to see Miss Louise Gyles for dinner at one of Sydney's finest restaurants, but he felt a twinge of uncertainty. Matthew Duffy rose into his thoughts. There had been something about Louise's reaction to meeting the aviator at the regimental ball a week earlier that disturbed him.

George Macintosh was not a man who abided any competition in either his private or public life.

Randolph Gates watched a flock of seagulls rise on the wind over the beach, squawking a protest as he and Fenella approached. Beside him, Fenella had slipped off her shoes and could feel the wet sand squelching between her toes as she walked along the edge of the cold, grey sea rolling in from the Tasman.

'Manly has always been the family's favourite place to retreat from the world,' she said, avoiding a sharp-edged sea shell washed ashore by the winter winds. The two were virtually alone on the beach and behind them was the picturesque village of Manly itself, a place popular all year around with the citizens of Sydney who could take a ferry from the southern shore to lose themselves in the beauty of the northern one. 'Our family maintains a little cottage here.'

Randolph stopped and gazed out to sea. A coastal trader was steaming south. For a moment he was reminded that within weeks he would be departing on a dangerous mission north into German territory. He had been sworn to secrecy by Matthew on the nature of their mission and could not even tell Fenella.

'You are miles away,' she said, noticing the distant expression in his eyes. 'A penny for your thoughts.'

Randolph turned to face her, a slow smile spreading across his face. 'It is nothing,' he said, dismissing his gloomy thoughts of having to leave this beautiful woman's side. A woman whom he had decided he would settle down with and spend the rest of his life loving. 'I was just thinking that I love you.'

Fenella glanced away and frowned before looking back into his face. 'I wish that you would not say that,' she said softly. 'We have enjoyed a grand time together for the past few weeks but love is not something I am able to entertain in my life just now.'

'Is it Wilkes?' Randolph growled.

'No,' Fenella quickly reassured. 'What was between Guy and myself is long over. It is just that there are things you do not know about me.'

'What should I know?' Randolph asked, exasperated by Fenella's continual avoidance of his declarations of love for her. 'All I know is that I have never met a woman like you, nor had I really known what love means until I first looked into your eyes.'

'You are very sweet,' Fenella said, reaching up with her gloved hand to touch his face. 'But I bear a secret that I cannot tell even you. I must find a way to overcome my problem before I can ever allow myself to feel whole again. Please do not ask me any further questions and let us just enjoy this beautiful day together before we return to the ferry.'

Randolph shook his head but accepted her plea not to interrogate her any further about 'her secret'. He had lived a life facing danger but considered surviving those experiences easier than learning more about the daughter of Patrick Duffy. He would be patient, however, and maybe one day she would trust him enough to confide whatever haunted her.

The two continued to walk northwards along

the beach as small sprays of sand whipped around their legs and a seagull drifting above called with a mournful cry on the winter wind. They would be at the ferry terminus at Manly before dark, travelling together across the harbour to separate – Randolph returning to the hotel and Fenella to her home in the city.

Randolph was now considering his future. He had been bitten by the movie bug and seriously considered accepting Arthur's offer to work on his projects, as an all-round cameraman, stunt man and sometimes fill-in for the other male actors. Arthur had even thought about making a film with Randolph in the leading role as an Australian stockman. Arthur had identified the American's ruggedly good-looking face as one that would appeal to the women who sat in the dark theatres, dreaming of romance away from the constricted lives they led as servants to their husbands. Randolph had a natural, masculine grace and sex appeal that could translate to the cel-luloid film and onto the silver screens.

To accept such an offer would mean Randolph breaking his partnership with Matthew. But all things had a life expectancy, he consoled himself. He was growing older and it was time that he thought about a steady life away from his drifting from one danger-ous place to another. He was a little uncomfortable with his thoughts as he felt like a traitor. At least he would share this one, final mission with the young man he had protected for so many years on behalf of his employer, Kate Tracy. But he needed to see Matthew that evening and explain his decision to settle down in the employ of Arthur Thorncroft after their mission into German territory. It would be the first evening in weeks that he was not spending with Fenella, he mused as they strolled arm in arm along the beach. The tough and independent American felt nervous about facing his friend and informing him of his decision.

Alexander Macintosh sat in the living room of his father's house re-reading the letter from Giselle for the third time, lingering on her words and sentences as if she were speaking them to him in person. She missed his company and was counting the days until she arrived in Sydney with her mother from New Guinea. Alex sighed when he considered that was still months away. Only the ticking of the grandfather clock in the hallway outside the living room made any sound, marking the seconds of the late evening.

Since Alex had met the young woman he had not been able to get her out of his mind and even spent his spare hours plotting a way to return to her father's plantation. But he was reminded from time to time of the mission he was involved in and its importance to Australia's future security. Although he was a militia soldier he was still a commissioned officer and took his responsibilities seriously.

'Your brother has arrived unannounced, Mr Macintosh,' came the voice of Angus MacDonald from the doorway, interrupting Alex's pleasant thoughts. 'Shall I announce him?'

The former soldier was a stickler for protocol and

even a member of the immediate family still required permission to enter Colonel Duffy's house. Angus MacDonald would have preferred that George Macintosh sent his card first – or even made a telephone call to say that he would be visiting. He had done neither which annoyed his sense of right and wrong.

'Certainly, Angus,' Alex said, looking up from his letter which he now carefully folded to return it to the envelope with the German stamps adorning it. 'Show him into the living room.'

When Angus ushered George Macintosh into the living room Alex was standing in the centre of the room wearing his smoking jacket. George had surrendered his coat to Angus and stood wearing an expensive suit.

'What brings you to the house so late?' Alex asked his brother.

'I did not expect to see you here,' George replied. 'I came to see Father about a rather disturbing matter, but I suppose you also should be privy to what I have to inform him of.'

Alex frowned. 'What matter is that?' he asked.

'I would rather have Father here before I say anything,' George replied, searching around the room for a drink. He could not see any liquor bottles. 'Angus,' he called loudly. 'Fetch the colonel and then also fetch a bottle of his best whisky.'

'I shall do so,' Angus called back from the hallway while George settled down in a large, comfortable leather chair opposite a small fireplace. Alex watched his brother make himself at home and thought he had that smug look Alex remembered so well from when they were much younger. It was the look of knowledge of one who had bad news.

Angus entered the room accompanied by Patrick who was also wearing a smoking jacket. The valet placed the bottle of whisky and three crystal glasses on the sideboard and left the room.

'Hello, George,' Patrick said. 'What has brought you here tonight?'

George rose from his chair and walked over to the sideboard where he poured three generous tots of whisky. He handed his father and brother a glass each. 'I think what I have to tell you tonight is going to require a stiff drink to hear,' he said. 'I am afraid that I am the bearer of very bad news concerning Nellie,' he continued, staring at his father. 'My sister is both pregnant and a drug addict.'

Patrick's face paled and Alex could see his father's hand tremble. For a moment he said nothing.

'Where in bloody hell did you hear this piece of absolute rubbish?' Alex responded before his father could recover. 'I don't believe it.'

'Nor did I want to believe it,' George replied innocently, taking a sip from his whisky. 'But I am afraid it is true – Nellie is addicted to heroin and carries Guy Wilkes' baby.'

'How in hell did you learn this?' Patrick said, rage written across his face. He stepped towards George who suddenly felt fearful of the sudden shift in his father's demeanour.

'I would rather not disclose how I have come to learn of the situation,' George quickly answered, taking a step back. 'Except that Mr Wilkes is prepared to make a written statement corroborating what I have said.'

Patrick placed his untouched glass of whisky on the sideboard. 'You are speaking about your only sister, and my beloved daughter. Nellie is very special and it is the duty of her brothers to protect her.'

'Alas, Father,' George said, 'I suspect that it is the influences she is exposed to in that immoral industry of film-making that have brought about her condition. I am afraid that you have been remiss yourself to allow her to work for that old sodomite, Arthur Thorncroft.'

'Uncle Arthur would not abide Nellie being allowed heroin,' Alex said in defence of the man who was as close as family. 'If he had known I am sure that he would have informed Father.'

'Whether he knew or not is rather irrelevant,' George said. 'The matter stands that Nellie is both a drug addict and pregnant outside wedlock. I feel that we must do something to attempt to redeem the family's good name before it is smeared across the tabloids.'

'What do you suggest?' Alex countered, watching with concern. His father appeared to be on the verge of exploding in an uncontrollable rage.

George shrugged and returned to the leather chair. 'That is why I have come here,' he said. 'I was hoping that you and Father might have some idea of what to do about the situation.'

'I still cannot believe that little Nellie is what you say she is – let alone pregnant outside of marriage,' Patrick said quietly, balling his fists in frustration at the confronting news. 'I will speak to her personally and clear up this matter which I know is an outrageous lie. I never liked Wilkes and suspect that the man is an adventurer prepared to blatantly blackmail us. When I get my hands on him I will extract the truth – and damn the consequences in doing so.'

Patrick's last statement alarmed Alex who had never seen his father so angry. There was something in his father's eyes that said he meant every word he had threatened. 'What if I see Nellie and find out the truth,' Alex suggested, hoping to deflect his father from any meeting with Guy Wilkes – or Nellie for that matter.

'No,' Patrick replied. 'It is my duty to see your sister and ascertain the truth of the matter. I will organise to drive over to Nellie's place tonight.'

Neither brother attempted to stop their father from leaving. The expression on his face warned them not to interfere.

Patrick drove himself to his daughter's house, arriving late in the evening. A steady rain fell and Patrick turned up the collar on his coat, unfurled an umbrella and walked towards the front door. He could see that the lights in the house were on and hoped that meant Fenella was still up. He knocked but there was no answer. He tried the door knob to find that it was not locked. Patrick opened the door and stepped inside, shaking the rain from his coat.

'Who is that?' Fenella asked in a muffled voice.

'It's your father,' Patrick replied. 'May I come in?'

A short silence followed as Patrick stood waiting. 'Yes, Father, just wait a moment,' Fenella replied. In a moment she appeared, wrapping a long silken dressing gown around her body.

Patrick was shocked at the change in his daughter's physical appearance since he had seen her two weeks earlier at the regimental ball. She had lost weight, her skin was a deathly grey colour and there was a distant look in her eyes as if she could not focus on the world around her.

'Are you ill?' Patrick asked, striding to his daughter's side and embracing her. Fenella did not resist his loving gesture, and broke into a sobbing fit against his chest. Patrick led her gently to a sofa and sat her down beside him, his arms around her shoulders as the tears welled and rolled down her cheeks.

'Is it the opiates you take?' he asked and Fenella nodded, reaching for the handkerchief her father produced.

'Are you with child?' he asked, barely able to muster the question. Fenella did not answer and looked away.

'Whose child do you carry?' her father asked in a controlled voice.

'Do you think that I am some kind of whore?' Fenella flared between tears. 'Yes, it is Guy's child.'

Patrick released the embrace of his daughter and sighed. 'Then you must marry him,' he said. 'And immediately desist from the use of opiates.'

Fenella rose to her feet and turned away. 'I do not love him, Father,' she flared angrily. 'What happened between us was a terrible mistake. Guy took advantage of me against my will when I was under the influence of the drug. He is the last man on earth that I would marry. I love another man.'

Surprised at his daughter's announcement, Patrick rose to take his daughter by the shoulders, forcing her to confront him. 'Who is this other man?' he asked, feeling guilty that he had not taken more notice of what had been occurring in his daughter's life.

'You don't know?' Fenella asked, almost bursting into bitter laughter. Patrick shook his head.

'I love Randolph.'

'Texas Slim!' Patrick gasped.

'Yes, Texas Slim, as you call him,' Fenella replied. 'But I doubt that he would be able to love a woman carrying another man's child. He is a man of great honour.'

'Does Wilkes know that you carry his child?'

'Yes,' Fenella answered. 'I have told him.'

'Don't you think that he would marry you under the circumstances?' Patrick asked quietly, causing his daughter to stare at him in disbelief.

'Did you not hear what I said?' she answered angrily. 'I do not love him.'

'Love has little to do with marriage,' Patrick answered weakly.

'Is that why Mother left you and went to Ireland all those years ago?' Fenella asked. 'Was your marriage a matter of duty?'

The rebuke caught Patrick off guard and memories of his dead wife flooded him with sorrow. It was as if history was repeating itself and that the family was truly cursed. He had loved his wife with a passion but had neglected to show it often enough to convince her that she was the high point of his life. She had left him for another man and eventually died in the cold waters of the Irish Sea. It was not known if she had died by accident or suicide.

'I loved your mother more than life itself,' he answered in a choked voice. 'I have not courted any woman since.'

'Then you would understand why I cannot marry Guy,' she said. 'Love is a greater force than duty. I can see that my predicament is causing you and the family shame and I promise you I will do something to rectify that.'

Alarmed, Patrick stepped back. 'You are not considering taking your own life?' he gasped. 'I love you, as my daughter, and you are more precious to me than you will ever know.'

'I did not say that I was going to kill myself,' Fenella answered bitterly. 'I said that I would rectify the situation so that no shame comes upon the family name.'

'What are your intentions?' Patrick asked.

'You may not have noticed, Father, but I am a grown woman living independently and able to make my own decisions without your permission. I have plans that I do not wish to reveal – to you or anyone else in the family.'

'Know that I will always be there for you, as will your brothers,' Patrick reassured.

'George?' Fenella asked. 'Do you think George is not pleased at my sad situation?'

Patrick frowned. He did not know why Fenella

would ask such a question. Despite his eldest son's seeming indifference to suffering, Fenella was still his sister. 'I think you are being a bit harsh.'

Fenella just shook her head. 'I would rather that you leave me now, Father, as I have a lot to think about. I promise you that I will not do anything stupid.'

Reluctantly, Patrick respected his daughter's wishes and turned to leave the house. He had one more stop before returning home but this time for a confrontation.

When his father had changed and driven to Fenella's residence, George decided it was time to meet with Guy Wilkes and speak with him now that his father had learned of Fenella's drug addiction and pregnancy. Wilkes had been alone and received George, inviting him inside where they shared a whisky.

Guy Wilkes reassured George Macintosh that he had no intention of ever considering marriage with a woman who had betrayed his love for another – especially the American Randolph Gates. Satisfied, George bid his good evening and departed the house. His car was parked behind a thick hedge, out of sight of anyone driving up to Wilkes' house, and George was about to slip the car into gear when he noticed the approaching lights of his father's automobile. George turned off the engine and watched as his father parked his car near the entrance to Guy's house in the leafy affluent suburb of Sydney. George was suspicious by nature but now more than curious as he watched his father alight from his vehicle and make his way to the front door. When the door opened he could hear his father's voice raised in anger. Eventually, Guy ushered Patrick inside, closing the door behind him. George slipped from his car and moved stealthily to a window that looked into the living room where he saw his father and Guy Wilkes engaged in heated discussion. They stood face to face and George could clearly hear what was being said.

'How is it that my daughter has an addiction to opiates?' Patrick asked angrily. Wilkes reddened at the direct question to which he suspected the army colonel already knew the answer.

'She was a willing participant,' Wilkes answered, stepping one pace back from Patrick to make space between them. 'I merely supplied her need.'

'That does not sound like my daughter,' Patrick growled. 'I strongly suspect that you enticed her into using the drug. What is it, heroin?'

'Yes,' Wilkes replied. 'She needed it because of the pressures of her work.'

'You do know my daughter carries your child,' Patrick said. 'Do you intend to marry her?'

Wilkes walked across the living room to a teak desk and turned to Patrick with hatred in his eyes. 'I would not marry your whore of a daughter if she were the only woman left on earth, Colonel Duffy. Ask her friend Randolph Gates the same question.'

A cold fury came over Patrick, a feeling he recognised from his days on battlefields in Africa before he was about to kill. He checked himself. He would not kill this poor excuse for a man before him, but he would thrash him within an inch of his life. Patrick strode towards him.

Wilkes was startled. He was not used to men daring to challenge him. As a famous actor he led a somewhat protected life. The fury he saw in the other man's face now, however, told him that he was in serious trouble. In desperation, he opened a drawer of the desk, producing a small, pearl-handled derringer pistol just as Patrick reached him. With his trembling hand outstretched, he pointed the pistol at Patrick who stopped in his tracks just a couple of paces away.

'I do not intend to kill you,' Patrick said calmly, 'Merely teach you a lesson for the misery you have brought to my daughter and the shame you have inflicted on my family name.'

The threat of the gun had brought Patrick to a stop but Wilkes could see that any fear Patrick felt had been replaced with confidence. He was now in control. 'Do you know, Colonel Duffy, I could shoot you dead and claim self-defence,' Wilkes said with a weak smile. 'My story would not be far from the truth. I could simply say that you burst in and attempted to kill me because of your slut of a daughter's current situation. I doubt that any court in the land would not see me innocent and the publicity would be very good for my career.'

'Have you ever killed anyone?' Patrick asked calmly, staring into Wilkes' eyes.

'No, but I doubt that it can be very hard to pull the trigger of this gun and do so,' Wilkes replied.

'Then, do it,' Patrick challenged. Suddenly he

could see a flicker of doubt in the other man's eyes. That was enough time for Patrick to react. With amazing speed, he was on Wilkes, knocking aside the hand holding the derringer.

The gun went off with a crack and the small bullet ploughed into the wall. But Wilkes had not released his grip on the pistol and desperately fought to bring it up into Patrick's chest. Patrick still had a grasp on the other man's wrist, forcing him to turn the gun inwards. A second shot followed but this time the bullet did not pass harmlessly from the barrel.

Wilkes grunted, his grip on the pistol now gone, and it clattered to the floor as he slumped, clutching his chest. Patrick released him and, ashen-faced, Wilkes collapsed to the floor.

Patrick kneeled down beside the dying man. The bullet had entered his heart, rupturing it. Wilkes stared in surprise at the ceiling, sighed and closed his eyes. Patrick knew he was dead. In his lifetime he had seen many men die.

Outside the house, George watched in disbelief at the scene unfolding in the living room. His father had just killed Guy Wilkes! But he had also seen that he did so in self-defence. For a moment he was at a loss as to what he should do – but only for a moment. The devil had sent him an opportunity of a lifetime.

Patrick turned away from Wilkes' body only to see his son standing in the doorway with an expression of horror on his face. Patrick was at a loss for words. He rose to his feet with the blood of Wilkes on his hands.

'Father, what have you done?' George asked,

stepping into the room. 'You have murdered Mr Wilkes!' he continued, feigning his horror.

'It was not murder,' Patrick muttered. 'It was a terrible accident.'

George shook his head in mock sorrow, looking down at the body. 'I am afraid that it would not look that way to the police. You know that you could hang for the crime.'

Patrick stared at his son. 'How is it that you are here?'

George turned to his father. 'I drove up to visit Mr Wilkes and speak with him on a matter of business about Nellie. When I got out of the car I heard what I thought was a pistol shot and immediately entered the house to see you bending over his body.'

'I was struggling to relieve Wilkes of his gun when it went off,' Patrick explained. 'Had you been here only moments earlier you would have seen that happen.'

'What we have to do,' George said, reaching for the silver case containing his cigarettes, 'is to get you away from here as quickly as possible.'

'I think that I should contact the police,' Patrick said. 'I will tell the truth and trust my fate to a jury.'

'I don't think that would be a good idea,' George countered. 'To do so would mean the newspapers getting involved, and the whole sordid story of Nellie's condition being exposed for all the world to read about. You have to think about the family name. Think what damage it would do to your regiment's reputation if their commanding officer is arrested for murder.'

Patrick listened to his son. If nothing else, George was extremely capable of turning bad situations around in business and now he was applying some of that cunning to their current situation.

'Maybe you are right,' Patrick reluctantly conceded. 'I was never here.'

George lit a cigarette and patted his father on the back. 'It is time to leave and let the police think that maybe a jealous husband did the deed. I am sure that Mr Wilkes has bedded one or two married women in his life.'

Patrick wiped the blood from his hands on the same handkerchief he had used for his daughter's tears. He felt no remorse for killing Wilkes but did have some guilt that he had killed the father of his unborn grandchild. If only it had been Randolph Gates' child and that the American was not tied to the mission ahead, things might have had a happier outcome.

After turning off all the lights to cover his exit Patrick departed the house. He was reminded that his own father, Michael Duffy, had once fled Sydney after killing a man in self-defence. The incident had brought about a lifetime of wandering across the globe as a soldier of fortune before his life was eventually taken in the wilderness of northern Australia.

'The bloody curse,' Patrick hissed under his breath. His grandmother had always told a doubtful Patrick it was real, but now he truly believed.

The eagle...

13

Matthew was trapped in his trench as the Boer artillery scattered shrapnel across the rocky ground. He could see the projectile falling out of the sky directly towards him and there was nothing he could do about it. Suddenly, he knew he was flying on the wings of the great wedge-tailed eagle and that he was soaring high above the battlefield at the Elands River crossing. The young man tossed and turned under the eiderdown, moaning and whimpering. He felt great fear as shadowy figures reached up with deadly fingers to destroy him. He felt the bite of a bullet and woke, sitting up in a lather of sweat. 'God almighty!' he swore, shaking off the nightmare. He remembered now the things he saw in the company of the old Aboriginal warrior – war as he had experienced it as well as how it would be in the future.

The eiderdown fell away and the cold air of winter caused Matthew to shiver. He slipped from the bed to pad across the room to where he kept a bottle of whisky. Pulling a dressing gown around his shoulders, he poured himself a stiff drink and swallowed it, allowing the fiery liquid to spread through his body. In the morning he was scheduled to join his cousin Alexander Macintosh and his friend Randolph Gates, and depart on a Macintosh coastal steamer for northern seas. The mission was on and there was no turning back. Matthew shook his head. He was getting too superstitious. He put his terrible dream down to it being nothing more than a nightmare inspired by his meeting in the ancient cave.

Patrick Duffy stood in his library. Despite the whisky he could not dismiss his turbulent thoughts. Had he touched the pistol that had killed Guy Wilkes? he wondered. But he was able to reassure himself that Wilkes had still been holding the gun when it discharged the shot that killed him. Had anyone seen him arrive and depart? He couldn't remember anyone else being in the quiet street that night. Only George had been a witness to the body and he had sworn to provide his father with an alibi should questions be raised about his whereabouts at the time Wilkes was killed. George would say his father was with him that night in a business meeting. Maybe he had underestimated his son, Patrick reflected, taking a swig of the whisky.

The grandfather clock in the hallway outside

his office softly chimed 3am. Patrick realised that he would need to get some sleep if he was to oversee the departure of the Macintosh ship on its journey north into German territory. Already, the disassembled biplane was packed into crates and stowed aboard as well as other supplies for the expedition.

Patrick placed the empty glass on his desk and left the library for his bedroom. He had killed men many times before and had been able to live with what he had done for Queen and country. But this time it was different. He was no longer on a battlefield fighting the Queen's enemies, but in his own country. And this killing, albeit accidental, had occurred as a result of his sense of honour. Patrick knew that he would not sleep well. Thoughts of an ancient curse continued to dog him and he tossed and turned all night in his mansion on the harbour.

As arranged, they met with John Hughes at his office in Sydney's Victoria Barracks for a final briefing. Only Hughes was in uniform and the men stood around his office in silence.

'This afternoon your ship will steam for New Guinea and then on to German territory around Rabaul,' Hughes said. 'Your mission will be to go ashore at a pre-determined site, guided by Captain Macintosh, and assemble the BE.2. Once that has been accomplished, Mr Duffy and Mr Gates will fly a course along the coast, filming possible places for a naval landing. Once this is achieved, you will disassemble the aircraft and ship it along with yourselves back to Sydney. Tactical control will be in the hands of Captain Macintosh, who is to have overall command of the mission. Be assured, your efforts may prevent the loss of countless civilians here in the future. I don't have to say how important it is that you don't fall into German hands. If you do, I expect you to do the right thing by your King and country.'

'Your king is not my king,' Randolph said quietly.

'Then I am sure Mr Duffy will do the right thing and shoot you himself, if it appears your mission has been compromised by any sign of disloyalty,' Hughes retorted, but with just the faintest trace of a smile. Nervous laughter greeted the British officer's remark. 'Are there any questions?' Hughes asked in closing. There were none.

'Good,' Hughes said, reaching into his desk drawer to retrieve a bottle of fine Scottish whisky. 'Gentlemen,' he added, producing a glass for each man. 'I think it is appropriate that I raise a glass to you and the success of the task ahead of you all.'

The bottle was passed around and each man filled the glass he was given. 'Colonel Duffy, you should propose the toast,' Hughes said, turning to Patrick who stood for a moment in silence.

'Gentlemen,' he finally said, raising his glass, 'to the King, and the success of the mission – and that you return safely to reap the rewards of your good work.'

Each man raised his glass. 'Hear, hear,' they mumbled, each taking a swig.

'Well, if there is nothing else, I am sure that you

gentlemen will find a good watering hole before embarking this afternoon,' Hughes said, placing his glass on his desk. 'I will not be at the wharf to see you off as we don't want to draw attention to your departure. Sydney has many German eyes, and a few keep watch of our maritime movements. But I will be with you in spirit.'

'And the spirits of alcohol will be with us when we sail,' Matthew replied, causing the nervous tension to dissipate in low laughter. The men finished their drinks, leaving their empty glasses on the British officer's desk.

'Colonel Duffy, if I could have a moment with you,' Hughes said as the group departed.

Patrick stopped and turned to his friend. 'What is it, John?' he asked, his hand on the door.

'You don't seem to be yourself,' Hughes said with a frown. 'Are you well?'

Startled by his old friend's perceptiveness, Patrick stepped inside and closed the door to the office.

'I did not sleep well last night,' Patrick answered. 'I have had a lot to think about, sending my youngest son on what could be a very dangerous mission.'

'He is a soldier,' Hughes said. 'He knows the risks and has not asked to be left out.'

'I know,' Patrick sighed. 'But I am also a father.'

Hughes nodded his understanding. He did not have children of his own and young Alexander Macintosh was the closest to being considered his own. He, too, had little sleep the night before but when he looked again at Patrick he sensed that there was something else bothering his friend. He knew him too well. They had marched together across the deserts of the Sudan so many years earlier. He would simply wait until Patrick was ready to confide in him.

He wore a cheap suit, threadbare in patches, and it appeared to have been slept in. Detective Sergeant Jack Firth stood over the body of the famous – and now dead – actor as a sobbing housekeeper wrung her hands.

'I found Mr Wilkes jus' layin' here, Sergeant,' she said, barely able to look at her former employer. 'I come in every day, 'cept Sunday, to clean his house. I was here about eight o'clock and jus' saw him layin' like he is with the blood on his chest.'

Jack Firth was a New South Wales policeman who had risen through the ranks. He'd had his fair share of years on the street in uniform, battling drunken workers and violent husbands. He was a highly intelligent man, which belied his coarse looks, and he had seen many deaths before. This one puzzled him, however. At first glance it appeared that the actor had shot himself through the chest as the small pistol was still in his hand. But his keen eyesight had spotted a second bullet hole in the wall. When he looked closer he could see signs of a violent struggle: a vase on the floor spilling flowers, a wrinkled carpet.

'What do you think, Jack?' a voice asked from behind him. It was the uniformed sergeant who had been initially summoned to the house. 'Suicide – or a jealous husband?'

'The latter, Frank,' Jack Firth replied. 'Or a very irate lover. From what I can see this was no suicide.'

'It's goin' to make good news for the morning papers,' the uniformed sergeant said, thrusting his hands in his trouser pockets. 'Dead actor killed by person or persons unknown.'

'Our job is to make that person or persons known,' the plainclothes policeman said. 'In the meantime we have to get Mr Wilkes here booked in for an autopsy and have some fingerprints lifted off whatever we can. Tell any of your boys that if I catch them taking souvenirs I will kick their arses until their noses bleed. Just leave everything alone until I say it is okay. You wouldn't know if our dead friend had any particular close lady friends, would you?'

'Jesus, Jack, for a good copper you mustn't go to the pictures very much,' the uniformed sergeant answered. 'Everyone knows that Wilkes was stepping out with Miss Fenella Macintosh. It's in all the gossip rags. Australia's darlings, they write of them.'

Jack Firth was not one for the movies. He was happier spending his spare time playing rugby union for a well-known Sydney club, where on Saturday afternoons he excelled as a front row forward. 'Then Miss Macintosh is at the top of the list of people I most want to meet,' Jack Firth said, reaching into his pocket for his battered pipe. He was a systematic man who worked his way from those closest to the dead man out until he found what he was looking for – a suspect. In his experience, most people died at the hands of someone they knew. Random killings were very rare. In this case, according to the housekeeper who had looked around the house for him, nothing appeared to have been stolen.

Arthur Thorncroft stood in his office staring down at the single-page letter written by Fenella and left that morning before he arrived in the afternoon to go through accounts. 'Oh, you silly child,' he moaned, folding the letter neatly and placing it in his breast pocket. 'Why must you go away so mysteriously?' He slumped into his chair and gazed at the telephone on his desk. Did Patrick know his daughter had opted to disappear?

'You Mr Arthur Thorncroft?' a gruff voice asked from behind him in the doorway. When Arthur turned he saw what could be mistaken for an over-sized thug in a bad suit.

'I am,' Arthur replied, rising defensively from his chair. 'Who, may I ask, would like to know?'

'Sergeant Jack Firth of the Criminal Investigation Branch,' the policeman answered without offering his hand. 'Do you have a Miss Fenella Macintosh working for you?'

'I have,' Arthur answered. 'But I am afraid I do not know of her whereabouts. It seems she has chosen to take a holiday without leaving a forwarding address.' Arthur noticed that his statement appeared to cause a discernible reaction in the police officer's battered face.

'I believe that a Mr Guy Wilkes was a former employee of yours,' Firth continued. 'Were he and Miss Macintosh involved in any illicit relationship?'

Arthur flared at the burly policeman's inference

that their romance might be a crime. 'If you are here about what occurs between Mr Wilkes and Miss Macintosh I suggest that you start by asking them the questions – not me.'

'Can't do that, Mr Thorncroft,' Jack Firth answered. 'Not in one case, at any rate. Mr Wilkes is dead. He was found this morning with a bullet in his chest and is currently lying on a slab at the morgue. I would very much like to speak with Miss Macintosh about the matter, though.'

Arthur gripped the edge of the table to prevent himself collapsing. He now realised that his initial statement made it look as if his beloved Nellie was deliberately attempting to avoid any confrontation with the police. 'I am sorry but I cannot tell you where Miss Macintosh is, because I do not know.'

The policeman glared at Arthur, telling him with his eyes that he did not believe him. 'When you next see Miss Macintosh I would appreciate it if you could let me know,' Sergeant Jack Firth said. 'I will speak with you at a future time, Mr Thorncroft.'

Arthur waited until the policeman had left the studio before he reached for the telephone on his desk. He prayed that his good friend Patrick Duffy would be at home to take his call. Time was of the essence and Arthur had already figured out that Fenella had been identified as a prime suspect in the death of her lover, Guy Wilkes. It was imperative that she be found and the matter settled with the police. A major scandal would erupt in the morning papers if she could not clear herself.

★

The ship rocked gently at its moorings. Her name, the *Osprey II*, had been handed down from the days when the Macintosh companies owned a blackbirding ship of the same name that sank off the coast of Queensland many years earlier as a result of a mysterious explosion.

The strong smell of brine and fish permeated the dock as the three men stood by their kit bags waiting for Colonel Duffy to present any final orders before they embarked. They had spent a few hours in a hotel but had not consumed an excessive amount of alcohol. Rather they had reflected on what lay ahead of them and chatted about subjects such as cricket, football and the social scene in Sydney, trying to keep their imaginations distracted from what could possibly go wrong.

Finally, the colonel's car arrived and Patrick alighted, his face already registering concern.

'Gentlemen,' he said, approaching the trio. 'I must apologise for my lateness but something of a personal matter has cropped up to delay me.'

'What is that, Father?' Alex asked.

'Your sister has disappeared without leaving any notice other than a letter to Arthur,' Patrick replied, turning to his youngest son. 'It appears that the police have found Guy Wilkes shot in his home and they suspect Nellie may be the killer, which we know has to be absurd. However, her sudden disappearance makes them suspect that she may have had a hand in taking his life. I must find her as quickly as possible to prove her innocence.'

'That is also my duty, Colonel,' Randolph said,

stepping forward. 'Under the current circumstances, I must excuse myself from the mission.'

'But we need you to operate the camera,' Alex protested. 'Without you the mission is doomed to failure before it has even commenced.'

'I think that I have a solution,' Matthew interjected. 'There is another man I would vouch for to fill Texas Slim's role. A man I have had the opportunity to get to know over some time, and can swear to his reliability.'

'Who is that?' Patrick asked.

'Mr Robert Houston,' Matthew replied. 'He was once a sergeant with the New Zealand Mounted Rifles in the South African war. I got the impression from our chats that he would jump at a bit of excitement and a chance to do something for King and country. With your permission, Colonel, I would like to speak with him and request he join the mission in Randolph's place.'

Patrick frowned and mulled over the idea. He only knew the cameraman briefly through his visits to Arthur's studios but the man had impressed him as being fairly solid in his work. 'We will need to postpone the operation by twenty-four hours but no longer,' Patrick replied. 'I will let you speak to Mr Houston. It was bad enough that we had an American aboard on this one but a New Zealander! I suppose they have their merits.'

'Good,' Matthew grinned. 'I will make contact with Bob and offer him Randolph's role in the operation. I am ninety-nine per cent sure he will go for it. All you have to do is clear his leave of absence with Mr Thorncroft.'

'Thanks, pardner,' Randolph said, offering his hand to his friend. 'I didn't want to let you down but finding Fenella is more important to me than serving your king and empire. Fenella is my whole world and her welfare all I really care about at this point in time. I hope you can understand.'

Matthew nodded, gripping the American's hand firmly. 'I think I know how you feel,' he said. 'Some things are worth going absent for but you do so with my blessings and I am sure that is also the sentiment of Nellie's father and brother.'

Randolph turned to Patrick, whose surprised expression at the American's decision was still on his face.

'Well, old chap,' Alex said, stepping forward to the American and offering his hand. 'I think that my sister is fortunate to have your concern for her in her life. If anyone will find her safe and sound I am sure it will be you and Father. Good luck.'

Relieved, Randolph accepted the gesture from the man he hoped would be his future brother-in-law.

The mission had not started well and Patrick felt ill at this unexpected interruption to the military plans as well as from what Arthur had read to him over the phone from the letter Fenella had left. At least Patrick could be one hundred per cent sure that his beloved Fenella had no involvement in Guy Wilkes' death but he had to find a way of ensuring that the investigating police understood her total innocence too. That would be difficult if the real killer was not found.

★

Alone, Arthur waited by the telephone in his office. When he had read the contents of Fenella's letter to Patrick he had not read the last two sentences to him. He had to respect Fenella's trust in him and the agony of not telling his dear friend what he knew was eating away at the film producer.

Every noise around Arthur made him jump and he was relieved when the telephone finally jangled its demand that he pick it up. As arranged, Fenella was at the other end and Arthur could hear the terrible pain in her voice. He agreed to meet her as she requested. He would not be informing the police of the young woman's whereabouts as very soon it would not matter. With his help, by the time the sun rose over Sydney the next morning, Fenella would no longer be upon Australian soil. He would have to learn to live with the guilt of his knowledge.

14

Twenty-four hours after its scheduled departure the *Osprey II* steamed away from the wharf. Standing on the wharf watching the ship slowly swing around to head into the harbour for its voyage north were Colonel Patrick Duffy and Randolph Gates – and at the rail of the coastal steamer stood Matthew, Alex and Bob Houston. They waved to the men on the wharf as if the three were on a liner heading off on a holiday voyage instead of destined for a deadly mission in German waters.

When the ship passed out of sight behind a small headland, Patrick turned to Randolph. 'We have our work cut out for us,' he said in a tired voice, 'if we are to find my daughter.'

Randolph nodded. Where did they start? He knew they were in a race with police investigators to get to her first.

Even as he pondered the search for the woman he loved more than his own life, an innocuous-looking man stood some distance away watching the Macintosh ship depart. He was the assistant to the German consul in Sydney and the information he had been passed proved to be correct. Something had happened and the American had been replaced by one of Mr Arthur Thorncroft's cameramen, Bob Houston. The fact that the replacement was a highly experienced photographer appeared to support the theory that the men were on a mission to film German territory in the Pacific, and that their destination was the waters around Rabaul. This at least pinned them down in time and place.

Herr Bosch walked away to make his report destined for the Imperial German Navy. Somehow they would disrupt the British operation and, if needs be, kill those involved. He shook his head sadly with a touch of sympathy for the three young men. Their mission was already doomed.

Even as the *Osprey II* ploughed through the heavy seas east of the harbour, a young woman leaned on the rail of the English-registered liner ploughing into the heavy seas of the Tasman. The salty air whipped at her hair and caused her long dress to cling to her legs. The sky was overcast and she experienced the misery of sea sickness. Her face was unduly pale but she had succeeded in fighting her nausea.

'I say,' a male voice said behind her. 'Aren't you Miss Fenella Macintosh?'

Fenella half turned to see a rather good-looking young man in his late twenties wearing a well-fitted suit and straw boater hat which he held with one hand to avoid having it blown over the side.

'Many people mistake me for her,' Fenella replied. 'I only wish I were she.'

'I don't think you would want that right now,' the young man said. 'Not if one is to believe what one has read in yesterday's papers before we left. It appears that the police would like to speak to her about the death of that actor, Guy Wilkes.'

Fenella was glad that she had been able to change her name for the sea voyage. She had done so to avoid her father locating her. She was leaving her country of birth to avoid bringing shame on her father's name with her addiction and unwed status with the baby she carried inside her. The only person she trusted to keep her secret was Arthur Thorncroft who was not only a close friend but almost an uncle to her. He had informed her of Guy's death and that the police were wishing to speak with her. Fenella had already made her plans – and had the financial means to carry them out – before the sudden and terrible incident. Although she had stopped loving the actor she still sobbed in Arthur's arms over his tragic death. He was, after all, the father of the child inside her. Arthur had pleaded with her to stay and allow her father to help, but Fenella was the daughter of the esteemed soldier and well-known philanthropist Colonel Patrick Duffy. She knew that she was innocent of any crime but also realised that if she stayed to confront the police she would be the target of malicious gossip that would hurt her father and family. Better that she disappear to prevent any chance of the tabloids smearing the family name. She had, however, promised Arthur that she would keep in constant contact with him and he had further helped by providing her with references for her future.

'I say, are you travelling alone?' the young man asked eagerly, changing the subject.

Fenella raised the faintest of smiles. 'That is a very forward question from a man who has not been introduced to me.'

'Oh, I am sorry,' the young man apologised. 'My name is Sean Duffy. I am a solicitor with my uncle's firm in Sydney, currently travelling to America to represent our firm on legal matters. I hate dining alone and noticed that you also were dining alone this morning when we departed Sydney.'

'Mr Duffy, it is a pleasure to meet you,' Fenella answered. 'I am Fiona Owens from Melbourne. I am a teacher of music.'

'It is an honour to meet you, Miss Owens,' Sean said, extending his hand. 'I would be grateful if you would meet with me tonight at the captain's table for dinner.'

'I think that would be nice, Mr Duffy,' she replied. 'But for now I would like to be alone if you do not mind.'

'I will leave you, Miss Owens, with the pleasure of knowing that we will break bread together tonight.' Sean lifted his hat and made his way down the virtually deserted deck.

Fenella was still feeling ill and did not want

to show so to the charming young man who she guessed to be in his late twenties, and whose face was not unlike those of her father and brothers. She had been clever in concealing her shock at meeting Sean Duffy. After all, she was an actress. She knew of the law firm and her father's relationship with his Irish-born cousin Daniel Duffy, son of a partner of that legal enterprise. Of all the places to bump into someone related to her, albeit distantly, she reflected. She even felt a little paranoid at having accepted the invitation to share a meal at the captain's table. But it did not hurt her cover to be seen in the company of a handsome young man when she was travelling by herself.

Then Fenella felt the tears rolling down her face. She really was alone, leaving all she knew. She desperately missed her father and Alexander and, above all, Randolph. The tears turned to soft sobbing but no one heard or saw her other than a couple of seagulls drifting on the wind off the ship's railing. She prayed that the sea voyage that divorced her from a supply of heroin might help stave off her addiction to the drug. After all, she was now responsible for the life growing inside her and suspected that the narcotic might be injurious to her baby's health. Even now, the terrible desire to use the drug haunted her and only her seasickness took her mind off her craving for its euphoric daze.

Colonel John Hughes read the de-coded cable from England's Secret Service chief. He rubbed his forehead. The pain in his face was evident. According to the message intelligence sources in England had stumbled on information that the covert operation in the Pacific had been compromised. The three men steaming for German Pacific territory were probably journeying into a trap.

He stood and paced his office, arms clasped behind his back. How in hell could the mission be compromised when the only persons who knew of its existence were just the five conspirators?

For a moment Hughes suspected Randolph Gates. He was, after all, an American and pro-German feeling was strong in his native land. He had pulled out at the last moment although that was understandable considering the Yank's infatuation with Patrick's daughter. The English soldier had been some years in the world of espionage so for him anything could have a sinister meaning. Did Gates arrange to have Fenella Macintosh abducted to give him a reason not to join the mission north? He shook his head. There had to be easier ways to excuse himself from the operation. He only had to feign illness. If the American had not betrayed them, who had? He instantly dismissed suspicion of either Matthew Duffy or Alexander Macintosh. Both men were soldiers at heart and prepared to die for their country. Matthew had proved that in South Africa and it was unimaginable that Alex would bring any shame on the family name and as for Colonel Duffy, his friend and colleague – impossible.

But then there was George Macintosh, Hughes thought. Not a likely suspect as he too would not do anything to jeopardise his standing in society – let alone want to be acccused of treason. However, he did have access to Patrick's work. And even for a moment Hughes thought about Fenella but dismissed her as a suspect despite her mysterious disappearance. She did not really have access to what they were doing, just as George Macintosh had not been involved in any of their planning – as far as he knew. However, George Macintosh might have the means to monitor matters . . .

John Hughes returned to his desk and folded the cable for destruction at a later date. He could only think of one other man he could confer with about the contents of the coded cable.

'Major Oaks,' he bellowed from his office to his aide. 'Fetch the car.'

Angus MacDonald greeted Colonel Hughes at the front door and immediately invited him to enter. The former Scottish soldier had served under John Hughes when they were younger and he respected the man for his close friendship with Patrick Duffy.

'I suppose you heard the news, Colonel,' Angus said, taking the officer's cane and coat. 'It's in all the papers, sir,' Angus said, holding up a copy he had kept in the foyer. 'The mad Serbians have killed the Austrian archduke and his wife. Do you think it will mean war in Europe?'

John Hughes accepted the paper from the valet and carefully read the account of the assassination of the heir to the throne of the Austro–Hungarian

Empire. It appeared that a plot by Serbian nationalists had been carried out in the Bosnian city of Sarajevo. The English officer's quick mind took in the ramifications of what this spark may have set off. There had always been bad blood between the Balkan Serbians and the occupying Austrians. So long as the old Emperor of Austria did not seek revenge against the Serbians they might avoid a war in that part of Europe. But another small voice told him that the religious and cultural relationship between the Russian empire and the Serbian Orthodox church might be a dangerous factor in mobilising the Tsar's armed forces to immediately provide the Serbians with moral support. Sabre rattling was not uncommon in these times.

'All going well, Sergeant Major MacDonald,' Hughes finally commented, 'I think cooler heads will prevail and a Balkans war will be avoided.'

'I dinna know, Colonel,' Angus mumbled. 'There is a lot in Europe spoiling for a war. I will announce to Colonel Duffy that you have arrived.'

With that, Angus escorted the British colonel to Patrick's library where he knocked, opened the door and ushered him inside.

The two soldiers greeted each other warmly.

'I suppose you have heard by now,' Patrick said. 'About events in the Balkans.'

'I only just read it in the paper Mac showed me,' John Hughes answered, taking a comfortable leather chair by the fire. 'It seems that we in the army are always the last to know. No doubt a paper will be on my desk when I return to the barracks. How is the search for Nellie going, old chap?'

Patrick walked across to his liquor cabinet to retrieve a bottle of whisky and two glasses. 'Mr Gates is making inquiries with all Nellie's friends and acquaintances. I have provided him with a list,' Patrick said, pouring two generous glasses. 'He keeps me up to date on his progress which has been very little as yet, I regret to say. But he is a good man with a clear head on his shoulders.'

'I wish you well and am sure that Nellie has her reasons for taking some time away to avoid the public scrutiny that dreadful Wilkes thing has caused,' Hughes said, accepting a glass from Patrick who now sat opposite his friend. Both men raised their glasses in a silent toast to what they thought most appropriate.

'You said on the telephone to Mac that you have a very important matter to discuss with me,' Patrick started, taking a swig from his glass.

Hughes moved uncomfortably in his chair before answering. 'I have just received news from England that they believe our operation is compromised and that the Germans are well and truly aware of our plans,' he replied.

Patrick looked sharply at his friend. 'Are you saying that the boys are in danger of betrayal?'

'I'm afraid so,' Hughes replied. 'We have to make a decision today as to whether we abort the operation or chance that they will be able to carry it off without incident. That is one of the reasons I am here today.'

'What is the other reason?' Patrick asked.

'To discuss with you the matter of a security breach – possibly from someone close to us.'

The pained expression on Patrick's face told his friend a story. 'I think that we should consider your first matter,' he replied, 'before exploring the second issue.'

'Do we abort?' Hughes asked bluntly.

Patrick put down his glass and stood to pace his library, rubbing his face in his anguish. So many months of hard work had gone in to coordinating the vital mission. But what about the fate of his beloved youngest son? He was forced to choose between being a concerned father and a professional soldier. 'How reliable is your information?' Patrick asked.

'It is from the highest sources in London,' Hughes answered. 'There was a note of urgency in the cable. I don't think the people in Westminster want us to embarrass them before the Germans. We might be disowned as renegade military men and that would be disastrous for both our careers.'

'I am more concerned about the fate of three very brave young men,' Patrick said, slumping into his armchair. 'But if we had even a fifty per cent chance of pulling off the mission we would have in our hands vital intelligence that could change the course of history in this part of the world. I have to consider that my son is also an officer of the King and has a duty to risk his life – if necessary.'

John Hughes waited patiently, sensing that Patrick was mulling over all the alternatives. 'There is an option,' John Hughes offered. 'That we alert Alex to the intelligence we have and he can then consider another approach to the situation. Maybe he can find an alternative way of completing the mission. He is a very astute young man.'

'Maybe,' Patrick mused. 'They should be docking in Port Moresby very soon. We could cable them with what we know and ask Alex whether he wishes to continue with a new course of action.'

Hughes nodded. It was not as if Patrick was avoiding the decision but rather trusting his son to consider the outcomes. Still, Hughes felt sure that the young army captain would reply that he could continue under another plan. Such was the sometimes reckless nature of men with blood like Patrick's.

'That decided, it will be done,' Hughes said. 'I will send off a cable today. Now, the second issue is equally as serious. I strongly believe that there is a security leak close to us.'

'Do you have anyone in mind?' Patrick asked warily. 'Do you consider me a security risk?'

Hughes laughed softly. 'I would hardly be discussing the matter with you, Patrick, if I suspected you in any way. No, but I am sorry that I have to even bring up the subject with you. However, I must do so as a servant of the Crown. We have known for many years that your Irish side of the family is openly critical of England. You saw that for yourself in your trip to Ireland only a few years ago in your meeting with your Jesuit priest cousin.'

'That was resolved,' Patrick reddened. 'There is no one close to me whom I could think of as harbouring treasonous leanings.'

'Can you vouch for George?' Hughes asked, clearing his throat.

'George?' Patrick asked, puzzled. 'Despite his manner my oldest son is more interested in making money than putting himself in harm's way. No, not George.'

Hughes frowned. Patrick was thinking like a protective father and not a professional soldier. 'Do you know that George has strong links with German industrialists?'

'The Macintosh companies are not alone in trading with German interests,' Patrick retorted. 'I am sure half of England's aristocracy has German links in one way or another. After all, King George and Kaiser Wilhelm *are* cousins.'

Hughes raised his hand to placate his friend. 'I am not accusing you or the Macintosh companies of treachery, but simply asking if you are aware that George has doubled your German trading interests.'

'You and I both know that Alexander's trading trip earlier this year to German territory was a ruse for him to establish our current mission.'

'I am not talking about that,' Hughes said. 'Are you aware that George has shifted a substantial amount of money into German chemical investments?'

Patrick did not answer immediately. He had always allowed George a free hand in business dealings as his son had a way of doubling their fortunes. The information about the German chemical investment was news to him. 'No, I did not,' Patrick finally replied. 'But it might be a good thing for a sound return. The German scientists are among the best in the world.'

'Sadly, I must agree,' Hughes said. 'It's just that

in his dealings George may have innocently revealed bits and pieces about the operation we had planned.'

Patrick stood up suddenly. 'Despite the fact that they do not like each other very much, George would never endanger his brother's life,' he said. 'How is it that you seem to know more than I about the family company dealings?'

'I am sorry, Patrick, but I have had to initiate inquiries into every avenue close to you for possible answers,' Hughes replied. 'It sickened me that I had to have your private business dealings looked into but you must understand my position.'

Despite his anger at his long-time friend, Patrick understood what he was saying in his apology. Would he have approached the problem in any different way? 'I will speak with George,' he said quietly. 'I promise that I will do so as a loyal officer of the Empire and not as a father.'

Hughes rose to his feet. 'I think that enough has been said,' he commented, offering his hand. 'I am sure that you will find that your son has not inadvertently revealed our operation to the Germans he deals with.'

Patrick accepted the gesture and the two men walked towards the library door. When John Hughes had left, Patrick walked back to the liquor cabinet and poured himself another drink. The conversation had almost cost the two men their longstanding friendship, he thought. How could anyone even consider that a person of his blood could betray his country? He would confront George with the absurd accusations and clear his son of any suspicion.

Just the smallest voice nagged at the back of Patrick's thoughts, however. Had his son been in a position to reveal the operation? The same small voice answered that Patrick had been too trusting. Now his son was in a position to blackmail him over the death of Wilkes. Patrick fully knew that he was not the man to question George. But blood was blood and Colonel Hughes trusted him to do the right thing. Patrick shuddered. What if his son had betrayed them all? It was not something he wanted to think about.

The Macintosh steamer lay at anchor off Ella Beach in the Port Moresby harbour under a hot, tropical sun. Alexander Macintosh returned to his ship by row boat and was helped aboard by Matthew Duffy and Bob Houston.

'How did it go with the governor's man?' Matthew asked.

'We need to have a conference in my cabin straight away,' Alex replied, wiping down his cotton slacks and shirt with his sweating hands. 'Something has cropped up.'

Bob and Matthew followed the young army officer to his cramped cabin and jammed themselves in as best as they could. It was fortunate that Alexander's cabin had a porthole to allow the tropical breeze to air the stuffy space. The two companions waited in silence.

'It appears that the Germans know we are coming,' Alex said quietly. 'Somehow, the mission has been compromised.'

Matthew knew that his cousin was to meet with the military attaché assigned to decode messages in Port Moresby but thought that this would merely be routine before setting off on the last leg of their operation. 'So, what do we do?' he asked.

Alex, sitting on his bunk, frowned. 'I have the option of choosing whether we call off the mission or proceed with another course of action.'

'What course of action?' Bob asked.

'First, I have to send a cable as to whether we go ahead or turn the *Osprey* around and return to Sydney,' Alex answered, wiping at the sweat on his face with a small hand towel. 'If I choose to continue I can only request that you trust me and follow me into what appears to be very hostile waters. It seems things are hotting up over in Europe over the assassination of the Austrian archduke. If we are not careful we might just find ourselves at war with Germany – if they choose to side with the Austrian emperor in any war that has the potential to bring the Russians in on the side of the Serbs.'

'The Germans would be fools to do that,' Matthew said quietly. 'The Austrian empire is already in decline and I doubt that they could muster an effective force to fight even the Serbs.'

'How do you know that?' Alex asked, looking with interest at his cousin.

'Texas Slim and I were visitors to Vienna a couple of years ago,' Matthew answered with a grin. 'Other than dancing the waltz, the Austrians did not impress me with their show of arms. However, I was impressed with the ladies I met.'

Alex shrugged. 'I am not going to return,' he said. 'With or without you both, I will go on with the mission. You have an hour to decide whether you get off at Port Moresby and take another boat home or continue with me to Rabaul.'

'You had better have a bloody good plan, cousin,' Matthew said lightly. 'I have all the intentions of returning home in one piece to take your brother's lady friend away from him.'

Alex looked at his cousin with gratitude for his unflinching loyalty and held out his hand.

'You think you Australians could do better with your crazy patriotism than us New Zealanders,' Bob Houston butted in. 'I think it is best that I stick with you to show you how New Zealanders really are superior to you Australians. After all, we fought together in the last war.'

His response brought forth light laughter from the two Australians. Matthew punched Bob playfully in the shoulder. 'I don't ever remember you New Zealanders being around when things got hot for us from the Boers, but if you stick with us, you just might learn a thing or two about handling dangerous situations.'

Despite their apparent levity each man knew how much the deck was stacked against them. Each was well aware that what had once been a dangerous mission had now become suicidal. But the bravado of young men was something they lived with.

'Go and find a cold beer,' Alex said. 'I am going to need one to think this through. And I don't have to remind you that the conversation we just had stays in this cabin. Not even the captain of the ship is to know what may lay ahead of us.'

Matthew and Bob nodded their understanding and left Alex alone to agonise over how he would carry out his mission and somehow avoid the waiting German armed forces. At the back of Alex's mind was just one nagging question: how in hell had they been betrayed?

15

An overhead fan in the Rabaul Club stirred the tropical air, pleasantly cooling the spacious room deserted of its patrons in the mid morning except for two. Both men sharing coffee wore civilian clothing although they were relatively senior officers. A Tolai steward hovered in the background prepared to provide more coffee should the pot empty or more late breakfast pastries be required.

Major Kurt von Fellmann sipped from his cup, watching the older and slightly overweight officer facing him. They had exchanged courtesies, and Major Paul Pfieffer, the resident intelligence officer, had politely enquired as to Kurt's sea voyage back from Sydney and his experiences while in Australia.

'I chose to cut short my inspection,' Kurt had replied, 'considering the news coming out of Berlin concerning the Serbian incident.'

'During your short stay in Sydney were you able to make contact with our man in the consulate?' Pfieffer asked.

'We met,' Kurt replied. 'He was very helpful.'

'So,' Pfieffer said, reaching for a small, sweet pastry. 'Do you think that we are moving towards war with the Serbians?'

Kurt shrugged. 'From the little that I have gleaned from the British newspapers nothing much seems to be happening on either side. I would presume that you know more than I considering your role here.'

The German intelligence officer shook his head. 'My information equates with your knowledge,' he said, taking a napkin to brush away the pastry crumbs from his mouth. 'I suspect that the Austrians will demand that the Serbians turn over the conspirators to maintain what the Orientals call face. The Austrians are looking for any excuse to teach the Serbs a lesson.'

'And if the Serbians refuse?' Kurt asked, leaning forward.

'Then that is another matter,' Pfieffer answered, placing his napkin on the table beside his coffee. 'Who knows what will happen after that. However, as you are to return to the Fatherland I am sure you will be in touch with matters further. I believe that you are scheduled to leave us tomorrow morning.'

'That is correct,' Kurt answered. 'I will be submitting my report on the woeful defensive measures in this part of the Kaiser's empire.'

'I doubt that they will listen in Berlin,' Pfieffer said. 'All attention is on Europe. However, we will soon enough find ourselves embroiled in a confrontation with the English in our little outpost.'

Kurt placed his coffee cup on the wooden table and gazed at the open doorway at the end of the room. Outside, he could see the soft glare of the tropical sun and the shady, evergreen trees. It was hard to imagine that this little piece of paradise could shortly be one of the first battlegrounds if war broke out between Germany and England. How the world had shrunk, he mused. Was it possible that the events in Europe could impinge on God's garden in the Pacific? The ominous feeling was not unlike living in the shadow of the volcano behind the German settlement; there was always the chance that it would erupt without warning. 'You are sure of your intelligence concerning Captain Macintosh and Mr Duffy?' Kurt asked.

'I am sure,' Pfieffer answered. 'Our source is so close to their planning that we have known every move since the English mission was initiated by Colonel Hughes.'

Kurt thought about the ramifications to his distant Australian relatives' lives if all that was known by the intelligence service of the Imperial German Navy was correct. As he had met both men and taken an instant liking to them, he wished that the information had proven to be incorrect. He sensed that both men would be killed and that Berlin would use their spying activities to embarrass the English government on the other side of the world. 'It is a pity,' he sighed.

'I know of your relationship to Captain Macintosh,' Pfieffer said. 'I regret that we have to deal with this matter but I suspect our adversaries are just as knowledgeable about what the Serbian matter could lead to. In a sense we are already at war.'

Kurt understood the portly intelligence officer's statement. Despite there being no declaration of such the intelligence community always perceived themselves to be at war. He finished his coffee and excused himself. When Major Kurt von Fellmann stepped into the sunlight he blinked and gazed around. Life was going on as if tomorrow would be the same. He did not want to think about tomorrow.

There was blood with the pain and Fenella doubled over in her cabin gasping. Although she had never experienced a miscarriage, she instinctively understood what was happening to her body – it was expelling the partially formed baby.

She cried out but in the luxurious cabin she was alone. The ship rolled gently beneath her in the calm waters and she collapsed on the bed, grasping her stomach. 'Please,' she gasped. 'Please, God, help me.'

As if answering her prayer she heard the knock on her cabin door. 'Miss Owens,' Sean Duffy called cheerfully from the other side of the doorway. 'Are you ready for some games of shuffleboard?'

Fenella remembered that she had made a date with the young Sydney solicitor and he had turned up punctually to escort her to the games deck. With all the effort she could muster, Fenella forced herself off the bed, and doubled over, made her way to the door to unlock it.

Sean Duffy's cheerful expression disappeared immediately when he saw the trail of blood and the ashen colour of Fenella's face. 'Oh my God!' he gasped. 'You need to lie down while I fetch the ship's doctor.'

He stepped inside and assisted Fenella to her bed where he lay her gently down on her back. 'I will be straight back,' he said, taking her hand. 'Just hold on.'

Fenella nodded weakly as Sean disappeared from the cabin to return within a few minutes with the ship's doctor, carrying his black bag. Sean hovered in the cabin until the doctor turned to him and with a gesture of his head, indicated that Sean should leave so that he could attend to his patient.

With expert hands he examined Fenella, ascertaining quickly the source of her distress. It had not been the first time on the ship that he had attended to miscarriages. 'You are losing your baby,' he said, opening his black bag to retrieve what he needed. 'I am sorry. Where is your husband?'

Fenella did not answer and the doctor did not ask any further questions. He understood that his patient was unwed and probably wealthy, using the voyage to America to avoid a family scandal.

Standing outside the cabin with a gentle breeze in his face, Sean Duffy experienced a flood of emotions. He had spent over a week in the young woman's company and had convinced himself that he was falling in love with her. He had not once suspected that she was ill and wondered at the reason for her serious haemorrhage. It did not occur to him that she might be pregnant.

The doctor stepped out onto the deck with his black bag and a bloody towel with something wrapped in it. 'Are you a friend of Miss Owens?' he asked.

'We have known each other for a little over a week,' Sean answered. 'I would like to consider myself as a friend on this voyage.'

'Miss Owens will require bed rest for a couple of days,' he said.

'Am I able to speak with her now?' Sean asked.

The doctor's expression reflected his hesitation. 'I have given her a strong sedative,' he finally replied. 'It might be best that you attempt to speak with her in the morning.'

'Thank you, doctor,' Sean replied. Sean stood for a moment trying to take in what had happened. When he saw the bloody bundle in the doctor's hand it dawned on him what he had witnessed. But he was at a loss as to what to think about the situation.

Closer to Rabaul the *Osprey II* altered course for its destination into German territorial waters. On the bridge the ship's captain, Ernest Delamore, scowled at the instructions given to him by young Alexander Macintosh. Although he had not been privy to the actual mission of the Macintosh ship he sensed that trade was not the priority as he had been briefed in Sydney. The mysterious crates in the ship's hold were carefully guarded by his three passengers but it had been his chief engineer who had volunteered what he thought they contained.

'I think the laddies have one of those flying machines stowed away,' Jock McLeod had said over a cup of coffee on the bridge. 'Dinna know why they would be carrying an aeroplane on this trip when we will be needing the space for copra.'

The ship was now to anchor off a beach identified on the charts by Alex Macintosh but the captain did not like the look of the alteration at all. Changing from their original course along the east side of the German island to the west side stank of nefarious practices. But he was subordinate to the ship's owner, Patrick Duffy, and had no choice but to accept the orders.

Alex joined Bob Houston and Matthew Duffy at the bow of the ship as it chopped into a deep trough before punching through a wave. Fine spray swept over the three men.

'It's done,' Alex said above the hiss of the spray swirling around them under the grey skies above.

'So we take the Germans by surprise,' Matthew said. 'Are you going to cable the colonel of our change of course?'

'I can't do that,' Alex replied. 'If there is a breach of security close to us it is better that only we three know of the final plan.'

'I don't like the sound of the word final,' Bob said. 'Maybe alternative plan is a better choice.'

Matthew smiled. 'I'm with you on that, Bob,' he said, slapping the New Zealander on the back. 'So, who goes on to Rabaul with the ship?'

'We all will,' Alex replied. 'The German authorities will probably be waiting for us on the other side of the island with their navy if what we know about being compromised is correct. Instead, we will turn up in the harbour as innocent traders and any search of the ship will find no trace of our cargo. We will stay a couple of days and then depart. Needless to say, that should convince the Germans the information they have been fed is completely erroneous and they will stand down their operations to intercept us.'

'Sounds good,' Bob said, frowning. 'But where do we dump the aeroplane?'

For the first time in days, Alex broke into a broad smile. 'That, gentlemen,' he trumpeted, 'is all under control. You are about to meet the woman who will one day be my wife.'

Startled, Matthew looked sharply at his cousin. Had he gone mad? 'You do not mean that young lady you met on her father's plantation up the coast from here?'

'Yes,' Alex answered. 'Miss Giselle Schumann.'

'But she is German!' Matthew exclaimed. 'Why do you think she and her family will help us?'

Alex bit his lip. He did not know but this was the only chance he could see in carrying out his mission to reconnoitre the German territory he had been assigned. He understood how important it was to military planning to know what lay ahead of any beach landing. 'I think that I might be able to persuade her to help us,' he said, ignoring the expressions of doubt on the other men's faces. He prayed that he was right; it was the only option he had short of a suicidal mission.

★

Despite his promise to John Hughes to question George, Patrick Duffy had avoided confronting his eldest son with any questions concerning the security breach. He had convinced himself that his eldest son had no way of learning anything about the covert operation. John Hughes had to be wrong and should be exploring other possible sources, Patrick thought as he thumbed through the newspaper before him on the breakfast table. Outside the French windows the heavy rain pounded with a steady beat.

'Master Macintosh is here, Colonel,' Angus MacDonald announced from the doorway.

'Send him in,' Patrick said, closing the newspaper.

'Father,' George greeted, shaking off the cold as he entered the room. 'I have come to remind you that we have a meeting with the board of directors before noon.'

Patrick had forgotten many of his business commitments which had been sidelined in favour of his duties as commanding officer of the city's infantry regiment. 'Thank you, George,' he said and watched as his son poured himself a cup of tea and took a seat at the end of the highly polished table.

'It seems that we have lost contact with the *Osprey II*,' George said, sipping the lukewarm tea. 'I was wondering if you could cast some light on the matter?'

Patrick looked sharply at his eldest son. 'Why is that of any interest to you?' he asked. 'You know the radios on our ships have a limited range. No doubt the captain will signal his position in good time.'

'As Alex is on a trading venture back to Rabaul it

is my concern that everything runs smoothly,' George countered. 'After all, it appears that I am the only one worried about keeping the family fortunes afloat.'

'Don't forget,' Patrick flared, 'I am still the final decision-maker when it comes to how the companies are run. I have trusted that you have obvious talent when it comes to making money and therefore do not interfere in your decisions. But ultimately I am responsible for what happens.'

'I did not mean to say that you are not,' George answered quickly. 'But considering the incident with Guy Wilkes and the sudden disappearance of Nellie, I feel that you are under a lot of pressure. My question regarding Alex's current whereabouts was born out of a natural desire to coordinate the trading venture with the Germans.'

'How much do you know about what Alex does for me?' Patrick quietly asked.

George frowned, feigning surprise. 'I am not sure I know what you mean,' he replied. 'Naturally I know that he shares a lot of your time playing soldiers with the regiment.'

'We don't play soldiers,' Patrick retorted indignantly. His son had cunningly caused him to go on the back foot, defending his part-time military duties and not pursuing the former line. 'I am hoping that Alex will consider choosing the regular army as his career.'

'It seems to be a family tradition,' George said and Patrick understood that he was making reference to Patrick's own father, the legendary soldier of fortune Michael Duffy. 'It is fortunate that I inherited some of that Macintosh blood rather than the Papist, Irish blood of the Duffys.'

Patrick realised that his son was baiting him and cautioned himself to keep a calm head. He felt guilty that he could not truly warm to his eldest son and often looked upon him as a total stranger. Patrick knew that it was not right for a father to differentiate his affections between his children, favouring one over the other.

'I will ask you again,' he said. 'Tell me precisely what you know about recent events with your brother's activities.'

George put down his cup of tea, rose to his feet and pushed the chair from the table. 'We have an important director's meeting very soon,' he said, ignoring the question. 'I hope I will see you there.'

Patrick watched as his son walked out of the room and brooded on the fact that George had not answered his question. As if reading his thoughts, George paused at the door and turned to his father. 'You should not be quick to forget that I am your alibi when the police eventually come to speak with you about the murder of Guy Wilkes,' he said with the trace of a sneer.

Patrick felt his blood run cold. There was no mistaking the blackmail his son had inferred: *don't ask me any more questions concerning your military operation.*

Then George was gone and Patrick could hear his son speaking with Angus as he left the house. Patrick sat staring out the French windows that framed the dining room at the incessant rain. Somehow George had confirmed his knowledge of his covert military life but Patrick had also realised just how fragile was his future in the hands of his eldest son. He was right. Sooner or later the police would come with their questions and only George could clear him of suspicion.

Patrick sighed heavily, rose to his feet and walked to the large window overlooking the manicured garden. Alex had not revealed his new plan to carry out the original aim of the mission. For all Patrick knew he could have fallen into German hands and already be dead. Nellie's whereabouts could not be ascertained and she could be anywhere in the world. His hands were trembling. He had not experienced such a physical manifestation of his fears since the battlefields of Africa. How could a father accept that he had a son who was a traitor to his King and country? He wished that he could believe in God as much as he was becoming a believer in the ancient Aboriginal curse on the family. It was as if a giant wheel was turning in time, repeating the events that had so tragically dogged the Duffys and Macintoshes in the past.

Sean Duffy waited a day and accompanied the ship's doctor to Fenella's cabin. After examining Fenella – and at Fenella's request – the doctor invited the young lawyer into the cabin, leaving them to speak in private.

Sean pulled up a chair beside Fenella's bed and reached for her hand.

'I spent a sleepless night worrying about you, Fiona,' he said with genuine concern in his voice.

'When I saw the blood yesterday I did not know what to think.'

Fenella gently squeezed his hand and responded with a weak smile. 'I am touched that you were concerned, Sean,' she replied. 'I do not feel so alone with you beside me.'

'Should I have the captain communicate your distress to family in Australia?' Sean asked.

Fenella glanced away and stared at the cabin wall with its paintings of English rural scenes. Sean realised that his question had touched a raw nerve. 'I do not wish to intrude and am sorry if my question caused you any concern.'

'I appreciate your sentiments,' Fenella said, turning to him. 'But it seems my whole life has been lived as a lie – even now I am not who you think I am.'

'You really are Fenella Macintosh,' Sean ventured and was not surprised when the beautiful but pale young woman in the bed did not react with surprise.

'You know one of my secrets,' she said. 'The second I tragically revealed yesterday, losing the baby.'

Sean felt his heart beating. 'Are you running away from that unfortunate business in Sydney with Mr Wilkes?' he asked, clearing his throat. He was surprised at Fenella's weak smile.

'I can assure you that is not the reason I left Sydney. I am innocent of the death of the father of the child I have lost. No, that has been a sad coincidence. You must know the scandal my former condition would have caused my family.'

'You do realise that your father and my Uncle Daniel were once close friends,' Sean said, still holding

Fenella's hand. 'I have often heard the stories of the past from my uncle's family.'

'I confess that my father spoke very little about his family on that side,' Fenella said. 'I think he carries much pain and will do so until the grave.'

'You must know how fond I am of you, Fenella,' Sean said.

'And I am very fond of you but I am afraid that I would like us to remain friends. Are you able to accept that?' Fenella asked.

Sean looked down at the floor lest she see the pain in his face. It was obvious that his strong feelings for her were not reciprocated. He looked up. 'I would hope that you accept my friendship and company on our voyage,' he choked, causing Fenella to squeeze his hand.

'I need to be alone in my life for a while,' she said. 'Much has happened and I am unable to make any commitments other than getting through the present. I pray that you will understand.'

Sean nodded. He could accept her words but deep down he held on to a glimmer of hope that Fenella Macintosh might see him in a different light when the voyage was over.

'I think that we should work towards having you back on your feet,' he said with a cheery smile. 'I need my shuffleboard companion to reign as champion on this voyage.'

Fenella felt his hand slip from her own. At least this young man of whom she was very fond could share one of her secrets and that made her feel less alone in life. He had not laboured on whether she had been involved in the death of Guy, accepting her innocence on face value. Still, Fenella could not think who would kill her former lover.

Sergeant Jack Firth was feeling the bruising results of the previous weekend's rugby match and his ear throbbed from a bite he had received from an opposing player in the scrum. He found the office he was looking for in the gloomy, cramped interior of the building. The imposing, convict-constructed sandstone building was behind the even more impressive courthouse designed in the Greco-Roman style. Darlinghurst police station had a sinister history. Seven years earlier the last man had been hanged inside the gaol. Now hangings were held elsewhere but for many years the public spectacle of the condemned dropping through the trap door had provided Sydney-siders with a macabre form of entertainment.

'You have something for me?' he questioned the young, blue-uniformed police officer assigned to the Wilkes murder investigation. The constable was ambitious and had his sights set on a career as a plain clothes investigator.

'Yes, Sergeant,' he said, producing his notebook from his breast pocket. 'I proceeded to the shipping offices as you ordered and showed the booking people the photograph of Miss Macintosh. One of the clerks remembered her booking a berth on the liner leaving Sydney the day after Wilkes' death. Except that she gave her name as a Miss Fiona Owens. He remembered her as she booked a single cabin that cost a lot of money.'

Despite his throbbing ear, Sergeant Firth smiled grimly. 'She must have planned to kill her lover and then skip the country,' he said, thinking out aloud. 'Definitely a *mens rea*, wouldn't you say so, Constable.' Firth liked to demonstrate his knowledge of legalese in front of junior men and using the Latin helped remind them of his great knowledge of law.

Suitably impressed, the constable nodded. Miss Macintosh's act of leaving the country under an assumed name certainly spoke of a guilty intent – especially when it coincided with the death of the Australian actor. 'What do we do?' he asked.

'You find out where the ship is currently heading,' he said. 'Then you find out when and where it next reaches land.'

'I have already done that,' the constable beamed, hoping his initiative would demonstrate his ability to be an investigator. 'The ship is supposedly two days out of Hawaii and is scheduled then to steam for America.'

'Good work, Constable,' Firth said with the hint of a smile. 'Your efforts will be suitably noted.'

'Is there any chance of getting our suspect back?' the constable asked, returning his notebook to his breast pocket.

'In these modern days of communications,' Jack Firth said, 'all we have to do is cable the Yank police in Pearl Harbour to detain Miss Macintosh, and then extradite her from American territory back to Sydney where we arrest her for the murder of Guy Wilkes.'

The constable did not want to ask further questions. His knowledge of the law extended to understanding that such an action required the suspect to be under arrest at the time of the extradition. After all, Sergeant Jack Firth had a reputation of almost a hundred per cent conviction rate in the courts and was a legend in his own right – on and off the rugby field.

16

Herr Schumann heard from one of his workers that a ship was anchored just offshore and rode down to investigate. He recognised the Macintosh trader immediately and warmly welcomed the boat load of young men who rowed into the beach.

'Herr Schumann,' Alex said in German, 'these are my good friends, Herr Duffy and Herr Houston.'

Schumann shook hands with each man and turned to Alex.

'My young friend,' he said, 'your visit to us is most unexpected. May I ask how you honour us, although you must know that my house is always open to you and your comrades.'

'My family companies have decided that we should explore the sisal trade with German businesses in your part of the world,' Alex lied. 'And, I must confess, I was hoping that I may visit with your daughter.'

The planter nodded his head in his understanding of impetuous young love. 'You are fortunate, Herr Macintosh,' he said. 'My daughter has just returned from the inland where she has been seeing to her patients. I suspect that she already thinks she is a doctor although I must admit she has proven to be very astute in her medical ministrations to the natives – especially concerning the diseases that ail the old and young.'

'I think that Giselle will one day make a fine physician,' Alex replied.

'Come,' Schumann said, gesturing towards his bungalow beyond the coconut trees waving in the mid-morning breeze. 'Bring your friends to the house and I will arrange for you all to eat. I am sure that you will appreciate some home-cooked food.'

The three young men followed the solidly built German as he led his horse up the beach and onto a trail that went to the green lawns of his sprawling house surrounded by rows of coconut trees, storage sheds and worker compounds. Within ten minutes they had reached the house and Alex was pleasantly surprised to see Giselle standing on the verandah gazing at them. Her hand shaded her eyes against the tropical sun's glare and when she recognised Alex she bounded down the steep steps from the verandah and ran across the lawn with her long dress flowing around her legs.

Breathless, she came to a stop in front of Alex but aware of her father and the two strangers with Alex she restrained herself from kissing him. 'Hello, Mr Macintosh,' she said, beaming. 'What has brought you to this part of the world unannounced?'

'I missed you,' Alex answered simply in English, causing Matthew and Bob to smirk. 'And I am also on a mission to explore the sisal trade.'

Giselle slipped her arm boldly into Alex's, leading him back to the house with her father and the other two men following. So stunned had she been by the appearance of the man she had been regularly writing to that she had hardly noticed the other two with him.

'I am Matthew Duffy,' Matthew said by way of introduction, as he walked beside his cousin. 'I had heard from my cousin that you are beautiful but he failed to say just how stunningly beautiful you really are.'

His flattery brought a scowl from Alex but Matthew simply grinned mischievously back at his cousin. 'This other gentleman is Mr Robert Houston,' Matthew continued. 'But it is hard to describe someone from New Zealand as a gentleman.'

'I think New Zealand is a far prettier country than Australia,' Giselle replied in perfect, unaccented English, addressing Bob. 'And the men from your country are far more polite than those of Australia. I will ignore Mr Duffy's comment.'

'Thank you, Miss Schumann,' Bob said. 'I hope that I might confirm your impressions of New Zealand men compared to our cruder Australian cousins.'

The good-natured banter between the young people continued until they reached the verandah where they were met by Schumann's wife who also impressed Matthew and Bob with her beauty. They were surprised to hear that her English was also excellent although her husband's was not. Within minutes, a young girl brought pots of coffee and tea on a tray. Settled on the verandah, the conversation drifted to copra prices, the social scene in Sydney and, like the picking of a scab, the news from Europe. It was at this mention that Alex sensed a tension creeping into what had hitherto been a light-hearted conversation.

'What do you think will happen if the Russians mobilise in support of the Serbs?' Schumann asked, leaning forward to pour himself a fresh cup of coffee. As he had asked the question in German, Alex answered.

'That has not happened,' he said. 'I am sure that cool heads will prevail in Europe and the world will go on rattling sabres as it seems it is doing a lot of lately.'

'But if the Tsar supports the Serbs that will mean the Austrian Emperor will call on Germany for assistance,' Schumann said. 'In turn, France will side with Russia and who knows what England will do. It could be that we are moving towards a war in which you and I will be on opposite sides.'

'War between France and Germany does not necessarily mean England will side with France,' Alex said. 'It would be well and truly in England's interests to remain neutral in such an event. After all, England did not interfere in the 1873 Franco-Prussian war.'

'*Ja*, that is true,' Schumann said, partly reassured by the historical example the young Australian had cited. 'I served the Fatherland against the French in that war as a cavalry man, and it would be very much in England's favour to remain neutral if we went to war with France. After all, Germany and England were comrades almost a century ago against Bonaparte. I pray that you are right, Herr Macintosh.'

Alex could see that his host was a little more relaxed as he sat back in his cane chair.

'Father, I think that you should offer our guests the hospitality of our guest rooms,' Giselle said. 'Mr Duffy has informed me that they are able to take some leave here before travelling on to Rabaul.'

'That is a good idea,' Schumann beamed. 'You may have the housemaid prepare their rooms.'

Alex thanked the planter on behalf of them all. Schumann rose from his chair and excused himself to speak with his supervisor at the packing sheds, leaving the two women and the three young men to finish afternoon tea. Alex kept glancing at Giselle, wondering how long they would have to carry on this charade of acting as if they were little more than merely friends. Each time he caught her eye he could see that the feeling was mutual. They needed time alone to express their feelings for each other. That time did not come until after dinner when Matthew and Bob Houston retired to Herr Schumann's living room to share coffee and cigars.

Giselle and Alex slipped out of the house and walked down to the beach under a clear sky ablaze with the twinkle of stars. A gentle breeze made the evening perfect and the couple removed their shoes to walk barefoot along the dark beach.

'I could not believe my eyes when I saw you today,' Giselle said. 'I have missed you so much and your letters have kept me sane counting the days until Mother and I travel to Sydney in September.'

'All I have thought about was some reason to see you again,' Alex said. 'Every day and hour has been an agony without seeing you.'

'How long will you be able to stay?' Giselle asked.

'I think at least three days,' he replied. 'But we will require a favour of your father. We need to leave some crates in storage so as to make space in our ship's hold for cargo. Do you think he would allow us to unload the crates and store them?'

'I cannot see why not,' Giselle answered. 'But why speak of these matters now when we have so much to say to each other in such a brief time.'

'I do not know whether I should broach the subject,' Alex said awkwardly. 'I know that we have known each other for such a short time, but events in the world seem to be conspiring to disrupt our lives.' He stopped walking and turned to face Giselle in the dark. 'Would you consider becoming my wife?' For a moment his heart beat at such a rate that he experienced a tightness of the chest.

'You would consider marrying a Jewish girl?' she asked softly, taking Alex by complete surprise. He was glad that she could not see the look of shock on his face.

'You are a Jew?' he asked. 'But I did not see any sign of that.'

'Are we supposed to look different?' Giselle countered with just the slightest trace of anger. 'Are we supposed to be born with dark skin and big noses?'

'No, I did not mean that,' Alex hurried to defend

his question. 'It is just that my family has Jewish friends in business and, well, they act differently . . . I don't care that you are Jewish . . . all I am saying is that your revelation was a surprise – that is all. I love you and would convert to your religion if that was necessary. That is how much I love you.'

Giselle leaned forward and kissed Alex on the lips with gentleness rather than a passion. 'You do not have to do so but it would be necessary that our children be raised in my faith. My father is a Lutheran, but my mother is a Jewess, if you were wondering. My father chose to come to this part of the Empire to save my mother from the constant disapproval of his family back in Germany. My father accepts her beliefs and in our tradition I am Jewish because my mother is a Jewess. How will your family react to your choice of a wife?'

Alex had to think about that. His family was restricted to his father, brother and sister. It was only his father's approval that he really worried about. But then, he was an adult and to hell with what his father might think. 'I don't really care,' Alex replied. 'All I know is that I had decided from the moment I set eyes on you that there would be no other woman in my life.'

'Then I will marry you, Alexander Macintosh,' Giselle replied. 'But I will also study to be a doctor.'

Alex swooped her up in his arms, dancing a parody of a waltz with the sand squelching under his feet. 'Anything you desire, the future Mrs Macintosh,' he whooped. 'Now all I have to do is convince your father that I am a worthy son-in-law.'

'Put me down,' Giselle gasped. 'Or I will suffocate before we are wed.'

Alex placed her gently on the sand and kissed her. This time it was with passion. They could feel the water around their ankles and in the tropics of German New Guinea the world was at peace.

'You wish for my daughter's hand in marriage,' Schumann said rather than asked as Alex stood in the planter's office in the late hours of the evening. A moth crawled across the desk where Schumann sat. Alex had never felt so nervous in all his life. So far his hopes for being the man's son-in-law did not look good.

'I love your daughter more than my own life,' Alex offered in his desperation to impress the formidable man.

'You do know that she has always had a dream to help the sick,' Schumann continued. 'Would she be able to do that as your wife?'

'I am not a man without property and income,' Alex countered. 'I may not understand her desire to become a doctor, but that does not mean I will not support her work.'

Schumann rose from behind his desk and Alex shifted nervously on his feet. The planter walked to a sideboard, paused then turned to the anxious young man. 'She is my only child and I love her in a way you are yet to learn of. At the moment the world appears to be on the brink of a war and we do not know what will happen. Both you and I know that there still exists a terrible chance that your country and mine may find each other on opposite sides of the battle lines. Do you think it is wise to propose when you have known each other for such a short time?'

'We have learned much about each other through our correspondence,' Alex replied, attempting to defuse the older man's argument. 'We are at peace now and that should continue into the future. All I know is that your daughter is the only woman that I will ever love.'

Schumann clasped his hands behind his back and stared hard at Alex. 'I feel that you should wait a while longer before planning to wed my daughter, and I am sure that her mother would feel the same way. After all, they are both travelling to Sydney in September when you could see my daughter under proper chaperoned circumstances. I do not ask much.'

Alex was forced to concede to Giselle's father's wishes. Much of what he said made sense but his desire to be with the young woman still over-rode reasoning. 'I take it that you do not grant your blessing on my proposal,' Alex said flatly. 'But I do accept your logic.'

'I am sorry, Herr Macintosh,' Schumann said sympathetically. 'You are a fine young man and under other circumstances I might have celebrated your desire for marriage to my daughter but for now I feel you have not known each other long enough and the present state of world politics may interfere with your relationship. You cannot forget that my daughter is a German citizen.'

'But she was born in Australia,' Alex countered.

'That may be so,' Schumann responded. 'However, by German law she is also a citizen of the German Empire. I am sorry, Herr Macintosh, but come again to me in a year's time and tender your case for my daughter's hand then.'

Alex let out a deep sigh, turned and walked out of the office to where Giselle waited with an intense expression of anticipation on her face. With a sad look and shake of his head, Alex answered her unspoken question, causing the young woman to burst into tears.

'Papa, how could you refuse my happiness?' she sobbed, brushing past Alex to rush into her father's office. When Alex looked across the room he could see Giselle's mother standing at the door, a sympathetic expression on her face. They nodded to each other before she turned to walk away.

Giselle spent the night crying in her mother's arms, while Alex lay on his bed, staring up at the dark ceiling in a state of despair. He slept very little and when the house came alive with the sounds of servants arguing, a rooster crowing and the banter of plantation workers outside his window he rose.

When Alex ambled into the dining room he was met by the solemn faces of his two friends who looked up from their plates piled with fresh bacon and eggs.

'I gather things did not go well last night,' Matthew said gently as Alex slumped in a chair at the table.

The housemaid attempted to place a plate in front of him but he waved her off, reaching for the coffee pot. 'How did you know that?' he asked in a dull voice.

'Hard not to hear the sobbing of a distraught young woman into the early hours of the morning,' Matthew answered. 'I am sorry, old chap. I guessed that your late night meeting with our host was to ask for Miss Schumann's hand in marriage.'

'You guessed correctly,' Alex answered, pouring a cup of hot coffee. He reached for the jug of fresh cream. 'Mr Schumann feels that we have not known each other long enough and that the world is in so much of a mess it would not be wise to wed until everything sorts itself out.'

'He has a point there,' Bob observed, entering the conversation with a shrug. 'After all, why are we really here?'

Alex glanced at the New Zealander. He had a point. After all, part of the reason for anchoring off the Schumann plantation was to conceal their cargo and then proceed to Rabaul. He was forced to remind himself that the aim of their voyage was to spy on German territory. But his feelings for Giselle were quickly taking precedence over the military mission, and he had to remind himself that the lives of the two men at the table with him were in his hands.

'At least one thing was resolved last night,' Alex sighed, sipping his coffee. 'Herr Schumann has agreed to provide us with storage space for the BE.2. We can unload today.'

'What did you tell him would be in the crates?' Matthew asked.

'Machinery parts,' Alex answered, wiping his lips with a linen napkin. 'I do not doubt that he will accept my word, considering I have conceded to his wish to delay any plans of marriage.'

'I am sorry that it did not work out with the wedding plans,' Matthew said. 'But, I think that you two are fated to be together one day.'

Alex did not reply. There were more ways of being together than simply seeking the permission of a father for his daughter's hand. There was such a thing as eloping and, like a good military planner, he was already considering that option.

Sean Duffy had been summoned to the bridge for a meeting. The ship's captain had been visited by representatives of the American police hours earlier, inquiring into one of the passengers, a Miss Fiona Owens. Although the captain was fully acquainted with the rules of the sea he wished to seek advice from the man he knew was a lawyer regarding police rights to come aboard and take by force – if necessary – one of his passengers.

'Well, Captain Howard, that is an interesting question,' Sean had replied. 'I doubt that even the Americans have the right to forcefully disembark a non citizen of their country from an English-registered ship. May I ask why they wish to take Miss Owens into their custody?'

The captain was a stout but solid man in his early fifties with piercing grey eyes and a reputation among his crew for strict discipline. 'It seems, Mr Duffy, that they have information that Miss Owens is wanted by the Sydney police on a murder charge under her real name of Fenella Macintosh, who I have been informed is an actress of some talent.'

Sean felt his blood run cold. He was aware of Fenella's true identity but did not believe she could be capable of a premeditated murder. 'I am afraid that the American police have been misled on Miss Owens' identity,' Sean lied. 'I have known Miss Owens – and her family – for many years and can swear to that fact.'

'If I allow the police to take Miss Owens in for questioning I am sure that they will also come to that conclusion,' Captain Howard said.

'That is true,' Sean agreed. 'But, if you allow that to happen I am sure that Miss Owens – whose family are of considerable influence in the Australian shipping trade – would take your concession to the American police as a terrible slur on their name and take appropriate legal action for damages.'

'I must admit that I am not aware of the Owens name in our business,' Howard said. 'But I have heard of your uncle's fine legal reputation from friends who have had dealings with him. I am sure you are right and that I should deny the police rights to come aboard and take Miss Owens.'

'To keep in goodwill with the American authorities,' Sean offered, 'I can represent Miss Owens' interests and personally meet with whoever is in charge of the investigation in Pearl Harbour. I am sure I will be able to clear up any misunderstandings and at the same time keep Miss Owens' family from any scandal that might cause recriminations against your shipping line.' Sean could see that the liner's captain was eager for a way out of this awkward situation and would seize on any reasonable offer made.

'Your idea has merit, Mr Duffy,' he replied. 'I know you will speak with Miss Owens and sort out the matter with the Americans.'

'Thank you, Captain,' Sean said, realising that he was sweating as much from the warm day as he was from tension. It had been touch and go and now he must warn Fenella of the unexpected development in port.

Sean met Fenella on the upper deck where she stood by the rail gazing over the busy Pacific port. Huge American warships and smaller commercial vessels crisscrossed between the pretty inlets. Fenella turned to him but her smile faded when she saw the worried expression etched on his face. 'Is something wrong?' she asked as he approached.

'The American police have spoken with Captain Howard,' he replied. 'It seems that they wish to take you into custody.'

'You know that I had nothing to do with Guy's death,' Fenella said softly. 'I cannot afford to be taken home in chains, as they say. It would bring shame to my father.'

'I understand,' Sean answered. 'Although I have not met your father personally I do know how highly my family thinks of him. I guess you could say that as extended family it is my duty to protect you now.'

Fenella reached out to take Sean's hand. 'I think God sent you to me as a guardian angel,' she said sweetly but with sincerity, although Sean was not sure if he was hearing the words of a good actress or the woman herself. 'You are in my prayers every day for all that you have done for me.'

Sean froze. Over Fenella's shoulder he recognised the walk of plain clothes police officers. No matter what country they came from the demeanour seemed to be the same. 'Miss Fenella Macintosh,' one of the tough-looking men said, holding up an identity badge. 'We have a warrant to arrest you.'

17

Officer Amos Devine had the kind of face that reflected the clientele he policed. It was tough and battle-scarred from years of dealing with unruly American sailors on shore leave. He had been born into a share-cropping family in Georgia and had escaped the poverty of the cotton fields by shipping over to Hawaii, where he was recruited into the island's police force. Now he had been told by some Limey ship captain that he could not take one of the passengers from the ship temporarily in port on its voyage to San Francisco. He had brushed aside the captain's objections to find the woman wanted by the police in Sydney, Australia.

'You Miss Fenella Macintosh?' he asked.

'Who are you?' Sean demanded, placing himself between them. The American policeman stared hard at the young Australian lawyer.

'If you don't step aside, buddy,' the tough police officer snarled, 'then you can join Miss Macintosh downtown in the cells.'

Sean wisely moved back, realising that he was both out of his depth and jurisdiction with the police officer. Fenella had not even identified herself when the American reached out to grip her wrist and it seemed that he did not care if she owned up to who she was or not. He had a job to do and seemingly liked the idea of throwing his weight around when it came to dealing with foreigners – especially Limeys. 'Just come with us, without any fuss.'

'Let go of me,' Fenella flared. 'My name is Fiona Owens and I am a citizen of Australia.'

'I don't care if you are a citizen of Timbuktu,' Devine growled, reaching behind his back to retrieve a set of handcuffs. 'We can do this the easy way or the hard way, it's up to you.'

Fenella looked at Sean with desperation in her eyes but he shook his head, warning her to cooperate for the moment.

'Do as they say, Fiona,' he cautioned. 'And I will organise to have you released immediately.'

Fenella relaxed slightly, knowing that Sean would attempt to carry out his promise.

'Wise move, lady,' Devine said, leaving the handcuffs tucked into his belt near his holstered pistol. 'You can sort out any problems down at the station.'

With these parting words, Devine and his offsider escorted Fenella along the deck to the gangplank. Sean watched them walk away, his mind racing as to how he would get Fenella out of the custody of the American police. He realised that his task was almost impossible and wondered at the modern power of communications that the police in Hawaii could be waiting for her when the liner docked. He cursed the arrogance of the Yanks for their total disregard of an Australian's citizen's rights.

Sean turned and hurried to his cabin. He had work to do.

On a winter's day in Sydney George Macintosh stood with his hands in his pockets against the cold. The meeting had been arranged through a note delivered to his office in Kent Street and he felt that it was not going to be in his favour. He watched as his contact strolled along a pathway bordered by flower beds until he reached George.

'Good afternoon, Mr Macintosh,' Maynard Bosch greeted, his hands also in his pockets.

'What is this all about?' George snapped, attempting to take the high ground in his dealings with the assistant to the German consul.

'Your information concerning your brother's plans appears to have been somewhat erroneous,' Bosch replied, staring across the park at a flock of pigeons strutting under the cloudy skies. 'I would like to know why.'

George shoved his hands deeper in his trouser pockets. 'It seems that I am under suspicion in my dealings with you,' he replied. 'In turn, I suspect that you have problems with your security.'

'I doubt that,' Bosch frowned. 'Who has raised this with you?'

'My father,' George answered. 'He has not directly accused me of spying but I know he has doubts about my loyalty to the Empire.'

'I can vouch that there have been no security breaches on our side,' Bosch shrugged. 'But I am here to see what you may know about the fact your brother's ship has not arrived off our eastern coast as you originally informed us it would.'

'I don't know,' George answered. 'From what I could find in the papers that my father so carelessly leaves in his desk, the last report he received was that our ship had docked in Port Moresby last week. There's been nothing else since. However, if I am under suspicion of treachery, my father would have taken measures to conceal anything else about the mission into your territory.'

Bosch kicked at a pebble on the ground with his toe. 'It is imperative that you endeavour to find out what has happened to your ship and report immediately back to me. Otherwise your investments in Germany may be jeopardised in the event of a war between us. I have information that you have banked a lot of money without your father's knowledge of our industries. You have a lot to lose.'

'I do have something up my sleeve that might help,' George said, realising that if the Germans reneged on the deal to give his investments favoured treatment it could cost the family companies a lot of money.

'Then I will hear from you within twenty-four hours,' Bosch said. 'That is all the time we have if we are to embarrass the British government in these uncertain times.'

'You will ensure that you keep your word to have my brother meet an unfortunate accident?' George countered.

Bosch tensed. 'That was our deal,' he replied. 'Just get us the information before tomorrow. I will bid you a good afternoon, Mr Macintosh.'

With his parting words, the assistant consul continued his stroll through the park at the heart of Sydney, the bitter taste of murder in his mouth.

George knew that his father would drop into the office that afternoon. When his personal assistant told him that his father was in the building George informed him that he wished to meet with his father in his office.

Within minutes, Patrick appeared and was ushered in. His son greeted him, closing the door behind his father and gesturing to a leather chair for guests.

'Do we have a confidential business matter to discuss?' Patrick queried, noticing the way his son closed the door behind him.

'No,' George replied, removing a bottle of whisky from a side cabinet and producing two crystal tumblers. 'I was hoping that you may have news of my brother and sister. How is Mr Gates going with his investigations?'

Patrick accepted the glass. 'Mr Gates seems to have hit a brick wall,' Patrick sighed, sipping the whisky. 'He has questioned just about everyone known to

Nellie and so far no luck. I have authorised him to use an account to fund his expenses in continuing with his search.'

'Good,' George lied. He was at a loss to know what had happened to his sister, although he hoped it had been something very bad. 'I noticed the authorisation go through this office.'

Patrick glanced at his son and realised just how closely he monitored anything to do with the business management. Was he using that same acute sense for detail to monitor what he could glean from his military activities? The answer made Patrick uncomfortable. He still could not bring himself to consider his eldest son a traitor. 'And as for your brother's whereabouts,' Patrick said, 'I suspect that we will hear from him soon enough.'

'I need to make urgent contact with him,' George said, walking to a large window that looked down over the street and across rooftops to the harbour. 'Is there no way of learning of his position at sea?'

'What is so urgent that you need to make contact with your brother?' Patrick asked. 'After all, he is simply working to expand our trade in German territory.'

'I know that,' George replied, forcing himself not to lose his temper. 'But I still have a need to contact him.'

'Why would that be?' Patrick asked.

'There has been a development,' George answered, turning to face his father, the whisky untouched in his glass. 'A deal has cropped up in Rabaul that we cannot afford to let slip out of our hands for a cargo of sisal. It is important that Alex direct the company trader to get there as soon as possible and I need to be able to reach him immediately to let him know the details.'

'I was not lying when I said I do not know your brother's exact whereabouts,' Patrick answered. 'And even if I did, I think you must understand why I could not reveal what I might know.'

'You do not trust me?' George scowled. 'Do I not keep our business interests in the black? Do you suspect me of being a traitor to my country?'

Patrick waved off the questions. 'Both you and I know that Alex works closely with me for the interest of the regiment and his country,' he said. 'I would prefer that you have no involvement in that part of my life and work only to keep the family businesses running. Otherwise, you may leave yourself open to accusations of treason from certain parties.'

'You mean your friend, Colonel Hughes,' George said with a bitter edge to his voice. 'Do you put more stock in what he thinks than me, your son?'

'It is not that,' Patrick attempted to defend himself. 'I love you as a father loves his son, but sometimes I admit to myself that I hardly know you.'

'Probably because you spend all your time with Alexander,' George said, taking a long swig from his whisky. 'And yet it is I who has put my neck on the chopping block to lie for you if the police come knocking about Wilkes' murder.'

'It was not murder,' Patrick replied softly. 'What happened was a terrible accident.'

'Do you wish to go to the police and explain

what happened?' George asked with a crooked smile. 'Or would you rather the family name stay out of any scandal that may ruin your reputation as the commanding officer of the regiment?'

'You know why I would prefer to remain silent on the subject,' Patrick said, feeling the whisky sour in his stomach.

'Then think carefully,' George said, approaching his father and standing over him. 'I am the only person who can keep you out of the hands of the police and possibly off the end of a hangman's rope. I need to know where my brother is right now.'

Patrick placed his glass on the small side table by the armchair and slowly rose to his feet. 'Then it is you who has been feeding information to the Germans,' he said. 'Traitors are still executed in this country.'

Both men stood facing each other.

'I am not a traitor,' George said. 'The little I gave the Germans was to influence favourable trade concessions and investments. It was not an act of treachery.'

'That is not how some would view it,' Patrick answered in a cold tone. 'You are fortunate that I am your father and that my operation can never be revealed to the public for scrutiny. Otherwise, I would have you arrested the moment I stepped through that door,' Patrick said, gesturing to the entrance to George Macintosh's office.

'And you are fortunate that I do not go to the police and inform them that I saw you kill Guy Wilkes,' George said.

'You did not see me kill Wilkes,' Patrick said, puzzled by the statement. 'You arrived after Wilkes was killed.'

'No, Father,' George said. 'I saw the whole affair through the living room window, including your attempt to take the pistol from Wilkes and the struggle in which the gun went off.'

'Then you are a witness to the fact that it was an accident,' Patrick gasped. 'You are able to help me clear up this whole horrible matter.'

'That depends,' George replied. 'On whether you ever speak of your suspicions of me being a traitor.'

'I would say that we are at what the Americans call a Mexican stand-off – neither of us may reveal what we know of each other.'

'Very well said,' George answered, turning to walk away. 'But, if you are able to tell me where my brother is before tomorrow morning I am sure we will be able to clear up the Wilkes matter in a way that it never comes to public attention.'

'How is that possible?' Patrick scoffed.

'You are rather naive for a man who has seen much of the world,' George snorted. 'We have at our means the most powerful weapon in the judicial system – money – and its ability to pay a poor policeman in one day what he would earn in ten years. I just happen to know about the leading investigator on the murder inquiry, and from what I have learned he is in dire financial circumstances. Just accept that I would never betray my country nor risk the safety of my brother,' George continued convincingly. 'Trust me when I say my need to know where

Alex is has nothing to do with your military affairs. I merely wish to make money for us.'

Patrick stared at his son, wanting to believe his words. Politics had never been an interest to George and he could understand why he might provide certain information to the Germans. After all, it was beyond comprehension that one brother would want to harm another – no matter how much they may dislike each other. 'I will help you,' he finally replied. 'So long as you swear on your own life that the information will not harm Alex or compromise what I am doing.'

'I swear,' George answered, holding up his glass of whisky. 'Alex is my brother. I could not do him any harm – despite our differences. I just need to clinch the deal with the Germans for a cargo that Alex may be able to return for us.'

Patrick left the office with his eldest son's oath echoing in his head. But he could not shake from his mind a story his grandmother Lady Enid Macintosh had once read to him from her much-used Bible. It was the story of Cain and Abel.

Now working as Herr Schumann's chief overseer, Gerhard Schmidt had been recruited from the dock-lands of Hamburg. He was a heavily built man whose strong physique had equipped him well to lay on the lashes of less than cooperative workers. He was also a man born with an innate suspicion of the world around him, a suspicion which had helped keep him alive as a young man scraping a living in the tough working area of Hamburg's docks.

He stood in a spacious storage shed normally used to stack copra and stared at the large wooden crates taken from the English ship and now occupying the space where he felt only Schumann property should be stored. Machinery parts, he mused picking up a steel bar to jemmy open one of the smaller crates that smelled strongly of a substance he could not identify. The wooden lid came off with a protesting squeal as the nails ripped through the pine timber.

For a moment Schmidt was puzzled. He had not seen an engine of the type in the crate and wondered if it might be some kind of pump. To satisfy his curiosity he went to a larger crate and repeated the procedure. This time he was in no doubt as to what the boxes contained. Before him lay a wooden propeller. The German overseer had seen such machines before in pictures and guessed that the strange smell had to be the remnants of aviation fuel. It was a disassembled aircraft. Schmidt did not bother to replace the lids but hurried to the main house where he knew he would find his boss.

Alex Macintosh watched wistfully from the stern of the Macintosh ship as the shoreline disappeared in the distance. He knew that Giselle would be on the beach watching his ship steam over the horizon and with each nautical mile he experienced the pangs of parting. When it was no longer possible to see the shore but merely the jungle-clad mountains behind the Schumann plantation, Alex turned with a sigh and went below to meet with Matthew and Bob in the small mess room for the crew. He found both men engaged in a card game with a pile of coins between them.

Matthew glanced up at Alex. 'It all seems to be going well,' he said. 'The plane is safely stored and we have nothing to hide from the Customs people when we reach Rabaul.'

Alex took a seat at the end of the tiny table. Bob was frowning as he perused the hand that he had been dealt. 'Overall this alternative plan has set us back a bit,' Alex said. 'But I think it will be worth it when we double-back to the aircraft. Hopefully by then the Germans will have become impatient and called off any security measures to intercept us. I can't see anything going wrong.'

'You want to sit in?' Bob growled. Alex politely declined, knowing that his cousin had a fearsome reputation for winning with cards.

'How long before we reach Rabaul?' Matthew asked, rearranging his hand. They were playing gin rummy and the aviator was flying high on what he had.

'Two, maybe three days,' Alex replied. 'We stay around for a couple of days buying enough cargo to fill the holds, and then we leave as the traders that we are. If the German authorities have been tipped off to the mission they will soon conclude their intelligence was faulty and call off any measure they may have set in place to trap us.'

Matthew heard his cousin's confident words but still did not feel easy about the plan. What if the security leak in Australia kept abreast of their new plan?

Although that did not seem possible when Alex had gone to great measures to bring about a blackout on information back to Sydney. No radio traffic had been allowed from the ship's signal officer. He smiled when Bob picked up a low card from the pack. If he was going to be killed on this operation, he might die a wealthy man on his winnings from the likeable New Zealander.

Hauptmann Dieter Hirsch stood behind the communications officer of the Imperial German Navy, hunched over his radio and morse key. The young sailor adjusted his headset and leaned forward, listening intently to the keystrokes emitting from a ship within the radius of his set's ability. In the cramped room the air was hot and sweat trickled down both men's faces.

'Has there been nothing from the English ship?' Hirsch asked. The sailor turned to his superior officer. 'Nothing for over two weeks, Herr Hauptmann,' he replied.

'Would you say that was unusual?' the German officer asked.

'Yes sir,' the young communications sailor answered. 'All the English trading ships talk to each other in our waters. This one has been unusually silent.'

Hirsch frowned. His last intelligence on the where-abouts of the Macintosh trading ship was that it had left Port Moresby. According to his calculations it should have been in their waters by now and yet the patrolling gun boat had reported no sighting of their target.

The sailor resumed his duties as the dots and dashes continued to flood the airwaves. Suddenly he reached for his pencil and began scribbling on a pad. Many messages were being sent to his station lately from cruising German warships and traders. Hirsch took a deep breath and sighed. It was time to return to his office and resume his duties for the governor administrating the island. He placed his cap on his head and turned to make his way to the door.

'Sir!' the young signaller called to him. 'I have just received an urgent message from the Schumann plantation. I think you should see it.'

Hirsch took the sheet of paper and read the deciphered signal. 'God in heaven!' he exclaimed. 'You have just sentenced yourself to death, Captain Macintosh,' he said aloud as the radio officer watched him in expectation. Hirsch glanced across at the young man. 'Are you in contact with our patrol boat?'

'Yes, sir,' the sailor replied.

'Then get a signal off to them to return to Rabaul immediately,' Hirsch commanded.

The communications officer began tapping out the signal as Hirsch scribbled the formal signal for transmission on an official message pad. He turned to a map on the wall covering the immediate area of German interests around Rabaul that also stretched to German New Guinea. He knew the Schumann plantation from formal visits in the past and it had just recently installed a radio set. With his finger he drew a line between it and Rabaul, calculating how long it would take a coastal steamer to arrive. He knew that he must now hurry to the governor's office and brief him on developments. He was certain that the Australian ship was on its way to carry out an act of espionage against the Kaiser's interests in the Pacific. With the current international situation as shaky as it was he was convinced that they had to be moving towards inevitable war in Europe although he still prayed England would remain neutral. No matter what the rest of the world was experiencing he was at least certain his war had already started.

18

George Macintosh stood by the window of his office, his hands behind his back. Patrick Duffy held the telegram in his hand, reading its contents while Randolph Gates hovered, waiting for the reason he had been asked by Patrick to accompany him to the Macintosh offices in the city.

'I believe that you may know something of the man who has sent this telegram regarding the situation Fenella has found herself in,' George said to his father without turning to face him.

'I do not know him personally,' Patrick replied. 'But I do know his uncle's firm. It enjoys a very high reputation and for many years in the past our companies used their legal services. When did you receive this?' Patrick asked, holding up the telegram.

'This morning,' George said, turning to face the two men in his office.

'What is it?' Randolph asked, sensing the tension between father and son.

'Nellie is currently in the custody of the American police in their territory of Hawaii,' Patrick answered. 'It appears from the telegram that she is safe and well but she is to be extradited home to face a murder charge.'

'Fenella did not kill Wilkes,' Randolph blurted. 'That is impossible.' He noticed that neither man disagreed with him but that was to be expected when it was a family matter. 'I will vouch that she was with me the night Wilkes was killed.'

'Is that true?' Patrick asked eagerly.

'No,' Randolph replied, shifting uncomfortably for the perjury he knew he would commit in any court of law as he suddenly remembered something. 'God damn it!' he swore. 'I am not in a position to do that. I have already given a statement saying Fenella was not in my presence for that time.'

'Could it be that you left out Nellie's being with you, to protect her reputation,' Patrick offered hopefully.

For a moment Randolph thought about the idea but dismissed it. 'I was at my rooms in the hotel and the night porter confirmed that when the police spoke with me,' he said. 'I doubt that I could include Fenella.'

'We could bribe the chap,' George said quietly. 'He could swear that Nellie was with you.'

Patrick shook his head. 'We would be creating too many loose ends that could easily unravel, and we know that my daughter did not kill Wilkes.'

George nodded. 'Then all we can do is wait until Nellie is returned to us, and employ the best defence lawyers in Sydney to represent her.'

'That would have to be your distant cousin's firm,' Patrick said, wondering at the strange turn of events. He had let his contact with the Duffys from Redfern lapse over the years. Now that he would need their help to save his daughter he felt the pangs of crushing guilt. All he had to do was go to the police and tell them the story of what actually occurred on that night and his beloved daughter would be free. But that would also mean seriously jeopardising the military mission so vital to Australia's future security. He knew that he was caught between saving his daughter and saving his country. The only hope he now had was that the Duffy blood of his father would be strong enough to save both his daughter and his country.

Patrick glanced at Randolph and could see the pain in his face. At least little Nellie had met a man worthy of her, he thought. He placed his hand on the American's shoulder, regretting that he could not share his terrible secret with him. 'Come, old chap,' he said. 'We have much work to do.'

'Do you know that Mr Thorncroft spoke with me yesterday?' Randolph asked as both men left the office and stepped onto the busy street shrouded by heavy winter clouds and whipped by a cold wind from the harbour. 'He has completed the film and wants to release it in Australian theatres as soon as possible.'

Patrick thought about Arthur's dilemma. 'I want

you to go to Arthur and tell him that we will not be releasing the film until this matter concerning Nellie is cleared up. If he needs money to get through until then you can inform him he only has to speak with me and it will be approved.'

The three men standing at the bow of the Macintosh ship scanned the harbour waters that were shimmering under the tropical sun on this cloudless day.

'Look there,' Matthew said, pointing across the bay to the clean lines of what from a greater distance might have been perceived as a millionaire's yacht. The upper structure of the two-masted, single-funnelled craft with its clean white-painted upper hull, lay at anchor but there was no mistaking the three deadly four-inch naval guns on her decks or the ensign of the Imperial German Navy fluttering in the breeze at her mast.

'It's the *Komet*,' Alex said. 'She is Governor Haber's gunboat in these waters. 'At least we know where she is and apparently not on station looking for us.'

The comment did not take away Matthew's unease. The German gunboat had the capacity to blow them out of the water and there was nothing they could do to defend themselves; .303 Lee Enfield rifles were pea shooters compared to what the formidable gunboat carried.

Bob Houston lit a cigarette and watched as the smoke swirled away. 'What do we do now?' he asked, taking a puff.

'We go ashore as the innocent traders that we

are,' Alex said, turning from the bow rail. 'I think that once we have cleared the port authority and Customs we should go to the officers' club in town and look up a man I met on my last trip. I am sure that he will provide us with some hospitality.'

Ashore, the three men watched a column of uniformed German men wearing slouch hats and with Mausers slung over their shoulders marching along a tree-lined avenue.

'Interesting,' Alex muttered as the men paraded smartly by under the command of a junior officer.

'What do you mean?' Matthew asked his cousin with a note of suspicion in his voice.

'They look like reservists,' Alex replied. 'Maybe it's just a routine training exercise,' he concluded. When the column had passed the three men continued their walk towards the German club in the settlement.

'Captain Macintosh,' an accented voice called from across the avenue. The three men turned to see a smartly dressed German officer hurrying towards them.

'Hauptmann Hirsch,' Alex greeted warmly in German, extending his hand. 'It is good to see you again.'

'Ah, Captain Macintosh, what brings you back to Rabaul?' Hirsch asked, eyeing Matthew and Bob.

'Maybe we should have a discussion in your wonderful club,' Alex said. 'But not to the extent of last time.'

Both men laughed lightly at the reference to the generous hospitality and even more generous amounts of schnapps Alex had consumed on his last visit to the club.

'I should introduce my companions,' Alex said, turning to Matthew and Bob. Introductions made, Hirsch invited the three to join him at the officers' club where it seemed that half the island's military had gathered for a drinking session. The rowdy party of uniformed and civilian-clothed Germans fell silent upon Hirsch and his guests' entrance.

'Gentlemen,' Hirsch proclaimed. 'I would like you to extend our hospitality to our guests, one of whom many of you are already familiar from his last visit . . .' A murmur of agreement met his words. 'Captain Macintosh and his companions, Mr Robert Houston and Mr Matthew Duffy. Both men have served their country in the South African campaign.'

Matthew had a good grasp of German and was surprised to hear that this stranger already knew about his past, as he also did of Bob Houston. That knowledge made him feel uneasy but he did not show it. A tall, good-looking young man stepped forward holding out glasses of clear liquid to Matthew and Bob while Alex accepted the same from another of the club's patrons.

'Schnapps, my friend,' the tall German said in halting English to Matthew. 'I am Lieutenant Klaus and I had the honour of serving as a volunteer gunnery officer to our Dutch allies in that war. We drink to brave men, *ja*?'

'On both sides,' Matthew replied diplomatically, raising his glass as did Bob.

'Where did you campaign?' the former artillery officer asked.

'I saw most of my action at the Elands River,' Matthew replied, causing the German to raise his eyebrows.

'You were at Elands River,' he answered with a note of respect. 'I heard much about your gallant defence from our Dutch brothers who were also there.'

'Well, I am glad not to be there now,' Matthew responded.

The German officer turned to Bob and his questions took the three men into a deep conversation about shared war experiences, albeit from opposite sides. The conversation made Matthew feel just a little easier and he was growing to like the men he met around him. No wonder Alex had suggested that they go to the club to mix with men not unlike themselves.

Alex found himself mostly in Hirsch's company and the two men exchanged idle news on many matters. But when Hirsch noticed a new arrival in the club he excused himself to walk over to a slightly portly German officer wearing his dress uniform and the insignia of a major.

'So, those are the men who have caused so much consternation to our governor,' Major Paul Pfieffer said, accepting a drink from a junior officer.

'Yes, sir,' Hirsch replied. 'But from what we have learned I doubt that they will be able to do much as they have left their aeroplane at the Schumann plantation.'

'Not now,' the intelligence officer replied, sipping the drink. 'I suspect that their visit is an attempt to throw us offguard. They know, as do we, that there will be nothing incriminating aboard their ship anchored in the harbour. After we are satisfied that they pose no threat they will steam back to the plantation, pick up their aircraft and return covertly to our shores to complete their mission. They are still as dangerous as ever and must be eliminated.'

'Sir, all we have to do is use the *Komet* to shadow them and its presence will deter any attempt they make to carry out their mission,' Hirsch said, hoping that the matter could be resolved without recourse to violence. The reappearance of the Australian militia officer had caused the German to remember how likeable Alex was. It would feel akin to treachery on his part if he was forced to have the Australian killed – it would be like murder.

'I am afraid that we have lost the use of the *Komet*,' Pfieffer replied, taking a cigarette from a silver case adorned with a regimental badge. 'Governor Haber has directed that the ship be used to carry out an inspection of our islands here. I suspect that he does not wish to be involved in any dealings we may have with the English that may be viewed by civilians as being a dirty job. No, we have to use other means to once and for all finalise this matter. To that extent I am going to organise for a fairly powerful explosive device to be placed aboard their ship with a timing mechanism so that by the time the bomb goes off their ship will be a long way out of our waters. Its sinking will be seen as an accident and nothing will be able to be traced back to the German government.'

Hirsch listened to the senior officer whose calm expression had not changed as he described the sabotage he had planned to kill off the three young men who, as he spoke, were partaking of the Germans' hospitality.

'What if I send a signal to the Schumann plantation to simply destroy the aircraft,' Hirsch countered in quiet desperation.

'That has already been done,' Pfieffer replied. 'I had a signal sent as soon as their ship anchored today. It seems there was a tragic fire in the storage sheds and everything was razed to the ground.'

'To blow the bottom out of a ship of that size will require a very large explosive device,' Hirsch said.

'I have arranged for a couple of our sea mines to be re-engineered for the task,' Pfieffer said. 'I have also arranged for them to be placed aboard using means that will not raise their suspicions. Trust me, Hauptmann Hirsch,' Pfieffer continued, 'I am very good at what I do in the interests of the Fatherland.'

Although frustrated at not being able to spare the lives of the three guests of his club, Hirsch realised that they were, after all, a threat to German strategic interests in a very uncertain time. He sighed and excused himself, rejoining Alex who was now sharing drinks with two other German officers. The laughter came easily in the club as the sun set over the placid tropical waters where the Macintosh ship rocked gently at anchor.

★

George Macintosh stared at the bottle of Scotch on the shelf in his library. In the past he had dismissed the use of alcohol as the crutch of the weak, but now he was wondering if it could help his depression. His plan to discredit Fenella seemed to have gone wrong. His father showed nothing but paternal concern for his daughter despite her failings. The latest cable from the Hawaiian Islands had said that Fenella was to be returned on the first available ship back to Sydney, escorted by a member of the American police. Patrick had expressed elation at having Fenella returned to him and, ironically, the death of Wilkes appeared to have only strengthened the bond between father and daughter.

At least his brother's life was still in extreme peril, George consoled himself. At his meeting with the assistant German consul at Hyde Park that afternoon he had been assured that the authorities in Rabaul had the situation in hand. The German agent had not elaborated on how but George was satisfied he may not ever see his hated brother again.

George walked over to the cabinet and retrieved a crystal glass, filled it with whisky and swigged a mouthful. It was his toast to the possible eradication of at least one of the stumbling blocks to his eventual sole ownership of the Macintosh fortunes.

The Scotch consumed, George pulled a cord to summon his valet from his quarters. Within a minute, the man appeared.

'Curtiss, have my dinner jacket laid out for me,' he said.

'You will not be dining at home tonight, Mr

Macintosh?' the man asked.

'Not tonight, Curtiss,' George replied. 'I will be dining with Miss Gyles.'

The man nodded and hurried away to prepare the clothes, leaving George alone to ponder on the return of his sister. He would have to think of some other way to discredit her in his father's eyes. Failing that, a fatal accident may befall her too.

The meeting of Colonel Hughes' staff officers concerning the developments in Europe and the possible ramifications to Australian security had ended and the grim-faced men filed out of the office leaving Patrick alone with the British officer. When the room was cleared, Hughes turned to him.

'You should have informed me, Patrick, about the matter concerning Nellie. From what I hear she is being transported by the American authorities back to Sydney to face a murder charge. It's not possible . . . I have known Nellie practically from the day she was born. I attended her christening and she is like a daughter to myself and Mrs Hughes.'

'She did not kill Wilkes,' Patrick responded. 'I am very sure of that.'

'I could never imagine that it would have gone this far,' Hughes said. 'Nellie is not capable of killing anyone, despite the apparent evidence against her. The newspapers are having a grand time splashing their lurid conjecture across the pages over the matter. I pray that you have taken on good legal services for when she returns.'

'I have decided to employ the services of Solomon & Duffy for Nellie's defence,' Patrick said.

'You are employing your cousin's firm?' Hughes asked.

'It has been Sean Duffy who has been looking after Nellie's interests,' Patrick said. 'I have not met the man but it appears he is aware who Nellie is and has expressed an absolute belief in her innocence.'

Hughes shook his head. 'No matter how much he may have faith in Nellie's innocence it will not help in a court of law,' he said. 'The evidence may be circumstantial but a good prosecution could make a jury believe she had motive as well as means and displayed guilt by fleeing the scene under an assumed name.'

'It was not because of Wilkes that she was fleeing this country,' Patrick said. 'It was because of me and the family name. She has been addicted to heroin and is pregnant.'

'That will not convince a jury of her innocence,' Hughes responded pragmatically.

'They cannot convict an innocent woman,' Patrick said.

'I know that you must be blinded to the possibility that Nellie could have committed the killing, but as we know women are capable of crimes of passion.'

'I know that my daughter is innocent as it was I who killed Wilkes,' Patrick said quietly.

'Good God!' Hughes blurted. 'What can I say? At this vital point in time we cannot expect you to sacrifice yourself – even for Nellie. Although I can understand why you might choose to confess to something that you have not done for your daughter.'

'I am speaking the truth,' Patrick said and recounted the events leading up to and including the accidental death of the actor. He excluded George's presence at the house on the night to avoid dragging his son into the affair, despite his potential to corroborate Patrick's story.

'I think we should sit down and talk about this,' Hughes said, slumping into a chair. 'You realise that if you go to the police your story will seriously interfere with our operation in Neu Pommern.'

'I know that,' Patrick said. 'If it was not for the fact that the mission is underway I would have gone to the police already and expected to be cleared of any charge of murder.'

'Did not your own father face a similar situation back in the sixties in Sydney?' the British officer asked.

'Do you know, John,' Patrick said, taking a chair and crossing his leg, 'there is a family story that an old Aboriginal curse dogs the Macintosh and Duffy bloodlines. When I look at what is happening to my own family I can understand why my grandmother died believing we were cursed for killing the Aboriginals who used to roam the Glen View lands. It is as if history is repeating itself and I do not know why we deserve this.'

'Poppycock,' Hughes said. 'That is all superstitious nonsense and you are a modern man. We both know that there are no such things as blackfella curses. I also believe you when you say you have kept quiet to protect our operation and so what you have confessed to me tonight will be forgotten. It will be up to you to decide what to do when the mission is over. Your secret is safe with me. We have soldiered through too many campaigns not to trust each other.'

'Thank you, John,' Patrick said, rising from his chair and extending his hand to his friend and superior. 'Our priority is to complete the operation and get the boys back safely. I will ensure that my daughter receives the very best counsel money can buy and that she is found not guilty, should the matter go before a jury.'

Hughes watched the Australian officer depart. He knew emotional pain when he saw it. He'd seen that kind of pain on the faces of young officers leading platoons and losing men they were responsible for in battle. That was the pain in the face of his friend.

Alex, Matthew and Bob had been treated with the utmost of hospitality while ashore and had been billeted with the families of their German hosts at Hauptmann Hirsch's insistence. Each day the three from Australia would meet at the Rabaul Club and breakfast on a fine meal before seeking out possible trade contracts with planters who, with the assistance of those they met in the club, they had arranged to meet. The offers Alex made were genuine. He was now experienced at trading negotiations and his excellent grasp of the German language helped him establish contacts for future deals.

Matthew made himself useful by spending the

days wandering around the German settlement, observing all that he could in the eventuality that the township may have to be taken by force of arms. He carried in his head dispositions of armed institutions, such as the constabulary and reservist depots. He was careful not to engage the colonial reservist officers in conversations concerning their armed forces, lest that attract attention but, even so, Matthew had the feeling his and Bob's movements around the settlement were always under scrutiny.

On the morning of the fourth day the three men met to prepare for their embarkation on the ship in the harbour. Aware that they were leaving Dieter Hirsch made a point of walking with them to the wharf where a longboat from the Macintosh ship was waiting for them.

'Well, my friends, I will be sad to see you leave us so soon,' Dieter said, shaking each man's hand. 'I hope that we may see you again.'

The three Australians agreed that they would like to once again enjoy the hospitality of the Rabaul Club and its members.

Pushing off in the boat, Matthew and Bob rowed while Alex took the rudder. The waters were calm and within minutes they reached the side of the ship. The chief engineer greeted them from the deck and called the crew to assist with the bringing aboard of the longboat using the davits affixed for cargo.

Alex, Matthew and Bob clambered up a rope ladder thrown to them.

'Welcome aboard, Mr Macintosh,' Jock McLeod greeted with a slap on his boss's back. The Scot's grin spread across his ruddy face. 'We dinna have fun and games while you were ashore with the ladies drinkin' an carousin''.

'What do you mean?' Alex asked as Matthew climbed aboard behind him.

'The wee ladies from the German Customs and some soldier lads did pay us a visit yesterday afternoon,' Jock replied. 'They ordered the captain and all of us to go to the mess with all our papers. They held us there for some time before they left.'

'A bit out of sorts for the Customs people to carry out their duties when we have been in port for at least three days,' Alex puzzled. 'I thought they would do that the first day we anchored.'

'Well, they did,' Jock replied. 'I thought it was a wee bit strange to have us muster in the mess when they could have done the same on the bridge. They were adamant that we were all together – all the crew.'

Alex shrugged. It did seem a bit suspicious but he dismissed the variation from routine as a consequence of the tensions arising from the current world situation in far-off Europe. 'I will speak with the captain,' Alex said. 'In the meantime, do we have a brew going in the galley?'

'That we do,' Jock replied and wandered bow-legged towards a steel door.

'What was that about Customs?' Matthew asked.

'Just a bit strange the way they went about a routine inspection,' Alex replied. 'I don't think it's anything to be concerned about. After all, you can see how friendly they were to us ashore and in an hour we will be steaming out of here and returning to the Schumann plantation to put stage two of the operation into place.'

'Okay,' Matthew replied, satisfied that Alex knew what he was doing. He had to agree that everything was going to plan. Within weeks they would have completed their mission and be returning home. Matthew glanced over at the volcano that cast its ominous shadow over the German settlement. He had to admit that every day he awoke on the covert operation he experienced the same pangs of fear he'd known as a soldier in South Africa fourteen years earlier. Sometimes the waiting for something to happen sharpened an already stretched imagination. Was it that the Germans were just leading them on, and that they were walking into an ambush? Matthew had a healthy respect for his adversaries. Something did not smell right.

19

Sean Duffy had been able to convince the American authorities to release Fenella on a substantial bail while she awaited transportation back to Sydney. His telegram to the Macintosh office in Sydney had been transmitted courtesy of the Macintosh agency office in Hawaii. The agent had arranged for Fenella to be put up at one of the best hotels in the Hawaiian capital and Sean had visited her every day, dining with her at night and discussing her situation. To all intents and purposes they could have been on a wonderful tropical vacation – except Fenella was forced to report her whereabouts each day to the police.

They sat on a balcony overlooking the beach waiting for the main course to be served. A gentle breeze stirred the candle flames on the table and the moon slid from behind a bank of dark clouds lighting up the sea with silver.

'I am grateful for all you have done,' Fenella said, gazing across the dining patio to the shimmering ocean. 'I only wish that my family had not learned of my predicament.'

Sean felt a little awkward. He had taken it upon himself to send telegrams informing his distant relative of his daughter's whereabouts. 'It was only inevitable your father would learn of your situation, considering that you had been taken into custody,' he answered in his defence. 'Knowing your father's rather fierce reputation I believe he will be of considerable help to us . . . you, when you have been returned.'

'Do you truly believe that I am innocent of the charge the police wish to level against me?' Fenella asked, turning to gaze directly into Sean's eyes.

'I do,' Sean replied. 'Don't ask me why, but I do believe that you are innocent of the charge.'

'That is very important to me,' Fenella said, reaching across the table and taking his hand. 'I don't know how I would have coped under the current circumstances, and you have proved to be a true friend.'

Sean was disappointed in her words. He had hoped that she might see him as something more than just a friend to her. It was becoming obvious that there was something Fenella had not told him and he felt the sickening pangs of jealousy. There had to be someone else in her life, he brooded, holding her hand without much enthusiasm. 'I think you know how I feel about you,' he said quietly as Fenella slowly withdrew her hand.

'Right now I cannot entertain your thoughts

about me nor return to Sydney,' Fenella said in a whisper, as if thinking out aloud.

'Why?' Sean asked with a frown. 'You will be able to clear your name of the charge and be home for the release of your latest film.'

'The film does not matter,' Fenella replied. 'But the shame I seem to constantly bring on my father does.'

'I am sure that he is totally convinced of your innocence,' Sean said. 'And he must be worried sick about your unheralded exit from Sydney. Already he has cabled to say that he has employed the services of my uncle's firm to provide for your defence. I can proudly say that they have a reputation second to none for criminal defence matters. We always win, which reminds me that I must leave on the next ship to San Francisco if I am to complete my original duty to the firm.'

'I will miss your company and conversation,' Fenella said with a sad smile.

'Tonight we shall dine and I will raise a toast to your gleaming future,' Sean countered with a warm smile.

Despite his assurances the evening passed with the couple in a sombre mood.

Sean found himself occupied with legal matters and business the next day meaning he was unable to visit Fenella. He did leave a note at her hotel to arrange a final evening together before they parted company. However, when he returned to his hotel that evening to prepare for his meeting with Fenella at her hotel he was surprised by the appearance of the tough American police detective who had arrested Fenella. The man was waiting in the foyer and from the scowl on his face Sean immediately knew that the American was angry.

'Mr Duffy,' the detective said, approaching Sean. 'You wouldn't happen to know of the whereabouts of that Macintosh dame you got out on bail, would you?'

Stunned, Sean was at a loss for an answer. What in hell did the detective mean?

'Maybe you can explain this,' the detective said, thrusting a sheet of paper under the young Australian lawyer's nose. Sean scanned the few words written in Fenella's copperplate hand.

> *I am sorry, Sean, but I must do what I can to avoid bringing shame on my father's good name. I pray that you will understand.*
> *Your grateful friend,*
> *Fenella Macintosh*

'It was left at the counter of Miss Macintosh's hotel when we went in search of her to find out why she had not reported in,' the detective said when he was sure that Sean had read the note. 'Maybe you can tell us what it means.'

'I am as much at a loss to explain what it means as are you,' Sean spluttered. 'I have no idea of where Miss Macintosh may be located.'

The detective stood facing the young man almost nose to nose, trying to intimidate him. Sean did not back down and eventually the American police officer realised that this man would not be easily browbeaten. He was, after all, a goddamned lawyer.

'If you get to hear anything about her whereabouts,' Devine said, 'be sure to inform us. You are, after all, an officer of your legal system and duty bound to work within the law. It ain't wise around these parts to cross me.'

The detective turned and walked away, leaving Sean mystified. A thousand thoughts swirled through his mind. Had Fenella done something drastic and taken her own life? This was the most disturbing thought. Or had the American authorities underestimated the abilities of the daughter of Colonel Duffy to elude them? He prayed that it was the latter, but knew now that Fenella would not attempt to make contact. Sean uttered an obscenity under his breath. He would have to carefully compose and cable Sydney with the news that Fenella had once again disappeared. He only prayed that she was still alive. After all, there was a rumour that Fenella's mother had taken her own life so many years earlier.

Matthew Duffy could not shake the dream. He tossed and turned in his cramped bunk as the *Osprey II* ploughed through the tropical Solomon Sea. The sky was dark, a storm threatening. Old Wallarie was in his head and Matthew had flashes of an ancient ochre painting of a warrior with raised spear. Wallarie was trying to tell him something and Matthew awoke, bathed in a sheen of sweat. In the dark confines of his tiny cabin he could hear the ship's metal creaking around him, and the constant thump, thump, of the engines below. Easing himself from the bunk he stood uncertainly as the ship rolled and pitched in the rising seas. He placed his hand against the bulkhead to steady himself and pushed at the cabin door which swung open. Half-dressed in his shorts, Matthew made his way to the deck where he was surprised to see Alex standing at the bow, silhouetted against the night sky.

'You couldn't sleep either,' Alex said when Matthew joined him. The wind moaned around them and the freedom of the open deck was a welcome change from the stifling heat in the cabin.

'Bad dreams,' Matthew muttered. 'I suppose you are thinking about reaching the plantation in the morning and getting to see the love of your life.'

'Yeah,' Alex answered. 'That, and the second stage of our mission. Did you ever experience that kind of fear that causes your stomach to churn?'

'Funny question,' Matthew answered. 'Why do you ask?'

Alex continued to stare at the darkness of the cloud-covered night sky above and dark waters below. 'I have always envied the fact that you served in South Africa and saw action. I am an officer in my father's regiment and have seen nothing of war. I suppose I will always wonder how I would perform leading men under fire. Now we have this mission ahead of us and all I feel is fear.'

'I was always scared out of my wits when the Boers were taking pot shots at us at the river,' Matthew answered. 'But it was even worse when they rained their artillery down on us. The shells going off all around started to send me mad with terror. I was so frightened I made sure I kept my head down. Every sane man experiences fear but few are prepared to admit the truth of their emotions. Even now I am feeling utter fear for what lays ahead. I think the unknown does that to us.'

'Thank you, Matt,' Alex said. 'I thought I was alone.'

Matthew slapped his cousin on the back. 'No, old chap, even our New Zealander cousin has admitted the terror he felt out on the veldt when we served in the Transvaal. We will get through this. You will elope with the beautiful young lady you have met, and Bob and I will be at your wedding in Sydney.'

'How the dickens did you know I was entertaining the thought of eloping with Giselle?' Alex asked in surprise.

'I just think that it is in that Irish blood of yours – that you deny to yourself – to consider the option given you are thwarted by her stubborn German father,' Matthew grinned at his cousin. 'Anyway, it is something I would do in your situation and I don't think that we are much unalike from what I have learned about you on this mission.'

'We have a job to do, first,' Alex said. 'Then I will broach the subject with Giselle.'

A silence followed, the two men gazing out at the swirling sky and rising sea. Behind them the lights on the bridge burned dimly as the chief engineer steered the ship west into a choppy sea. Wallarie's presence haunted Matthew – even so far from the cave – and he closed his eyes, thinking hard on what the message might mean.

'Bloody hell!' Matthew swore, opening his eyes.

'What is it?' Alex asked, alarmed by his cousin's sudden exclamation.

'I think that we are in great danger,' Matthew said, turning away from the bow rail. 'You and I should have an urgent talk with Jock.'

Alex followed his cousin across the rolling deck to the bridge. They climbed a metal ladder and opened the door. Stepping inside they found the Scottish engineer at the ship's wheel.

'Come to spend some time on the bridge?' Jock asked cheerily. 'I could do with the company.'

'Mr McLeod,' Matthew said, 'what do you remember about the visit you got from the Customs people back in Rabaul a few days back?'

Jock looked at Matthew with an expression of surprise. 'Not much,' he answered. 'Just that they herded us all into the mess like I told you when you came aboard in Rabaul.'

'Did you see the Customs boat when it approached the ship?' Matthew persisted.

'I did that, laddie,' the engineer replied. 'Come to think of it,' he continued, 'it was a bit unusual because I remember seeing a couple of German soldiers in the boat – or they might have been marines. They looked like they were guarding a large wooden crate. I just got the feeling that they a bit anxious about the big crate in the boat.'

Matthew's expression tensed. 'Did you see the

boat return to the shore with the Customs people?' he asked.

'We were allowed to leave the mess when the Customs were finished with us,' Jock answered. 'I saw them motor away. There was nothing un . . . the crate was gone! It wasn't in the boat anymore!'

Listening to the conversation between his engineer and cousin Alex had been at a loss to understand where Matthew was going with his line of questioning, but suddenly the Scot had comprehended what Matthew was leading to.

'You canna be thinking that the Germans have planted a bomb aboard the ship,' Jock gasped.

'I don't bloody well know,' Matthew replied in exasperation, for nothing but a bad dream without a clear message had prompted the interrogation of the ship's engineer.

'We must organise a search,' Alex said. 'I will wake the captain and inform him of our suspicions.'

Matthew glanced at his cousin. Alex had the aptitude for quick judgement and an equally fast response to any situation. He was a good leader.

The captain was shaken awake and he listened intently, as Matthew explained that he thought it would be wise to immediately conduct a search of the ship. Alex reinforced the request by having the rest of the crew, mostly Indian and Malay deckhands, gather in the mess cabin. Once they were briefed a systematic search was put into place.

The first place the engineer suggested they search was down in the engine room where any explosive device might do the most damage. Jock, Bob,

Matthew and Alex clambered into the confined space. The stokers, bathed in sweat, continued to shovel coal into the great furnace that provided heat for the steam engines thereby creating the power to turn the great shaft of the ship's propeller. It was Bob who found the device near the end of the shaft housing.

'Down here,' he hollered so as to be heard above the noise.

The others scrambled into the cramped space between the engines, getting covered in oil and sweat.

'It's not something meant to be here,' Jock said, squatting over the black metal ball with a height just above his knees. Affixed to the sinister sphere were gauges and wires.

'What do you think?' Alex asked over the engineer's shoulder.

'I would be thinking it is some kind of naval mine that has been modified,' Matthew said, recognising the deadly explosive he had seen in his travels to war zones. 'Probably has a timing device attached, designed to go off before we reach the Schumann plantation.'

Wide-eyed, Bob glanced at Matthew. 'As we are due to anchor tomorrow that means it is about to explode.'

'What are our options?' Matthew asked, looking to Alex.

'We only have one option,' Alex answered. 'We have to somehow render the mine harmless – we have to disarm it.'

'Anyone here disarmed a mine before?' Matthew asked, not really expecting a reply in the affirmative.

'Maybe I could have a go,' the New Zealander said quietly. 'I have a fair bit of experience with the mechanics of cameras, and from what I can see of this thing it has a bit in common with some of those.'

'I can help you,' Jock volunteered. 'It might take an engineer to give assistance taking the wee beastie apart.'

Alex wiped at his face with the back of his hand to clear away the sweat dripping into his eyes. It was hot and stifling jammed into the stern of the ship's engine room. 'I will inform the captain to get all the crew to muster at the bow away from the mine while Jock and Bob have a go disarming it.'

Matthew understood why the young militia officer had so readily agreed to Jock and Bob volunteering without protesting about the danger they would be in. He was the leader of the mission and as such understood that men's lives might have to be sacrificed for the greater goal of completing the covert operation.

'I'll shout you both a cold beer as soon as we get back to Sydney,' Matthew said, slapping Jock on the back as he squatted, peering intently at the tangle of wires. 'Just don't take any bloody stupid chances. If you feel that it is too dangerous to take this bastard apart head straight for the upper deck and we will consider abandoning the ship.'

Bob nodded and, with a grim smile, turned to his friend. 'You see, it takes a New Zealander to show you Australian bastards how to get out of trouble. I will take you up on your shout.'

'Take care, Jock,' Alex said to his engineer and

friend. 'The same goes from me. Any sign of trouble, leg it to the deck.'

Alex stood down the stokers and ordered them above. He found the captain in the cargo hold with two deckhands searching through the piles of wooden crates with torches. Alex briefed him on the situation, and the captain passed an order for all crew to assemble on the forward deck.

The frightened men huddled against the rising seas, waves crashing over them in great sprays of salty water while the captain remained on the bridge, guiding his ship skilfully through the tropical storm. Alex and Matthew said little. Alex wondered how time could just seem to stand still as they waited for the two men from below to come up and tell them everything was in hand. The ship's single lifeboat was large enough to carry them all and had already been swung out in the event that it would have to be used. Alex hoped that they would not have to resort to it in the heavy seas. Although he was not particularly religious, he prayed with all the conviction he could muster that the men below would disarm the mine. As if answering his prayer, he saw Jock's head appear through a hatchway. A wide grin spread over his face as he waved a jumble of wires over his head.

'God almighty!' Matthew exclaimed in his relief. 'They did it!'

Jock scrambled out of the hatch and walked unsteadily towards them. Behind him, Bob Houston's head appeared as he clambered up from below.

'We beat the wee beastie,' Jock shouted victoriously. 'It had a timing device we . . .'

His words were never completed. Simultaneously the men at the bow felt the deck shudder under their feet and heard the ear-splitting explosion of metal and timber tearing apart in the bowels of the ship. In a split second Alex realised that a second mine must have been planted in case the first failed to explode. The heat and shock of the blast hurled him off his feet and he was thrown violently through the air and into the raging sea below.

She was not a pretty sight as she rocked at her moorings in a dock in Sydney's harbour. Rivulets of rust ran down her hull like dried blood from a wounded animal, but the Macintosh ship was due to steam out of the harbour at first light.

In the early morning chill Randolph Gates lit a cigar. He was standing alone on the wharf with his swag at his feet, awaiting permission to board. Only a few hours before he had been lying on his bed in the hotel room when he received the call. At the other end of the telephone had been Patrick Duffy briefing him on Fenella's disappearance in Hawaii and the colonel's urgent request that Randolph take a berth on a Macintosh steamer heading for the Pacific islands.

Hasty arrangements had been made to finance the American in his search and the berth booked. Randolph did not hesitate in accepting the task, packed his few belongings and made his way to the moored ship.

As Randolph puffed on his cigar, he became aware

that a man huddled against the chill was approaching him along the dimly lit timbered wharf. When the man was a few feet away Randolph recognised him as Arthur Thorncroft.

'I didn't want you to leave without a farewell party,' Arthur said, producing a silver hip flask.

Randolph accepted the gesture and took a swig of what proved to be gin. He passed the flask back to Arthur. 'How did you know I was leaving?'

'Patrick telephoned me,' Arthur replied, swigging from the flask. 'He told me that you would be away for some time and not available at the studio. He was kind enough to tell me when you would be leaving and from where.'

Randolph gazed at the ship. 'I suppose you have heard how Nellie was located in Hawaii and has again disappeared,' Randolph said quietly. 'I guess the colonel suspects that she may have done something terrible to herself.'

Arthur shook his head. 'I don't think so,' he said with a sigh. 'Patrick is still haunted by the death of Nellie's mother. I have known him for many years and feel that my friend is at the end of his tether. I fear more for his welfare than that of Nellie, who I know is a strong and very capable young woman. She would never consider harming herself, no matter how bad the situation became. No, I suspect that my Nellie has simply slipped from the hands of the Yank police.'

'I think so too,' Randolph responded.

'I have to make a confession,' Arthur said, staring at the ship. 'I knew about Nellie skipping Sydney as she came to see me on the eve of her departure. I helped her with papers for her visit to the USA. At the time of our meeting neither of us were aware that Guy had been killed. Nellie is innocent of what the police here want to charge her with.'

'God damn it!' Randolph exploded. 'Why didn't you tell me? You must know how I feel about her. I would have kept your confidence.'

'She is pregnant,' Arthur said. 'You did not know?'

For a moment Randolph was at a loss for words. 'No one told me,' he said in a strangled voice.

'I am sorry,' Arthur said. 'She told me it was Guy's baby, and that she was leaving so as not to bring shame on the family. I also think she ran away because she did not want you to know she was carrying another man's child – and not just on account of the scandal she thought might be brought down on her father's name.'

'I wouldn't have cared that she was carrying Wilkes' child,' Randolph said, but knew inwardly it had torn at him as a betrayal of love.

'She fell pregnant to Wilkes before she met you,' Arthur said as if anticipating the tall American's feelings. 'But she is a woman who puts great stock in life and felt that she must go away to have her child. What she planned after that . . . I do not know.'

'Have you been in correspondence with Nellie since she left?' Randolph asked, attempting to put his pain aside.

'No, nothing since our meeting,' Arthur answered. 'But I may have information that might help you find her – if she has somehow escaped to the USA.'

'Anything,' Randolph said.

'I gave her papers to give to a friend I have in the industry in California,' he said. 'She was hoping to have an introduction into their studios when she arrived. She was travelling under the name of Fiona Owens. Don't ask me how she organised her documents but she had them. If you do not locate her in Hawaii I would strongly suggest that you continue on to California and go to Los Angeles and look up my friend there. It's the place they appear to be making most of their films out of these days.'

Randolph pocketed the paper with the contact details Arthur had given him just as he heard his name called from the deck of the ship. He turned to Arthur, extending his hand. 'Thanks for the information,' Randolph said.

'I wish that things could have worked out a little better than they have for you and Nellie,' Arthur replied sadly, shaking his hand. 'Just find her and bring her home. She means a lot to more people than just her father and brothers.'

'I know,' Randolph said, bending to shoulder his swag. 'Take care, Arthur,' he said, preparing to walk to the gangplank up to the ship's deck. 'Your secret is safe with me.'

Arthur nodded gratefully. It had eaten away at him that he had sworn not to tell his friend, Patrick Duffy, what he knew of his daughter's disappearance. At least now one other he could trust knew the truth. As he turned to walk away he could hear the coal-fired engines of the ship thump into life. Arthur felt like the loneliest man on earth.

20

Matthew had just the vaguest impression that he had seen Bob Houston's body shredded into pieces when the explosion went off below. Much of the shock wave had exited itself through the hatch that Bob had been climbing through and his body had taken the full impact of the blast.

Matthew found himself slammed against the railing and fought to remain conscious. His hearing had turned to a ringing in his ears, and as he slid into a sitting position, he could taste blood in his mouth. The light from the bridge was still on, casting enough illumination on the deck below for Matthew to see the Scottish engineer attempting to rise to his feet. Blood poured down his legs and when Jock McLeod turned away Matthew could see that the man had terrible injuries, probably caused by flying metal. Matthew had seen shrapnel wounds before and knew that Jock required urgent medical treatment if he were to live. Staggering to his feet he stumbled towards the engineer who was in a state of shock. Matthew could hear the screams of other wounded crew members who had taken the brunt of the explosion.

'Jock,' Matthew shouted at the wounded man, 'you have to sit down and let me fix you.'

The tough Scotsman heeded Matthew's order and buried his head between his knees. Matthew tore his shirt off and quickly ripped it into bandage strips to stem the bleeding on Jock's lacerated back. Then he glanced around to try to locate Alex. The ship was listing to one side and with its engines silent wallowed helplessly. The captain appeared on the deck beside Matthew.

'Mr Macintosh went over the side,' he shouted at Matthew. Already the captain was holding a lifebuoy and peering over the railing into the dark, rolling sea. 'Mr Macintosh!' he roared at the top of his voice. But to Matthew it sounded almost a whisper. 'Mr Macintosh!'

Satisfied that he had done as much as he could for the engineer, Matthew turned his attention to the wounded crew members.

'I see him,' Matthew heard the captain call and Matthew immediately looked to the railing, where the captain was leaning towards the sea with the lifebuoy in hand. With some difficulty Matthew staggered along the listing deck to the railing. He peered over. For a second he thought that he saw something in the water.

'Give me the buoy,' he shouted to the captain who passed it to him. Matthew took the buoy and, without hesitating, leaped from the deck into the sea. He hit the surface with a splash and with one arm commenced swimming in the direction that he had last seen what he thought was Alex. Matthew was a strong swimmer and was rewarded for his efforts by reaching his cousin within seconds. He reached out and gripped Alex by the hair, rolling him as best as he could onto his back. Alex struggled weakly, gasping for air and vomiting sea water. Matthew thrust the lifebuoy between them.

'Get a hold of this,' he said to Alex who responded by grasping one side of the flotation device.

'I'm okay,' Alex spluttered as a great wave swept them upwards only to thrust them down into a trough, obliterating the ship from sight. 'That you, Matt?' he asked.

'Yeah,' Matthew answered. 'We have to get back to the ship, so start swimming.'

On the deck the captain knew his ship was taking in water at a faster rate than any of his sea pumps were capable of dealing with. He had watched as Matthew Duffy dived into the ocean with the lifebuoy and now he could only return his attention to the welfare of his crew.

'Mr McLeod,' he called to Jock who was attempting to regain his footing. 'Organise to get the lifeboat over the side and get the crew in it.'

Jock looked at the lifeboat which was now dangling against the side of the ship. It had been a good decision to have it swung out in anticipation of an emergency.

'All you heathens get into the boat,' Jock barked

at the frightened crew members who did not need a second warning to abandon ship. They scrambled up the tilting deck to the side and slid over into the dangling lifeboat.

'You coming, Captain?' Jock called to Ernest Delamore who was making his way like a crab on sand towards the stairs to the bridge.

'As soon as I get a distress call off,' he called back to Jock. 'Just get the boat adrift with yourself and crew, Mr McLeod.'

Jock turned to claw his way up the sharply sloping deck towards where the lifeboat dangled against the ship's hull. When he reached the railing he clambered over painfully and with some difficulty slid down the hull and into the lifeboat, slamming into an unlucky crew member.

'Cut the ropes,' he bellowed to a sailor who swung a hatchet at the lines securing the boat to the ship.

With a heavy jerk, one side of the boat collapsed, hurling all its occupants into the water. The second rope gave way, bringing the boat down on the men floundering below, killing one of them with its heavy weight as it smashed into the sea, bobbed and then crashed against the hull, revealing the exposed keel. Jock felt the captain had little hope of joining them in the lifeboat. The ship groaned and creaked, keeling over to begin settling into a death dive below the waves.

Matthew stopped swimming when he saw the ship keel over. He calculated that he and Alex had been washed a good hundred yards away from the stricken vessel by the heavy seas but now the little light they had to guide them had disappeared, leaving them alone in a dark and angry ocean.

'She's gone,' Alex gasped weakly, hugging the lifebuoy.

Matthew did not respond. The pain from the injury he received when he had been thrown backwards was now making itself known.

'Thanks, cobber,' he heard Alex say. 'Thanks for coming after me.'

Matthew ignored his cousin's gratitude. Perhaps it would have been better if they both had suffered the same fate as their New Zealander friend – one minute alive and within a split second obliterated. As far as Matthew knew, no radio call had been made regarding their situation and they were now adrift in seas infamous for the sharks patrolling the channels. That could possibly be a better death than dying of thirst, Matthew thought grimly.

'Anytime, old chap,' Matthew finally answered. 'Just hope that you are a good swimmer and know which way is west.'

The rain came in a tropical squall and then the sun over a suddenly placid and warm sea. When Matthew and Alex gazed around all they could see was ocean. They were well and truly alone. There was no sign of the rest of the crew – nor the ship's lifeboat. Then they spotted the first fin slicing through the water towards them.

Angus MacDonald awoke Patrick and summoned him to the telephone.

'Colonel Duffy,' Patrick said, accepting the call.

'Patrick, I have some disturbing news,' John Hughes said. 'A radio station up north picked up an SOS from your ship. Not all the message got through but from what could be ascertained the captain was able to give his position and say that the ship was sinking rapidly, that they had lost at least two men. He transmitted that an explosion had holed her and then the communications with her were lost. That was about two o'clock our time last night. I have contacted the navy and requested their nearest ship make haste to the last reported position to see if survivors could be found.'

'What was her last position?' Patrick asked.

'From what I could see on the charts she was just off the Schumann plantation. At least that is a good thing.'

'You don't know who the dead were?' Patrick asked, feeling a tightness in his chest.

'I'm sorry,' Hughes replied. 'Not at this stage.'

'I will get dressed and see you at the barracks,' Patrick concluded. 'I feel that the Germans were somehow behind her sinking.'

Patrick returned the telephone to Angus who stared at his boss intently. 'I gather we have bad news about Captain Macintosh, sir,' he said sympathetically.

'I'm not sure, Angus,' Patrick answered. 'We will have to wait for developments.'

Angus nodded his head. He was not a praying man but he prayed that the young militia officer was safe and well. The colonel had suffered enough for one man.

★

The black fin drew closer and it was followed by many others. Both men clinging to the lifebuoy braced themselves for the inevitable attack.

'A bloody dolphin!' Matthew burst into laughter. 'Wallarie has sent a fish to guard us.'

'It's not a fish,' Alex rebuked. 'The dolphin is a mammal – and what do you mean about Wallarie sending us a guardian?'

'You must know the stories about the old Nerambura warrior,' Matthew said, relieved at the presence of the guardians of stranded sailors now circling them. 'It was he who warned me of the danger and now he is continuing to protect us.'

Alex shook his head. 'I find that a bit hard to swallow, old chap,' he scoffed. 'I thought that the old bugger was long dead.'

'I made a visit to him some weeks ago when I was up in Queensland,' Matthew replied. 'I was able to visit him at the cave.'

'You really believe that Wallarie has magical powers?' Alex quizzed.

'I know it may sound like lunacy but there are some strange things in this world that we do not understand,' Matthew replied. 'Just say that Wallarie can be both a guardian angel and an avenging demon – depending on the orders he receives from his ancestor spirits.'

Alex did not pursue the subject and the two men watched as the dolphins rolled and turned playfully in the clear tropical waters around them.

They had scanned the surrounding sea for any sign of the rest of the ship's crew but had been unsuccessful. The heavy seas the night before had swept them apart and they had no way of telling if the crew had been successful in abandoning the sinking ship as the lifeboat had been on the opposite side of the hull to where they had been in the water.

'Look at that and tell me I am not dreaming,' Matthew suddenly said. Alex turned his gaze in the direction his cousin had indicated.

'I see it,' he said excitedly. 'It looks like land on the horizon. And the current is taking us in.'

'Time to start swimming,' Matthew said, kicking out in the direction of the bobbing strip of green they could see.

Escorted by the pod of dolphins, it took them the better part of the day to reach the beach. Exhausted, dehydrated and burned by the sun they crawled ashore. Grateful to be alive, both men lay on the hot sand, attempting to regain their strength.

Matthew heard the soft clop, clop, of a horse's hooves on the sandy beach. Someone had found them! Now they would have some desperately needed water. With a great effort, Matthew raised himself onto his knees. Behind the approaching horseman trotted three Melanesian workers carrying machetes. Matthew recognised the horseman immediately as being the foreman from the Schumann plantation and raised his hand to wave. 'We are truly saved,' he croaked to Alex who lifted his head to observe the party of men.

The German plantation foreman brought his mount to a halt a few yards away, dismounted and drew a carbine from the scabbard attached to the saddle. Alex and Matthew watched in amazement as he levelled the rifle at them.

'You are not to attempt to escape,' he snarled. 'You treacherous English are my prisoners.'

Alex rose unsteadily to his feet. 'Could we have some water?' he asked.

The foreman said something to the man nearest him who fetched a water canteen from the saddle attachments and handed it to Alex who immediately passed it to Matthew. Matthew took a long swig before passing the canteen back to Alex.

'Our ship has been sunk and I do not understand why we should be considered prisoners,' Alex said, handing the water bottle back to the plantation worker.

'Your plot to carry out subversive activities against the Kaiser has been revealed,' Schmidt replied. 'Your aeroplane has been destroyed.'

Matthew understood enough to realise that his aircraft had been destroyed and felt a rage building inside him. 'The bastards,' he growled in English.

Sensing his cousin's anger, Alex placed a hand on his shoulder to calm him.

'I do not know what you are talking about,' Alex continued calmly. 'The aircraft was not intended for anything subversive. We were going to see if we could use it to fly between islands seeking trade.' He knew his story was flimsy but it was the best he could think of, staring as he was into the barrel of a rifle.

'We received orders from Rabaul that your aircraft was to be destroyed,' Schmidt said. 'The orders came from our administration.'

'I demand that we are taken to Herr Schumann to sort out this misunderstanding,' Alex said, controlling his anger. 'You have no right to hold Australian citizens as your prisoners.'

'Just in case you are not aware,' Schmidt responded with a crooked smile, 'you are on German soil and subject to the Kaiser's law.'

'I still demand to speak with Herr Schumann,' Alex continued. 'I am sure that he would be enraged to hear of your treatment of us.'

'Herr Schumann sent me when you were spotted by one of our workers attempting to get ashore,' Schmidt explained. 'He gave me orders that you were to be apprehended and treated as spies. You will be handed over to our military as soon as they are able to come here and take you off our hands. In the meantime, Herr Schumann has told me that you are to be shot if you should consider any attempt to escape. I hope you understand what I am telling you.'

'I understand,' Alex replied. 'But I would still like to speak with Herr Schumann.'

'When you are secured I will see if Herr Schumann wishes to speak with you,' Schmidt replied. 'Now, you can march up the beach to the plantation.'

Alex and Matthew obeyed. They had little choice, being on German territory and a long way from home. How had it all gone so wrong? Alex asked himself. Worse still, if she was aware that he was a prisoner of her father, what was going through Giselle's mind?

★

'Well, we have some good news,' John Hughes said, gazing at the large map on his office wall depicting the German territories in the Pacific.

Patrick stood behind him, dressed in his military uniform. He had read the report cabled in code from a northern radio station and received by the British intelligence officer. 'It makes no mention that my son and Matthew were among the survivors,' Patrick said. 'Only that they were last seen in the water.'

'Your engineer was badly wounded,' Hughes said. 'He was a bit vague about everything that occurred after the German mine went off aboard the ship. I know it's hard, Patrick, but do not give up hope. The ship went down practically off the Schumann plantation and they may have been found by a native outrigger. After all, it was a coastal trader that located the ship's lifeboat and all the surviving crew members with the exception of the captain, Alex and Matthew. What's to say that the three are not already found but we have not yet been informed.'

Patrick stared at his friend and then the map on the wall. 'I pray you are right,' he said.

John Hughes turned to Patrick and gestured for him to take a chair. 'We are in a bit of a political pickle,' he said. 'We cannot accuse the Germans of sabotaging your ship because we know that they will most probably counter with an accusation of us spying. It is obvious that the leak here, in Sydney, has kept them up to date on our every move. With the way things are going in Europe the subject is very touchy. I am to prepare a report for your Prime Minister and am in a dilemma as to how much I include about the whole operation. You realise that politicians will put their interests before the security of the country if it means votes and leave you and me out to dangle as renegade military men acting without orders.'

Patrick tended to agree with the British officer. 'What happens now?' he asked. 'To all intents and purposes the mission has failed and it may have cost me a son.'

'I think that we are left only with the choice of trying to find Alex, Matthew and Captain Delamore,' Hughes replied. 'As far as I am concerned, the operation is now called off and I will use everything within my power to bring the boys home safely. I promise you that, Patrick.'

Matthew and Alex were immediately secured in a storage room within one of the large sheds at the plantation. They were not mistreated and in the evening a good meal was brought to them by one of the housemaids, but a fierce-looking worker with a rifle had been posted at the entrance to ensure that they did not attempt to escape when the door was opened.

'I want to see Herr Schumann,' Alex said to the girl. He figured she was around fifteen years of age but she shook her head, not comprehending English. Alex tried again, this time in German. But he received the same response and the girl left.

'It's bloody obvious that your future father-in-law is not very happy with us,' Matthew said, scooping a spoonful of pork and cabbage from his tin plate.

'I just wonder what in hell they have specifically planned for us.'

'I suspect that Schumann has notified their government in Neu Pommern that he has us in custody,' Alex replied, wiping the sweat from his face with the sleeve of his shirt. 'No doubt they will send someone to take us back to Rabaul and who knows what will happen after that.'

'Maybe a quick trial followed by a slow drum roll and a firing squad,' Matthew said with a wry grin. 'But be assured that you will probably get full military honours because you are a commissioned officer.'

'I doubt that the Germans would try us as spies,' Alex said, but without much conviction. 'It would cause too much of a political rift between Australia and Germany. Maybe they'll just ship us home with orders never to return to German territory.'

'If they were prepared to blow us up at sea I don't think that they really want us around to talk,' Matthew countered. 'Think about it.'

Alex settled himself against a pile of hessian bags. 'I just don't understand why Giselle has not at least come to see me,' he sighed. 'She must have heard that we are here.'

Matthew did not comment. He had already considered that the love of Alex's life would now see Alex in a different light. He had not informed her of the contents of the crates when they were brought ashore to be stored and no doubt she felt betrayed by the fact – not as a German citizen but as a woman who expected to be told everything. Alex did not know as much about the complex thought processes of women as he might think, Matthew mused, relishing the pork in its rich stew. He smiled, catching Alex's attention.

'What's funny?' Alex asked.

'Nothing much,' Matthew replied, putting his plate aside. 'I was just thinking of a Yank story about an Indian princess called Pocahontas, and how she saved Captain Smith from the wrath of her father.'

Alex shook his head. 'What's that got to do with our current situation?'

'Nothing, I suppose,' Matthew shrugged. 'I think that we should get a good night's sleep before tomorrow. It's been a long and eventful day.'

Alex watched as Matthew made a crude bed out of hessian bags, curled up and dropped into a peaceful sleep. Alex was not afraid of what they might have to deal with when the sun rose but he was in emotional agony because Giselle had made no attempt to contact him. His despair was more painful than even the thought of being executed. It was a terrible feeling that kept him awake until sheer exhaustion caused him to slip into a troubled sleep.

Before sunrise, the door clattered open, waking both men.

'Good morning, gentlemen,' Schumann greeted in a less than friendly tone. Beside him stood his foreman with his carbine.

Both men rose into a sitting position, blinking away the night's sleep from their eyes.

'I have had breakfast prepared for you and it will be delivered very soon,' Schumann continued. 'I must say how very disappointed I am with you, Captain

Macintosh. You have betrayed my trust and used my family to carry out a blatant act of war against the Fatherland. However, that matter will be dealt with by our government when they come to escort you back to Rabaul. In the meantime, despite your act of treachery, you will be dealt with courteously and not harmed. I expect you, Mr Macintosh, to give me your word that you will not attempt to escape and if you do so I will allow you out of your current prison. You will be able to roam the plantation under the guard of my people. Do I have your word?'

Alex glanced at Matthew, who had attempted to follow the conversation spoken in German.

'I gather that Herr Schumann is asking for your parole,' Matthew said.

'That is correct,' Schumann said in English.

'I can't see what is wrong with that,' Matthew replied, smiling at the German planter. 'After all, where can we go?' Alex stood and held out his hand to Schumann. 'You have my word as an officer and gentleman that I will not attempt to escape,' he said.

'And you, Mr Duffy?' Schumann asked.

'The same,' Matthew shrugged, but did not extend his hand.

'Good,' Schumann responded. 'You are now free to take advantage of your limited freedom,' he said in English. 'You will remain within the borders of the plantation. Herr Schmidt will show you where they are. At night, you will be confined to this place and you will not, under any circumstances, attempt to speak with any of my family or workers. Do you understand what I am saying?'

'We do,' Alex answered. 'I will respect your wishes and add that I am truly sorry if we have caused you or your family any embarrassment for what you perceive as an act of betrayal. That is the last thing I would want to happen between us.'

Satisfied that he had settled the issue of the Australians' captivity, Schumann nodded to the foreman and turned on his heel to leave.

'You stop here, *ja*,' Schmidt said in heavily accented and fractured English. '*Kai kai* come.'

He left, closing the door, and moments later the housemaid appeared with bowls of porridge which both men devoured. Then the foreman returned, waving with the rifle barrel for them to exit the shed. Matthew and Alex stepped into the tropical sunlight. Plantation workers were moving about, chattering in their language as they prepared to go to work among the coconut palms.

'I did not exactly promise not to escape,' Matthew muttered in Alex's ear as they walked in front of the armed foreman. 'After all, I am neither an officer nor a gentleman.'

Alex turned his head quickly towards Matthew. 'I kind of thought that,' he said softly. 'If you do make it, tell my father that I attempted to do my duty.'

'I will be getting you out of here,' Matthew said.

'No, I gave my word,' Alex answered. 'Besides, I have to see Giselle and explain that I never intended to hurt her with my actions. You will have to go alone.'

Matthew did not respond. After all, he knew his cousin was a man in love and blinded to the realities of their dire situation. Matthew suspected that they would be quietly disposed of when the authorities from Rabaul arrived. After all, they had already tried once to kill them.

Throughout the day they roamed the plantation, Matthew scheming to escape while Alex plotted to see Giselle. Always they were followed by either the foreman or an armed worker.

21

For almost the week that he and Matthew had been allowed the freedom of the plantation, with the exception of being permitted near the main house, Alex had not seen Giselle. Alex observed that Matthew was forever noting all that occurred around them and it was obvious that his cousin was plotting his escape. They had learned from Schumann on one of his visits to their makeshift prison that the German navy was sending a ship to pick them up and take them back to Rabaul; the transport was due in three days. This news spurred Matthew on in his plans to escape and made Alex consider a desperate plan to speak with Giselle.

In the evening the two men were confined to the storage shed and brought their evening meal of baked sweet potato and roast pork.

'I have worked out that Herr Schumann owns a

cutter – the one we have seen in the harbour,' Matthew said, putting aside his plate. 'And from what I have seen in the last week Schumann has relaxed his guard on us. They don't even post a guard at the shed by night anymore.'

'I know you can fly, but what are you like at handling a large sailing boat?' Alex asked.

'It has an engine,' Matthew answered. 'I expect that I would get the boat out of here on the engine and with the right winds sail her south.'

Alex knew they were on a countdown and the pain he felt at not being able to communicate with Giselle had not abated. 'I will do anything I can to help,' he replied. 'What do you need?'

'I am going to make my move tomorrow night,' Matthew told him. 'Around midnight when most of the plantation is asleep I will break out of here and make my way to the bay. With any luck the boat will not be guarded and all I have to do is take her out. Hopefully, I will not be missed for at least six hours and that will give me a head start. All I have to do is get the boat into Papuan waters and the Germans are powerless to act against me.'

'Sounds fairly straightforward,' Alex agreed. 'If all goes well you will be able to get back to Sydney and brief my father on the situation.'

Matthew and Alex played a couple of hands of cards from an old pack they had been given by Schumann, and then put out the lantern to get a good night's sleep.

Matthew did not know what it was that caused him to awaken, sit up and look across to where Alex normally slept, but when he did he could clearly see that his cousin was gone. Confused, Matthew tried to fathom what had happened to Alex.

'You old dog,' he muttered. 'Be bloody careful.'

A couple of hundred yards away, Alex moved stealthily along a wall of the main house to a window which he knew from his previous visits was Giselle's bedroom. The window was wide open and he cautiously hauled himself over the ledge to drop softly to the wooden floor below. In the dim light cast by a lantern outside the room he could see the huge mosquito net over the young woman's bed.

'Do not shout,' Alex ordered, his hand clamped over Giselle's mouth. 'It is only me, Alex.'

Giselle attempted to struggle against him but he used his strength to pin her down. 'If you cry out I will be surely shot,' he pleaded. 'I just wanted to speak with you before your people come and take us away.'

Giselle's struggles ceased, but her eyes were angry. Slowly, Alex took his hand away.

'How could you have done it?' the young woman demanded angrily. 'Betrayed me and my family?'

'I am a soldier,' Alex said. 'I have my duty to my country. I never intended to hurt you or your family.'

'Well, you have,' Giselle snapped. 'How do you think I felt when I saw that aeroplane burned in the yard? To hear from my father that the authorities in Rabaul knew you were on some kind of spying mission against my country? Do you know what the penalty is for spying?'

'I do,' Alex replied. 'I could lie to you and say that I am innocent of the charges but I will confess to you – and you alone – that I was doing my duty as best as I could, under the current circumstances. That does not mean that I don't love you with my heart and soul. I am sorry, Giselle.'

'What will happen to you now?' Giselle asked with concern creeping into her voice. Her anger was gone and Alex sensed that she still cared for him.

'You know the answer to that,' Alex replied with a shrug. 'Anyway, Matthew is under the impression that we won't even make it back to Rabaul.'

Giselle gripped his arm. 'I cannot see you come to any harm,' she said with fierce conviction. 'Despite your misguided actions I still love you.'

'I gave my word to your father that I would not attempt to escape,' Alex replied. 'I just have to take my chances.'

'I could not bear to think that you could be hurt,' Giselle said, moving to put her arms around him and laying her head on his shoulder. They clung to each other, tears rolling down Alex's face. He stroked her hair and smelled the depths of her sweet scent.

'I will help you to escape,' Giselle said, pulling back to face him. 'I don't care how many promises you made to my father, I love you more than life itself.'

'They are the only words that I wanted to hear,' Alex said gently. 'That you love me as I do you. That love overrides any oath that I might make as an officer.'

'How will we do it?' Giselle asked.

'Matthew has a plan,' Alex revealed. 'I only have to join him and when I am in a better position, return to take you away from here. I want you to be my wife and share my life.'

'I want to come with you when you escape the plantation,' Giselle said with a note of determination that told Alex she would be very hard to dissuade.

'That would be too dangerous to consider,' Alex countered gently, stroking her face. 'Matthew plans to steal your father's cutter and sail for Papuan waters. What if your navy on its way here goes in pursuit of us?'

'I know the boat and waters around here better than both of you,' Giselle said. 'I also know of places ashore where we could hide by day.'

'I will have to discuss your involvement with Matthew,' Alex replied. 'How can I communicate with you before tomorrow evening?'

Giselle thought for a moment. 'I will ride to the western edge of the plantation where my father is planting more trees. Do you know where I mean?'

'We have walked there,' Alex answered.

'Good,' Giselle continued. 'I will be there mid afternoon when most of the workers and my father take a break.'

'I will meet you,' Alex said, realising that he should leave before much longer. There was a chance that an early rising house worker might spot him departing the house. 'I will leave now and see you later this day,' he said, taking Giselle in his arms. He kissed her passionately and she returned the gesture. Reluctantly they broke apart.

'I love you,' Alex said, slipping from his position by the bed to go to the window.

'I love you,' Giselle echoed softly across the room as Alex slipped through the window into the yard to make his way carefully back to the storage shed.

'Good morning, Romeo,' Matthew greeted in the dark as Alex tiptoed through the doorway. 'Hope the risk was worth it.'

'It was,' Alex answered. 'Giselle has expressed her desire to join us in our escape.'

'Us?' Matthew asked softly. 'Do I rightly deduce that you and Miss Schumann plan to flee with me in the cutter?'

'That's right,' Alex replied. 'Three can handle the cutter better than one. We would have a better chance of escaping.'

Matthew stood and stared through a crack in the wall at the yard beyond now under the soft glow of a rising sun. 'I have no problem concerning you breaking your parole,' he said. 'But you would be risking Giselle's life if we get caught. Have you considered that?'

'We love each other,' Alex answered. 'I cannot live without her.'

Matthew shook his head. It was obvious that his cousin was acting like an infatuated school boy and not the commissioned officer he was supposed to be. 'We have a duty to report back to your father,' Matthew reminded his cousin. 'You cannot let your personal feelings interfere with why we are here.'

'Giselle knows the cutter better than either of us could learn under the hasty conditions,' Alex defended. 'Surely you can see that.'

'Okay,' Matthew sighed. 'She comes with us.'

'Good,' Alex said and lay down to rest. He had an appointment that afternoon with Giselle to tell her the good news – if putting her life on the line could be considered good news! The plan that Matthew had set out earlier was simple. They would wait until midnight, leave the unguarded shed and make their way to the beach where the cutter lay moored to a small jetty. All going well it would be unattended and they would push it off and set a course south. It all seemed so straightforward. With the wind and luck on their side the cutter would sail into Papuan waters which were under the administration of Australia. Here they would be safe and Giselle free to wed him in Sydney regardless of her father's opposition. With these final reassuring thoughts, Alex dozed off until he was awoken for breakfast.

The day passed without incident and Alex was successful in meeting with Giselle and explaining what Matthew had planned. They parted with a passionate kiss and unspoken fears for what may lie ahead. Giselle mounted her horse and rode back to the house leaving Alex to gaze after her, afraid that he could lose her if the plan failed. However, he shook off his doubts and tried to feel confident in his cousin's plot to escape.

When evening came Matthew noted that there appeared to be no change in the routine around the plantation. Neither man could get any sleep as midnight approached. They sat and spoke softly on a myriad of inconsequential subjects to calm their nerves.

'It's time,' Matthew said quietly, glancing down at the pocket watch in his hand, a present from his mother for his twenty-first birthday. It had survived many dangerous situations and even the long swim to shore, wrapped as it had been in an oilskin wallet.

They rose and cautiously exited the shed. Moving across the dark yard they reached a row of tall, uniformly spaced coconut trees which they followed until they reached the natural vegetation adjoining the beach.

'Where is she?' Matthew hissed. 'You said she would meet us here.'

Alex crouched in the rotting vegetation and just beyond the beach below they could see the dark outline of the cutter secured to the small jetty. 'Giselle will be here,' Alex replied. 'She must have been held up.'

'We cannot wait for very long,' Matthew warned. 'According to what I was able to find out from a worker the tide will be coming in within the hour. If she is not here in ten minutes I am afraid we will have to leave.'

'Give us ten minutes,' Alex pleaded, swatting at the clouds of mosquitoes rising in the still, humid air.

They waited with only the buzzing sound of the mosquitoes and the gentle hiss of the sea surging onto the beach disturbing the oppressive silence. Finally, Matthew rose to his feet. 'Are you coming? I am sorry, but we can't afford to wait any longer for Giselle,' he whispered.

Confused, Alex continued to crouch in the tropical night. Why had Giselle not joined them as they had planned? Had she become lost in the dark? Was she safe? The questions tumbled over each other in his mind. No matter what the answer, Alex realised that time was running out if they were to use the tide in their escape. 'I'm with you,' he said, following Matthew towards the small single-masted ship secured to the wooden jetty.

The two men moved cautiously, each step dogged by the fear of being recaptured. In a short time they found themselves on the wharf. A lantern flared and both men froze.

'Hands up!' a voice commanded from the cutter and in the lamplight Matthew and Alex could see the German foreman levelling his rifle at them. 'I have been expecting you.'

Obeying the command, both men raised their hands. The big German stepped off the cutter onto the wharf, followed by two of the plantation workers, also armed with rifles.

'How did you know?' Matthew asked.

'Fraulein Schumann gave you away,' Herr Schmidt sneered. 'Herr Schumann is extremely angry that you have broken your parole, Captain Macintosh.'

'Giselle?' Alex uttered in his shock at the news she had betrayed their escape attempt. 'I don't believe you.'

Schmidt shrugged and gestured with his rifle for them to turn around and march off the jetty. For a moment, Matthew considered the possibility of attempting to overpower the German, but dropped the idea when he considered the two armed men accompanying the foreman.

'Lie down and put your hands behind your back,' Schmidt commanded when they were on the beach.

For a terrifying moment both men entertained the thought that they were about to be executed. Instead, they felt rope being wrapped roughly around their wrists, securing their hands. When the task was completed they were hauled to their feet.

'As much as I would dearly like to shoot you both here and now I am under orders to return you to the shed,' Schmidt said, prodding Matthew in the back with the rifle barrel. 'We have news that the navy will take you off our hands tomorrow and your treacherous activities will be revealed to the world.' Stumbling forward, Matthew and Alex marched in silence to see Herr Schumann awaiting them at the shed, a pistol strapped to his belt. The expression on his face told the two escapees that they were lucky to be alive.

'It was my idea to escape,' Alex lied but was cut short by Matthew.

'Captain Macintosh is lying to protect me,' he said. 'The escape was my idea, not his. He only came under threat from me to expose him as a coward if he did not.'

'Your sentiments to protect your cousin are very noble, Herr Duffy,' Schumann said. 'But I have ascertained Captain Macintosh was a willing participant in your plan. I could have intercepted when you left the shed but I wanted to be sure that you really were going to steal my cutter. You certainly confirmed that by your actions and I will be glad to see the last of you both. A soldier who breaks his parole loses any right to claim his commission.'

Herr Schumann was indeed stating a fact in the rules of war. Alex felt deeply ashamed. He hung his head and remained silent, glancing at Matthew to see the anger directed at him from his cousin.

'Inside, both of you,' Schmidt ordered, pushing at Alex who stumbled forward to collapse against a wooden pole supporting the tin roof. Matthew followed as the door slammed behind them and they heard Schumann order that the guard be doubled for the night.

Matthew remained standing while Alex sat on the earthen floor. 'We would have made it had it not been for your misguided trust in your beloved,' he snarled. 'No wonder she did not turn up at the rendezvous point. She was selling us out.'

'I don't believe that she did,' Alex said softly but with a pain of doubt he would not admit to. 'I think that they are lying.'

'Maybe her father had her whipped to force her to confess,' Matthew said sarcastically. 'We were so bloody close to getting away and tomorrow the German navy picks us up. I doubt that we will have any chance of escape then.'

Alex did not respond but sat staring into the dark depths of the shed. He was not thinking about the imminent arrival of the German authorities the next day. He was more concerned about how the woman he loved, and whom he had thought loved him, could have betrayed them. Despite his attempts to deny that she had, the thought still crept into his mind. His thoughts were in turmoil; there had to be an explanation.

★

Hauptmann Dieter Hirsch found that he was spending more time in uniform than he was performing his civil duties for the governor. Dressed in his field dress and covered in grime, he dismissed his junior militia officers from a debriefing of the latest military exercise on the outskirts of the German frontier town. The young officers ambled away to their units of Tolai soldiers, to stand them down after a gruelling two weeks in the surrounding jungle.

Dieter retired to his tent where he would spend the day writing up reports on the observed strengths and weaknesses revealed by the exercise designed to repel an invasion. He opened the flap, sat down in a folding field chair behind the table where he formulated tactics and issued orders at briefings. He had hardly taken off his hat when Major Paul Pfieffer appeared dressed in his field uniform. Dieter stood and snapped off a salute to his superior officer.

'At ease,' the intelligence officer said. Dieter had not seen Pfieffer during the exercise, guessing that he was preoccupied with intelligence matters.

'Good morning, sir,' Hirsch said.

'Hauptmann Hirsch,' Pfieffer said. 'I have learned that the mines intended to sink the Macintosh ship appeared to have either been faulty or interfered with. It seems that they did not detonate until the ship was almost within anchorage of the Schumann plantation. I was wondering if you knew anything about the delay to the timing devices of the detonation fuses.'

Hirsch had been dreading the question and had hoped that the delay might be written off as the devices being faulty. But he should have known that the man questioning him was no fool.

'I am sorry, sir, I do not know what you mean,' Hirsch lied.

Pfieffer stared hard at the officer. 'Then my source that has informed me you made a visit to view the mines just before they were taken to the ship is wrong?' he questioned. 'That you were alone with the mines before they were rowed out to the English ship is also wrong?'

Dieter Hirsch could feel the sweat trickling down the back of his neck and knew it was not just because of the rising heat of the morning in the tropics. Yes, he had altered the timing devices so that the men aboard the ship would be ashore when they went off. They were not at war and his conscience would not allow him to murder a man he had befriended. The report had returned that the ship had been delayed by a storm and the mines exploded just off the plantation. At least Captain Macintosh and Matthew Duffy had survived. It was not as if he had completely sabotaged the operation – after all, the ship was at the bottom of the Solomon Sea.

The intelligence officer continued to stare directly at Dieter Hirsch. 'If it could be proved that you in some way tampered with my mines I would not hesitate to have you court-martialled, Hauptmann Hirsch, for an act of treason. You would join your English friends before a firing squad. Do we understand each other?'

'Yes, sir,' Hirsch replied stiffly.

'Good,' Pfieffer replied and in a chameleon-like

manner suddenly changed persona. 'Now, I think it is time to retire to the club for a good breakfast and a cold beer. You will be my guest, in recognition for all the good work that has been reported to me for the exercise you have conducted with our boys.'

Hirsch blinked. One minute he was threatened with a court martial and possible execution and the next the same man was inviting him to breakfast as if nothing had been said. 'Sir, I must complete my reports and . . .' Hirsch attempted to protest.

Pfieffer held up his hand. 'That can wait for the moment, Hauptmann Hirsch,' he said. 'You have earned a good breakfast where we can discuss the fate of the two prisoners soon to be returned to us.'

Hirsch realised that arguing his case was not an option and followed his superior officer through the tent flap. Major Paul Pfieffer worried him. He had a devious mind and even the breakfast invitation must have some significance.

Like a young German officer in far away Rabaul, Colonel Patrick Duffy found himself spending more time in his uniform than his civilian suit. International events were drawing the world closer to war in Europe and he found himself briefing government committees, answering questions from the politicians responsible for defence about the status of his militia unit, as well as holding conferences with John Hughes. At least the Macintosh companies were in the capable hands of his son who was also monitoring the search for Fenella.

Patrick marched down the sandstone colonnade of Victoria Barracks, taking a salute from a smartly uniformed warrant officer. He entered John Hughes' office complex to be cheerfully greeted by the English officer's assistant, Major Oaks. 'Good morning, sir,' he said, bracing at his desk. 'Colonel Hughes is expecting you, so just go straight through.'

'Thank you, Major Oaks,' Patrick replied.

'It's official, Patrick,' Hughes said by way of greeting. 'A cable came through last night. The Serbians have made a formal request for the Tsar to mobilise forces to help them defend against the Austrians.'

Patrick slumped in a chair. 'It has to mean war,' he sighed.

'Maybe we will stay out of it,' Hughes responded. 'From what I have been able to glean from my sources in England, it does not appear that we are all that keen to get involved in a Balkans war – even if the Kaiser commits forces in support of his Austrian allies.'

'What about the French response?' Patrick asked.

'The French might go in on the side of the Russians and there is a pact for the French to side with the Tsar if they go to war with Germany. Maybe the Kaiser will show some commonsense – who knows.'

'Have we any further news about my son and Matthew?' Patrick asked. Days earlier, he had been informed that an intercepted message between the Germans in the Pacific had mentioned their survival and subsequent detention on the Schumann plantation.

'Only that they are to be shipped back to Rabaul

today,' Hughes answered. The fact that they had been able to intercept German naval radio traffic in the region was classified top secret. They had not been able to read coded transmissions but some of the messages had been transmitted in clear on the logistics airwaves when not considered of tactical importance. Or had the signal transmitted in clear been the Germans' way of ascertaining whether their electronic mail was being read? A reaction to the message would have exposed the Australians reading their signals and Hughes clearly knew that. That the two Australians were in German military custody was not officially recognised in order to conceal the intercepts being made. As much as it frustrated Patrick he fully understood the importance of keeping secret their reading of the German transmissions.

'At least they are alive,' Patrick responded. 'What do you think the Germans will do with them?'

John Hughes frowned. 'Considering that they most probably know they might be on the verge of war with the Russians I am sure that they will be more concerned about those matters. After all, we are not at war with Germany and if all goes well England will remain neutral. If so, as a gesture of friendship I am sure that the Germans will be very quick to hand Alex and Matthew over to us.'

'But what if England gets tangled up in a war on the European continent?' Patrick asked quietly.

John Hughes did not respond.

22

The Macintosh ship made good time to the American territory of Hawaii and Randolph found himself at home among the accents of his former countrymen. As the trading ship was scheduled to remain in the harbour for a week to load cargo he chose to use it as his base in an attempt to locate Fenella.

Clearing Customs, he made his way to the street. His first port of call would be the hotel Fenella had been staying in before she mysteriously disappeared. As it was not far from the shore he was able to walk the distance, stretching his legs on land to eliminate the swaying stance he had adopted from the rolling deck of the ship. The sun was pleasantly warm and the island had a holiday atmosphere. In the foyer of the plush hotel a balding young man was busy behind the reception desk.

'My name is Randolph Gates and I would like to ask some questions about a past guest of your hotel,' he said.

The young man looked suspiciously at the imposing stranger on the other side of the desk. 'Are you a policeman?' he asked.

'No, but I am in the employ of an important Australian searching for his daughter, a Miss Fenella Macintosh who may have also gone under the name of Fiona Owens,' Randolph said. 'I would like to ask if you knew of the lady.'

The clerk glanced down at his log of accommodation bookings. 'I am sorry, sir, but I am unable to answer any questions concerning the lady you ask about,' he replied politely. 'I would suggest that you take up your enquiries with our police department. I think that a Detective Amos Devine might be able to help you. I can direct you to the police station.'

'I know where it is,' Randolph answered. He had once been a guest of the Hawaiian Police Department on an earlier trans-Pacific voyage to Australia to take up employment with Kate Tracy. There had been a bar room brawl and Randolph had laid out two sailors. He had been arrested but was able to make bail before skipping on the next ship to Australia.

'Well, sir, if I cannot help you any further . . .' the man said without looking at Randolph, making himself look busy with his paperwork.

From his pocket Randolph slipped a wad of American dollars he had been given before leaving Sydney and peeled off a generous sum. He noticed that the clerk had seen his gesture. 'All I need to know is whether Miss Macintosh made contact with anyone that you could tell me about?'

The clerk eyed the money on the shiny desk top between them. He licked his lips like a hungry man and placed his hand casually over the notes, pulling them towards him. 'There was one man, an Australian,' he said in a quiet voice. 'A Mr Duffy; I think he was her attorney. He would visit and they would dine together.'

Randolph felt a twinge of jealousy but knew that the clerk was not far from the truth when he said that Mr Duffy was acting as her legal representative, having learned this for himself back in Sydney. Randolph slipped an equal amount of money onto the desk.

'I will double this if you can provide me with something more substantial,' he said.

The clerk glanced around the foyer nervously. He stepped away from the desk, leaving the booking counter unmanned. Randolph waited patiently for the clerk's return. When he reappeared he slipped a couple of letters into Randolph's hand. 'These came after Miss Macintosh booked out of the hotel. She had paid in advance and so we had no interest in pursuing her for unpaid accommodation, although she had said that she would be staying longer than she did.'

True to his promise, Randolph peeled off a few more notes and handed them to the clerk who quickly concealed the bribe in his trouser pocket. Randolph thanked the man for his assistance and walked from the hotel foyer into the bright sunlight of a day that promised to be pleasantly warm with a cooling sea breeze.

When he returned to the ship he went to his tiny cabin and sat on the bunk. From his pocket he retrieved the letters. One was from Arthur Thorncroft but the second had been posted from the USA. Randolph opened the American-posted envelope first and when he scanned the letter he smiled grimly. Carefully placing the folded letter in the envelope he hoisted himself from the bunk to depart for a shipping office. He would need to take the next available ship to San Francisco and then make his way to the town of Los Angeles. The letter was from a film producer stating that he would accept Arthur Thorncroft's recommendation and provide Fenella with an opportunity to demonstrate her talents in his studios. From his time working with Arthur, Randolph was well enough acquainted with the workings of a movie studio to know what to do next. All he had to do was get to Los Angeles. But first he would go to the Macintosh office on the Pearl Harbour waterfront and cable Colonel Duffy, informing him that he was on his way to the USA to find and bring Fenella home. So far everything had fallen into place.

When he had ensured the cable would be sent, Randolph returned to the ship. In a fine mood, he walked to the gangway of the Macintosh trader to see two tough-looking men obviously waiting for someone. The larger of the two intercepted Randolph at the bottom.

'You Randolph Gates?' he asked.

'Who wants to know?' Randolph retorted, sensing trouble.

'Detective Amos Devine,' he replied, reaching for the handcuffs jammed into his trouser belt and revealing a holstered pistol next to them. 'Put your hands behind your back,' he continued.

Randolph tensed. 'What in the hell is going on?' he demanded.

'I have a warrant for your arrest on a matter a few years back when you skipped bail,' the police detective said. 'Thought Uncle Sam had forgotten, did you?'

For a moment Randolph was confused until he remembered the case a little over thirteen years earlier. To resist would be futile and so he surrendered to the detective's order. He felt the cuffs bite into his wrists. 'It's not really about the warrant, is it?' Randolph said as he was roughly spun around.

'You're goddamned right about that, fella,' Amos said with a smirk. 'Heard that you were asking around at the hotel about that Australian dame we would like to find ourselves. Then I got lucky when I found the outstanding warrant for your arrest in our files. You know that you will most probably go down on the charge and, I can assure you, this island is no tourist paradise for men in prison. You could end up doing a few years' service to repay Uncle Sam.'

'What do you really want from me?' Randolph asked as he was marched across the wharf.

'You tell me where the dame is and I might just let you escape – so long as you are on the next ship back to Australia,' Amos said.

'I can honestly say that I do not know where Miss Macintosh is,' Randolph replied, glad that he had not yet booked his passage to the United States. 'I was intending to return empty-handed to Sydney anyway.'

'Too bad,' Amos answered. 'Looks like you will have to do your time here, before you return.'

Randolph knew that all he had to do was inform the American police detective of the letter in his cabin and he might just be freed. But to do so would also put the police on her trail. It had been too easy and now he was forced to decide between his freedom and Fenella's.

'How long do you reckon I will get?' Randolph asked. But he did not receive a reply.

A cutter, similar to that owned by the Schumanns, had been employed by the Imperial German Navy to retrieve Matthew and Alex. Aboard the sailing ship the two prisoners were shackled hand and foot and guarded by a small contingent of Tolai police under the command of an officer neither man knew from their time at the Rabaul Club.

As they sailed away from the plantation Alex noticed that the Schumann cutter was no longer at its jetty. Sitting on the deck in their chains Alex gazed across the water to where it had been moored the night before. 'I can see it has gone,' Matthew commented quietly beside Alex. 'That is kind of unusual.'

'What do you think is going to happen next?' Alex asked, not wishing to dwell on the last twenty-four hours, especially the pain of betrayal on the part of the woman he still loved.

'Well, I don't think we are going to disappear at sea again,' Matthew replied, watching a flying fish hover between two waves rolling off the starboard rail. 'I figure that we will be taken to Rabaul where the Germans will decide what to do with us. I think it is all going to depend on what is happening in Europe.'

'So, what alternatives do you think the Germans have?'

'Maybe our chances are good if the Germans want to stay in with the English,' Matthew replied, juggling what they had last heard of the European crisis. 'I truly think that the Germans feel more at home with their English cousins than the English do with their old enemies, the French. Maybe we will be forgiven and released.'

'What do you, as a well-travelled Australian, consider will happen to us if for some reason Germany finds itself at war with England?' Alex asked, respecting his cousin's knowledge of international affairs.

Matthew did not reply immediately but continued to gaze at the gently undulating Solomon Sea. Above them the rigging creaked and the soft splash of the bow ploughing through the waves belied the situation they were in. 'Do you really want to know what I think will happen to us?' he asked.

Alex instinctively tugged against the manacles around his wrist. 'Then we cannot waste any time in planning our escape,' he said in a whisper.

Matthew glanced sideways at the younger man.

'How in bloody hell are we going to make an escape under the current circumstances?' he asked with a frown.

'Not now,' Alex said. 'But when we get to Rabaul we have the Italian priest up in the hills. He might be able to help us. All we have to do is escape the Germans in the town and head for the mission.'

Matthew did not comment. At least his cousin had not given up but he doubted that the Germans would allow them any chance to slip from their custody. Their fate was in the hands of those faraway emperors, kings, kaisers and tsars currently fighting what could be seen as a very vicious family war but for the moment they were being treated well. They had not been beaten or starved in the custody of the German police and navy.

Patrick first saw the awful news in his morning paper – the Austro-Hungarian Empire had declared war on Serbia.

'You have seen the news, Colonel,' Angus said over his shoulder. 'I have laid out your uniform.'

'Thank you, Angus,' Patrick replied, appreciative of how his valet instinctively knew what and where he would be on this day after reading the headlines.

'Sir, could I be mentioning something?' Angus asked in a way that Patrick knew was more a question from a friend than a servant.

'Speak whatever is on your mind, Angus,' Patrick replied, turning to face the big Scot standing in the dining room.

'I think we are going to be in a war,' he said with conviction. 'When we are I want to serve alongside you again. We were always a good team back when we was fighting them Fuzzy Wuzzies in the Sudan. You were the best officer we lads had.'

Patrick was touched by the Scot's commitment. 'How old are you now, Angus?'

The Scot bristled at the question. 'I'd be around fifty-four,' he replied defensively. 'But I'm as fit as any man younger than me. Besides, I've seen more wars than all of them young whipper-snappers put together.'

'No dispute about that,' Patrick answered. 'I will see what I can do – if we go to war.'

'Beggin' your pardon, Colonel, but I would appreciate you considering my offer pretty quick, because if we go to war it will all be over by Christmas.'

'I think that England will show some sense and stay out of any European war,' Patrick replied, knowing through his friend, John Hughes, that the English government was actually seeking a way to remain out of the impending conflict. Were not the German Kaiser and English King cousins?

'Will you be returnin' home this evening?' Angus asked, switching the subject.

'I am not sure,' Patrick replied. 'It will depend on my duties today with the regiment.'

'I will tell the cook to put aside some of the lamb cold cuts for supper if you make it home tonight,' Angus said. 'Don't forget that you will be needin' a batman when we go to war, Colonel,' Angus said in parting as he returned to his duties in the big empty house. There had been no news on the fate of Captain Macintosh since he had heard from the colonel that the young man and Mr Duffy were being held at a German plantation in New Guinea. If war was coming he fully realised that the lives of both men were in dire peril.

Matthew and Alex were brought up on deck as the German cutter manoeuvred to make anchorage in the deep water port of Rabaul. As the anchors clanged down the cutter's hull to splash into the placid waters both men could see a large open launch motoring out towards them. Alex was able to make out Hauptmann Hirsch in the bow of the launch and when the motorised boat swung alongside the cutter, a rope ladder was lowered over the side. Hirsch was the first aboard and received a salute from the German officer assigned to escort the two Australian prisoners back to Rabaul. He then walked over to Matthew and Alex, still manacled hand and foot.

'Captain Macintosh,' he said stiffly, 'I deeply regret that we should meet this way again, but you must realise that you are prisoners of the Kaiser, and it would be my duty to shoot you if you attempt to escape.'

With a wry grin, Alex held up his manacled hands. 'I doubt that I will be attempting to escape in my present condition.'

'I have been informed that you have broken your parole to Herr Schumann so I can no longer accept your word that you may not try to do so again.'

'I am sorry that I broke my parole, Hauptmann Hirsch,' Alex said. 'I know it was not becoming of my commission.'

'I doubt that you would have been privy to the latest news out of Europe,' Hirsch said in a less formal tone. 'Germany is now at war with Russia and it appears that France has mobilised its forces against us. It is inevitable that we must declare war against the French.'

'What about England?' Alex asked.

Hauptmann's face brightened only a little at the question. 'So far England has remained silent,' he replied. 'I pray that she will stay out of any war between us and the alliance we must face of Russia and France.'

'Do you know what our fate will be?' Matthew asked.

Hirsch turned to him. 'I have been led to believe the governor will release you both as soon as he returns to Rabaul as a goodwill gesture towards the English, despite your attempts to spy on us.'

'When will that be?' Alex asked eagerly.

'I am not sure,' Hirsch sighed. 'He is currently touring the islands on the *Komet*. However, you will be well looked after until then, albeit that you are still prisoners of the Kaiser.'

Inwardly, Matthew groaned at the delay. The world was about to explode in Europe and anything could happen in the Pacific. His dream of testing the idea of aircraft as active weapons of war seemed a lifetime away.

'In the meantime, I will have your shackles taken

off,' Hirsch said, turning to the officer who had acted as their escort aboard the German cutter.

The officer stepped forward and released the locks. The shackles clanked away and both men massaged their ankles and wrists.

Hirsch indicated they should board the launch and as the boat puttered towards the township's wharves Matthew felt the wind in his face. Maybe Alex was right, he mused. They might yet have a chance to escape. He did not want to take the chance that their neutral situation might not change given the way things appeared to be developing in Europe. As they approached the shore Matthew could see an officer standing with his hands behind his back, obviously waiting for the boat to land.

'Ah, Major Pfieffer is expecting us,' he heard Dieter Hirsch comment to Alex. 'But not an expected pleasure,' Hirsch added.

Matthew felt an instinctive fear for what was ahead. Please God, he prayed silently, keep England and hence us out of this war in Europe. Around him onshore the world remained in an idyllic tropical peace.

Through the bars of his cell Randolph Gates heard the news that Germany was at war in Europe. He was still reeling from how fast he had been brought before a judge without the opportunity to ask for legal representation. The judge had glowered down at him from his bench and declared him a low life for avoiding the judicial system in the country of his birth. Randolph realised that he was already judged and attempted to throw himself on the court's mercy as a man who had served his country with Teddy Roosevelt's Rough Riders on the slopes of San Juan Hill. The judge was obviously not of the former American president's political persuasion and sentenced him to six months in prison with hard labour for the old charge of assault against members of the American navy.

When Randolph turned around in the court he could see the detective smirking at the sentence. Handcuffed, he was returned to the gaol to await transport to the island's tough prison.

'You're damned lucky not to be back in Australia,' a fat, sweating gaoler said when he pushed Randolph's meal under the bars to him. 'If them Limeys get mixed up in what's happening over their way you might have got yerself shanghaied into the army. Isn't Australia one of their colonies?'

'Not anymore,' Randolph replied, retrieving the tin plate with a slice of stale bread and some kind of cold stew. 'The Australians got their independence from the British back in '01.'

'Never heard that,' the gaoler replied, waddling away from Randolph's cell.

Randolph had been informed that they would come for him that afternoon to take him to the island prison where he would be forced to serve out his time. He sat down against the rough concrete wall with the plate in his lap and dipped at the cold stew with the piece of bread. He ate slowly. The stew was mostly water and gristle and he expected he would be dining in a similar fashion for the next six months. As he ate, his thoughts drifted to Fenella. Where was she and was she thinking of him? How could he get the opportunity to convey to Colonel Duffy what had happened? Hopefully the American detective had not searched his cabin and found the incriminating letter. He doubted that he had, so Fenella's secret was still safe for the moment.

Randolph had hardly finished his meal and gulped down some brackish water when he heard his name called. 'Prisoner Gates, Randolph.' It was time to commence his sentence.

George Macintosh paced his office. He was agitated but not because of the news arriving from Europe that the continent was on the verge of a major war and massive armies were being mobilised. The telegram from Randolph Gates addressed to his father lay on his desk. So, his sister was apparently alive and well and possibly already in the United States. His attempts to discredit Fenella had failed. In a sense, his sister's tragic situation had only endeared her more to his father who had rallied to provide love and support for her.

George had been informed that his brother was also alive, albeit in the custody of the German authorities in New Guinea. There was still a hope that he just might be found guilty of spying and dutifully executed. George could only live in hope.

But his sister was still a problem and George continued to pace the office. He stared out the window at the busy street below where people went on with their business, untouched by what was occurring in far-off European cities. George knew that Fenella would never be found guilty of murder if she returned to Sydney but rather would fall into her father's arms as the prodigal daughter.

Frowning, George returned to his desk and considered the single sheet of paper from the American. The world might be facing horrific times ahead but still George felt desperate about wanting sole claim to the Macintosh empire after his father's death. If anything should happen to Fenella in America who would know of her fate? She had so carefully concealed her flight from Sydney. But now he had a clue as to where she might be and when all traces of the telegram were destroyed he alone in Sydney would know where to find her.

The thought came to George as he heard in the distance a paperboy calling the headlines that Germany had declared war on France. If only he could despatch an assassin to America to kill his sister her death would be swallowed up in the over-riding international events. George leaned back in his leather chair, considering how he might go about organising such a thing. With a grim smile, he sat up and leaned forward. Of course he had the means to make that happen, he gloated. All he had to do was make his contacts and the matter of his sister's demise would be assured. The only obstacle was Randolph Gates. So the job would also entail disposing of the American but the financial cost would be worth it.

George picked up the telegram from his desk and reached for a box of matches. Carefully he held the edge of the paper until it burned away. He dropped the ashes in a waste paper bin and reached for his telephone to make a call.

23

Matthew and Alex found themselves secured in the town's gaol for the first night. They were still being treated with courtesy but they both knew that they were also considered as spies. The German police had not bothered to separate them and they had the opportunity to discuss matters.

'What is the date today?' Alex asked, having lost track of time since the Macintosh ship had been sunk.

Matthew thought for a moment. 'I think it's the fifth of August. Why would you ask?'

'It is Fenella's birthday, today,' Alex sighed. 'And I don't have a clue where she is — or even if she is well.'

Matthew stared at a translucent gecko high on the wall above their heads but was distracted by the sound of cheering coming from the streets. A bugle was blasting out discordant notes and somewhere someone was beating a drum. He turned to Alex with a puzzled look.

Already Alex was straining to hear what the people outside were shouting but could not pick up any words in the background of what appeared to be celebrations. Eventually the noise subsided and Hauptmann Hirsch appeared at the door to their cell.

'Good afternoon, Captain Macintosh, Mr Duffy,' he said with a grim expression. 'I gather you would have heard the celebrations a moment ago.'

'What is going on?' Alex asked. 'Are you celebrating the Kaiser's birthday?'

Hauptmann Hirsch shook his head. 'I am afraid that England has declared war on us,' he said sadly. 'You can now consider yourselves as our first prisoners of war as I strongly suspect that your country will quickly follow in the footsteps of your mother country.'

'What do you intend to do to us?' Matthew asked, gripping the bars on the cell door. 'I gather you will put us on trial.'

'I am afraid so,' Hirsch answered. 'We have enough evidence to support a charge of espionage against you both, and the fact that you are a civilian matters little in this case, Mr Duffy.'

'And if we are found guilty?' Matthew persisted. 'What then?'

Hirsch looked away. 'The penalty for spying is death. But you will receive a fair hearing by authorised German officers. I have volunteered my services as your defence counsel and I promise that I will do my best to have you both acquitted.'

'Can a military court try Matthew?' Alex broke in.

'Yes, in time of war it can,' Hirsch replied. 'I am sorry, my friends, that it has come to this, that we should be enemies.'

'So am I, Dieter,' Alex said sorrowfully. 'Why can't the rest of the world just leave us alone out here in the Pacific?'

'I echo your sentiments, Alex,' Hirsch said. 'I dread the thought of Rabaul being turned into a war zone. This is a paradise – not intended to become a hell. I must go and speak with Major Pfieffer; he is arranging the military court for your trial.'

Hirsch left the two men frowning at each other.

'You realise that the Germans have enough evidence to convict us,' Matthew said. 'Between the security leak in Australia and the aircraft stashed at the Schumann plantation they will be able to make a case. I doubt that it will even have to be beyond a reasonable doubt.'

'I know,' Alex said, squatting in a corner of the cell. 'If only we had got away when we could. I am sorry, Matthew, for getting you into this situation.'

Matthew was tempted to remind his cousin that it had been his beloved Giselle who had betrayed them, but bit his tongue. He could see that Alex was on the point of despair. 'Don't worry, old chap,' he said. 'I believe that the tradition is that before we are either shot or hanged, our executioners grant us a good meal and a smoke. I could do with both right now.'

But Alex did not laugh at his cousin's morbid sense of humour.

★

'We are facing a probable invasion of our territories by the English,' Major Pfieffer said to Dieter Hirsch as they stood in the shade of a large mango tree in the street in front of the major's office. 'I doubt that we have time to set up a trial for the two prisoners.'

'Then we put them on the first available ship back to Germany as prisoners of war,' Hirsch concluded, only to have his superior stare at him as if he were a child.

'No, you organise to have them both shot,' he said. 'We have better things to do than worry about the fate of two spies.'

Hirsch was shocked at his senior's response to the lives of the prisoners. 'That would be murder,' he blurted. 'I cannot condone the execution of two prisoners who have not been given a trial.'

'You don't think it is inevitable that they would be found guilty and executed anyway?' Pfieffer asked. 'Organising a trial is a waste of valuable time and resources. Make sure that they are both dead before the sun rises tomorrow. I don't care how it is done but I want to hear they have been disposed of.'

'Yes, sir, I will organise for their disposal,' he replied, saluting his superior officer.

Pfieffer stared hard at the German militia captain. 'You failed to kill Captain Macintosh on his first visit to Rabaul some months ago,' he said icily. 'The Fatherland is not so forgiving of a second failure.'

Pfieffer returned the salute and left Hirsch considering the punishment for disobeying orders – legal or not. Germany was at war and he knew that any concepts of justice came a poor second to the national aims of winning. He had only hours to think of some way of saving the two men currently in the police cells, men who were now declared enemies of his country.

The heat shimmered across the plains of the tough, stunted scrub of Queensland's central west. Shadows baked and the kangaroo rose from the hot earth where it had been dozing. It was alert to something alien stalking it and its large ears twitched, attempting to locate where the threat was coming from.

Wallarie knew that his eyesight was poor, but the desire to return to the hunt brought him out from the cave with one of his old hunting spears. He could see the big marsupial stirring and realised that it might be long gone before he was within range to hurl his weapon and impale his prey.

Beyond the resting kangaroo Wallarie could see the swirling shape of a column of wind twisting skyward, dancing between the stunted scrub, picking up red earth and desiccated grass. He lowered his spear and gazed at the dust column and, as if in a trance, crouched and began chanting a song almost forgotten by his long-lost clan. The fabric of the universe was changing in places he did not know, but the ancestor spirits had been there to tell him. Before the old warrior swarmed the faces of long dead friends and family. Wallarie was frightened. He could see the face of Matthew Duffy among those of the dead. The pastor at the mission station on Glen View would have told him he was seeing evil, heathen things better confessed about for the sake of his eternal soul. Wallarie had been told he must recognise Jesus Christ before he could be granted eternal salvation otherwise he would forever burn in the fires of the whitefellas' hell.

The kangaroo would be safe this day. Wallarie continued to squat in the dust of the brigalow plains, chanting his song for the dead.

Evening had come to the German town of Rabaul and the two prisoners in their cell had been fed. Neither spoke much but sat with their fears for what might be their fate.

Before midnight, Matthew and Alex attempted to sleep on the concrete floor; no beds were provided, nor any mattress. In the background they could hear the sounds of the town celebrating the proclamation of war against the English, French and Russians, but Alex thought the cheering sounded rather subdued now as the citizens realised just how vulnerable they were on the fringes of the German Empire to the larger forces of the British in the Pacific. Their only real chance was their navy operating out of China and many privately prayed that the Imperial navy would suddenly materialise in the harbour to protect them.

Hauptmann Dieter Hirsch did not pray for the appearance of the big battle cruisers. He knew that they took time to arrive and would no doubt be assigned to other tasks. He had spent the daylight hours pondering the steps he must take to ensure two defenceless men were not taken from their cells and executed with a bullet in the back of the head. He realised that what he was doing amounted to treason, plotting to give assistance to an enemy combatant and his assistant civilian spy. But Dieter Hirsch was also part civilian and believed that even in war one could not simply execute a man for the fact he was on the other side – even if he was a spy. To do so would simply condone the same thing happening to his comrades in other places, should they also be captured. No, even war had rules to keep some semblance of humanity in hellish times.

'Are you awake?' Hirsch asked softly through the cell door. Matthew and Alex scrambled to their feet.

'What is happening?' Alex asked, gripping the bars of the cell door.

Hirsch glanced around him to ensure that they could not be overheard. The gaoler was a fat German police officer who was more used to locking up local Tolai and a few drunken civilians for the night – not dangerous English spies. He stood at the end of the short corridor, dangling a set of keys from his leather belt, idly watching the German militia captain talking softly to his prisoners and annoyed to hear him speaking in English, which he did not understand.

'I am going to get you out of here. You must make a break for the hills to Father Umberto's mission station,' Hirsch said. 'Captain Macintosh, I know that you will remember the trail,' he continued. 'I am sure that the Italian priest will give you sanctuary.'

'You know about Father Umberto?' Alex asked.

'We have for some time,' Hirsch answered. 'You

have to get away from here as fast as possible. I have orders to shoot you before the sun rises.'

'You do realise what you are doing?' Alex asked. 'You could be arrested and even executed for helping us escape.'

'It will not look as if I was helping you,' Dieter Hirsch replied with a crooked grin. 'I have decided that your execution should be carried out by me alone, so as not to involve any other member of the Imperial Army in this disgrace. So listen carefully and I will tell you how it will be done but, unfortunately, I have been forced to bring two of my men with me for the task. I suspect that Major Pfieffer has ordered me to do so in order to have witnesses to your deaths.'

Matthew and Alex listened to the German officer outlay his plan. It was dangerous but it was their only hope if they were to survive.

Hirsch walked back to the gaoler at the end of the corridor and the two Australians watched as he engaged him in conversation, noticing the shocked expression on the policeman's face. He waddled towards their cell and, stony-faced, opened the door, gesturing to Matthew to come out. He then locked the door behind him, leaving Alex alone.

'The chains will not be necessary,' Hirsch said when the gaoler held them up. 'I have an escort out-side.' The gaoler shrugged and returned to his desk in his office at the end of the cell corridor.

Hirsch fell into place behind Matthew, his pistol covering him as they exited the police station. Matthew saw two uniformed soldiers with rifles waiting for them.

'Now,' Hirsch said softly.

Matthew looked quickly to the two German soldiers standing to one side before falling into their positions as escorts. Their rifles were slung on their shoulders as commanded by their officer. He had stood them at ease outside the gaol before entering to fetch his prisoners. The Australian swung around and snatched the pistol from the German officer's hand. Had Hirsch been uncooperative, Matthew was fully aware that his rash act would have proved fatal to himself. The startled escorting soldiers saw what had happened and immediately reached for their rifles, unslinging them from their shoulders. But before they could level them on Matthew, Hirsch had called on them to refrain from shooting. Matthew had the pistol pointed at Hirsch's head and hoped that it did not discharge accidentally.

'Put down your guns,' Hirsch commanded his men. 'Or the prisoner will shoot me.'

With some reluctance, the two men lowered their rifles to the ground. 'Step away from them,' Hirsch continued. 'Go into the gaol.'

Obediently, the two soldiers walked into the gaol to be met by a confused gaoler who then saw Matthew with the gun at Hirsch's head. 'Release the other prisoner,' Hirsch said. The gaoler picked up the key set on his desk, went to the cell and unlocked the door. Alex stepped out.

'All of you,' he said in German. 'Get into the cell.'

The gaoler, two soldiers and Hirsch entered the tiny cell which Alex locked. 'No noise or we will shoot you,' Alex said, tossing the keys to the end of the building, knowing that he had no intention of carrying out his threat. He glanced at Hirsch but did not betray his thoughts of gratitude for what the officer had risked to save their lives.

Outside the gaol, Matthew scooped up the rifles and passed one to Alex. 'Stick close with me,' he said. 'I think I know a way out of town to the track up into the hills.'

They had the cloak of night to conceal their flight and only the barking of town dogs might have betrayed their presence to the occupants of the houses they slipped past in the night. Very soon, Alex found the path and their trek began. They struggled in the dark through rainforest gullies and climbed steep ground. The more distance they put between them and the township before first light the better. Many times they slipped in the dark, knocking skin off exposed flesh. Desperation kept them immune from both the pain they were suffering and the stench of rotting vegetation. Exhaustion dogged them. By dawn they had put a respectable distance between themselves and Rabaul and they collapsed into the leaf-carpeted floor of the thick forest surrounding them.

'How much further is the mission station?' Matthew gasped, fighting the need to drift into sleep, despite his terrible thirst.

'A fair distance yet,' Alex replied, also suffering dehydration. 'Coming back down the trail with Jock I remember that somewhere along here was a spring. I think we need to find water before we go mad with thirst.'

Forcing himself to his feet, Matthew followed Alex who had already set off in search of the spring. They stumbled forward, sometimes on their knees and hands, clawing up steep, overgrown slopes of tropical vines that tore at their exposed limbs. From time to time they were stung by insects. Matthew wondered if they would make the mission alive. It was Alex who set the example to keep going. Plodding on, he stopped at the base of a small incline. 'It's here!' he exclaimed.

Matthew watched as Alex broke off the track to plunge into the forest. 'Over here,' he whooped.

When Matthew joined his cousin he saw him gulping from a clear trickle of water running down a small crevice in the rocks. Matthew staggered forward to drink as much as he could. Refreshed, he fell back against the warm, rainforest floor. 'Good on you, Alex,' he said with a sigh. 'You're a bloody marvel.'

'I don't think we can stay here very long,' Alex said, leaning against the trunk of a forest giant. 'No doubt the Germans will be following close behind. They seem to know about Father Umberto's collaboration with us. Maybe we have had a chance to make a good gap between us and Rabaul but I figure they would have headed after us as soon as the sun rose.'

'What do you think we should do?' Matthew asked, staring with bleary eyes at the thick canopy blocking the sun.

'I think our best bet is to continue deeper into the forest, get off the track, covering any evidence of our path as we go, and then rest up for the day. With any luck the German patrol that's likely to come after us will stick to the track and pass us by.'

Matthew glanced around. He could see how someone could easily hide in the forest. 'Not a bad idea,' he agreed. 'But we are going to need more water before too long or we will be too weak to continue.'

'We could get that at the mission station,' Alex replied. 'It's not that far off and I don't think we will die of hunger before then.'

Moving cautiously at a right angle from the track, the two men found a place to hold up for the day and rest. They were in luck. There was a source of water only a short distance from their location and now it was a matter of evading the enemy until they could receive help from the Italian priest. Secured in their hide, both men quickly fell into a deep sleep, unaware that an armed patrol of Tolai police were already searching for them along the mission station track.

Hauptmann Dieter Hirsch stood at attention before Major Paul Pfieffer. Hirsch could feel the cold sweat of fear trickling down his spine as the senior officer scanned the reports he had compiled from the two soldiers who had been released from the gaol along with Dieter. He sighed and looked up at the young militia officer.

'It does not look good for you, Hauptmann Hirsch,' he started. 'From what the two men accompanying you last night have told me in their reports, I am having trouble accepting that the prisoners escaped by their own devices. We are at war, and to aid the enemy is an act of treason punishable by death.'

'Sir,' Dieter attempted to explain, 'I was overpowered by Herr Duffy and disarmed. I decided that the most appropriate action to take to avoid one of my men being killed in an exchange of gunfire with a desperate man was to fully comply with his demands. I knew that the prisoners could not go very far without help and as they are visitors to the island I felt that they would not receive assistance from the local populace.'

Pfieffer rose from behind his desk and walked across to a window that had a view of a large mango tree shading the backyard. He turned to the officer, still standing rigidly at attention. 'You and I both know that Captain Macintosh has been in contact with that Italian priest and I have no doubts that he and Herr Duffy are making their way to his mission station. I have already despatched a patrol of our native police to capture them. I may be unable to prove that you abetted the prisoners in their escape,' he said. 'But I do have the power to place you on close arrest for negligence in your duties, Herr Hauptmann. As of this moment you are confined to your quarters at the barracks. I will convene an official inquiry into your actions last night in due course. That is all.'

Hirsch saluted, turned and marched out of the office. His fate was now in the hands of his fellow officers. Apart from a charge of negligence in his duties he knew full well that he could be found guilty of treason.

24

In the mid-morning sun of late winter, Colonel Patrick Duffy completed his inspection of his regiment. The proclamation of war by the Prime Minister, Mr Fisher, had inspired many to enlist, eager to join the battles being fought in Europe.

Saluting the regimental second in command, Patrick left the parade ground to go to the reviewing dais for the march past. His men gave the traditional eyes right salute under the command of their sub unit commanders as they swung past the platform where the senior military guests sat.

Patrick returned their salutes until the last unit passed and then went to join John Hughes among the spectators, proudly watching the sons of the Empire dismissed to their barracks. It was a scene repeated across the Empire from Canada to New Zealand, from India to South Africa. Fresh-faced young men could see an opportunity to travel and find glory under the British standard, proudly displaying their own brand of nationalism to the Mother Country, Britain.

'They will require more training,' Patrick said to John Hughes. 'But they are keen and I am sure will display the same soldierly character we did in South Africa.'

'I am certain they will,' Hughes agreed. 'I have orders on my desk. The government intends to raise what is to be called the Australian Imperial Force, and that means you and I will be tied up with our recruiting people for the next few weeks.'

'What about the German navy's operational order?' Patrick asked. 'You and I know that if they are able to carry it out, we won't have any recruiting halls still standing along the east coast – let alone military depots. We both know the terrible power of the German cruiser guns.'

Hughes took Patrick by the elbow and guided him away from the throng of civilian and military spectators attending the parade. 'I have it from good sources that we are raising a combined army and navy expeditionary force to deal with the problem,' he said quietly. 'Its task will be to take out the German radio stations and cut off all communications in the Pacific for the German navy on their China station.'

'Have we heard anything in the radio intercepts concerning my son and Matthew?' Patrick asked.

Hughes shook his head. 'Sorry, old chap,' he replied. 'Nothing since we heard they were being taken to Rabaul.'

'My son is now officially a prisoner of war,' Patrick reflected. 'They would have to treat him under the terms of the Hague Convention.'

'I am sure they will,' Hughes reassured. 'As Matthew is a civilian the worst that could occur is for him to be detained as an enemy alien and simply confined. The Germans are a civilised race, despite our differences with them. They cannot afford to mistreat our people when they know so many Germans live in this land. Tit for tat, one could say.'

'They were not so civilised when they invaded neutral Belgium,' Patrick countered.

The invasion of Belgium had forced Britain's hand as they held an old but valid treaty with that country in the event of invasion. Somewhat reluctantly, England had been forced to declare war against Germany and her allies when German troops had crossed the Belgian border in a sweeping movement aimed at the heart of the French nation. Paris was in the German sights and crossing neutral territory a necessity to achieve that aim.

'Would not you and I have used the same strategy if we were on the German planning staff?' Hughes asked. 'Military men are guided by wanting decisive victories on the battlefield – not political ends to satisfy the men sheltered in their party rooms.'

Patrick reluctantly agreed. He might have formulated the same strategy, now known to them as the Schliefflen Plan. 'I don't want a desk job in recruiting,' he said, changing the subject to a matter weighing heavily on his mind. 'Either I lead my regiment in battle, or I am included in the staff of the expeditionary force for the Pacific region of operations.'

'I regret that you will never have the opportunity to lead the men of your militia regiment,' Hughes replied. 'I have been informed that your soldiers are to be absorbed into the soon-to-be-raised AIF, but I will do my best to get you included in the expeditionary force for operations against German territory in our part of the world.'

'Thank you, John,' Patrick said. 'Do you personally think that the war will be over by Christmas?'

John Hughes stared across the now empty parade ground. 'Take what you and I saw in South Africa and multiply it a hundred thousand times. I doubt it. The way things are going in Europe the Kaiser might be sitting on a newly resurrected French throne in a matter of weeks. The Belgians are fighting back, but I doubt that they will be able to hold the German advance, and our own small army, as well trained as it is, is no match for the sheer weight of German numbers that will be arrayed against them. The Germans are not the primitively armed Fuzzy Wuzzies you and I faced in the Sudan and Egypt. They are crack troops, well armed and motivated, and Lord Kitchener is already calling for at least one hundred thousand volunteers to enlist, which will put a huge strain on Britain's workforce. I fear that we will be in for a protracted war.'

'My own thoughts,' Patrick said. 'But still the politicians are boasting to the papers it will be all over before the year is out.'

'How many politicians have you known who

have ever been on a battlefield and seen what we have?' John Hughes reflected sadly. 'The stupid bastards are only thinking about popularity and votes garnered by jingoism. A lot of them will make a lot of money out of this war, along with their cronies, while good young men will die to help them boost their profits.'

The British colonel's last words struck a chord with Patrick. He had no doubts that his son George would come to him and explain how, as one of the captains of industry, he must stay out of military service in the interests of his country's economy. The thought sickened Patrick. He had seen it all before where young men died so that a handful of already wealthy men could further prosper.

Patrick made his excuses and left the barracks in his chauffeured limousine. He needed to stop off at the Macintosh offices on his way home. He was let off in the street and noticed that the civilians who had hardly given him a glance before when he was in uniform now respectfully dipped their hats. Even the occasional, 'Good on yer, cobber' followed him.

George was at the offices when Patrick arrived. The outbreak of hostilities had caused some panic among shareholders, as their sources of income were now under threat of being cut off by naval blockades. Patrick greeted familiar faces as he made his way up the stairs to his son's office. He knocked before walking in and was surprised to see his son in the company of Miss Louise Gyles. She was standing close to his son by the window. George glanced at his father with a look of annoyance.

'Hello, Miss Gyles,' Patrick greeted, ignoring his son's expression. 'How is your father, Sir Keith?'

'He is well,' she replied sweetly. 'You should reacquaint yourself with him when you can.'

She turned back to George. 'I must excuse myself as I have an appointment with my mother for afternoon tea,' she said. 'George dear, I will see you on the weekend at the Grants' – don't forget.'

Patrick could smell her perfume as she brushed past him. When she was gone, he turned to his son. 'A truly wonderful young lady,' he said.

'One whom I hope will agree to become your future daughter-in-law,' George replied, walking back to his desk. 'I intend to speak to Sir Keith and ask for his daughter's hand in marriage and I have a strong feeling he will be agreeable to having me as a son-in-law.'

Patrick registered his surprise. 'Is that a bit sudden considering we have just gone to war?'

'Father, we both know the best thing I can do for the country is to remain out of uniform and run the family companies,' George said. 'We have vital commercial interests tied up in war production and England is going to need many of our primary products to feed the masses. We have a huge stake in providing that important service and for me to enlist would be a disaster for the business. So I do not think asking for Louise's hand in marriage is out of place. I will not be in harm's way as you and Alex will probably find yourselves in the future.'

George's speech chilled Patrick. His son was so clinical about what he was doing and the final sentence about him and Alex being in harm's way was delivered as if his eldest son were talking about share prices rather than the possibility of losing a father and brother.

'Have you any further news from Mr Gates?' he asked, shrugging off his son's speech.

'Nothing,' George replied. 'My last communiqué from him was that he had reached Pearl Harbour and was looking for Nellie. Since then nothing has been heard. You know that you gave him access to a lot of funds against my advice. I would not be surprised to learn our American friend has decided to abscond with what Macintosh money he can lay his hands on and is now, as the Yanks say, living the life of Riley.'

'Randolph Gates is not that kind of man,' Patrick retorted angrily. 'I have known a lot of men in my life and consider myself a relatively good judge of character. Mr Gates loves Nellie dearly. He would not desert her.'

'Sorry, Father,' George said from behind his desk, 'but I do not share your opinion of him. And on the matter of my siblings, have you heard anything of Alex?'

'Only that he may be in Rabaul and, if so, then he is probably a prisoner of war of the Germans,' Patrick replied.

'Well, at least we have not heard any news concerning his death,' George said, hiding a scowl of disappointment for not hearing such from his German source at the consulate. As it was, at the last meeting with Maynard Bosch two days earlier, the German had informed him he expected to be interned and, with any luck, possibly repatriated to Germany, as he had semi diplomatic contacts. Bosch had been evasive about Alex's fate. All he could tell George was that he believed Alex was being held in custody in Rabaul along with Matthew Duffy.

'Are you sure Miss Gyles will accept your proposal of marriage?' Patrick asked, changing the topic of conversation.

George blinked in surprise at his father's question. 'Why would she not accept?' he countered.

'Oh, just that I felt she may be holding a candle for Matthew Duffy,' Patrick answered. Although he was making a guess, based on Matthew's attention towards Louise at the ball, he knew it would unsettle his smug son. 'No other reason.'

This time George's scowl was apparent. 'Why would she be interested in a Papist drifter like Matthew Duffy?' he asked.

'Papist as he might be, he is a rather handsome and dashing man and believe me, son,' Patrick said smugly, 'in times of war such men have an appeal to the ladies.'

George sensed that his father was deliberately needling him and refused to let his feelings of anger show. 'That may be so,' he answered mildly. 'But there is a very large part of a woman which desires the comforts and stability such men as myself can offer. Now, if that is all, I have to prepare for a meeting with a representative of our shareholders.'

Patrick left his son's office knowing that his eldest son could be a dangerous adversary. But beneath his son's calm exterior, he knew, was a troubled and insecure man.

Matthew slept through to early afternoon until the crawling insects annoyed him out of his repose. When he awoke he noticed that Alex was already up and about. He was sitting with his back against a tree and from his demeanour Matthew sensed that the young officer was suffering a bout of melancholy.

'What's up, cobber?' Matthew asked, scratching at the numerous bites to his arms and face.

'It's all gone so bloody wrong,' Alex replied in a faint voice. 'We have failed miserably to carry out the mission, I have lost Giselle and now, here we are, on the run from the Germans whom I have no doubt will shoot us on sight.'

'Cobber,' Matthew said, standing and stretching his legs, 'despite what has happened to us in the last few weeks, we are still alive. That is at least something to celebrate.'

Alex glanced at the man who had grown as close as any brother could. 'I suppose that you are right,' he replied with a weak smile, struggling to his feet. 'Someone is looking over us.'

'A black angel called Wallarie,' Matthew said, causing Alex to cast him a quizzical look. 'Why not?' Matthew shrugged. 'It might be my Irish blood that makes me believe in the unseen forces around us. After all, we have relatives back in the old country who still believe in the little people and banshees. So why not believe in the mystical powers of our new land?'

Alex was surprised to be reminded that, despite his very Protestant upbringing under the guidance of his great-grandmother Lady Enid Macintosh, he still had Irish blood through his father as well as Celtic blood from the Scots side. 'You could be right,' he conceded. 'Maybe our guardian angel is Wallarie, but from what little I know about our mutual family histories he has not been so accommodating in the past.'

'Not a good thing to talk about the dead,' Matthew warned. 'It might piss off Wallarie's ancestor spirits – he told me that once.'

Alex grinned, picked up his rifle and started walking towards their water supply near the track. 'You coming?' he asked over his shoulder and Matthew shouldered his rifle to follow.

They refreshed themselves at the spring and, proceeding very carefully, found the trail leading to the mission station, fully aware that any patrol sent for them might be just up ahead of them on the track. This was the most dangerous part of the trek. They would be groping in the dark and could stumble upon a camp that the patrol might have set up for the night.

Then the skies opened and the rain bucketed down on them through the canopy above, soaking them through. They plodded on for hours, staying within a couple of paces of each other, until they were too exhausted to take another step in the mud that gripped their boots. They eventually agreed that they should pull off the track and struggled in the pitch blackness and under the heavy tropical downpour to find a piece of ground to stretch out on. When the rain eased, clouds broke above the canopy allowing the moon to shine through, casting eerie shadows on the forest floor. A clinging mist rose around them and they lay on the soggy earth shivering. Clammy, sticky leeches attached themselves to their skin. Then Matthew heard the noise. It was a man coughing, followed by a soft murmur of voices and the clink of metal. He recognised the sound as a Mauser rifle bolt being locked into place. Unwittingly, they had pulled up just short of the German patrol's camp site. Had they continued along the track they would surely have found themselves stumbling into the heart of the enemy unit.

Alex smiled grimly in the dark. Had the old Nerambura warrior – so far across the sea – sent the rain to save them? He was beginning to think like his cousin!

The following morning their fears were confirmed when they heard the unmistakable sounds of a camp being broken. They lay in their improvised hide listening as the patrol had their breakfast and moved on. At least now they could gauge where the patrol was. They found the camp but were disappointed to discover that the Germans had ensured they left no scraps behind. Hunger was becoming an increasing concern. If they did not eat soon it would be difficult to continue on their flight to freedom.

'What do you think?' Alex asked.

Matthew was poking around the camp site looking for anything that might have been left behind.

'We get off the track and continue to the mission station using the path as a guide off to our right,' he answered.

Alex agreed. He was not sure how the Germans operated but there was just the chance they might leave a rear patrol to keep an eye on the jungle trail for anyone coming up it.

They broke away from the track to push into the dense forest. Ahead were ridges, valleys and cloying mud to fight. After some hours in the dense scrub they had lost sight of the trail they needed to guide them to their destination. Alex was first to admit that they were now lost. The country was devoid of landmarks and sweat rolled down their bodies as the humidity rose with the sun. They would need water to stay alive and reaching the mission station now took second priority to finding water.

By sunset they had travelled an unknown distance.

'Got to have a break,' Matthew gasped, collapsing to his knees and using his rifle as a support.

Alex also slumped to the ground. From where they stopped they had a magnificent view across a steep valley. 'There has to be a river or creek down there,' he observed. 'All we need to do is have a short rest and then make our way down.'

Despite his thirst, Matthew closed his eyes and drifted into a short sleep – as did Alex. He did not know how long he had closed his eyes or dozed but something woke him with a start. His time as a soldier on active service had trained him to listen for sounds out of place in the environment. It was the soft sound of stealthy foot falls on the rotting vegetation. Cautiously, Matthew felt for the rifle beside him and wrapped his hand around the stock, his finger curling around the trigger. He needed to roll over towards the direction of the sound. As casually as he could, still gripping his rifle, he rolled onto his back. 'Alex!' he said in a loud voice as he looked up into the dark face of a man holding a deadly machete at his side.

'I see them,' Alex replied quietly from a few feet away behind him. 'They have my rifle.'

The man towering over Matthew was not alone. Any attempt to fight would result in him and Alex being overwhelmed. He sat up, glanced around to count three more Tolai men armed with machetes standing in the tiny clearing. They were naked except for the loincloths they wore.

'Father, he send us,' the oldest man, the one who had stood over Matthew, said with a broad grin. 'Me think you lost,' he said in fractured German. 'You two men come with us.'

Matthew glanced at Alex. The Tolai warrior had passed his rifle back to him and Matthew did not sense that they were in trouble.

The leader of the men who had found the two Australians identified himself as Joshua and told them that he had no love for the Germans who had invaded his people's lands. He was a proud Tolai warrior who still bore the scars on his back of a whipping he had received for his defiance to the German occupiers. He and his family had fled into the hills, avoiding contact with the Europeans and their police. His family had been joined by others resisting the occupation. In all, his small village now numbered around eighty men, women and children eking out a living from the gardens they established to grow root crops and raise pigs. The village was well hidden and not known to the Germans. He had befriended the Italian priest who ensured that the people received medical aid when needed.

'How did you know about us?' Alex asked in German. He estimated the Tolai man to be in his early thirties.

'Germans come to Father's mission,' he replied as they wended their way along a hidden path. 'They say they look for you and any native boy who help you be hanged. Father, he send mission boy to us to say we must find you and look after you. You not to go to mission station.'

Alex wondered if the Italians were in the war and, if so, on which side. He felt that the Italian king would most probably ally his country with Britain should they go to war.

Just before sunset the two Australians, escorted by the machete-wielding young men, entered the village. It was a typical Melanesian village with log huts on stilts with sloping palm-frond roofs and open to the air. They were met by wide-eyed, curious children and their bare-breasted mothers.

The Australians smiled to their silent welcoming committee of Tolai villagers and were quickly brought baskets of cooked tubers and gourds of water which they accepted gratefully, squatting by a fire that Joshua had ushered them to. The people watched them dine and a few of the children overcame their fear and touched the skin and hair of the two strangers.

That night they slept on woven mats above the ground in a hut set aside for the men. At all times the two Australians kept their rifles close. It was not the people of the village they feared but a sudden appearance of German soldiers. Alex and Matthew both knew that they would not be taken alive and the rifles ensured at least they would go down fighting. Despite their fears a heavy downpour of rain lulled them to sleep.

When they awoke next morning the sun was shining and food was provided for them. After they had finished their meal Joshua reiterated that they were to stay close to the village. Matthew and Alex asked if they could find a place to bathe and Joshua led them to a stream not far from the village at the end of a well-worn track through the forest. They stripped off and washed themselves. Both men were covered in rashes and swollen insect bites but the cold water helped ease their discomfort. When they had dressed they rested on the bank of the small stream.

'You realise that it is our duty to mount a military campaign against the Germans on Neu Pommern,' Alex said, his rifle resting in his lap.

Matthew looked at his cousin with an expression of disbelief. 'You realise of course, Captain Macintosh, that between us we have ten rounds of 7.92mm ammo for the rifles and my Mauser pocket pistol has nine rounds in the magazine of fairly useless 6.35mm ammo. I doubt that we are really ready to take on the German army.'

'We will have to persuade Joshua and his men to aid us in the fight,' Alex said, ignoring Matthew's summary of their arms status. 'With their help we may be able to ambush the Germans or at least steal some of their supplies. I have studied the tactics of the Spanish guerrillas in Wellington's Peninsula campaign and think that our small numbers could tie up the Germans until Australia sends a force to seize the island. It's the least we can do for the cause.'

'You forget,' Matthew said, 'that I am a civilian. Simply keeping one step ahead of the Germans is all we need to do until our cobbers come to save us.'

'You were once a soldier,' Alex countered. 'And you have more combat experience than I have. I cannot see why you should not join me in fighting our war.'

'Your war,' Matthew snorted, realising how hopeless any confrontation with the Germans and their indigenous police would be. 'Don't include me and Joshua's mob. He has women and children to protect. If the Germans suspect he is aiding you they will surely carry out reprisals against the Tolai. They have a long record of doing that in this part of the world.'

'I will discuss the matter with Joshua,' Alex persisted stubbornly. 'And see what he thinks.'

Matthew did not respond but hoped the Tolai leader would show some sense and reject his cousin's call to arms. He looked closely at Alex. His cousin wore the unsettling expression of a man who was out to prove his worth – or was it of a man who had lost the most important love in his life?

They made their way towards the village but were

met by Joshua on the track. He had obviously been running. Sweat streamed down his face and body.

'You must not go back to village,' he panted. 'German man has come with guns looking for you. They say they know we help you. You must run away.'

Matthew and Alex looked at each other, wondering how the Germans could have known where they were. Perhaps the Italian priest had betrayed them. Then they heard the soldiers crashing through the undergrowth and advancing towards them.

25

Colonel Patrick Duffy returned to his home in
a dark mood. He had been officially informed
that he was not to be posted to the newly raised
expeditionary force being assembled for the invasion
of German territory in the Pacific. The Australian
Naval and Military Expeditionary Force, as it was
known, would be separate from the recently formed
Australian Imperial Force to which he was being
transferred. He had wanted to be an active part of
the armed forces which would attack Rabaul but
John Hughes had told him that by accepting his
transfer he would most probably be given command
of an infantry battalion. At least he would be back
on active service and not confined to a staff officer's
posting, he tried to console himself as he stepped
from his limousine onto the gravel outside the front
door of his house on the harbour.

His valet was outside the door waiting for him and when Patrick caught his eye he noticed an enigmatic expression on the old former soldier's face.

'What is it, Angus?' he asked.

'You have a visitor, Colonel,' Angus replied with just the slightest hint of a smile. 'And a very pretty lassie, if I say so myself. She is waiting in the drawing room for you. She would not give me her name but said that she had come because of young Alex. I have settled her down with a wee cup of tea while she awaits you.'

Intrigued, Patrick stepped inside and went directly to the drawing room where he saw a very beautiful young woman sitting in a chair, sipping from a fine porcelain cup. When she saw Patrick she placed her cup on the polished table and rose, delicately extending a gloved hand to him.

'I am Miss Giselle Schumann,' she said.

'Ah, the young lady my son is so smitten by,' Patrick replied warmly as Giselle's hand lingered in his own. 'It is a pleasure to meet you.'

Giselle slid her hand away and Patrick could see a hint of pain in her expression at the reference to Alex.

'Colonel Duffy, you must realise that although I was actually born in this country I am considered German and thus an enemy alien in the eyes of your government. I was reluctant to come here as I know how my presence might compromise you, but I could not remain in my mother's company any longer when I had a need to tell you something of great importance.'

'You are with your mother?' Patrick asked. 'The last that I knew of you was that you were staying on your father's plantation and not due to visit Sydney until September.'

'I am here now because of matters that happened at my father's plantation some weeks ago, and I fear Alex may have interpreted my actions as a betrayal of him, and Mr Duffy. I was forced by my parents to come to Sydney prematurely because of something that happened on the last night that I saw Alex.'

Patrick could see that the young woman was on the verge of tears and led her to a settee. She did not resist and he sat down beside her.

'Something happened,' he said gently. 'Tell me.'

'Alex and I planned to escape in our cutter to sail with Mr Duffy into Papuan waters and on to Port Moresby,' she said, fighting back tears. 'I organised a supply of rations for the sea voyage and was seen to be doing so by our foreman. He informed my father and I was confined to my room which prevented me from joining Alex on the boat. I heard the next morning that Alex and Mr Duffy were captured at the cutter. My father had sent a party to intercept them. He assigned a crew and I was accompanied by my mother to our cutter. We sailed for Port Moresby to take a ship to Sydney. I fear that Alex may have been led to think that I betrayed plans of his escape attempt and I cannot live with that knowledge. I had to tell you what had really happened. I would never betray the man I love more than my own life.' Giselle's hard-fought attempt to control her tears broke down and she began to sob, wringing her hands.

Gently, Patrick placed his arms around her and held her to his chest. With soothing words he told her that it was all right to cry. For a moment he felt that he was holding Fenella in his arms, just as he had done when she was but a little girl in need of love.

Eventually, the crying subsided. Patrick produced a clean handkerchief and Giselle attempted to regain her composure.

'I fear that very soon my mother and I will be arrested and sent to a concentration camp, like those I heard the British had in South Africa. We were forced by the police to register as soon as we stepped off the boat in Sydney. It is only a matter of time before we are sent away and I wanted you to know that I did not betray Alex. I may not be in a position to tell him what happened that night, but I know you will.'

'As soon as Alex returns I am sure that you will be able to tell him yourself,' Patrick reassured, realising nonetheless that Giselle was right about the inevitable internment of enemy aliens. Already an act of parliament had been pushed through to ensure this happened. 'Believe me,' he continued. 'If the worst comes to the worst I will fight tooth and nail to ensure that you and your mother are looked after. I have powerful friends in government.'

Giselle gazed into Patrick's face seeking the conviction of his words and was satisfied to see that he was so much like his son. She saw an honesty in his eyes that immediately made her feel just a little safer.

'Thank you, Colonel,' she whispered. 'But I do not want to compromise your position. I know that Alex was involved in a plot to spy on us. My father had the aeroplane destroyed on the orders of the government in Rabaul.'

'Do you know what happened to my son?' Patrick asked hopefully.

Giselle shook her head. 'I only know that he and Mr Duffy were to be taken back to Rabaul under military guard. After that I do not know any more.'

Patrick sighed deeply. 'If you would like to use one of our guest rooms you are welcome to stay,' he said.

'Thank you for your kindness, but I must return to my mother,' Giselle said, rising from the settee. 'She does not know that I have come to visit you and I know that she will be very distressed if I do not return to her before dark. We have rooms at a good hotel in Sydney.'

'If there is anything I can do for you or your mother just telephone me,' Patrick said, placing his card in her hand. 'May I ask where you are staying?'

Giselle provided the address of the hotel which Patrick knew as one of the best in Sydney. It certainly meant that the Schumann family were well off. He escorted her to the door and ordered his chauffeur to drive her to her hotel. Giselle suddenly turned to Patrick, surprising him with a warm kiss on the cheek.

'Thank you,' she said.

Patrick felt the softness of her lips and as she stepped into the car. He turned away lest any on the driveway see the tears welling up in his own eyes. The young woman reminded him so much of his own lost daughter. How could it have come to this?

★

Matthew gripped his rifle, glancing at Alex to see his reaction to the sound of a large party of men beating their way through the heavy undergrowth towards them.

'We have to get out of here,' Alex said, also hoisting his rifle. 'Too many of them from the sounds of it.'

'This is best way,' Joshua said, regaining his breath. 'German man not know this way.'

The Australians did not question the Tolai warrior's suggestion and followed him off the small, winding trail back to the village, plunging into the tangled bush. It was hard going but there was some kind of cleared trail through the scrub. Joshua was ahead of them and led them on to the base of a steep slope.

'In here,' he whispered, indicating a narrow earthen tunnel under the twisted roots of a large forest tree. The three men crawled into the tiny space and jammed up against each other, before Joshua pulled over a thatch of cut saplings. The sound of the soldiers searching for them was very close but in the cleverly constructed hide they had seemingly been absorbed into the very earth itself. Now they could clearly hear the voices of the men searching for them and even a conversation between a senior NCO and his patrol. It was obvious that the Germans were tired, irritable and looking forward to returning to the civilised comforts of Rabaul township.

They waited until the voices drifted away before crawling out from their concealed hide, brushing off the damp earth and standing to stretch their legs. Alex turned to Joshua and thanked him.

'We make this place to hide,' Joshua explained. 'It work well. Me think that the soldier man go home soon. Then safe to go back to village.'

'How did the soldiers know to come to your village?' Alex asked Joshua.

'Me think someone at the mission tell them about you staying with us but it is not one of my people,' he replied thoughtfully. 'It must be a bad kanaka who know about Father sending message to us to find you.'

Alex was puzzled. He had suspected the Italian priest but that did not make sense. There must be a traitor in the mission who had betrayed them to the German patrol. If so, that person would have to have the priest's trust. Treachery seemed to dog him and Matthew.

'I have a feeling that the Germans are not going to keep up looking for us,' Alex said to Matthew. 'I feel that they will be more needed down in Rabaul to defend their radio station in the event of an assault by our forces.'

'You are probably right,' Matthew agreed. 'I think we should just hold out in the hills until our cobbers arrive and forget organising any guerrilla movement.'

'We can't just sit around doing nothing when I am a commissioned officer,' Alex replied. 'It is my duty to fight.'

Matthew shook his head sadly. 'If you wait until we are rescued I am sure there will be plenty of war left for you to fight somewhere other than this hellhole.'

Alex glanced at his cousin sheepishly. He knew

that Matthew had seen war at first hand and his insistence to fight must have sounded like a drunk spoiling for a brawl. 'Well, we could use our time to collect intelligence on the Germans,' he countered. 'I know of Englishmen living in Rabaul and they must feel motivated to assist the Empire.'

'I wouldn't be so sure of that,' Matthew said, hoisting his rifle over his shoulder. 'They are civilians and right now probably locked up. Besides, even if we did collect any information of worth how would we transmit it to our people in Australia?'

Alex knew that Matthew was speaking sense. It frustrated the young army officer bent on serving his country to stand idly aside while the war went on. Had he been back in Australia he might be now considered for a company command.

'Maybe we could make contact with Father Umberto,' he finally replied. 'He may have ways to relay any intelligence we are able to collect to Australia.'

Matthew rolled his eyes to the sky. 'Wallarie, protect me from men with good but misguided intentions.'

'You really believe in that heathen rubbish?' Alex asked.

'What else should I believe in?' Matthew answered sarcastically. 'The fidelity of women?'

'Touché, old chap,' Alex muttered and began to walk back to the village.

After last light Alex asked Joshua to guide him and Matthew to the mission station. They moved cautiously through the undergrowth lest a German patrol remained in the area but did not see any sign of such. Around midnight they found the neatly laid out Tolai structures and Joshua led them to the priest's house. He knocked on the door and announced himself. Very shortly the priest answered the door, holding a lantern aloft to illuminate his late-night visitors.

'I thought that you might pay me a visit,' he said, seeing Alex. 'It might be best if you come inside.'

The three men entered the house and Father Umberto fetched a bottle of Scotch.

'Who is your friend, Captain Macintosh?' he asked as he poured three glasses. It was obvious that Joshua would not receive an alcoholic drink.

'My cousin Matthew Duffy,' Alex replied, accepting the glass.

'The Germans did not tell me who they were searching for,' Father Umberto said. 'They just said that a couple of Englishmen were on the run from them. No doubt they meant you two. One of my people coming up from Rabaul told me that the Germans had two Australians in the gaol.'

'Did you tell them that we were in Joshua's village?' Alex asked directly.

The priest frowned. 'Why would I tell them when it was I who sent you help to hide out with Joshua and his people?'

'I thought so,' Alex replied. 'But somebody here must have informed the Germans of our whereabouts.'

The priest stared past Alex at a crucifix on his wall. The night had a stillness promising a storm.

Insects fluttered around the kerosene lantern now on the sturdy table in the centre of the room. 'I am very sure I know where the information came from,' he said sadly. 'One of my Irish nuns, with no love for the Empire, has probably passed on the information to the Germans.'

'But we are not English,' Alex protested. 'We are still loyal to the Crown but we are Australian.'

'Your loyalty to the Crown is enough to place you in their camp,' Father Umberto said. 'The good sister lost a brother to English soldiers in Ireland. She is yet to understand the meaning of forgiveness.'

'Who is she?' Matthew asked.

'It does not matter, Mr Duffy,' the priest answered. 'The sister is my responsibility and, at last report, my country has not entered the war on either side. But if I continue to assist you I will put in jeopardy that neutrality and be subject to arrest by the Germans.'

'I understand, Father,' Matthew replied. 'We do not want to put you in any danger of arrest for aiding and abetting us. We were hoping to just hide out until Australia sends a force to seize the island.'

'Do you think that will happen?' the priest asked.

'I am sure of it,' Matthew said. 'It is vital to Australia's security that the Imperial German Navy be neutralised in the Pacific.'

'My only suggestion is that you continue to avail yourselves of Joshua's hospitality until that time comes,' Father Umberto said. 'I will let it slip to the sister in question that I have heard you both have trekked to the eastern side of the island to acquire a boat to sail back to Port Moresby. That might take a bit of pressure off you when she passes on the information – as I know she will do – to the Germans.'

'That would be a help,' Alex replied. 'I am sure that we will be able to compensate Joshua and his people when we are rescued by our forces.'

'One thing, Captain Duffy,' the priest said. 'I would drop any ideas of attempting to wage war against the Germans here. It could mean terrible reprisals against Joshua and the Tolai. I have seen in the past what the Germans are capable of when it comes to putting down native insurrection.'

'How did you know?' Alex asked in a surprised voice.

'I just guessed that a man like you could not be comfortable just simply sitting out in the jungle doing nothing until your comrades came,' Father Umberto replied with a slight smile. 'I would expect your word on that matter before I provided any further help.'

'As one of the Chosen Faith,' Matthew answered in lieu of Alex, 'I can give you our word on that matter.'

'You are a practising Catholic?' Father Umberto asked.

'Well, I was baptised a Catholic and did a stint as an altar boy,' Matthew replied with a wry grin. 'That must count for something when it comes to giving your word to a priest.'

The priest nodded and swallowed the last of his Scotch. 'I accept your word, Mr Duffy,' he replied. 'Now, I would suggest that you make your way back to Joshua's village with him. The last I heard from the German patrol commander was that they were more urgently needed back in Rabaul. They, too, expect your comrades to arrive in force very soon. I will send messages to you of any developments we hear up here. Go in peace and with God.'

Matthew, Alex and Joshua left the house under cover of the night and crept out of the mission station compound to make their way back to the village. During a quick rest en route, Alex turned to Matthew.

'My father was once a Roman Catholic,' he said. 'He promised to renounce Papist ways so that we could inherit the Macintosh family assets, but I sometimes wonder if my father still harbours Papist sympathies.'

Matthew smiled in the dark. 'I guess by now you are starting to understand my so-called religious beliefs.'

'I think that I have more in common with the beliefs of old Wallarie and his ancestor spirits than I do with Christianity. Maybe it is that we aviators tend to be a fairly superstitious lot.'

Hoisting themselves to their feet the three men continued to plod through the night towards the sanctuary of Joshua's village. Alex had tacitly agreed to the Italian priest's request not to wage armed resistance, but he had not promised not to continue his intelligence war. After breakfast the next day he would put to his cousin another idea of how they could fight the Germans until their rescue by invading forces. Needless to say it would be risky.

26

George did not want to be in the park. Now that war had been declared against Germany, he was extremely nervous meeting the assistant consul, Maynard Bosch, but he also realised that the German diplomat had enough knowledge to blackmail him.

George stood at the edge of Hyde Park facing a busy road. Bosch had delivered a written message that they were to meet at this location and George was to appear to be reading a newspaper.

'Thank you for coming,' Bosch said, slipping in beside George without appearing to be talking to him.

'You realise that it is dangerous making contact with me,' George growled. 'What if we are seen together?'

'That is a possibility,' Bosch conceded. 'But I doubt we'll be seen. Your government is preoccupied with other matters for the moment. We have been forced to register with the police but at this stage nothing more has happened.'

'What do you want of me?' George asked, pretending to peruse the newspaper he held up before him.

'I suspect that very soon your police will round us up and send us to internment camps,' Bosch replied. 'I will need someone on the outside in a position of power to carry out certain tasks from time to time.'

'That is impossible,' George replied. 'That would be an act of treason.'

Bosch restrained himself from laughing. 'What do you think you have been doing since we first met?'

'I have never intended to act against the Empire's interests,' George retorted, indignant at the inference.

'Well, consider your help to me as a way of protecting your investment in our chemical industries,' Bosch replied. 'That way you may sleep better at nights.'

'What do you want of me for now?' George asked, glancing fearfully at the people on the footpath on the opposite side of the road and those occupied with horse-drawn wagons and noisy automobiles. A uniformed policeman stood at an intersection directing traffic.

'We would like you to accept this,' Bosch said, slipping a small, thick, brown paper package into George's coat pocket. 'Just say it is both a token of our gratitude and expenses in advance for tasks you may undertake for the Fatherland.'

George was startled by the gesture but remained calm. He already suspected the package contained a lot of cash. 'When we are victorious,' Bosch continued, 'you will be suitably recognised by the Kaiser for your contribution to our war effort. Now, I must leave you but remember, you are in our pay whether you like it or not.'

George did not respond, nor look to see where the German agent was heading. He folded his paper and walked towards his office north of the great spread of parkland, unaware that he was being followed.

The plain clothes constable drew his small, stiff police-issue notebook from his coat pocket and flipped open to the page covering entries for the day. Standing before the newly posted detective sergeant he began to read out what he had observed, having been assigned to covertly track the German diplomat.

'At approximately eleven o'clock this morning I followed Mr Bosch from the consulate to Elizabeth Street, where he stopped by an unknown male person and on careful observation it appeared that he was speaking to the unknown person, whom I have now identified as a Mr George Macintosh. I cannot confirm it, but I thought I saw Bosch discreetly place a small package into the pocket of Mr Macintosh, who did not appear to acknowledge receipt of the article in question.' The constable paused, flicking through his notes.

'Go on, Constable,' Detective Sergeant Jack Firth

prompted from behind his desk. 'Did this Mr George Macintosh happen to have any link with the Macintosh Companies in Kent Street?'

'He did, Sarge,' the constable answered, glancing up from his notebook and seeing an expression of extreme interest in the face of his supervisor in the enemy aliens department of the police force. Jack Firth had fought against being taken off his investigations of criminal matters in Sydney but was convinced by his superiors that this was his significant contribution to the war effort against the enemies of the British Empire. He had been flattered with the idea that only the best men had been chosen for such sensitive duties and settled into his new role, but the Macintosh name was still fresh in his memory regarding the slaying of Guy Wilkes.

And now this suspicious incident had cropped up linking the Macintosh name to possible cooperation with a known enemy agent. The British Secret Intelligence Service had cabled a list of suspects operating in Australia to the government and Firth had been assigned the task of putting Herr Maynard Bosch under close surveillance until the time he was to be interned. Firth had felt it was a good idea to allow the man the opportunity to lead them to any other possible enemy agents and now the mention of one George Macintosh had stunned him. He already knew of the Macintosh name around Sydney. The highly influential family had as its patriarch Colonel Patrick Duffy who was considered above reproach for his services to the British Empire and the Australian government. However, his eldest son was known as a man of expensive tastes and strange behaviour. Rumours picked up from prostitutes on the city streets claimed that he had peculiar sexual tastes.

'Constable,' Firth said, 'I want you to continue your surveillance of Bosch and report immediately if you see him in the company of Mr Macintosh.'

'Right, Sarge,' the constable said, placing the notebook back in his coat pocket.

Alone, behind his desk Sergeant Jack Firth pondered the meaning of what his man on surveillance duties had observed. To all intents and purposes it appeared that Mr George Macintosh was in cohorts with an enemy agent. Firth was astute enough to know that any investigation of a member of the Macintosh family would have to be carried out with great delicacy and discretion. He would pay George Macintosh a visit at his office and maybe, if he played his cards right, get a break in the Wilkes case. Chasing enemy aliens might be an important duty in these troubled times but he was still a copper who knew more about criminals. Jack Firth was not a man who liked to leave loose ends.

Patrick Duffy stood in the foyer of the hotel feeling just a little self-conscious.

'A message has been sent up to Miss Schumann's room,' the concierge said politely, deferring to the tall, distinguished officer. The colourful ribands on his chest denoted his considerable campaign service to the Empire in three wars.

Within minutes, Giselle appeared in company

with a striking older woman whose beauty had been inherited by the daughter.

'Colonel Duffy, may I introduce my mother, Karolina,' Giselle said with a sweet smile. 'Mother, this is Colonel Duffy, Alexander's father.'

Patrick felt uneasy at the frosty expression on Karolina Schumann's face. She was polite in extending her hand but behind the eyes Patrick could see animosity.

'My pleasure, Colonel,' she said, her gloved hand briefly in Patrick's. He did not believe she was telling the truth.

'I must apologise for the unexpected visit but I was in the neighbourhood and thought that you may accept an invitation to attend my eldest son George's residence this Saturday for afternoon tea,' Patrick said, clearing his throat. 'My son has an important announcement to make about his future intentions with Miss Louise Gyles.'

'Louise!' Giselle exclaimed. 'Louise and I were at school together. How exciting! I have not seen Louise in ages.'

'It is a small world,' Patrick said, suddenly remembering that the German girl had spent more time among Australians than her own people in Germany. 'I am sure that she will be pleased to see you again.'

'Mother, we must accept Colonel Duffy's invitation,' Giselle said, turning to Karolina. 'Sir Keith Gyles and Isabel will be pleased to see you again.'

'We are German,' Karolina said. 'Do not be so sure, Giselle. Times have changed.'

'Countries may wage war against each other but

friends remain for life,' Patrick said lamely, receiving an angry look from Karolina Schumann. 'You will find that you will receive the hospitality you have known in the past from all at my son's residence. I give you my word.'

'Your son's word was not to be trusted, Colonel Duffy,' Karolina retorted, anger flashing in her eyes.

'Mother!' Giselle remonstrated. 'Alexander had his reasons.'

'What did my son do, Mrs Schumann, that no good German officer in his shoes would not have done?' Patrick asked, controlling his anger at the slur on his son.

'Your son lied to my husband and all of us about the cargo he left in our safekeeping. And he promised not to attempt to escape the lawful custody of my government and then proceeded to break his parole. I am sorry, Colonel, but the word of your family is accepted with some reservation.'

'My son is an officer in our country's army and I am sure that he acted at the time in the interests of this nation's security,' Patrick countered. 'However, I would like to put all that aside for the moment to reiterate my invitation to you both. I think that you will see we are not all anti-Teutonic in this country. I have left the invitations at the desk with the concierge and pray that I may see you both at my son's house on Saturday. I must excuse myself for now and return to my duties.'

Patrick turned on his heel and departed the luxurious hotel foyer to step back onto the bustling street. He was still smarting from Karolina Schumann's bitter words regarding the honour of his family. As he strode along the crowded street his mind was with his youngest son. Where was he and was he even still alive? Patrick felt helpless. Not just one child had been lost to him but two.

Three weeks had passed since Matthew and Alex had escaped German custody. In that time they had lived among Joshua's people and from time to time had received messages from Father Umberto's mission station keeping them in touch with what was happening in Rabaul.

Alex had acquired a map of the island from the priest and this he saw as being worth its weight in gold. He would pore over it with great interest, identifying locations he felt would make ideal observation posts.

Matthew had returned with Joshua from a hunting trip during which he had used one of his precious rifle rounds to bring down a large feral pig. Joshua was pleased with the meat to be shared with the villagers and Matthew's status in the village was raised. He was no longer just a guest but also a contributor.

Matthew flopped down beside Alex who was sitting cross-legged in the dirt in front of the hut they slept in at night with the single men of the community. Hens strutted around pecking at the insect life they found and a couple of contented, mangy dogs lay in the sun a few feet away, scratching at fleas. Around them they could hear children at play and the laughter of women gossiping as they went about their duties.

'Do you know,' Alex said, staring at the map spread out in his lap, 'if we can get to this ridge here, overlooking Rabaul, we would be in an important position to observe troop movement in the town.'

Matthew glanced at the location Alex indicated. 'The Germans hardly have a force worth observing,' he said. 'I have no doubt that our troops will roll them up in a day.'

Alex looked up at his cousin. 'We have to do something,' he said. 'We just can't sit around here. I promised that I would not agitate for an armed resistance, but I did not promise the priest I would not be active in our war against the Germans.'

Matthew sighed. It was growing obvious that Alex would go insane just simply waiting for the troops to arrive and liberate them. 'I will go along with your idea, but how in hell are you going to be able to pass on any information we glean from our observation post?'

Alex carefully folded the map. 'I have an idea. We collate what we have and if one of our ships is sighted then we send a native boy out in a canoe to pass on our intelligence in a written note.'

'You realise, of course,' Matthew responded, 'that if we spot one of our ships it will probably be on its way to invade. I doubt that a small canoe will be heeded by one of our battle cruisers steaming at full speed.'

Alex leaped to his feet and stared angrily at his cousin. 'So we just sit around here all day and ignore our duty to the Empire?'

'Okay, okay,' Matthew said, holding up his hands in surrender. 'I will go along with your idea. It will take some planning for us to get from here to that ridge and we will need a reliable supply of food and water – not to forget convincing Joshua to support us.'

'I have already spoken with Joshua,' Alex said. 'He has agreed that one of his boys will paddle out when the time comes.'

Matthew did not reply immediately. His cousin had everything in hand and he knew that he could not let him down. 'When do we start?' he asked.

'Tomorrow morning,' Alex said, the tension of his angry outburst easing away.

Matthew rose to his feet, noticing Joshua hurrying towards them with a frown on his face.

'German man has Tolai people who help them look for you,' he said when he was close to the two Australians. 'Father send message that German man pay any Tolai who capture or kill you.'

'What does that mean?' Alex asked.

'That mean we must be very careful,' Joshua replied. 'Many Tolai man know that you are here. Maybe they raid my village looking for you. I think they will just kill you and take your heads to the German man for money.'

'Good idea of yours to get out of here,' Matthew reluctantly conceded to Alex. 'I don't want to see Joshua's people caught up in the middle of our war.'

'We will go this afternoon to that place that you and I discussed,' Alex said to Joshua. 'You can spread the word among the Tolai that we are no longer here and that they are welcome to see that for themselves.'

Joshua nodded. His prime responsibility was to his villagers and he would be glad to see the last of the two Australian guests. He turned and walked away to arrange an escort for them to the ridge over-looking Rabaul.

It took little time to gather together a few baskets of food and gourds of water for the journey. Joshua organised for two young men to accompany him and his guests to the ridge and the small party set off.

Within hours they were swallowed by the jungle along an almost hidden hunting trail in the direction of Rabaul. Joshua and his two warriors were armed with spears, slings and clubs while Matthew and Alex carried their firearms. Near sunset the party stopped to make camp and the leading young warrior spoke softly to Joshua. Alex could see Joshua tense up as they conversed.

'What is it?' Alex asked.

'We travel in another clan lands,' Joshua replied. 'My man think we are being watched.'

Nervously, Alex glanced around at the rapidly darkening forest. Before he could reply the ominous silence was shattered by a hair-raising yell he imme-diately thought was a war cry.

A spear hissed through the air between Joshua and him, narrowly missing them. Alex brought up his rifle in time to see a small party of warriors clam-bering through the undergrowth only feet away. He fired at point blank range at one warrior wielding a vicious-looking club and the man threw up his arms before falling to the ground. Alex was vaguely aware of Matthew firing his rifle and, when he had run out of ammunition, switching to the pistol for defence.

As suddenly as it had exploded on them the attack fell away. The rifles and pistol had killed at least three of the attackers. But Alex realised that he had also emptied his meagre supply of ammunition at the attacking rival clan and of the three Tolai men only Joshua still stood. His two warriors lay dead from fatal wounds inflicted by spear, axe and club.

'Matthew,' he yelled.

'I'm here,' came the reassuring reply as Matthew stepped from the cover of the scrub, holding the pistol.

Alex was relieved to see that he did not appear to be injured. The attack had been swift and short and when Matthew saw the battered and slashed bodies of their two escorts he groaned, squatting down beside the lead boy. 'I only have two rounds left for the pistol,' he said. 'If they mount another attack, we are goners for sure.'

Alex realised that the rifle in his hands was now useless, except to be wielded as a club. 'Maybe they do not know that,' he said. 'I think that we should push on through the night to get out of this area.' He turned to Joshua and explained his idea. Joshua agreed, although he was reluctant to leave the bodies of his two men in the forest. But he was also pragmatic about the chances to recover them deep in rival tribal territory. The warriors would be mourned when he returned to his village.

By midnight they had agreed that they were far

enough away from the scene of the bloody clash. The three men made camp and slept until the dawn.

George Macintosh was extremely annoyed that the plain clothes policeman standing in his office should insist that he speak with him. He had a full schedule of work for the day and now this uncouth detective, whose reputation he already knew about from the city's lurid crime columns, had interrupted his day.

'What can I do for you, Sergeant?' George asked coldly. 'You must realise that I am a busy man, with the war and all calling on the services of our companies.'

'Does that time also include meeting suspected German agents, Mr Macintosh?' Firth countered, and was pleased to see the colour drain from the arrogant man sitting smugly behind his desk.

'I do not have a clue what you are talking about and I must warn you that your insinuation smacks of accusing me of treason. I am sure you are aware of my standing in the community.'

'You were observed, and the meeting in company with Herr Maynard Bosch near Elizabeth Street noted, by one of my men yesterday, Mr Macintosh. You accepted a small brown paper parcel from the aforesaid person.'

'Oh, you mean the assistant German consul,' George countered quickly, realising that his best course of action was to lessen the known facts. 'I had almost forgotten about that. He owed me a sum of money from before the declaration of war and I

418

agreed to meet with him and receive back what he owed in a way that did not appear we had any contact with our current enemy. I suspect that you might do the same had you been in my position.'

Firth was taken aback by Macintosh's explanation and grudgingly conceded the man was smart. This was not going to be easy. 'That may be so,' he replied. 'But I will still have to pass the report upstairs and let my superiors make a decision on how they want to proceed in the matter.'

George rose from behind his desk. His frosty tone appeared to have evaporated towards the policeman. 'I am sorry that I may have appeared somewhat antagonistic towards you, Sergeant Firth, but I have been under a lot of stress lately. I would consider it a favour if what has been observed and mistakenly interpreted could be kept with you and go no further. Possibly I could donate a little towards a police charity.' George opened a drawer in his desk where a pile of fresh bank notes lay in neat bundles. It had been the money passed to him the day before and he had counted two thousand pounds. Quickly peeling off a wad of three hundred pounds he passed it to the policeman. 'I am sure that the amount will satisfy any charity you should think of.'

Firth stared at the wad of notes. It was a substantial amount – more than his pay for a year. 'I will need more,' he said quietly.

George turned to reluctantly retrieve another bundle of notes but was stopped by Firth. 'The money is sufficient but I want information regarding the Wilkes murder, Mr Macintosh.' Firth took the wad of bank notes from George, pocketed them and stood back waiting for a response.

'Do I have your assurance that the matter of me meeting with Herr Bosch will be, should we say, lost?' George countered.

'I can promise you that, Mr Macintosh,' the policeman answered. 'But I must also have information on the Wilkes murder if we are to seal the bargain of your donation.'

'What do you want from me?'

'For now I want very little – except any information as to the whereabouts of your sister.'

'That, I am afraid, I cannot tell you as I do not know myself,' George said. 'All I can tell you is that she is most probably in America, and possibly in the Los Angeles area. My father had a man assigned to track her down and it seems from what I have been told by our Pearl Harbour agency that he was arrested by the police there on an old charge and is currently doing hard labour on the island.'

'If I find out that you are lying to me, Mr Macintosh, be assured all bets are off and the report of your meeting with a suspected enemy agent will be passed up to higher circles,' Firth said slowly so that his words would sink in. 'We will let the matter drop for now but I will be keeping a very close eye on you. Since there is nothing else – and you are a busy man – I will leave you. Good day, Mr Macintosh.'

As George watched the detective leave his office he realised that he had been sweating. At least he had survived the close call of being reported for treasonous activities and the investigating officer seemed more obsessed with bringing someone to justice over the murder of the popular film actor than counter-espionage work. George knew that despite the way the war had changed roles for many people Detective Sergeant Jack Firth was at heart a true policeman, and not so much interested in the politics of war. It had been a damned close run thing, George thought, echoing the words of the Duke of Wellington after the battle of Waterloo.

27

Arthur Thorncroft was tortured by the dilemma. After a silence of ten weeks the letter from Fenella had arrived on his desk, and with trembling hands he had opened it to read the words from the other side of the Pacific Ocean. Fenella had expressed how well her life was progressing and that she missed him and all her family in Sydney. However, she had reminded him of his oath not to divulge her whereabouts to anyone until she felt that she was ready to return and face her father.

Arthur placed the letter on his desk and stared at a metal container in the corner of his office. Inside it was the completed film that Fenella and Guy had finished just before his death and Fenella's flight from Australia. Arthur was a showman and knew just how valuable the film was. It would attract a huge audience intrigued by the mysterious circumstances surrounding the leading man's death and the disappearance of his leading lady. Sex and violence were a powerful combination and although such things were not spoken of openly in polite society the film was guaranteed to draw in the crowds. But both Patrick and George had concurred that the film should not be released until Fenella was located and the matter of Wilkes' death settled – one way or another.

Arthur sighed in his frustration at the ban on its release. He was a man who believed that the show must go on but was also dependent on the Macintosh family for finance. His studio was temporarily closed and most of his young male staff had left to enlist for military service while the rest sought employment with rival film companies. But each day Arthur would journey to his empty studio and go through the routine of administering what was now the ghost of a thriving film production enterprise. As it was, the Australian market was being flooded with popular American movies, highlighting the talents of their own stars, and the Australian product was under threat.

One matter in Fenella's letter particularly disturbed Arthur. She had asked about Randolph Gates, and requested that Arthur pass on to him the message that he was constantly in her thoughts. It was strange, Arthur mused, that Fenella had not made contact with Randolph who he trusted was astute enough to be able to track her down with the information he had provided. As it was, from what he had been able to glean from Patrick and George, no one had heard from Randolph in a long time. George had even implied that the American had disappeared with a good amount of the money set aside to find Fenella. Arthur had trouble believing that Randolph would do such a thing as he was an honourable man and very much in love with Fenella.

Arthur pulled a page from a writing pad and scribbled a message addressed to the Macintosh agency in Pearl Harbour. Maybe they could throw some light on the whereabouts of Randolph Gates. He would telegraph Pearl Harbour and inquire as to what they may know of his whereabouts.

The afternoon for George's afternoon tea party was perfect – a sunny, unseasonal balmy day. The manicured gardens were filled with marquees manned by white-jacketed stewards hired for the big event. Ladies were wearing their finest fashions for the up-and-coming spring season in Sydney and the gentlemen had donned formal suits. The guests mingled on the lawns and under the canopies of the marquees for the grand occasion. George had ensured that he be surrounded by the city's most influential voices in politics and society, without any concern for the extravagant cost of the party.

Patrick attended wearing his colourful dress uniform as given his current duties he was rarely out of it. He was accompanied by Colonel John Hughes, also in uniform, and Gladys Hughes in her best dress. George greeted them and gestured to a waiter hovering nearby to supply his guests with a flute of champagne.

'This must be the first time that I have ever seen you looking just a little flustered,' Patrick said to his eldest son, taking a sip of the excellent imported French wine.

'It is not every day that one announces the fact that one is to be married,' George replied.

For a moment Patrick saw the son that he wished he had always known – a young man who was facing the huge responsibility of marriage and the probable birth of children.

'I only wish that your brother and sister could be here,' Patrick sighed. 'I think that they would approve.'

George did not respond. 'Father, Colonel and Mrs Hughes, I must excuse myself,' he replied. 'I see that Sir Keith, Lady Gyles and Louise have arrived.'

George made his way through the guests and went to his fiancée and her parents.

Gladys Hughes immediately waved to a friend from her bridge club and excused herself from the company of the two old soldier comrades, leaving them alone to discuss military matters as she knew they would.

'I am sorry to say that we have heard nothing of Alex and Matthew,' John Hughes said quietly. 'But I can get you up-to-date information on the progress of the AN and MEF,' he said, glancing around to ensure that their conversation would not be overheard. 'They have been tasked to capture the radio stations at Yap, Nauru and Rabaul. The New Zealanders are going after Samoa. Our navy friends have taken out all stops and we have the full support of our best surface ships to escort the invasion force north. The AN and MEF are currently laid up in Port Moresby. It will only be a matter of time, maybe a week, and they will be in Rabaul's harbour. When that happens, I am sure we will get the boys back safe and well.'

'I pray that you are right,' Patrick replied. 'Life is very lonely without my children.'

'Well, you have the consolation of knowing George will probably continue the Macintosh dynasty with that fine young woman,' Hughes said, nodding in the direction of George now in conversation with Sir Keith Gyles, who was standing proudly by his daughter and wife.

'Yes,' Patrick said without much enthusiasm. 'All going well he might make me a grandfather.'

Even as the two soldiers stood aside from the guests at George's afternoon tea party, Giselle Schumann and her mother arrived. Patrick noticed the two women and broke off his conversation with Hughes. 'I'm sorry, old chap,' he said. 'But I have to welcome a couple of guests that I have personally invited.'

John Hughes looked across at the two women who had attracted his colleague's attention. They were standing just a little awkwardly among the guests. 'I say, old man, a couple of true beauties. Would I be correct in assuming they are mother and daughter?'

'Yes,' Patrick answered. 'Mrs Karolina Schumann and her daughter, Giselle.'

Hughes turned to Patrick. 'You don't mean Frau Schumann and Alexander's young lady?'

'I do,' Patrick replied. 'They may be considered

enemy aliens but I doubt that two women are a real danger to our national security. Besides, Giselle Schumann was actually born in Sydney and holds British citizenship.'

'I did not intend to upset you,' John Hughes hurried to say. 'It's just that in your position it may not be wise under the current circumstances to be seen consorting with German nationals.'

'I believe that Alex is very much in love with Giselle Schumann,' Patrick said. 'I have spoken with her and it seems that she was prepared to escape with him from her father's plantation, except that things went a bit wrong for her. She is the only real link I have with Alex until he is returned – or we learn that he has been killed by the Germans.'

John Hughes patted Patrick on the back with a gesture of sympathy for the father agonising over the unknown fate of his youngest son. 'He will come home to us,' Hughes said reassuringly. 'Go to the ladies and be assured that I would also like to make their acquaintance.'

Patrick nodded, grateful that his friend was prepared to provide a public show of support. When he reached the two women they turned to greet him.

'Thank you for your invitation, Colonel Duffy,' Karolina said. 'It is a little warmer than that from some others I recognise here this afternoon. They seem to pretend not to see me, as if I were a ghost in the dark.'

'Don't worry about those people,' Patrick said. 'I am sure that when they see I am more than happy to have you both here on this day they will warm to you again.'

'Louise!' Giselle suddenly said.

Patrick turned to see Louise Gyles pushing her way through the guests towards them with a beaming smile.

'Giselle, Mrs Schumann, how wonderful to have you both here today,' she said, hugging both of them briefly in turn. 'How did you know . . . how did you arrive in Sydney, oh, I have so many questions . . . Do you remember Harold Quinn . . .'

The excited prattle between close friends continued and Patrick felt a warmth towards his future daughter-in-law for her uninhibited welcome of his two guests. It was obvious that Karolina Schumann was being gently pushed out of the exchange of gossip between the two young ladies and Patrick guided her across to meet John Hughes and his wife. He sensed that his act had thawed a little of the animosity she obviously held towards him as the father of Alexander. For a short time he left Karolina chatting in the company of Mrs Hughes who did not appear to hold any hostility towards the other woman on account of her nationality. In fact, he actually heard Karolina laugh as she and Mrs Hughes discussed holidays in the Bavarian Alps. Patrick found himself gazing at the mother of Giselle just a little more than he should. She was, after all, an enemy alien but still, Patrick admitted to himself, she was a damned beautiful woman.

Once the trivialities of gossip had been covered Louise noticed that her old school friend appeared sad.

'What is it?' she asked Giselle. 'You appear to be upset. Have I offended you?'

'Are we able to go somewhere private?' Giselle asked, touching her friend on the wrist.

'I am sure that we can go to George's sitting room to be alone,' Louise said, guiding Giselle by the elbow across the lawn away from the guests. When they reached the house they went inside and Louise sat Giselle down with a small glass of sherry from the decanter on the sideboard.

Giselle sipped gratefully at the liquor. Louise sat down beside her on the settee. 'What is troubling you?' she asked gently.

'Oh, I am sorry for being so melancholy on your special day,' Giselle answered. 'It is just that you were always my very best friend when we were at school and when I visited Sydney. And now, here you are, about to wed the brother of the man I love.'

'You are in love with Alexander!' Louise exclaimed. 'How bully!' Then she suddenly fell silent, remembering that George's younger brother had mysteriously disappeared on a voyage to German New Guinea. Neither George nor his father would speak about the disappearance, but Louise had gleaned from bits and pieces George had mentioned that there was a good chance that Alex might not be returning from some kind of secret mission.

'Oh, I am so sorry,' Louise said, impulsively rubbing Giselle's arm as one would consoling a child. 'I have heard that something may have happened to Alex.'

'I was with Alex on our plantation only weeks ago,' Giselle confided. 'We had talked of marriage and I was even prepared to defy my parents and elope with him to be married in Sydney. But everything went wrong and he and Mr Matthew Duffy were taken under armed guard to Rabaul. Since then I fear for his safety.'

'I was never told of your feelings for Alex,' Louise responded. 'If only the colonel or George had said something I might have been able to have been by your side for support.'

'There was nothing you could do,' Giselle assured her. 'Alex is a soldier and I fear that might have put his life in extreme danger.'

'I did not know that Mr Matthew Duffy was with Alex,' Louise said. 'The last time I saw him he promised to take me up in his aeroplane to touch the clouds. I must confess that I was very attracted to him but, without a word, he simply disappeared from my life.'

'Matthew is a fine man,' Giselle said. 'He and Alex were as close as two men could be when I knew him at our plantation. I hang on to the hope that their friendship will keep them safe as they look after each other.'

'It will,' Louise agreed. 'The little that I came to learn about Matthew Duffy impressed me. He is a man of action and has lived through many dangerous situations in his life. Just the man who should be with Alex.'

Giselle hugged Louise. 'Oh, I dream that one day you will be my guest at the colonel's house when Alex and I declare that we will be wed.'

'Louise.' The two women broke their embrace as George's voice carried through the house. 'Louise, it is time to join me as I make our announcement.'

'I am coming,' Louise replied, rising from the settee and patting down her dress. She extended her hand to Giselle. 'I would like you to be beside me when George makes his speech and next time it will be me beside you when Alex makes his.'

For three days after reaching a low ridge line east of Rabaul Matthew and Alex had little else to do other than attempt to observe the shipping anchored offshore from the German settlement. They were too far away to make notes on troop movements and the time passed slowly. Joshua had left them with enough supplies for four days and returned on the evening of the third with four of his young men. The rough living was taking its toll on the two Australians living under a fierce tropical sun on the monotonous rations of starchy food and poorly cooked pork. Their bodies were covered in weeping sores and they had both lost a considerable amount of weight.

Joshua remained with the Australians overnight and when the sun rose on the following day Matthew called him over to where Alex lay on his back in a fever, mumbling incoherently as he thrashed about.

'I think he's going through a bout of malaria,' Matthew said to the clan chief. 'We have to make a litter and get him back to the mission station.'

Joshua did not understand the English Matthew was speaking so Matthew switched to his crude German. Joshua nodded vigorously and shouted orders to his men who used their machetes to cut down saplings and string them together.

They rolled Alex into the improvised litter and the tough young Tolai men lifted it to their shoulders. It would be an arduous journey back into the hills, one fraught with danger from rival clans to say nothing of the rugged terrain itself. Matthew had seen malaria in many countries before and had from time to time fought the deadly sickness himself. What he saw in the attack on his cousin worried him. Weakened as they were from living on the diet of starchy vegetables, their bodies were prone to infection. He hated to think what they both looked like. The ragged clothes he wore had taken on a distinct looseness since their escape from the gaol in Rabaul.

They struggled along the trail, ever climbing up and clambering down the slopes, with Matthew taking a turn at one end of the litter to relieve the Tolai men. Only Joshua did not assist in carrying the litter; his task was to guide and look out for any ambush along the way.

It took two days of hard struggle along the bush trails to reach the mission. When they arrived late in the evening it was the Irish nun, Sister Bridget, who met them, holding up a lantern to provide light for the Tolai men to take Alex to the infirmary.

'And you would be returning to us, Captain Macintosh,' she said, lowering the lamp to identify the patient. 'You have learned nothing of being out of your own country. And who would you be?' she asked, glancing up at Matthew's gaunt, unshaven face.

'I am Matthew Duffy,' he answered. 'And my

grandfather was the big man himself, Patrick Duffy, who once roamed the north-east coast of the old country, son of Kate Duffy, sister to Tom and Michael Duffy.'

The Irish nun looked closely at Matthew with some interest, holding up the lantern to get a better look at the sunken eyes burning with a fierce challenge. 'I have heard of Patrick Duffy, a true son of Ireland who it was said was murdered by the savages of Queensland.'

Matthew was too tired to explain that it had been a treacherous police officer who had killed his grandfather. At least she had heard of his legendary grandfather and from the tone of her voice was suitably impressed by his pedigree. If she was the traitor in Father Umberto's tropical parish then she just might not betray a fellow Irishman who had such an impressive record fighting the British. 'We need your help,' he said. 'My cousin looks as if his fever is malarial. Do you have quinine?'

'We do,' Sister Bridget replied. 'I am surprised to hear that Captain Macintosh is related to you as I have heard he is a Protestant and not of Irish blood.'

'You are wrong on that point, Sister,' Matthew said with a weak smile. 'His grandfather was also Patrick Duffy. Captain Macintosh's father is named in honour of the big man himself, but I am afraid Captain Macintosh's side of the family dropped the rosary beads.'

'Heaven protect us,' the nun said, crossing herself as if she were in the presence of the son of Satan. 'Despite the fact that Captain Macintosh is not of the True Faith, I will ensure that he receives the best treatment we can give him, as he carries in his veins the blood of a true Irish patriot.'

Matthew rubbed his forehead with the back of his grimy hand, satisfied that he might just have gained them forgiveness for being supporters of the British Empire. He knew that Alex was beyond any hope of moving for some time but he would not leave his cousin's side until he was well enough to return to the jungle to avoid the German patrol. He prayed that Wallarie was still watching over them both.

The burly German reservist warrant officer saluted his superior. Major Paul Pfieffer stood by the machine-gun post in a trench reinforced with heavy palm tree logs and manned by the warrant officer's crew of young German reservist soldiers.

'I telephoned what I heard from a native boy we had come to our post yesterday, sir,' the warrant officer said.

'Yes, Sergeant Major,' Pfieffer answered, sweat trickling down his face from under his slouch hat. 'You said that the native informed you that they had suffered casualties last week when they attempted to ambush the two escaped prisoners. Did he say where?'

'We still have him here for further questioning,' the senior NCO replied. 'Thought he might also be of value as a guide.'

'Good thinking,' Pfieffer said. 'Hang on to him until I say otherwise.'

'Yes, sir.'

Pfieffer had finished his tour of the armed posts that had been established to defend the Rabaul region against the inevitable invasion ahead. He would return to his headquarters in the town and consider what was to be done about the two Australian escapees roaming about somewhere in the mountains east of the township. All non-German expatriates had been arrested on the declaration of war against England, France and Russia but then given their freedom for the moment. The intelligence officer knew from the news trickling through their communications centre that savage fighting was occurring on the other side of the world. He had a brother who was commanding a regiment at a place called Mons where the British were offering stiff resistance, and an uncle serving with the High Command at Tannenberg, fighting the Russian Tsar's vast army. And here he was with a pitifully small force expected to resist overwhelming numbers when the time came. He suspected that names like Mons and Tannenberg would be remembered in the future, when German soldiers sat around beer halls clashing pewters together like the old Saxon warriors of the past to celebrate their victories. None would raise a toast to the pitifully small garrison courageously standing its ground in a far-off place most in Germany had never heard of.

Pfieffer accepted the salute of a young soldier and pulled down on the pommel of his saddle to hoist himself onto his mount. He had a difficult decision to make about the young captain relieved of duty and currently languishing at the barracks. What was he to do? Under the martial situation on the island he could either execute Hauptmann Hirsch or give him back command of troops. He would decide what to do when he received the latest intelligence reports at his headquarters.

28

How could it have happened? Arthur Thorncroft fumed, reading the telegram received from the Pearl Harbour offices of the Macintosh companies. It seemed Randolph Gates was currently incarcerated in an Hawaiian prison. No wonder he had not had any contact with him.

More importantly, why had George not pursued the American's whereabouts? After all, Patrick had assigned the task of monitoring developments to his eldest son while Patrick was tied up with his military duties. Arthur reached for the telephone and rang through to George Macintosh's office.

'What can I do for you?' George asked when he was put through.

'I have just received a telegram from your offices in Pearl Harbour,' Arthur said. 'According to what your agency there has told me, Mr Gates is currently serving six months in prison on an assault charge. Why did you not telegraph your office in Hawaii to see if they knew of Randolph's whereabouts?'

In his office, George shifted uncomfortably in his chair. He suddenly remembered how he had quashed the information weeks earlier and pretended that he knew nothing of the American's sudden and mysterious disappearance from the scene. 'I am sorry, Arthur,' he replied. 'I knew nothing of Mr Gates' arrest. However, I will look into it.'

'Will you be telling your father what I have learned?' Arthur persisted.

'I don't think that it would be wise to upset my father at this moment. He has enough on his plate. It would be better that I take care of the matter but I would need your word that you will inform no one else of what you have learned of Mr Gates' fate. Do I have your word?'

Arthur took a deep breath. 'You do, so long as you promise to do everything in your power to help free Randolph. He is a good man and there must be something the Macintosh name can do for him – even in American territory.'

'As I said,' George reiterated, 'I promise to use all means at our disposal to chase up Mr Gates' unfortunate situation. If that is all, Arthur, I must return to my work.'

'Just one other thing,' Arthur added. 'Congratulations on the announcement of your engagement to Miss Gyles. I read about it in the social pages.'

A silence followed as Arthur knew it would. That he had not received an invitation to the afternoon tea party came as no surprise. He and George did not like each other and, deep down, George would not have wanted to have a man attend who was known to be a queer.

Arthur placed the telephone on the hook and sat back to stare at the poster for his latest film hanging on the wall of his office. It was just too bad the film would never be released.

Major Paul Pfieffer felt himself being shaken awake.

'Sir, sir,' the voice said with a note of urgency. 'The invasion has commenced.'

Pfieffer sat up in his bed and blinked at the dim light from the lantern being held by the German soldier whom he had left on duty at the military headquarters in town.

The German officer shifted his weight to place his feet on the floor. 'What time is it, Private?' he asked, rubbing his eyes.

'It is just after three o'clock, sir,' the soldier answered as Pfieffer stumbled across the room to retrieve his field uniform hanging beside his sword on a wooden hook. He dressed quickly while the soldier waited to escort him.

'What has happened?' Pfieffer asked when he was dressed and ready to depart in the early morning dark along the silent streets of Rabaul.

'Our lookouts spotted the shape of two enemy destroyers in the harbour, but they left,' the soldier answered. 'We thought it was important enough to disturb you.'

'You acted correctly,' Pfieffer answered. 'I want you to go to the officers' quarters at the barracks and wake Hauptmann Hirsch. Tell him to report to headquarters immediately.'

'Yes, sir,' the soldier answered and broke away to head for the barracks where the men were already awake because of the call to arms. Pfieffer continued his walk. At least now he knew what he must do about Dieter Hirsch.

Offshore the Australian navy conveying a battalion of infantry supported by armed reservist sailors cruised the tropical night. Two of the heavier ships, the HMAS *Australia* and HMAS *Sydney*, were escorted by Australian destroyers ready to launch their forces against the Germans in Rabaul. Their task was to capture the radio station just outside of town and force a surrender of all enemy forces. A sweep of the harbour for sea mines and enemy shipping had been carried out and the result was that there did not appear to be an immediate threat to the invasion force currently at sea.

Dieter Hirsch stood to attention before the intelligence officer at military headquarters.

'You are off the hook, for the moment, Herr Hauptmann,' Pfieffer said. 'From what I can put together we are now facing a full-scale invasion and we need every officer and soldier we have. I am assigning you the command of a contingent of our native police, and you will join with our other forces to defend the radio station at Bitapaka. Should you acquit yourself well I will dismiss any reports concerning your behaviour resulting in the escape of the two prisoners. Are we clear on my instructions?'

'Yes, sir,' Dieter replied. 'I promise to carry out my duties as expected of an officer of the Fatherland.'

'Good,' Pfieffer said, sensing that the young officer had answered with conviction. 'Now, go and draw arms and report to Warrant Officer Abanego. He will assist you in organising your men for the defence.'

Pfieffer rose from behind his desk and stretched out his hand to the young officer. 'I wish you all the best, Hauptmann Hirsch,' he said, shaking Dieter's hand firmly. 'As we both well know, it may be that we will never meet again in this world. Good luck.'

Dieter Hirsch accepted the gesture from his superior officer. They both knew that the defence of the island was hopeless in the light of what they suspected lay out at sea waiting to steam into the harbour. Dieter Hirsch may have only been a reservist officer but his courage was equal to that of any professional soldier. He stepped back and saluted the major, turned on his heel and hurried away in the dark to find his command of armed Tolai police. He did so knowing that once the Australians came in force he may not see the sun go down that day in his paradise.

Hours later, bleary-eyed, Major Pfieffer received news at his headquarters that an Australian destroyer identified in the morning light as the HMAS *Yarra* had cruised into the harbour to disembark a small party of troops near the jetty. He was also informed that the Australian troops had broken into a warehouse and looted it. As no opposition was offered by the defenders no shots had been fired. A surreal situation prevailed in Rabaul as the Germans watched the manoeuvrings of the Australian soldiers, sailors and ships in their territory. Pfieffer was kept up to date with intelligence reports, attempting to identify the intentions of the Australian task force off his shores. He was disturbed to see that telephone lines were being cut to Rabaul from outer settlements and concluded that the enemy task force was landing raiding parties to disrupt communications.

All day the German troops who came and went at his headquarters appeared demoralised. Maybe it was the fact that nothing appeared to be certain anymore in their lives, Pfieffer thought, watching a young German reservist staring wide-eyed at the harbour as if expecting to see the apocalyptic horseman of death ride directly toward him.

At around sunset an unconfirmed report came to Pfieffer that a small cruiser and submarine had been spotted in the harbour. All nerves were on edge as the sun set that night. Searchlights lit the harbour and Pfieffer retired to his private bungalow on the edge of town. The German officer sat at the edge of his bed and stared at his sword hanging from a wooden peg on the wall. If nothing else he could hand it over in any surrender ceremony as it was fairly useless against the big guns of the Australian cruisers out at sea that seemed at the ready to bombard the town into a pile of rubble. There were many civilians cowering in their homes, most likely praying that the military did not attempt to resist the overwhelming force arrayed against them. Damn the Kaiser's men who had ignored the defences in the Pacific, Pfieffer thought. He lay down on his bed. It had been an exceptionally hot day but Pfieffer suspected that hell would be even hotter if the naval guns opened up on the town.

The major was dressed and already at military headquarters the next day when the news came through mid morning that the Australian naval task force had entered the harbour. The news was not correct; only a couple of ships sat offshore. But after midday the full force was seen to steam into the harbour. By the time the sun set that day a battalion of infantry soldiers had landed and the German major knew it was all over. At least the Australian ships had not shelled the town and no one was killed.

He was only partly correct in his summation. South of Rabaul Australian forces and German-led reservists and police were engaged in a fierce battle to the death. Hauptmann Dieter Hirsch was learning what it meant to be an officer leading troops into a wall of gunfire and bayonets.

Although it had been expected, Karolina Schumann and her daughter were still in shock. The uniformed police had come in the early hours of the morning

443

and knocked heavily on their hotel door, demanding entry.

Karolina had dressed quickly before opening the door to a burly police sergeant backed by two young constables. He had spoken gruffly and when he was satisfied he had established her identity and that of Giselle ordered them to put together only the amount of personal property they could carry. He had made it plain that they were now officially under arrest and were to be transported to a place south-west of the city called Holsworthy, to be interned for the duration of hostilities as enemy aliens. Karolina had been half-expecting the day to come and had ensured that she had her parcel of valuables set aside.

They were escorted from the hotel where a few early risers reading newspapers in the foyer glanced at them with hostile eyes as they passed. Karolina met their stares with a cool demeanour, belying the terrible fear she felt for the safety of her daughter and herself. Karolina had heard of British concentration camps established in South Africa by Kitchener during the Anglo–Boer war at the turn of the century and knew that thousands of innocent women and children had died behind the barbed wire from malnutrition and disease. Dear God, she prayed silently, do not let this be so.

In the rear of the truck that carried them west out of Sydney they clutched their meagre possessions in their laps as the truck bumped and rattled along the poorly constructed roads, passing paddocks and lonely farmhouses.

By mid morning the truck arrived outside the

high barbed wire fence enclosing a small settlement of white tents set out on a dreary plain of grass and a few gum trees while armed guards manned towers and patrolled the perimeter. Karolina could see that in one of the wooden towers a machine gun was positioned, its squat barrel pointed inward at the tents.

'All out,' a soldier ordered in a loud voice and the frightened civilian men and women clambered down from the rear of the truck. None had spoken to each other on the trip by order of the armed soldier who sat in the back with them. They had cast each other terrified looks, but had obeyed the order to remain silent.

'Right, you lot, line up and you will be marched to the administration office for processing,' the soldier barked.

Karolina recognised the two stripes on his arm as marking him as a corporal in the Australian army. She fell in beside Giselle whose shocked expression was also that of disbelief. 'I have a British passport,' Giselle protested to the corporal.

'That don't count for much around here, lady,' he replied. 'Half the people going into here were born in this country, but a German is a German despite all that. Tell your story to the government officials.'

Karolina took her daughter's hand in her own. 'We will be safe, my little one,' she said with a weak, reassuring smile and never before had Giselle loved her mother more than now, when their world had been turned upside down.

Satisfied that his charges were under control, the

corporal gave the order to march. The small party of German internees – men, women and children – stumbled through the gates to be processed. Giselle was too stunned to cry. The tears of despair would come when they were assigned their tent quarters.

Sweating, reloading, yelling orders and feeling the thump of the rifle in his shoulder, Dieter Hirsch fell back with his contingent of Tolai policemen, against the steady Australian advance along the track to Bita-paka. Around him in the scrubby jungle, he guessed, were others experiencing the same fear that he felt. He had seen enemy soldiers fall from their bullets and knew that he had left many of his own men lying back along the track either dead, wounded or simply too terrified to react to the assault on them.

Dieter knew that they would eventually lose the fight. The sheer numbers of the assaulting force alone dictated this. He saw movement and swung his rifle onto the target. The firing pin clicked on an empty chamber and he reached for the bandolier across his chest, finding a clip and slamming it in the open breech, sliding the bolt forward to chamber a round. The Australian soldier had disappeared and for a moment the jungle fell eerily silent.

Dieter glanced around and saw that he was truly alone now. His ears rang from the constant gunfire. When he took stock of his situation it appeared that he had lost his command to bullets and capture. He knew that he was faced with a couple of grim alter-natives. He could go down fighting, or surrender to the advancing Australians. Had he not sworn to Major Pfieffer that he would acquit himself as a son of the Fatherland?

There was a third alternative, he thought grimly. He could simply slip away and head back into the hills where he might find others like himself, evading capture, and then move into a guerrilla war against the invading Australian forces.

When a man screamed in agony not far away Dieter recognised the terrible sound of a bayonet being withdrawn from a body. He had heard a similar sound when pigs were stuck. He lowered himself to the ground and cautiously moved aside some undergrowth to see an Australian soldier wiping the blood from his long bayonet on the trunk of a tree nearby. At his feet lay a Tolai policeman gasping out the last of his life, while gripping the terrible wound to his chest.

Dieter shrank back into the concealment of the undergrowth. Had the policeman surrendered, only to be murdered by the Australian soldier, or had he attempted to fight the man in hand-to-hand combat? Whatever the answer, Dieter was convinced to escape and continue armed resistance another day. He was not deserting – as his command no longer existed.

Very carefully, Dieter concealed himself while the advancing Australian soldiers and sailors passed by him on their way to capture the radio station. Gunfire broke out behind him where he deduced a handful of his fellow countrymen were still holding out. The rifle fire was answered by a fusillade of shots from the advancing Australians.

Suddenly, Dieter felt his side thumped as if he'd been stung by a giant hornet. He realised immediately that he had been hit by a stray bullet and lay gasping in the undergrowth. Dieter could feel the stinging pain along his ribs halfway down to his waist and gingerly probed the wound with his fingers. From what he could ascertain the bullet had grazed his side, smashing a rib. The pain came in agonising waves and he groaned softly, praying that his cries had not revealed his position to the enemy. He knew he was losing blood and applied a bandage from his kit, listening carefully and gritting his teeth as the Australians moved all around him, but fortunately intent on clearing the track to the radio station.

With the bandage applied securely, Dieter remained hidden until last light when he broke cover to escape into the hills. He at least knew the country better than the invading Australians and calculated that it would take him a good day and night to reach the mission station. From there he could make his plans to disappear in the jungle and continue waging war against the occupying Australian troops.

Unknown to those at the Catholic mission, the skirmishing against German resistance continued on the coast and, despite a clear intent by the few remaining German troops not to cede, a surrender ceremony was already being arranged in Rabaul by the commander of the invading force to mark the defeat of the Germans on Neu Pommern.

Father Umberto had organised to use his limited supply of malarial suppressant to save Alex who by now was out of the worst of the fever and sitting up to take soup administered by the nuns. He was thin and pale but still alive.

Matthew had sat by him day and night and the strain of worry had creased his face with worry lines.

'How is the patient?' Father Umberto asked, entering the lime-washed infirmary with a broad smile.

'Good, Father,' Alex answered with a weak smile. 'Should be on my pins by this afternoon and out of your hair by tomorrow.'

'Well, one of my boys returning from Rabaul has some astounding news that I think you two might like to know,' the priest said, his smile widening. 'It seems that your countrymen have landed and captured Rabaul, and that they have even conducted a surrender ceremony. You will be able to go home soon.'

Matthew leaped to his feet and grabbed the startled priest's hand, shaking it vigorously.

'Thanks, Father,' he said. 'The news could not have come at a better time.'

'However,' the priest continued, 'I would caution against Captain Macintosh attempting any trek to the coast in his present condition. He should rest a few days and gather his strength before doing so. In the meantime I will be sending down a message to your people to tell them that you are up here safe and well.'

Matthew looked to his cousin propped up in the

infirmary bed. 'That is good news,' he said. 'If a party comes for us Alex can be littered down to Rabaul.'

'Be damned if I am going to be carried out of here,' Alex retorted fiercely. 'I will walk out with you.'

Matthew sat down. He could understand his cousin's pride. 'Okay, we wait for them to arrive and walk out together.'

The Italian priest shrugged. At least now he did not have to fear reprisals from the German administration for harbouring the two Australians.

That evening the mission station had a visitor, but not one who was expected.

Matthew and Alex were stunned to see Hauptmann Dieter Hirsch helped into the infirmary by two of the native nuns and Sister Bridget and laid down on a cot next to Alex. With glassy eyes, he looked up. Matthew could see the dark shadow of a blood-soaked bandage strapped around his chest.

'Where did you get it?' Matthew asked Dieter.

'In the side,' Dieter replied hoarsely. The Irish nun was swabbing the wounded German officer's brow when Father Umberto arrived.

'Sorry to hear that,' Matthew said without rancour. 'We have heard that your cobbers have surrendered to our boys.'

'I have not surrendered,' Dieter replied, gritting his teeth against the pain when the priest stepped in to remove the bandage, exposing the ugly wound.

'That's a bit of a moot point,' Matthew said. 'Captain Macintosh over here is a commissioned officer and obliged to accept your surrender.'

'There are no prisoners under the roof of my

mission,' Father Umberto said, tossing aside the bloody field bandage and reaching for a sterilised swab to clean the wound. 'Your war is out there, not here. Italy is still a neutral country.'

'But you are now on land occupied by my country,' Matthew countered. 'You will fall under our administration.'

'When you and Captain Macintosh sought our help did not my people and I risk everything to protect you?' the priest asked.

Matthew felt embarrassed by his nationalistic enthusiasm but before he could reply Alex's voice cut across the tiny space of the infirmary. 'Hauptmann Hirsch risked his career to aid us in our escape,' he said. 'We owe him our lives and must honour the risk he took. As far as I am concerned, we never saw him brought into the mission.'

'That suits me fine,' Matthew agreed. 'But I never thought that you might see the matter from other than a military point of view.'

'Thank you, my friends,' Dieter said, gritting his teeth as Father Umberto bandaged the wound. 'I am grateful for your consideration.'

'How are you at chess?' Matthew asked, causing Dieter to glance up at him with a questioning look.

'I play well,' he replied.

'Good,' Matthew answered. 'Captain Macintosh is a lousy player and I need a bit of competition. Father Umberto has a chess set. You and I will have a few games while you are recuperating.'

'That should be a short time,' the Italian priest said, washing his hands in an enamel dish. 'Hauptmann

Hirsch has not suffered a life-threatening wound. The bullet has broken a rib and it will heal with some bed rest.'

That night the four men shared a bottle or two of the good French wine that Father Umberto had stashed away. For the night there was no war as they swapped stories of home.

Two days later, a patrol of Australian soldiers and sailors arrived under arms to make contact with their two countrymen rumoured to be holed up in the mission station.

When they arrived they were met by the sight of two very gaunt men with beards, wearing ragged clothes but exhibiting broad smiles of relief. They were not told of the German militia officer who'd been moved outside the mission station to an outlying hut where he was being cared for by an Irish nun.

29

It was a grand homecoming for Alex and Matthew in October. Guests filled Patrick's house and no expense had been spared in catering for the formal dinner to toast the return of Captain Macintosh and Mr Duffy. Only George Macintosh did not appear happy as the invited friends and guests celebrated the miraculous survival of the two Australians. Alex wore his military dress uniform while Matthew found that his formal suit still fitted him, albeit hanging just a little loosely on his frame on account of the loss of weight he had incurred in the jungles of the Pacific island.

'Good to have you back, m'boy,' a red-nosed guest congratulated Alex, slapping him on the back. 'Now you will have the opportunity to show those dirty Huns a thing or two.'

Alex smiled weakly and moved on. He found

that he was only comfortable in the company of his cousin who had shared so much with him on their failed mission. Even his father was now a distant figure – caught up in military duties for his newly formed battalion. Since returning home to Sydney he had barely had the chance to speak with Patrick in private.

'Alex,' a voice said and he turned to see his future sister-in-law smiling at him. 'Would you like to step outside for a little fresh air?'

'Certainly,' Alex answered, glad to have an excuse to leave the pack of well-wishers.

They made their way to the garden where they stood under a magnificent southern sky of twinkling stars.

'How are you?' Louise asked, and her question had a note of genuine concern.

'I am fine,' Alex answered, reaching for a silver case containing a row of small cigars. 'I'm just glad to be back.'

'You do know about Giselle and Mrs Schumann?' Louise asked.

Alex removed a cigar and noticed that his hands were trembling. He had tried to block Giselle from his thoughts for some time. 'I don't know how I could, since I saw them last at their plantation.'

'Giselle told me what happened when you were there,' Louise said. 'I am sorry that it all went so badly.'

'When could she have told you that?' Alex asked, attempting to light the cigar. 'Did she stop by Sydney after she betrayed Matthew and myself?'

Even in the dim light of the garden Alex could

see the expression of shock on Louise's face. 'She did not betray you,' she retorted. 'As one of her best friends, she confided in me that she is madly in love with you, and would have given her own life if it meant changing what happened.' Louise repeated the story of how Giselle had been intercepted with the supplies intended for the sea voyage south to Port Moresby.

'Is she back with her father and mother?' Alex asked, attempting to appear casual about her fate.

'No, she and Mrs Schumann are being held in an internment camp at Holsworthy and they have since been informed that Mr Schumann was killed in a native uprising at his plantation last month. I think that you should pay Giselle a visit as I suspect that she really needs to see you.'

'I didn't know,' Alex said quietly. 'The last couple of months have been a bit hectic and I have had little chance to follow up on anything since I returned home.'

'As her friend I would ask you to visit Giselle,' Louise beseeched. 'Most of her other friends have disowned her because in their eyes she is German. I only know my friend as a person with ambitions to make this world a better place.'

'I will see her,' Alex ceded. He was surprised at the depth of Louise's friendship for the woman whom, he had to admit to himself, he had never stopped loving. 'I will arrange to go to Holsworthy as soon as possible.'

'Good,' Louise said, satisfied that she had done something important for the sake of friendship.

'I think that we should be returning to your party before George starts thinking that you and I are having an affair.'

'You are really marrying my brother?' Alex asked as they walked back to the house.

'Your question has a disbelieving note to it,' Louise replied. 'Why would I not marry George?'

'Oh, nothing,' Alex answered, avoiding expressing his dislike for his brother.

Inside the house they were assailed by the pungent smell of tobacco smoke and the heavy perfumes of the ladies. 'I believe that you have not yet availed yourself of a flight in my cousin's aeroplane,' Alex said, causing Louise to glance sideways at him with a curious look.

'I have no doubt that Mr Matthew Duffy has a very strong charm and dashing appearance when it comes to the ladies,' she said with a smile. 'But he is a man destined to forever roam places where a lady cannot go. I will admit that when I first met your cousin I was almost swept off my feet, but when you and he just simply disappeared without telling anyone I was brought firmly back to earth.'

'So you admit that Matthew held some interest to you?' Alex asked with a smile. 'I would hate to think that he might be more attractive than my brother.'

'If you are attempting to play cupid, Alex, forget it,' she said, accepting a flute of champagne from a passing waiter. 'I am happily betrothed and the banns have been posted for what George has promised to be the social event of the year. I also know that it will be my duty to ensure that the Macintosh dynasty is continued with the presentation of a son to the family line.'

Maybe the reproduction of another George Macintosh, Alex mused. Not a pleasant thought. 'Well, I shall raise a glass to toast your happiness,' he said but without conviction, for Alex not only strongly disliked his brother but now had a gut feeling that he had some connection to their betrayal in the past months on the mission. Although he did not have proof, knowing his brother as he did, Alex could only think that he was responsible for the leak of information to the Germans.

Patrick saw his son chatting with his future daughter-in-law and excused himself from the company of a couple of Sydney's more prominent entrepreneurs who were already discussing what a bonanza the war meant to their future profits.

'Father,' Alex said when Patrick joined them, 'I was just telling Louise what a wonderful addition she will be to the family.'

'She will,' Patrick said. 'Louise, if you will excuse us for just a moment.'

'Certainly, Colonel,' Louise replied, sweeping away to join her father and mother who had been cornered by a fat banker and his equally fat wife.

'What requires the privacy?' Alex asked, sipping from his champagne.

'I have not had the opportunity to tell you that there is a vacancy for a company commander in my battalion,' Patrick answered. 'I have kept it open while you were away. That is, if you don't mind continuing your career under your father's command.'

'If it means my own company, I would serve the

457

devil,' Alex replied. 'No, I have no objection to serving under you, Father. Thank you for your faith in me, considering I let you down on the mission.'

'You did not let me down,' Patrick hurried to counter. 'What went wrong was because of circumstances beyond our control. As it is, the assault on Rabaul went very well and now the Imperial German Navy has had all its communications in the Pacific cut, foiling any plans to carry out raids on our Eastern seaboard.'

'We were betrayed, weren't we?' Alex asked quietly, casting a look at his brother engaged in animated conversation with a group of businessmen.

'We were,' Patrick answered. 'But it is nothing that I can prove.'

'You really mean that you suspect George somehow betrayed the mission to the Germans,' Alex continued. 'My own despicable brother, a traitor to his country.'

'You cannot say that,' Patrick said. 'He is of your flesh and blood, and no matter what happens, you have to remember that.'

Alex shook his head in disgust. 'The worst part of it all is that my brother is marrying a truly wonderful lady. I only wish that Matthew had been given the chance to take her up in his aeroplane then things might have worked out differently.'

'You are to report to BHQ tomorrow no later than midday, Captain Macintosh,' Patrick said, diverting the conversation away from George and his future with Louise Gyles. 'The adjutant will fill you in on your new command.'

'I am requesting leave for another forty-eight hours,' Alex countered. 'I have a vital task to do.'

'Given your past experiences, I think that I can grant that,' Patrick replied. 'Just be on parade no later than 0600 hours next Monday.'

'Thank you, sir,' Alex answered, reverting to his role not as a son but as a new company commander, obeying his CO's directions.

'But what is more important than taking command of your company as soon as possible?' Patrick asked out of curiosity.

'Love, Father,' Alex answered with the trace of a smile. 'Just love.'

Patrick immediately knew what his son meant and felt a shiver of apprehension. 'You know Giselle is interned as an enemy alien?'

'I didn't know until Louise told me a short while ago and that is a matter of politics,' Alex waved off. 'I plan to visit her and her mother at Holsworthy first thing tomorrow.'

'You do realise that if it is known you are consorting with an enemy alien it might reflect badly on your military career,' Patrick cautioned.

'What would you do, Father?' Alex countered. 'If you were in my shoes?'

Patrick extended his hand to his son. 'You go and see your young lady,' he said gently. 'Heaven knows that there is enough suffering and misery ahead of us in this war. I have long learned that life can be a fleeting thing, and if you can have just a little happiness in the meantime, you snatch it. I will get Angus to drive you out to see Giselle and her mother. Please pass on my condolences about Herr Schumann.'

Alex watched as his father turned his back and made his way over to John Hughes who had just arrived. Alex realised that beneath the exterior of the professional soldier was a loving father who was also prepared to put his own reputation on the line for him. He was overwhelmed with love for the tough, stern man who had always dominated his life and for a brief moment reflected on the grandfather he had briefly known when he was younger – a big, tough, man with a black eye patch who had roamed the world fighting other people's wars.

Alex realised that he was simply the next in line to a tradition of men prepared to put their lives at risk for a cause and wondered if he would be able to live up to the standard already set by his father and grandfather. 'I love you, Father,' he said softly and raised his glass to his father's back. 'And here's to you, Michael Duffy,' he continued. 'In whichever heaven allows the lonely a place of peace.'

On the other side of the crowded room, Matthew was at a loss among the strangers who congratulated him on his miraculous escape from the hands of the Hun, an expression he was hearing more and more often to describe the German enemy. He had noticed Louise escorted by George when they arrived at the house an hour earlier and found that he was still infatuated with the beautiful young woman. After an hour, Matthew smiled when she glanced over at him, and his gesture was returned before Louise turned again to George to say something. Matthew noticed George look in his direction and scowl.

'I don't think your brother is very pleased to see me back,' Matthew said when Alex joined him, bearing two glasses of good quality Scotch.

'I get the same impression from my brother about my safe return, too,' Alex said, passing a glass to Matthew. 'I suppose you are hoping to hear from your cobber, Randolph.'

'Yes,' Matthew answered. 'I asked your father had he heard from him but he appeared to be a bit evasive on the subject of his whereabouts. The colonel said that Randolph was last heard from in Pearl Harbour on a quest to find Nellie and then just dropped the subject. It makes me a bit uneasy that nothing has been heard since from Texas Slim. It's not like him to just drop off the map.'

'Maybe Uncle Arthur might know something,' Alex said, swilling his Scotch around in the crystal tumbler. 'After all, Randolph worked for Uncle Arthur and I know that Arthur had a good deal of time for him. You should try Arthur tomorrow to see if he can throw a bit of light on Randolph's uncharacteristic silence.'

'I think I will,' Matthew replied, his eyes fixed on Louise as she moved gracefully about the room chatting with guests.

Alex noticed Matthew's attention fixed on Louise. 'I tried to remind my future sister-in-law that she had not availed herself of a flight in your aeroplane,' he said with a wide grin.

'Who do you mean?' Matthew asked, feigning ignorance.

'You bloody well know what I mean, old boy,' Alex replied. 'Believe me, she is a good woman and deserves a better man than my brother.'

'You mean someone like me,' Matthew said lightly.

'Even you,' Alex answered, grinning at his cousin.

Dust rose in small puffs as the soldiers stamped down on the ground, changing the guard. The grass had long been beaten flat within the barbed wire confines of the internment camp on the outskirts of Sydney.

Outside the gate Alex stepped from the motor vehicle and received a salute from the slouch-hatted guard posted at the main entrance. Alex had opted to wear his uniform as he knew it would allow him to pass more easily through the system in the civilian camp.

'Want me to go with you, Captain Macintosh?' Angus asked in a growl, regarding the slovenly appearance of the guard at the gate with the eye of a former sergeant major of an elite British regiment.

'No, you stay with the car,' Alex replied. 'I shall not be too long.'

'Good then, sir,' Angus answered.

Alex made his way to the main administration building to obtain a pass from a clerk on duty and stepped outside with directions to the accommodation of Giselle and her mother. He walked along row after row of white tents and even a street of ramshackle huts which he could see were quickly becoming a tiny town of interned merchants. His uniformed appearance was met with indifferent stares by the internees or, in some cases, hostility from the younger men and women. Alex ignored the eyes that followed him. Then he saw Giselle. She was walking towards him, a small basket tucked under her arm. They both stopped walking when they saw each other.

It was Alex who then continued walking. Giselle had an expression of complete surprise on her face at his appearance in the camp and appeared transfixed by his presence.

'Giselle,' he said when he was within an arm's length of her. 'I know that you did not betray us and I have come to you to seek your forgiveness for even harbouring the slightest thought that you might have.'

A sad look crossed Giselle's face. 'I am so happy to see that you are safe and well,' she answered. 'I prayed that you would return to your family.'

'I have returned to you,' Alex said, aware of the many curious eyes upon them. 'I am going to get you and your mother out of here.'

'How can you do that?' Giselle asked with a note of despair.

'By marrying you as soon as possible,' Alex said, causing tears to well in Giselle's eyes.

'Oh, Alex, my love, I have dreamed so often that you and I would grow old together, but you are a soldier in your country's army and I am an enemy of your nation.'

Alex had an overwhelming urge to sweep Giselle into his arms but was also aware that any sign of affection from him could bring retribution down on her and her mother from their own countrymen interned in the camp. He withdrew his hand lest that indicate any intimacy between them. 'My father is a very powerful man in this country and I am sure he will help set you and your mother free. In the meantime I will move heaven and earth for us to wed – even if it must be in this place.'

Tears rolled down Giselle's cheeks. 'Oh, Alex, I would marry you in hell if that was required for us to be man and wife. I know that we cannot express our feelings for each other here in public but I want you to know that every fibre of my being aches for you. I only want to be held in your arms and loved – as I would love you. But I must leave you now and go to my mother before those watching us become suspicious and brand me a traitor to the Fatherland.'

'I will return,' Alex said, choking back his feelings. 'And when I do it will be with a rabbi.'

'You would do that?' Giselle gasped in astonishment.

'Of course, my love,' Alex answered. 'You are my main reason for living.'

Arthur Thorncroft had been unable to attend Alex and Matthew's homecoming party, as he had been away in the country on a business trip. So it was a pleasant surprise when Matthew Duffy arrived at his office first thing in the morning. They greeted each other warmly with hugs and back slapping and Matthew gave a brief description of his and Alex's experiences since they had departed Australia several weeks earlier.

Arthur called for his one remaining employee, Miss Myrtle Birney, to make them a pot of tea. Myrtle had remained behind and was now employed as Arthur's personal assistant although the job did not entail much these days.

'No one has heard from my cobber, Texas Slim,' Matthew finally got around to saying after exhausting his narrative concerning the failed mission.

'That is not true,' Arthur said to Matthew's surprise. 'George Macintosh has known for some time that Randolph is currently incarcerated in Hawaii on an old charge. He was sentenced to six months hard labour. So, George has told no other person of Randolph's whereabouts.'

'It appears so,' Matthew frowned. 'Why in hell would he not tell his father? The colonel mentioned nothing concerning Randolph when I asked him.'

'I am afraid that I do not trust George any further than I could kick him,' Arthur said, sipping his tea. 'But I cannot say anything because he is Patrick's son.'

'The bastard!' Matthew swore. 'George has known all along and from what I can guess has not lifted a finger to help get Texas out of prison.'

'George made me promise that I was to remain silent on the matter as he did not want to burden his father. But he said that he would do anything to free Randolph,' Arthur said, placing his tea cup on his desk.

'How do we spring Texas?' Matthew asked.

'Leave it with me,' Arthur said with a grim smile. 'I promise that Randolph will not be spending Christmas behind bars. I personally will speak with Patrick. I know he is good friends with the American ambassador and I am sure that a deal can be made.'

'I should travel to Hawaii,' Matthew said. 'Texas has never let me down in all the years that we have shared.'

'That will not be necessary,' Arthur reassured him. 'I am sure that you have immediate plans of your own and going to Hawaii is not as fast as a telegram transmitted across the Pacific, my boy.'

Matthew was grateful that he had been given an excuse not to spend the time travelling to Hawaii when, he considered selfishly, there was a possibility this war would be over before Christmas. He wanted a chance to try out some of his ideas of aerial warfare before it was all over. He had already spoken with the colonel about the air training being held at Point Cook in Victoria and had been assured he would be granted a commission along with a posting to the newly formed training unit. Because of his flying experience he was considered the right sort of chap to be an officer with the rank of Second Lieutenant.

'I trust you, Arthur,' Matthew said. 'All I ask is to be kept up to date with your efforts to free Randolph.'

'I promise that I will keep you abreast of any developments,' Arthur replied. 'I suspect that you are just itching to get back into the sky again, and I have a pretty good idea where you will be heading. I suppose that one day man will say that there are some born to fly,' Arthur continued kindly. 'You, my boy, are one such person.'

Matthew looked just a little sheepish that his quick agreement with Arthur allowing him to handle Randolph's bid for freedom should be so obvious.

He finished his tea, thanked Arthur with a firm handshake and stepped out of the office. He would return to his hotel and check out. The next day he would be on the train to Melbourne and back into the air where he belonged.

30

Four days before Christmas, Colonel Patrick Duffy sat alone in his library with a tumbler of Scotch at hand. It was late in the evening and he had returned from a meeting of battalion commanders at Victoria Barracks. A month earlier Patrick hoped that he would be sent to South Africa with the newly formed Australian Imperial Force to assist Botha's government put down an uprising of rebellious Boers in sympathy with the German cause. The uprising had been crushed and Britain had its first victory against a German colony on the Dark Continent. Where they would now be committed was still a mystery, but rumours of being deployed to Egypt to help defend the Suez Canal floated around the meeting he had attended.

Even with Christmas only a few days away the war was well and truly establishing itself in the green fields of Europe. The names of once obscure villages now began appearing in the newspapers: Mons, Marne, Ypres, and on the eastern front the decisive German victory against the massive Russian army in the swamps and forests of Tannenberg. Grass was being rapidly replaced by mud and the clean lines of farming land were now crisscrossed with the jagged lines of trenches.

The Canadians had landed in England and this annoyed many of the commanders Patrick spoke with who were eager to join the battle against the enemy. Why had not Australians been deployed?

Patrick sipped his Scotch, his feet up on a chair. He could hear the old grandfather clock in the hallway tick-tocking in its monotonous way as it had for an earlier generation of his family. So much had happened in his life since the outbreak of war. Alex had quietly married Giselle at a synagogue in Sydney after Patrick had pulled strings to have her released for a secret, forty-eight-hour supervised leave of absence. Their short honeymoon had been spent in an expensive hotel and then Alex had been forced to relinquish his bride back to the internment camp, leaving them with the sworn oath that he would have his bride and her mother released before the next Christmas arrived in 1915.

George and Louise had been married in November in a lavish wedding ceremony attended by the who's who of Sydney society. The pair had made a handsome couple, and their marriage dominated the social pages of the daily papers.

Alex had shared letters with his father from

Matthew Duffy who had kept in contact with Alex as he put in his hours flying at Point Cook for the newly formed Australian Flying Corps. Matthew had written that he was itching to get into action and because of his previous flight experience was at the top of the list for deployment into active service.

That left his beloved daughter, Nellie. Patrick sighed and raised his glass. 'To you, my darling daughter, wherever you are.'

Patrick felt the tears welling. Fenella was so precious to him and he still felt the pangs of guilt knowing that she was innocent of any crime and yet still a suspect in the death of Guy Wilkes. The war had wiped away any real interest in the case and its strong hint of scandal. Patrick knew that his military career would be over if he provided the police with the real story of Wilkes' death, even if he was cleared. It was not the done thing for an officer of the King to be embroiled in such sordid affairs and he would be requested to resign his commission should he reveal what he knew. But now the rapidly mounting body count of dead and maimed young men on the Western Front of Europe stunned the readers of Western newspapers and one man's violent end was lost in the long lists of other young men.

As for Randolph Gates, Patrick admonished himself for ever suspecting that he had skipped with Macintosh funds instead of continuing his crusade to find Fenella. A talk with his American friend, the ambassador, had solved that problem. Randolph had been released two weeks before Christmas and a telegram from him in Pearl Harbour assured Patrick that he was chasing down a strong lead on Nellie's whereabouts. Patrick had cornered George on the matter of why he had not been informed of the American's incarceration in Hawaii after receiving a phone call from Arthur. George had dismissed Patrick's anger with the explanation that he did not want to worry him any more and that he was looking into solving the problem. Needless to say, Patrick had reluctantly accepted his son's explanation as he was forced to admit his older son's astute business acumen was making the Macintosh companies more and more money each day with wartime government contracts. Patrick knew he was not in a position to oversee the day-to-day dealings any longer with his full-time duties to the army and so he desperately needed his son to keep the companies afloat.

Patrick took a sip from his glass and stared at the dim shadows on the library wall opposite. Life was so bloody lonely, he thought, but also knew that this had been so at his own choice. With the death of his wife fourteen years earlier he had sworn never to neglect his children. To that extent he had avoided any romantic liaisons and allowed his time to be consumed by his militia duties.

But now, there was a promise that he would have his family around him for the Christmas of 1914. Again, Patrick had been able to pull strings and have some unofficial leave granted so Giselle and her mother could spend the day with him and the others at his place. So he would have two sons and two daughters-in-law at the Christmas table, and a place would be left vacant for Nellie. Oh, if only she was with them, he sighed, wiping away a tear running down his cheek. At least here in the privacy of his library he could allow himself to feel emotion.

Patrick finished the last of his Scotch and settled back at his desk to flick through the messages Angus had left from the day he was away on military duties. Besides the usual accounts and company papers to be signed was a note scrawled by Angus saying that Arthur Thorncroft had an urgent request for Patrick to meet him on the morrow in the afternoon at his office. Patrick puzzled over the note. What could be so urgent?

But with regard to his lifelong friendship for the former film producer, Patrick had Angus deliver him to Arthur's office in the afternoon.

'I will be forwarding an invitation for you to attend the house on Christmas day,' Patrick said by way of greeting. 'I must apologise, old friend, for not keeping in contact more often.'

'You are a very busy man, Patrick,' Arthur said, taking Patrick's extended hand. 'And if I know the brash young officer I first met in the deserts of the Sudan, you are still eager to lead your men into battle.'

'Not so eager anymore,' Patrick replied. 'I know that the time will arrive that I will be overseeing those terrible letters to wives and mothers saying that their husband or son has been killed in the service of the Empire. I am just glad that I will be able to share some precious time in the company of dear friends and family on Christmas Day. I only wish that list extended to others whose whereabouts and welfare are not known.'

Arthur nodded. 'I think I understand,' he replied. 'But for now, you and I should go and see one of those Yankee films this afternoon, and then share a drink after it.'

'A bloody film,' Patrick said. 'I have many important things to do, and watching a film is not really a priority.'

'Just trust me,' Arthur said, taking Patrick by the elbow and steering him out into the street. 'Get that big, beautiful Scot to drop us off at the Odeon as I am sure that you need some light relief from your duties, and I can assure you that spending a little time in the theatre is the perfect way to leave the world behind for a short time.'

Reluctantly, Patrick let his persistent friend prevail and Angus drove them to the picture theatre, dropping them off. They were ushered to a seat on the sumptuous top balcony overlooking the cheaper seats below, and the lights went down. The patrons rose when the national anthem was played on a piano from the orchestra pit and sat down after it was completed. Tobacco smoke rose as patrons lit up and the silver screen flickered into life. Patrick was slightly annoyed that he had let Arthur talk him into watching the Yank film. He really was a busy man, and watching films was such a trivial way to spend his time. Despite his impatience he settled back as the piano player rolled off the notes to the score, setting the mood for what was being displayed on the screen. It was obviously an American melodrama about a working man who had just lost his job. He was now sitting alone at a table with a bottle of rum before him. Close-ups of his face showed his despair as his wife entered the room to go to him. It was then that Patrick almost bolted from his seat. 'Nellie!' he gasped, recognising his daughter up on the silver screen. He felt Arthur's hand on his arm.

'Now you can see that she is safe and well,' Arthur said gently. 'She may not be able to be with us for Christmas, but she is now with the world, wherever this film is seen.'

Patrick settled back and for the time the film ran admired his daughter's skill at acting. When the lights came on, he rose and shook Arthur's hand. 'Old friend, it is my shout at the pub,' he said as they mingled with the crowd pushing their way to the exits. On a personal level 1914 was ending on a good note for him, Patrick thought. But what did 1915 offer for all those he held dear?

Across the vast expanse of the Pacific Ocean, Randolph Gates strode along an avenue of shady trees. It had been many years since he had last passed through the town of Los Angeles and many of the houses around him still bore the architectural features of their Spanish heritage. The weather was pleasant and the skies clear blue – a marked difference to his home state of Texas which he knew a few days before Christmas would have a white sheet of snow across the prairies and in the hills. But the hills and canyons surrounding the town he now found himself in were covered in orange groves and tough, stunted brush.

He found himself joining a happy throng of

people walking under the ornate archway of a thriving film studio and into a world of people dressed in everything from cowboy outfits to pirate costumes as they strolled between the spacious buildings outfitted to make movies. It was an open day for movie fans to meet their favourite stars and Randolph was just one more tourist visiting this world of make-believe.

A uniformed elderly man, probably a retired policeman, Randolph thought, stood with his hands on his hips looking bored at the passing throng of visitors.

'Hey, buddy,' Randolph addressed the security man. 'Where do I find Miss Fiona Owens?'

'You mean the Scottish dame,' the security guard replied. Randolph thought it was amusing that his American countryman did not know that Owens was in fact a well-known Welsh name and not Scottish at all.

'Yeah, the Scottish actress,' he said.

'Just go down this road and you will see a building marked with an eight,' he replied. 'She should be in there doing a shoot.'

Randolph thanked the man and continued his walk along the road, passing a group of men dressed in the uniforms of the Confederate Army and leaning on old-style rifles. He found the building, a tall, huge structure where a couple of security guards were allowing a line of visitors to enter. Randolph joined the queue and was ushered inside into a world he was already familiar with from his time working with Arthur Thorncroft – cameras, sets and big lights on stands. Even the set of three walls constructed for filming looked as familiar as those Arthur would have done up for an indoor scene. The only thing about this set, Randolph noticed, was how elaborate and large it was compared to those which he was familiar with in Sydney.

At one corner of the cavernous building he could see a tight circle of men and women around someone he could not at first see. Then he caught a glimpse of who had attracted the crowd and felt his heart skip a beat. It was Fenella and she appeared radiant, signing autographs and chatting with her adoring fans. She wore a long, floor-length dress fashionable during the period of the Civil War and was in conversation with a young lady whose face beamed with delight at having Fenella's attention. Fenella's happy laughter drifted to him across the space of a mere twenty paces.

For a moment Randolph hesitated. She looked so much at home among her adoring public and he knew from reading the local paper that she was one of the studio's biggest stars. He had completed his mission for her father to find his daughter but now experienced some doubt as to how Fenella might view his sudden appearance once again in her life. It was obvious that she was on top of the world and being treated as some kind of American royalty on account of her popularity as a film star. What could she ever see in an old cowboy whose life had been spent wandering the world through dangerous places no sane man would consider going?

Randolph commenced to turn to walk away when a smiling Fenella glanced across the heads of her fans to meet his eye. Randolph suddenly felt both trapped and exhilarated when their eyes locked on each other. He could not move his feet. He could see Fenella mouthing his name and then she burst into tears, stunning those around her. She pushed her way through the crowd and ran to him, flinging her arms around his neck.

'Oh, my darling, I knew you would come for me,' she sobbed, clinging to him like a person drowning. 'I knew no matter where I tried to hide you would find me. I don't know when I last felt this happy.'

Randolph realised that his whole body was as rigid as stone as she held him and he relaxed. 'I would have been here earlier but I kind of got caught up,' he said, wrapping his arms around her. 'But I got here.'

The only thing that puzzled Randolph was the same thing that had puzzled men throughout time. If she was so happy why was she crying?

Epilogue

Lieutenant Matthew Duffy had his French-designed Caudron aloft and the fragile little biplane was at maximum speed of sixty-eight mph, soaring above the Mesopotamian desert at a height of 7000 feet, although it was capable of reaching a ceiling of around 14,000 feet. He had been tasked with reconnoitring the Turkish positions on the Euphrates River and was acutely aware of how alone he was flying into enemy-controlled territory. As a temporary member of the Australian Half Flight squadron he knew how vulnerable he was to engine failure or ground fire. But he did carry multiple machine guns attached under the wings and was itching to find a target of opportunity to swoop on and strafe.

In the air he had the chance to reflect on life and death although he tried not to think of the latter. The last he had heard from his cousin Major

Alex Macintosh was that he was frustrated by the delays in his attempts to be posted with a battalion overseas to fight the enemy. He had been held back and transferred to a training battalion, and was soon to become a parent. Giselle had been released from internment – thanks to Patrick's considerable influence. Alex had written that his father's battalion had suffered heavily against the Ottoman Turks on the beaches of a place called Gallipoli, but that the colonel was in relatively good health and making a name for himself in that campaign as a very competent commander with prospects of being promoted to a brigade in the future. Alex also mentioned that his father had written to say that a young former solicitor by the name of Sean Duffy had been sent to his battalion as a reinforcement platoon commander with the commissioned rank of Second Lieutenant and in an action on the Peninsula had been awarded a Military Cross for his bravery. Patrick had personally recommended him for the bravery award. He had written to Alex that he had done so with great pleasure for all that Second Lieutenant Duffy had done to help Nellie.

Also was the good news that Fenella was in touch with her family by letter, and that she had met up with Randolph Gates who had been able to gain employment as what they called a stunt man in Hollywood with the same film company that employed her.

Matthew received a regular flow of letters from his mother, Kate Tracy, whenever mail could be delivered to the miserable, swampy, fever-ridden country of the ancient land Matthew flew over on his missions. He had been informed that very soon he would be transferred for a posting in England and that this would be one of his last missions in the skies over the ancient land of Mesopotamia. When transferred to England he would have a better chance of replying to his mother's loving letters.

A wall of dust rose up ahead of Matthew's aircraft and he realised that he must break off his flight north in the face of the sudden and deadly storm. His fragile aircraft could not take on the ferocious desert winds and he peeled away to circle around an edge of the wall of swirling sand, if he could find one. He was successful. The desert storm was only a small one and Matthew checked the dials on the dashboard in front of him. His fuel supply was sufficient for him to complete his mission and return home to the airfield where he could have a good cup of tea brewed up for him by his Arab servant.

It was then that Matthew, looking down at the ground, saw the faint outline of what he guessed to be an ancient village or town, long gone from the historical record. Warping the wings, he swung around to fly over what the dust storm had briefly uncovered and marvelled at what he was viewing. The young aviator guessed that had he been on the ground he might have walked over the ruins without seeing them but from his vantage point in the sky he had the eyes of an eagle searching for its prey.

Fascinated by his discovery, Matthew used precious fuel to circle the outlines of what must have been a substantial fortified town. He was prompted to think about the stories of ancient civilisations where chariots and iron weapons changed the course of history in these very same lands. It was then and there that Matthew recognised his destiny as revealed by Wallarie. All he had to do for now was stay alive and outlive the war that the world was embroiled in to return and explore the ancient past. Lieutenant Matthew Duffy, Australian Flying Corps, turned his little biplane back on course and looked down to see the mighty artery of the ancient civilisations flowing sluggishly below under a fierce mid-summer sun of searing heat.

Glen View Lutheran Mission Station
Central Queensland
1934

The sun was a red ball hovering on the western horizon. The young man squatted in the dust under the bumbil tree, hardly aware that his legs were cramping from the long time he had been listening to the old Aboriginal warrior spin his story.

Wallarie had fallen silent and was sucking on a tobacco pipe that contained little else than grey ash. 'You got more baccy?' he asked, breaking the silence.

The young man rose to stretch his legs. 'I will fetch some from my grandmother,' he replied eagerly, in the way that youths sometimes do when they recognise they are in the presence of one who knows more than they.

Wallarie grinned. 'She is still here,' he chuckled. 'She and I are old friends.'

The boy returned with a generous supply of tobacco plugs and handed them to him. Wallarie immediately refilled his battered pipe and, reaching for a box of matches, lit it, puffing with an expression of contentment.

'You got no place to go?' he asked, staring with blind eyes at the boy. 'Me think you want to go to the cave.'

The boy shuffled his feet but did not reply.

'Mebbe one day you go to the cave and see the ancestor spirits,' Wallarie sighed. 'Mebbe you go alone, because ol' Wallarie be with the ancestor spirits up in the sky.'

Again, the boy did not reply. Death was not something he truly understood in his privileged world and this man he had heard so much about was almost immortal to the boy's thinking. It was impossible for the old Aboriginal to die. Had he not outlived all in the boy's own family with the exception of Kate Tracy?

'So, you want me to tell you more of the story,' Wallarie said, resting his back against the rough bark of the tree behind him, and feeling the comforting last rays of the sun against his face.

'Family stories take a long time,' he said. 'There are many stories – like the branches of the bumbil tree – and you are the new twig that will grow your own branches one day. But I will continue my story of the two families the ancestor spirits cursed. One day you will understand but for now I must sleep. When you come back in the morning time I will tell you more.'

Author Notes

There is a popular perception that at the outbreak of World War I Australians were divorced from the battlefields of distant Europe. This is far from the truth. Australia and New Zealand were well and truly within the military planning of Germany in the event of hostilities between themselves and the British Empire. It should be remembered that before the outbreak of the Great War Germany controlled a considerable number of islands as well as the northern section of Papua New Guinea as a part of their Pacific Empire. The Imperial German Navy had a sizeable naval force operating out of Southern China and within striking distance of Australasian waters.

I was fortunate in my research to find a fascinating analysis of the military situation relating to our part of the world in Jurgen Tampke's *Ruthless Warfare: German military planning and surveillance in the Australian–New Zealand region before the Great War* (Southern Highlands Publishers, Canberra, 1998). Translated documents set out the plan to launch attacks against the eastern seaboard ports of Australia and locations in New Zealand including the capture of the ports of Gladstone in Queensland and Westport in New Zealand for their coal supplies in order to fuel the German naval warships.

It is not my intention to provide a detailed explanation of those plans in these notes as any reader interested in the subject has access to further sources through their local libraries. Needless to say, however, the German operational plans against Australia and New Zealand were disrupted by a combination of factors. One was that Japan aligned itself with the Allies and its impressive navy was able to threaten the Imperial German Navy in the Pacific. As well, there were strikes by Australian and New Zealand forces against German territory in the region, capturing or destroying the vital radio stations needed by the German warships to coordinate their operations against the British Empire in the Pacific region.

Many months before the Gallipoli landings, Australia suffered its first battle casualties in the Great War as a result of fighting in the jungles of the Pacific islands. The sacrifice of these men has been mostly forgotten but they were killed and wounded directly in the defence of Australia and not simply for British interests. Their graves can be found in Rabaul alongside those of the heroic men who would die in New Britain a quarter of a century later resisting the

Japanese. This fact makes that war cemetery rather unique.

I must emphasise that my story of the operation around Rabaul is a work of fiction. In a twist of fate the great author Wilbur Smith's latest book, *Assegai* (Pan Macmillan, Sydney, 2009), is set in the same period of time, but on the other side of the Indian Ocean in Africa. Readers may be interested to know that Britain originally planned to send our newly raised AIF to Africa to assist the pro-British government of General Botha suppress the Boer rebellion. But at the last minute the AIF was re-routed to Egypt prior to the Dardanelles campaign of 1915. As Botha was able to crush the pro-German Boers and invade German territory, his region of the world did not require our assistance.

This story will continue in the next release of the family saga where the Macintoshes and Duffys face four years of campaigning in the European trenches of the Western Front and in the deserts of the Palestinian campaign.

Acknowledgments

A very special thanks for the significant support in producing this book must go to my publisher, Cate Paterson, editor Catherine Day, all at the Pan Macmillan company in both Sydney and Melbourne, and also all the reps on the road. And to my publicist, Jane Novak – a special thanks for being you.

I would also like to thank my agent, Geoffrey Radford of Anthony Williams Agency, for his ongoing support and advice. Thanks, mate.

There are other people in my life who have an indirect and yet important role in assisting in producing a book. My thanks go to the following: Kevin and Maureen Jones and all the Jones clan, Mick and Andrea Prowse, John and Isabel Millington, Pete and Kay Lowe, and Ty and Kerry McKee from Maclean.

Thanks also are extended to Debrah Novak of WoMEDIA for her wonderful assistance with last year's launch in Maclean, and also to Dr Louis and Christine Trichard from Yamba for their friendship.

I would also like to thank Graham Mackie who entered my portrait in this year's Archibald Prize at the Art Gallery of NSW. Alas, so as not to frighten people, the portrait was not exhibited, but thanks to Graham anyway for considering me a personality worthy of his artistic endeavour.

After ten books I would like to mention the support of a wonderful free paper, *The Outback City Express*, published by Ken and Barbara Hay in Queensland. Over the years it has provided publicity for many Pan Macmillan authors within its colourful pages and on the front cover.

Continuing thanks also go to Irvin Rockman CBE, Rod and Brett Hardy for keeping the visual media project alive in difficult times, and Fran McGuire from the Maclean Library for her assistance in my research. Also to Herlinde Kroth from Geelong for her ongoing advice concerning German matters.

On a sadder note I would like to mention three very special Australians who have passed from us this year. Peter John Dawson, whom I had the honour of serving with in the NSW Police many years ago and who may have saved my life in an ambush set up on a country road one night. Smokey – as he was known to his friends – will be missed by his family and many who knew him.

I have close connections to two writers' organisations. They are The Bush Curlews from Charters Towers and STARS from the Gold Coast. Respectively, the two principle founders of these organisations were Rosa Christian and Nerida Marshall. Sadly, both ladies lost their mothers this year and as I knew Rosa's and Nerida's mothers as readers of mine I would like to honour their memory by mentioning them here. Doris Thelma Christian and Irene Lorraine Maile – you will always be in our memories and hearts.

On a happier note, congratulations are extended to my brother, Tom Watt, and his wife, Colleen, for becoming first-time grandparents with the birth this March of Oliver James Herps to my god-daughter, Shannon, and her husband, Aaron Herps.

Finally, a thanks to my friends in the writing business: to Tony Park, Simon Higgins and Sandy Curtis. And a welcome to Steve Horne, a newcomer to the ranks of published authors; your company and conversation is always appreciated.